Though I Walk:
Book One in the Prescott Family Chronicles

Sheri Dean Parmelee
November 2023

I would like to thank the following people for their contributions to the background of the novel: Ellen Yang, M.D., Commander Jeff King USNA, Mrs. Sandra King, and Petra from Helzberg Jewelers at the Annapolis Mall.

I would also like to thank Nancy Dean, Dorothea Harrison, Marie Harrison, Marti Skogebo, Tisha Martin, and Betty Judd for their support. I am thankful for the suggestions of my First Year Seminar students at the College of Southern Maryland: Rita, Anita, and Michael. Many thanks for the unwavering backing of Sue Barbera, Doctor Tammy Brown, and Georgia Greer.

A special thanks to Barbara Horstemeyer, who served as my first reader for this edition of the book. She held me accountable for the flow of the novel and I truly appreciate her long hours of hard work.

I would like to dedicate this book to all of the women like Susan who live with a man like Kurt.

Prologue

As Susan Thomas Prescott neared the end of a completely routine day, she had no idea that, only hours later, her world would be rocked by an unexpected confession and that her husband would deliberately try to kill her. This, then, is her story.

Chapter I

Sue Prescott was setting out the dishes for their evening's repast that frigid midweek night in January 2012, when a quick, brusque phone call from her husband Kurt disturbed her preparations.

"I'm taking you to dinner in Annapolis. Be ready when I get home in fifteen minutes."

No greeting, pleasant or otherwise. Just an order. Boy, did that get tiring. Yes, he was a former military man, a Naval Academy graduate after returning home from Viet Nam, but did he really need to be so blunt? A little softness every now and again would go a long way. Not him. Not Kurt Prescott, thank you very much. What's his major maladjustment now?

Sue sighed, and then considered his statement with care before replying, not wishing to infuriate him further. "We don't usually go this time of the week." Sue can't you do any better than that? You're the queen of pathetic excuses. Sheesh.

"Who's to say we can't go now?" he replied. "The Federal House will be empty and quiet. We'll have our favorite town all to ourselves."

Sue gave a muted yet audible sigh to express her discomfort and angst, hoping against hope that he didn't hear it. Things would not go well, if he had. She was never one to speak up for herself, particularly to Kurt, who she preferred to placate rather than to annoy. Thank God, Kurt appeared to have ignored her sigh, once again. Their exchange, though short, delivered the final verdict: They were going out into the frozen temperatures for a night in an empty town.

"I want to go. We're going. That settles it."

He swore briefly, she supposed at the antics of a nearby driver, though it could have been directed at her. She held her breath. Nope, it was definitely someone else this time, judging from how long his horn sounded. She inhaled again. Relief.

"It's very, very cold out," she said. What was he thinking? This was a night for staying in, not going out. She had planned to pick up her favorite book and spend the evening reading in the family room, a fire in the fireplace to cheer her otherwise solitary evening. She supposed Kurt would head to his study after eating dinner, as he usually did.

"Wear your heavy wool coat and boots, then," he said. "You know how to dress yourself. Get ready. We're going, like it or not." He hung up on her.

Well, that command was nothing out of the ordinary, though the plan to go to Annapolis on such short notice was. Of course, he didn't particularly care for her cooking, as he constantly reminded her, so perhaps he simply didn't feel like eating what he sometimes called her "burnt offerings" tonight. Yes, that must be it. She climbed the stairs to go change her clothes, suddenly weary beyond belief. Being with him was such a drain. Into the closet I go, with no complaints now, Susan Margaret. Pick your warmest clothes and get on with this.

Sue chose her garments with care: navy blue wool pants, thick socks, a deep red turtleneck and cable knit sweater, her longest scarf, leather gloves, and full length red wool coat. As she dressed, she thought how peculiar his actions were. Within the sphere of their normal, everyday life, she would suggest a trip downtown if she felt he needed the military atmosphere to help calm him down. Living with him was like living with a time bomb. She never knew when or why he would blow up. She reasoned that his hostility was motivated by his service as a pilot in Viet Nam and

9

that, if he was around the town that catered to the Naval Academy from which he had graduated, he might be calmer. And he often was. But not always.

Sue heard him before she saw him. Kurt came inside, slamming the door to the garage. He ripped through a week's worth of mail in the kitchen. She heard the shredder going. Rejecting that stack of stuff, she told herself. He tromped upstairs. He entered their bedroom, dumping his suitcases and airline pilot jacket on the bed, then brushing past her as she sat at her dressing table, to enter the master bathroom. He scowled in her direction but did not speak. A normal part of their co-existence. He'd been gone for days, yet there was no conversation from him. She looked at his luggage. She wished he wouldn't put his dirty suitcase on their lovely bedspread.

"Hello, dear," she said, as she sprayed his favorite cologne on her wrists. No reply. Bathroom cabinets were slammed. She heard him brushing his teeth. Water splashed. He was washing his face, covering the countertop with water. She would have to remember to wipe it up later that evening.

This night was somehow different from other nights when he returned from his most recent trip. This evening was motivated by a peculiar kind of aggression that she couldn't quite put her finger on. Had she been asked, she might have described it as hostile. His aggression was not towards his environment or circumstances, however. He was hostile toward her. But why? What did I do this time? She shivered, afraid of what she might have done, or not done, that had him so ticked off. Sometimes it was better to not know.

Sue walked downstairs in silence and retrieved her boots from the entryway closet. Seating herself at the kitchen table to pull them on and wrestle with the bothersome laces, she contemplated entering the empty yet inviting breakfast room that was her solitary sanctuary. No one else in the house ever spent time in the sunny little room on the far side of the kitchen. Kurt felt it was too feminine and cramped, leaving the space to her alone. It was where she sat and read, wrote cards and letters, and enjoyed her first cup of tea each morning. It was a place where she found a sense of peace and contentment. All she had ever wanted was to be a mother and wife. She had no major ambitions after marrying Kurt, except guiding her children to be good adults and supporting her husband in all of his career goals. Often, however, her chief hope was to stay out of Kurt's way. He was mad all the time, these days.

"I don't understand why you're so slow, Sue" he grumbled at her as he entered the kitchen, having changed his clothes to something more suitable for a cold winter night, a black turtleneck sweater and black corduroy pants. He was impatient as always. She never moved fast enough for him.

"Sorry. Be right there," she replied.

"Get the lead out," he said. He threw on his heaviest coat.

Kurt went ahead of her to pull his car from the garage as he often did in his impatience. By the time she walked through the garage, he had already moved the vehicle out onto the driveway. Sue stepped into the dark blue sedan and buckled herself in as Kurt pushed the button on the garage remote, her body trembling due to the freezing temperatures. Good night, it's cold in here, even though he just got home from the airport. The car sure cooled off quickly. She rubbed her gloved hands together in vain, then held them underneath her thighs, hoping to gain some warmth as the car heated up. It didn't work.

Not a word was spoken that entire drive, just the sound of the asphalt passing below their vehicle and the silence of the dark, clear sky. Everything she saw felt far away as they made their journey to the quaint little town. The night always felt empty in winter. While the rest of the world was tucked into their homes with churning furnaces or cheery fireplaces, she was all alone, even with the presence of her husband nearby. She looked over at his profile as he drove. How had they come to the place where they were so far removed from one another? She quickly moved her gaze from him, lest he become upset with her scrutiny. No need to anger him any more than he already was. She stared at the street instead and sighed. She yearned to be near him, yet the gulf between them was greater than the distance in their car would make it seem. She felt empty, useless, old. She was emotionally running on empty.

They pulled into the Noah Hillman Garage and drove to the second floor, as was their custom. She opened her door in quietness and slipped out, her face meeting the cold air like a freezing octopus whose tentacles wrapped themselves around her and shot to the bottom of her lungs with every breath she took. Oh! The air was frigid. The cold wind would not be stopped, regardless of the layers she wore. Every part of her was freezing; even the earrings in her earlobes bit her skin with their frozen metal. Yet upon observing her husband, she saw his face was red as ever with annoyance. Where she was a calm cup of hot tea, he was the spoon in the cup that constantly stirred things up. He seemed oblivious to his environment and to her discomfort. What was on his mind that engulfed him so completely? Time would tell, she feared.

"Let's go," he said, marching toward the metal stairs. He clanked down the stairs as if they were his enemy. No, that title is reserved for me. She followed him.

Why didn't he take the elevator? It might have been at least somewhat warmer than taking the open stairs to the street below, but she remained silent as she followed her husband through the cold, quiet town towards the restaurant. She smiled a little at his pulling his coat closer and burying his hands deeper into his pockets to protect them from the frigidness of the evening. She smiled a bit more into her scarf, "serves you right," as he always told her.

As normal, Kurt kept a pace or two ahead of her as they walked to the restaurant from the garage, but tonight the distance between them was further, to the point of his crossing Main Street before she had even stepped into the crosswalk. Why couldn't he wait up? What's the rush, other than the freezing cold? Something's on his mind. The question is: Do I want to know? Probably not. It's better left unsaid.

Once inside the almost-empty restaurant, he further isolated her by choosing one of the larger tables in the restaurant to keep her at a distance. Sue got his message. This was not to be an intimate evening by any stretch of the imagination. It was cold, empty, and distant. They placed their drink orders and accepted the server's proffered menus without comment. Sue smiled quickly at the server, then looked at her menu lest Kurt become angered by her delay.

"What did you do while I was gone," Kurt asked, leaning back in his chair, with an undertone of accusation in his voice that she knew only too well.

After retiring from the Navy, he had a stint as a flight instructor for a year before becoming bored. He now worked for American Airlines as a pilot, making flights in and out of the country. His time away could last up to a week and even longer. She was used to being alone for long stretches. She stirred the ice in her glass of water before replying, "It was very low key. I cleaned, I read, I went to the library. Nothing particularly special."

They fell silent, smiling at the waitress from force of habit, as their drinks were delivered. Hot tea for her, a soda for him. Their stilted conversation continued, more like barely-polite conversation between two unhappy strangers than a loving husband and wife. What imagined slight had she perpetrated against him? Nothing came to mind. She could have asked him why they had come out that night, but knew better than to ask- don't ask the question unless you want to know the answer. It was better to hide behind her feigned ignorance than to face his brutal honesty.

"Most pilots' wives seek some kind of companionship when their husband is traveling," he said, taking a long drink from his soda.

"I feel no need," she sighed, sitting back in her chair. "I'm happy waiting for you to return." Sue wrapped her hands around the steaming mug, eager for some warmth. She held it close.

"I'm not happy," he said.

So that was it. Unhappiness. But why? The night was so tense, like a hostile cross-examination in a court of law. His suggestion that she had been unfaithful struck her, leaving wounds that stung. Had she ever given him cause to not trust her? The waitress returned, ending their conversation briefly. Sue sipped her tea as their meals were delivered. They both began eating, though her meal was tasteless in light of what he said. Moments later, she put her soup spoon down and decided to face whatever lay ahead.

"Kurt," she responded. "What are you not happy about?" She took a sip of tea to calm her nerves.

He glanced around the empty room, and then spoke so quietly that she had to lean forward to hear him. "I met someone on one of my trips," he said. "I've been seeing her for a while and she seems to be everything you are not." He took a bite of his burger, following it up with a swig of soda. Too fast. He coughed, sputtered, and cursed slightly under his breath.

She sucked in air. What? How could he confess such a crime in public? She looked around. Did anyone hear what he just said? No, the sole other guests were on the opposite side of the restaurant, laughing. The servers were in their station, playing with their cellphones. No one overheard him. Good. Sitting there, she didn't dare move for fear of giving away the internal struggle playing out in her mind. Her stomach was twisted in knots, her appetite totally demolished, as she sat and stared at him. Her hands and feet broke into a sweat, although she had been chilly just moments before. She put down her teacup. She grasped her hands under the table, trying to maintain an outward calm. What would happen to her? She bit her lip as she waited to hear what he had to say. What would the future bring for her? She started thinking of various scenarios. No, Susan, focus. You must pay attention. What was he saying? Oh. Nothing, for now.

She had guessed some time ago that he was seeing another woman, but even if his admission didn't blindside her, the pain was not any less real. It was not the action that hurt her most. She would be the first to acknowledge human weakness- she had misbehaved in high school, resulting in the birth of her first child at seventeen- and give forgiveness to a husband who had strayed. But forgiveness can only be given if it is desired; the man who sat before her enjoying his burger and fries looked contented and at ease, relaxed by his confession.

"How long?" she asked.

"Almost three years," His voice was quiet but haughty. "You really didn't know, did you?" He smiled, sneering at her trust.

"What do you want to do? Divorce me??" she asked, no longer wanting to enjoy her cream of crab soup. She pushed the bowl away, glancing down, then back up at him, to face the future.

"I don't," he said. "Divorce is difficult even in the best of situations and, besides, none of the money is yours."

"So," she paused. Her mind was racing, not knowing what alternative he might be seeking. "You don't want me, but you're not going to get rid of me?"

"I didn't say that." He sneered, then laughed, amused by his own joke.

Her hands, already trembling as he spoke, began to shake so hard she was afraid he would notice. She held them more tightly under the table. She unclasped them long enough to wipe away the sweat that had begun to form on her upper lip, pretending her nose was running. Her hands retreated to her lap quickly, lest he notice their quivering. The verbal blow he had delivered struck her deeply. She glanced in his direction. Yes, there he sat, cool and calculating, unruffled, eyeing her reactions. He picked up his burger again and calmly ate his food as if they had been discussing the weather instead of the end of their marriage. How could he be so nonchalant? Was he really so callous?

The attention he had given her over recent years had been so minuscule that she knew he couldn't read her face. Based upon his apparent interpretation of her body language, he seemed outwardly satisfied that she was taking his announcement of their marriage's end quite well. Another gulp of soda accompanied his examination. She felt her heartbeat speed up, though beneath the surface of her seeming calm, she was terrified and she could not understand what his plan was if not to divorce her. She did not know how to react. She did not speak further, afraid her shaking voice would give her fears away. Better to remain silent. It was safer. She folded her napkin and placed it next to her plate.

Kurt finished his food without further comment. Then, "You don't seem to be eating anymore, let's go," he said with abnormal kindness. He threw a wad of cash on the table, to speed their departure, she supposed.

Sue followed his lead out of the restaurant, after bundling herself up once more to meet the cold night. She hesitated, having difficulty moving forward, almost frozen in place by Kurt's news. The night, engulfing her in its darkness, seemed even bleaker after their dinner conversation. She found herself continuing to shiver, this time, for more than just the cold. She paused on the stoop of the restaurant, girding herself for the walk as Kurt pushed past her. Something was not right, she was certain. She was deeply troubled.

***

Susan's feet tapped the floor in patient nervousness as her mind retraced every word she had spoken in the interview. Two years of complication after complication had brought her to this quiet, empty, isolated moment of anticipation in the busy hallway of the Anne Arundel County Courthouse. Had it really been two years since that freezing night in Annapolis? Had she recounted all the events correctly? She smoothed her navy blue slacks with her middle-aged hands, pausing to look at the band of skin on her left ring finger. No wedding band graced her finger any longer. She had lost it when the accident happened. She missed it. Her hand felt denuded, empty.

How could I have predicted life would be reduced to this? Susan twisted her hands together. She looked down at her ring finger again, which bore testimony to the fact that no one loved her enough to place a ring there. Her engagement ring and wedding band had been taken to a pawn shop months ago by Kurt, for the money they would add to his bank account with his mistress Kelsey. His love- and his gifted rings- had departed. She was embarrassed by her forced singleness.

Susan wiggled on the polished wooden bench, trying to get more comfortable in an uncomfortable, tense situation that was compounded by the unforgiving hardness of the seat. As she waited to be called, she imagined how unrecognizable the circumstances might have been had a different case called her there and if the unimaginable events leading to this moment had not occurred. Things would certainly be different for her.

Sue held her hands tighter and furrowed her brow to concentrate and remember every detail she had related in the interview preceding the case she was now waiting to begin. Her jaw began to tremble. Did she say everything right? Did she miss anything? She didn't want to have perjured herself. Remember Susan, remember.

"Susan Prescott," the attorney had begun. "When were you first aware that your late husband wished you dead?"

Sue had drawn a deep breath to calm her nerves and gather her wits.

"January 12, 2012, on a very cold midweek night."

Chapter 2

Sue thought back once more to that freezing evening in Annapolis. The destruction of her marriage had happened so slowly that she was baffled by the abrupt nature of that January night. Kurt's blatant disregard for over thirty years of marriage struck her to the quick; her heart was breaking. Yet there she was once again being hurried along by her husband, who took her elbow and pushed her quickly out of the restaurant in a fashion that made no sense. Life with Kurt, though often unsettled, was normally unhurried. Nothing had ever been rushed, if for no other reason than Kurt's obsession with doing things perfectly and with precision. Tonight was different, weird.

Thinking they would return to the car and go back to the warmth of their home, Sue moved to the right as they exited the restaurant. She anticipated Kurt's late-night routine, while she planned to boil a pot of Sleepytime tea to calm her nerves. He would lock the door to his study and bury himself in his computer, ignorant of her existence in the breakfast room. This would give her time to collect her trembling thoughts by the light of her warm lamp in the comfort of her rocker with a soothing cup of tea. She would rehearse with herself how she must take everything one step at a time. Yes, that's what she would do. Nice and easy, Sue. Calm down, girlfriend.

"No, we're going down to the harbor, Susan," Kurt said as he grabbed and then squeezed the crook of her arm and rerouted her to the left. "We always take a walk before going home."

Their new course set, he pinched her arm hard and then released her. Ouch, that pinch hurt. He charged ahead as she fell in step behind him. I wonder if it'll leave a bruise. Probably. It had in the past when he gave her a "love pinch," as he called them. There was nothing loving about them.

Kurt resumed his position in the lead. Sue frowned a little to herself as she burrowed her face into her scarf, which itself had become icy against her face and offered very little respite from the wind that encircled them. Kurt had always complained that a walk down to the water after their meal was boring, claiming the monotony of the scenery as his excuse to return home to more important matters not concerning her. She always persisted for the sake of his health, saying that it was in his best interest. It was good for him, for them. He and his "Paunchy Pilot" friends, as she called them, could use a little workout time every now and again.

In the summertime, she would anticipate with joy the sight of the wide-open water, the lapping waves, and the boats rocking back and forth in the water. Yet when the wind had sunk what would otherwise be 36-degree weather to a below-freezing, bone-chilling night, Kurt, without notice, suddenly wanted to stroll along the dock. That made no sense. No one was out there. It was far too cold and dark.

"Are you sure you want to go down to the docks, given the weather?" she asked with a tinge of concern. What was he thinking? It's freezing out here. Was he nuts?

Kurt remained silent as he stomped down the sidewalk, not answering as they began their usual route. Sue sighed and quickened her pace to resume her submissive position behind him. Years had taught her not to question her placement behind him rather than by his side. They made their way without speaking down Market Space, passing McGarvey's Saloon and turning right onto Dock Street. They passed the Middleton Tavern, crossed Randall Street, and passed Dock's Bar and Grill where the street side tables were abandoned. Most of the restaurants appeared desolate and gloomy. They looked so forsaken; she thought they must be closed for the night, despite the early hour.

As she followed him through the night and down the dark sidewalk, she asked, unsure of herself, "So, what is she like?"

"Her name is Kelsey," he replied into his coat, avoiding giving any more detail than was necessary, it seemed to her.

Names like those weren't common among the generation she and Kurt belonged to, if present at all. They were their children's names. She must be very young, Sue thought to herself.

"We met on one of my flights, almost three years ago" he added.

Sue nodded, still silent. Of course. Sue was not a suspicious woman. She preferred to think well of people, especially her husband. Through the years, people had warned her that traveling husbands sometimes went astray but she waved them off. Not her Kurt. Not her straight-arrow husband. When it came right down to it, the fact that his mistress was met on a flight didn't surprise her in the least. Now Sue remembered the warnings of friends. Of course. They were right all along. How stupid, blind, I've been. How could I not know?

As they passed the Storm Brothers, she glanced into the empty ice cream parlor. Closed. No surprise that no one wanted ice cream tonight. She shivered. They pushed on against the frigid wind, passing Starbucks, Moe's South West Grill, and Eagle Souvenirs. They scooted across Craig Street, and passed the temporary location of the Annapolis Yacht Club. A few months back, AYC lost their usual location to a fire. A fire sounded rather nice, right about now. Sue buried her hands further into her coat. No one in their right mind would be out here tonight. The huge parking lot across from the storefronts was deserted, allowing them to cross uninhibited.

"What would you like to do about our... situation?" she asked. He already said he didn't want a divorce.

His steps became heavier, and he glanced towards the harbormaster's office. "It's an awful business, divorce."

"I don't understand." What was he talking about? He didn't want her; that was all too obvious.

His pace began to slow and he allowed her to catch up to him. "It's messy with splitting things up and inevitably it doesn't end fairly. One party gets what they don't deserve, one way or another. I don't want that."

Sue caught up after a few paces, but still maintaining the distance from him as he always preferred. "If it's a money issue, I don't need much at all," she said, trying to be gracious in the midst of this horrific night.

"What of the money do you think is yours?" he scoffed, glancing quickly at her and quickening his pace once again, to put her back in her place. "If your name is on an account then by all means, take it, but name one thing that says, 'Susan Prescott,'" he demanded.

She winced. He never called her Susan, only when he was very frustrated with her. She had been Sue while they were dating and had remained so for their entire marriage. "None," she murmured.

"Are any of my investments in your name?" he questioned.

"No."

"Savings accounts? Checking accounts?" he persisted, stopping suddenly in his tracks.

"No."

"And what about the house? Did you ever make any payments on the mortgage, the electricity, the water, the gas, the insurance, the taxes-"

"No, Kurt," she interrupted.

He looked at her satisfied. "You don't have a right to anything, woman," he said. A quick, sneering glance accompanied his pronouncement of her unworthiness. "That's why I don't like the sound of a divorce." He turned and continued walking through the parking lot. He muttered quietly, "I'd rather you just died instead."

Her heart almost stopped at the sound of his words. Never before had Kurt resorted to such biting language to express his unhappiness. What could he be thinking? She watched his movements with caution as he trudged against the cold. In the past, his thoughts seemed to always expose themselves in his demeanor. She observed him, trying to read his present state of mind. Nothing, except anger and some other emotion she couldn't quite read.

As her mind swirled through so many thoughts, she remembered how he often boasted to his sons as he sat in his armchair in the living room, pontificating that a true man was one who could control his every emotion. A man was strong, mentally and physically. "First a man makes a decision and then he makes it right," he told the boys. Sue would hear his words from the kitchen and sigh. A man never makes a mistake, in Kurt's world. That's so sad, so wrong, so completely foolish. She shook her head at the memory.

Sue watched him carefully now during their march down to the harbor, trying to read where he was, mentally. His walk was fast-paced, then slowed as if some inward battle was raging. There was some hesitation, it seemed. This apparent conflict in his mind confused her. She felt that something troubled his mind and left him uneasy, making her unsure of what would happen next. What worried her most was his desire for her to die.

They came to the boardwalk that wrapped around the stone courtyard, ended their walk, and embraced the icy harbor. The lights were dim, somehow made dimmer by the frozen night. She pulled her arms around herself tightly as she kept her eye on Kurt, who seemed to have finally won some side of his internal battle. He stepped up the six or so inches from the red brick of the lot to the pock-marked wooden dock. He turned towards her, pausing and waiting for her to approach from behind, his eyes intently fixed on her.

"Come here," he demanded in a quiet voice that left her uneasy.

Boats that would have been moored there in warmer weather were gone. The wind grew stronger, but that was not the sole reason for a shiver to slither down her spine.

"Kurt, please," she called, stopping dead in her tracks, and trying to control her tone so as not to sound too desperate. "Is it really necessary to spend more time down here?"

"I want to show you something, Susan," he replied, ignoring her obvious unhappiness.

There it was again, her given name spoken three times in one night. "Kurt, what could you possibly want to show me?"

"There's something in the water," he answered her without even a glance to the waiting waves that lapped against the pier. His voice was calm, even, measured. He motioned for her to join him on the dock. "I want you to come see it." He gestured towards her, indicating that she was to come up on the dock beside him. He waited.

She placed her feet together, remaining in the parking lot, and held herself tighter. "Please, let's just go home."

"I think you'll find this interesting. Come here!" he said with more urgency in his voice.

"I'm going back to the car. I can't stay here any longer. It's too cold." She took a step away, still looking at him. "You shouldn't either."

His face began to redden again with that same rage she knew so well. He stared her down before he at last relented and dropped his full weight in a frustrated step from the dock. He refused to make eye contact with her as he marched by her, roughly shouldering her aside. His pace was determined and quick as he headed for the parking garage. She tried to keep up, but somehow either he became faster or she became slower. Outpacing her, he disappeared around the corner leading to the Noah Hillman Garage. Moments later, she heard the clang of his angry footsteps climbing the metal steps to the floor where their car was parked.

As she came to Main Street, his car arrived, screeching, in the middle of the walkway. Kurt stomped on the brakes, allowing her to get in, and barely giving her enough time to shut the car door before taking off. He burned rubber as they left.

Later that evening after the silent drive home, when she found herself hidden away in the darkness of the breakfast room, the evening's confession and events replayed many times over in her troubled mind. The inexplicable desire to visit downtown Annapolis, the hurried walk to and from the restaurant, and the stubborn need to walk to the dock all confounded her. But above all, his demanding she join him on the dock to see something he hadn't even turned to look at was very unsettling. The more the night replayed in her mind, the more troubled she became.

Sue soon began to wonder what might have happened had she joined him on the dock per his request. He had told her about his mistress and made it clear he didn't want her around anymore, even going so far as to say that he wished her to die. A divorce was clearly not on the horizon. Yet there he was trying to draw her near and show her something, an act that would otherwise be considered sweet in mid-summer, but was now ridiculous and had the most inopportune timing. The temperature in the Chesapeake

25

Bay must have been frigid due to a freezing December followed by a brutal January. The entire town was deserted. What could possibly have been in the water? Even so, none of those details made a difference, considering he didn't look in the water, only at her.

He only looked at me. The thought swirled and enveloped her mind. He had focused his attention on her completely. What if it wasn't something already there that he wanted to show her, but something he wished to be there? The possibility of what might have happened caused a cold wave of sickening dread to wash over her. There was no ladder anywhere nearby if someone accidentally landed in the water. The nearest ladders were at least twenty feet away. In other seasons, the larger boats docked where they were standing and those ships had their own ladders.

Furthermore, not a single person was to be seen. If he had succeeded in pushing her in, her cries would have gone unnoticed. The harbormaster's office located about two city blocks away might have caught the sound of her voice, but it was doubtful the harbormaster would have reached her in time, if he even happened to be looking out his window as she fell.

Her breath would have been taken away by the shock of her entering the Bay. Her feet could not have found purchase on the Bay's ten-to fifteen-foot floor. She could not have survived treading the ice-cold water as her boots filled, her wool coat and scarf became saturated, and she began to sink. There would have been no escape, not with her leather gloves shrinking around her hands and making it impossible to free herself from her winter clothing. Her breath would have been quickly depleted, and she would have been lost to a watery winter grave.

"I'd rather you just died instead." Did he really say that? Yes, she knew she'd heard those mumbled words from her husband's mouth. After all the years of verbal abuse he had heaped upon her, those words cut Sue like no others. He wanted her dead.

The odds were against her survival. If she had followed him, would he have done it and fulfilled his previous, befuddling, muttered statement? Would he have walked away, driven home, and told some outrageous lie to her loved ones? Would he have even the smallest decency to throw her the one life preserver located on the other side of the dock, pretending to anyone who might have been watching that he cared for her life?

It's ludicrous! She reasoned with herself. Impossible. He wouldn't really do it, would he?

But there was a hesitancy that kept her from being sure he wouldn't. There was too much opportunity and risk, all defeated by her refusal to step up on the dock. The thought of pitching below the surface of the murky water and coming so close to being lost forever would not leave her mind. Despite all her contemplation, even if she put all that aside, one overarching truth remained that could not be ignored, no matter how hard she tried.

He could have.

Chapter 3

Sue thought back to her girlhood, trying to make some sense of her life as she sat in the breakfast room that night. How had the girl she had been as a teen turned her into the doormat of a woman she was today? Hum....It had probably started almost fifty years ago, forty-seven to be exact, when she was a junior in high school. She remembered going to dances at the Naval Academy as a teenager, where she would eventually meet Kurt. Those were the days!

The girls had heard about the Friday night dances at the Naval Academy. The prospect of dancing the night away with attractive Plebes in uniform filled the imaginations of every 16-year-old girl at the high school. Sue was not exempt. All the girls were so excited throughout Friday classes; they rushed home to prepare for their expected fun evening. Despite her bashful nature, she couldn't help imagining being asked to dance and perhaps meeting her own Prince Charming. She was not alone in such wistful musing, as none of her immediate circle of three friends was dating anyone at the time. They drove to the Naval Academy, almost beside themselves with anticipation.

The music was so loud they could hear it as they click clacked in their dress shoes, two by two, down the sidewalk towards Dahlgren Hall. "Oh, 'Stayin' Alive' – that's one of my favorites from the Bee Gees," Sue commented to no one in particular as they got closer. How thrilling!

All of them had been to the Naval Academy before, but this was the first time they entered this particular building. It resembled a huge train station, leading each one of the girls to look up to the dark metal trusses that seemed to tower over everything. As their gazes fell to the brick walls and polished wooden floors, they couldn't help but feel somewhat intimidated. They found a table to remove their coats and leave their handbags at, but each girl loathed de-coating, due to the cool temperatures of the room.

"Why is it so cold?" asked one of the girls, shivering.

"There's an ice rink underneath the flooring," Sue replied.

The girls quickly began chattering to one another about the strangeness of the architecture, trying to ignore the cool air soon enveloping them as they left their warmer layers on the table. Sue adjusted the seams of her dark blue skirt and pulled at the long sleeves of her fuchsia collared shirt as she observed the movement of the people filling the hall. She adjusted the clasp on her flowery necklace to the center behind her neck, while her meandering gaze spotted a group of midshipmen coming their way. Quick! She glanced down to make sure there weren't runs in her stockings or scuffs on her heels. The Plebes all looked so perfectly handsome in their ironed and starched uniforms, with their precisely-cut hair. Yes, she looked presentable.

"How Deep Is Your Love" began to play as the men crossed the hall with their cocky smiles and flirting eyes, apparently aiming for the beaming young ladies. Their focused attention sent a giggle like an electric surge through the girls as they eyed the men coming towards them in their handsome service blue uniforms.

"Hi, girls. I don't think we've seen you ladies here before," one of the Plebes said. "This is Bee Gees night, in case you couldn't tell." He winked at Sue. "Would you care to dance?" His friends repeated the question to her companions.

A resounding "yes" came back from the girls. Sue blushed as the others whispered over the flirting they had just observed and how she had been the recipient. As much as she couldn't help feeling excited that she had been winked at, she maintained that it was nothing more than playing. She couldn't get hung up over a wink when he didn't even know her name. Not yet, anyway. But he was really, really cute...

The men led them past the dark leather couches where less fortunate midshipmen were waiting to find acquaintances to usher onto the dance floor. Other sailors broke in on their dances, after waiting for their classmates to tire. While the Plebes would find themselves waiting and returning to the floor in cycles, the girls didn't sit down all evening. At ten o'clock sharp, the dance came to an end and they were escorted to their car. They giggled all the way home as the eldest gal of the group, grown up at eighteen years old, dropped each starry-eyed, breathless female off at her respective house.

Their chatter was continuous: "Did you see that guy with the red hair? He was *so* dreamy." "I can't wait to go back again. Those guys are absolutely outtasight." "They are all so far out! I love a man in a uniform!"

Over the next few weeks, they returned to the dances with half a mind to come home with a fella. Sue even gave out her phone number to a couple of the men, but things fizzled out, one way or another. It wasn't for lack of liking the few sailors who took her number and called her the following day, but time was the relationship destroyer. Classes at the Naval Academy were demanding and finding a moment for a lengthy phone call or an ice cream downtown was just not feasible. It didn't help that one of the first questions a girl was asked was her age and, no matter how mature she was, "sixteen years old" seemed an uncomfortable stretch for the older men who might have had the time for a relationship. So began her casual whirl of *almost* dating a Navy man.

An unforgettable moment presented itself in the midst of these adventures one day in the hallway of Annapolis High School, when she ran into her old friend, Daniel Walsh. Dan's family had moved away from the Annapolis area a few years before, when his father had been transferred. Dan had been a scrawny kid five feet tall with tousled dark brown hair and an awkward walk. Their friendship was one of mutual timidity and shared interests, but was put on a silent hold by his family's move. She had heard somewhere along the line that Mr. Walsh had gotten a new job a few weeks earlier and that the whole family would be back on the east coast again, but she didn't dare believe it until she knew for sure.

"Sue!" Dan had exclaimed with his undeniable boyish charm as soon as their eyes met. "How are you?"

Sue couldn't help laughing at the moment it took for her to recognize him. The boy of earlier years had gained a foot in height and thirty pounds, and somehow learned to order his unruly brown hair and improve his attire. Her cheeks flushed over how quickly he knew her face. She gulped. "Dan! It's been a long time." She hesitated for a moment before bracing herself to ask, "Are you back here permanently?"

"Yes," Dan smiled, his blue eyes sparkling with some secret delight that never ceased to thrill her. "Dad took a new job that meant coming back here. It's good to be home, even if we got here halfway through my junior year."

A moment passed between them in which Dan was silent, while she wished to the point of desperation that she didn't look as disheveled as she felt standing next to this attractive young man. Her brown hair felt frizzy due to the humidity of the day. She touched it to verify what she suspected. Yep. Frizz City. Groan. He looks so cute and I look so horrendous. Her outfit, a green plaid skirt and yellow blouse, was not what she would have preferred to wear when reuniting with her long-lost friend. Why a yellow shirt, on today of all days? This shirt is not my color. Mom! Why did I let you talk me into getting this Tweedy Bird wannabe?

"So...uh..." Sue tried to restart the conversation, fearing her lengthy silence had been too awkward. "What classes are you taking this semester?" She began kicking herself for asking such an uncreative question. Pathetic.

"Oh, you know, the usual," Dan replied, apparently not perceiving her discomfort. "History, English, Geography, Biology, Spanish..."

"Wait, who are you taking Spanish with?" She interjected in surprise.

"Mrs. Adams," he laughed at her enthusiasm. "Do you know her?"

"Yes," Sue blushed and wrinkled her nose. "She's a little weird."

Dan chuckled and shifted his weight from one foot to the other. "How so?"

"She's married to this really hot photographer guy." Dan burst at once into an amused chuckle at her description. "But she looks so straight-laced!" She said in protest. "She always wears the same kind of black skirt, battleship gray sweater, and worn-out flats. She's ...not very good-looking. The boys tease that she looks like a cow. She's always talking about reincarnation, claiming she was once British royalty or something. Watch out for your Spanish lab, though. She listens in on those earphones of hers and you never know when she's gonna pounce on you."

"I guess I'll find out about her," he said. She could tell there was something else behind his amusement and she couldn't quite put her finger on it. "I have her for third period, right before lunch."

"Really? Me too!" she said with far more enthusiasm than she intended. Embarrassing!

"How about if I save you a seat in class and then we can have lunch together?" he winked.

"Sure thing," she blushed, feeling her face turn beet red as she started to walk away. "Catch you on the flip side."

Over the next few weeks, their friendship took on new meaning. She was surprised at how fast she and Dan became a couple, despite how desperately she had hoped it would happen. In spite of how well they clicked, she had a secret fear that she wasn't good enough for him. In time, now always on his arm, she knew her fear was a silly thing to have considered.

It didn't take long for her to forget the Naval Academy dances and attractive sailors as she and Dan found themselves going everywhere together. The more time she and Dan spent together, the closer they became. They soon found themselves completing each other's sentences, turning down invitations from friends to spend time with each other, and loving the moments they could be together. But as time went on, their affection became far greater than either had planned. Every moment they had alone was another step across a forbidden line. Boundaries were drawn and redrawn after they violated them.

Yet, she couldn't help feeling guilt creep into those moments. She would shake her head and brush her fears away, resolving to focus on Dan alone. Their love was all that mattered to her, to him. Theirs was a timeless love, one that would never end. Why were their actions forbidden by their age and lack of a marriage license? They were married in every way that mattered, or so she told herself.

Prom came, and Dan took her to all the activities, including the Saturday night dance in the gym. The prom committee had somehow succeeded in transforming the gym from an athlete's sweaty playground into a romantic dinner and dancing club. Christmas lights hung from the high rafters with the hopes of softening the hard edges of scoreboards and basketball hoops.

Burgundy and navy-blue crepe paper swirled near the vents that were trying, with limited success, to blow enough cool air to make the room less sweat-provoking. Matching balloons were fastened in the corners, meeting in the middle like a gigantic plastic archway. Tables were laid, every other one, with burgundy or blue tablecloths; coordinating napkins and centerpieces completed the decorations. Everywhere they turned in the building there was a picture of the school mascot, the panther.

Sue had worn a long-sleeved light lavender gown with faux diamonds at the neckline and a corsage mixed with light and dark lavender carnations and a hint of baby's breath. Her hair was held back by a lavender headband. Before they had left her house, she helped Dan put on a lavender bow tie and secure a cummerbund that matched her dress. To top his outfit off, she had placed a single white rose in his lapel. Her parents had made such a fuss over them both, saying how nice they both looked. When they got to the dance, she was relieved to see that their outfits fit in perfectly with their friends.

Couples cuddled in front of the camera as a local photographer took their pictures for posterity's sake. In an attempt to dampen the romantic atmosphere on the part of the hawk-like chaperones, blaring rock and roll music was played by an enthusiastic and loudmouthed DJ, but the couples would not be deterred and took advantage of the soft light and formal atmosphere. With enough trying, they could ignore their surroundings and focus only on each other, regardless of the upbeat music.

The dancers bopped their hearts out all evening long, making their way every now and again to the punch bowl they wished had been fortified with liquor. The jocks had done their level best to add their stolen spirits to the concoction, but the principal, Mr. Williams, who stood six foot four and must have weighed about 240 pounds, made sure that the punch contained no "supplemental ingredients." His black Albert Einstein hair and stern countenance made him a force to be reckoned with. No one messed with him, not even the jocks, no matter how much they wanted to try alcohol. But they were willing to work behind his back.

In his determined effort to have a sober prom "for once in a dang blasted lifetime," Mr. Williams had guilt-tripped assorted teachers into spending the evening with deafening music and their recalcitrant students. Sue and Dan couldn't help laughing to themselves over the grumpy teachers who hadn't bothered to change from their school clothes, and who had gravitated toward each other at a table furthest away from one of the speakers. Sue imagined the conversations about the fun that the teachers wished they had been having and alcohol they wished they had been consuming. Neither, from the teachers' apparent state of mind, seemed to be at the function. Or so it appeared.

What Mr. Williams could not have envisioned was the determination of his students to fortify their evening with a substantial supply of liquor. The scuttlebutt was that a few members of the basketball team had older brothers who were only too happy to supply their younger siblings with whisky and vodka. It wasn't clear to her who had what booze, but Sue noticed there were quite a few boys who left the gym repeatedly, returning with increasingly unsteady steps. Others reached into their jackets quite frequently, pulling out small bottles stashed therein, augmenting their cups of punch, and then throwing the empty bottles into the trash can. The garbage cans began to smell of hard liquor. Couldn't these guys just enjoy the dance? Why did they have to drink?

One of the wayward young men, a football player named Douglas, approached her while Dan was off getting them some Mr. Williams-approved punch.

"You know, Sue, I have always said that you are the most beautiful girl in the school." Douglas burped through his alcoholic buzz. "That Dan Walsh shouldn't be allowed to keep you all to himself." He hiccupped. His speech became increasingly slurred. "I want a little kiss. Come here…" He fell towards her, wrapping one arm around her shoulder.

"No, Douglas. You smell like a booze factory. Get away from me." She pushed him away. Where was Dan? She needed to get rid of this drunk, pronto.

"Come on, baby. Give us a little kiss. Dan's not here. He won't see us." Douglas began pawing at the front of her gown. "Don't be shy, baby." He leaned in, puckering up.

"Go away. I don't want anything to do with you, loser." She tried to shove him away again or, in the very least move as far from him as possible, but his foot was entangled on the bottom of her dress. Rip! "My beautiful dress. What've you done? You big creep!" The bodice was torn away from the lower part of her gown. "Oh, no!" She felt like slugging the guy. She fiddled with the front of her dress. Ruined.

Douglas said, "Oh, baby, I'm so sorry. Here, let me help you fix it." Again, he barreled in her direction, barely able to stand.

She kicked him in the shins. Decked!

***

Dan looked over at Sue. Who's that talking to her? Not that he was jealous but… hey, it's that bum, Douglas. He's touching her. Man, wait till I get ahold of him. He dropped the cups of punch on the nearest table and headed for his date at a trot, weaving among the dancers.

36

"What's wrong Sue?" She looked like a mess. Her mom wasn't going to be happy about this. And he was the one who had to take her back home in this condition.

"Douglas grabbed at me and tore my gown." Sue started to cry, all the while trying to restore her dress. It didn't work.

"Oh, baby, I'm so sorry." Dan squeezed her arm gently. He turned to Douglas. "You can't touch my date. Get up on your slimy feet and fight like a man." He grabbed Douglas and pulled him up. Dan felt his neck and face turning red. The guy was a lot bigger than he was. Douglas outweighed him by a good two inches and twenty-five pounds. What did he think he'd accomplish by threatening the guy? Too late now.

"You ain't gonna hurt me, you pipsqueak." Douglas lurched in his direction.

"Fight!" one of the other kids yelled. A crowd began to gather, urging them on.

Dan felt the attention of the room focus on the encounter as dancers stopped dancing and encircled them. He had to fight the creep or lose face. He took his first swing. He connected with Douglas's mid-section. The boy sucked in breath and swung back. Douglas's alcohol consumption did not help his aim. Douglas struck near Dan's head, somewhere in mid-air. It was a lucky miss. Douglas could've done some serious damage.

He hit Douglas again. Splat! Right on Douglas's nose. Blood flew everywhere. The students standing nearby egged him to continue. "Way to go, Dan!' "Hit him again!"

Douglas grabbed his nose in an attempt to stanch the flow of blood and then torpedoed his opponent's stomach. Ouch! Man that hurt. Dan staggered several steps backward and fell on the floor in pain. Douglas jumped on him. The smell of Douglas's breath was about to knock him out. Good grief, what had the guy been drinking?

They wrestled for a few minutes. Slap! Punch! Dan was glad he had Douglas on the floor- he'd been on the wrestling team and Douglas was easier to manage down- Augh! Where did that strike come from? Oh, crud. Douglas had gotten the upper hand there and Dan was lying underneath the creep, again. Disgusting.

"You leave my girlfriend alone." Dan realized that he didn't speak from a position of strength here, but he had to defend Sue's honor. He drew his knees up to his chest and tried to launch Douglas off of his body. It worked, but was a temporary fix. He started to throw a punch Douglas's way but the fellow suddenly began to wretch and, the next thing he knew, Douglas had thrown up all over him. Dan backed off, standing to his feet and shaking the barfed food from his suit jacket. It was so gross, repulsive. The other boy finally stood to his unsteady feet. Dan punched the kid one more time. Douglas was not upright for very long. Good night, Douglas. Pleasant dreams.

***

"Gross, Dan! That stinks so bad!" Sue wrinkled her nose and then began laughing. She couldn't help herself. The picture she had was of her dress in tatters, Dan's suit a mess of vomitus, and Douglas looking unconscious and very green. Somehow, it struck her sense of whimsy. It was better to laugh than to cry. Then Douglas awoke and vomited on the front of her tattered hemline. Not so funny. The stench worked its way up to her nose in droves. The next thing she knew, she upchucked on Douglas, who was kneeling on the floor in front of her. He was now wearing her dinner all over his heaving back.

Just then, Mr. Williams arrived. "What in the world's going on here? I smell liquor. Whisky, I'm guessing. What do you young people have to say for yourselves?"

Sue wiped her mouth on her partially-destroyed sleeve. She and Dan began talking at the same time. She said, "Please, Mr. Williams, we haven't been drinking, but Douglas has." Dan added, "Please sir, this isn't our fault." They explained the circumstances and Mr. Williams allowed the two of them to go get cleaned up in their respective bathrooms, after smelling their breath. They were in the clear, but Douglas wasn't so lucky with the sniff test. She heard Mr. Williams telling Douglas that his parents would be called and that a suspension was in his near future.

One of the female chaperones had a small sewing kit in her purse and, though much the worse for wear, Sue's dress was made at least somewhat presentable. Sue got stitched up and cleaned up and emerged quite damp from the girls' room a short while later.

Dan, in his wet, squeaky shoes and ruined suit, walked over and said, "Sue, this isn't what I had planned for prom night."

"Me neither."

"Shall we dance?" Dan tried to smile but their mutual stench was still lingering.

"Of course," she told him. "Maybe we'll dry off a bit."

They had both looked so nice when they stepped out that evening, but now, thanks to Douglas's interference and the resulting kerfuffle, her gown dripped with water from the girls' bathroom and her headband was askew. Her lovely corsage was catawampus, though otherwise relatively intact. Dan had tried to straighten it for her, but his ministrations had met with limited success. Dan's suit was spotted with water, his bow tie was askew, and his shoes were leaking black shoe polish on the floor. His boutonniere was reduced to a single twig of greenery, the rose long-since departed, probably mid-fight. She realized that there was nothing she could do to help, so she left his outfit alone. They danced their way through several tunes when the announcement was made regarding the presentation of the prom court.

"Oh, no, Dan. We look horrid. What if we win?"

"Sue, we will hold our sober heads high and wear the crowns with dignity. . . or something like that. My dad talks like that all the time." Dan smiled at her, but his smile was as crooked as her hemline.

"Come on, Dan." Disheveled though they were, they lined up with the other prom queen and king candidates, glad that the voting had taken place during the last class on Friday. The other candidates, especially the boys, were in various stages of inebriation, so maybe no one would notice their bedraggled appearance.

Mr. Williams seemed less than happy with his charges, even as he announced the prom court, leading up to the queen and king of the night. It was narrowed down to them and one other couple. Sue trembled at the thought that they might win. This must be what it would be like to be in a beauty contest. Dan squeezed her hand as they waited for the announcement. First princess and first prince would be nice...queen and king would be better still. Her teeth chattered in nervous anticipation. Her knees knocked. It could have been nerves but, more likely, it could have been because she was freezing in her wet dress.

Mr. Williams shouted, "And the winners, your prom queen and king for the year are...Susan Thomas and Daniel Walsh!"

How exciting! Everyone applauded and cheered. She was very glad that the rose bouquet she received from Mr. Williams was large enough that, with the royal cape, her gown was covered enough for her to look presentable in the requisite pictures. Thank heavens. They would be gracing the cover of the local newspaper by tomorrow afternoon, and she was relieved that she would look queenly instead of unkempt.

She laid her bouquet aside for one formal dance by the queen and king. More photos. Groan. Would they never end? Dan held her tight enough that the rips in her dress were hidden. The photographer moved on to other dancers and she began to relax a bit.

They kissed and snuggled a bit on the dance floor. Okay, so my dress is less than flawless. I don't think Dan cares about that right now. I'm glad the DJ slowed things down a bit. I love being held by Dan. I could stay like this the rest of my life...well, maybe take a shower and change my clothes first. Dan kissed her forehead.

Dan smiled down at her and said, "You know, this evening hasn't gone exactly as I hoped but maybe we can get some romance into it, after all." He started singing into her ear, his incredible baritone voice blending perfectly with the music, his lips gently touching her ear. She could listen to him sing all night. Perfect. During the last slow dance, Frankie Valli's "My Eyes Adored You," Dan drew her behind a pillar encircled by Christmas lights and opened a black box containing a tiny chip of a diamond, set in yellow gold. Dan knelt down on one knee. Her heart was beating so loudly, he could probably hear it. She had only dreamed about this moment.

"Sue," he swallowed. "I love you. I want us to be together forever. I've never loved anyone the way I love you and I can't imagine loving anyone else. I know it isn't much, but I want this promise ring to be my pledge that I will always love you. I want to take this first step towards making you my wife." Her eyes filled with tears as her heart soared far away from the fear that had caused her so much worry. Without a word, he slipped the ring onto her finger and she stepped into his embrace, wrapping her arms around his neck and kissing his cheek.

"I promise to always love you, Dan," she whispered in his ear as his arms encircled her waist. "If you asked me to marry you now, I'd say 'yes' in a heartbeat."

They left the prom a little while later, making sure to be home by their parents' curfew. They had some explaining to do but had clearly not been drinking, so she got into her house without any rebuke. Dan left a short time later. She had never felt so happy in her whole life. She was promised to Dan Walsh. Life couldn't get any better.

With that ring upon her hand, all worry over their previous private activity quickly dissipated. She no longer wondered if she was simply an object of his affection and nothing more. She used to worry Dan might turn out to be someone he wasn't and talk about their dates to others. Of course, she knew the guys who did that were losers who didn't do half the things they claimed. Dan was different, and he proved it every day, though he didn't have to. He was not the kind to "kiss and tell." They both bore a sense of responsibility for their forbidden actions, but she felt all of her concern melt away in the promise of a lifetime covenant. It made up for everything, it seemed.

The rosy colors of the future began to fade one day as late summer moved into fall, a day that would remain vivid in her mind for the rest of her life. A few years prior, in her solemn duty to her daughter, her mother had handed her a booklet explaining the menstrual cycle with a hasty aside regarding the "birds and the bees." Her mother preferred to remain aloof about the whole subject and not give too many more details or explanations. Health class provided not much more information, just a pathetic film strip about menstruation. Sue began to experience what she had been told about and eased into her cycle without many problems. Not long before the fall homecoming dance of her senior year, she was surprised when she didn't have to go to her mother's bathroom for some monthly supplies. Sue was very surprised when she missed another month. However, she was not the only one shocked by her lack of need.

Sue was in her bedroom that late afternoon, adding the latest Bee Gees poster to her wall. She loved to get the latest issue of *Tiger Beat*, check out the centerfold photo, and tape the newest Bee Gees poster to her wall, amid her vast collection. The deep purple paint on the wall behind the pictures reflected against the high gloss white paint of the other three walls, making her room a perpetual lavender color that she loved. Recently, though, it made her feel a bit queasy. No, it must be her imagination. She shook her head. Dizzy. She loved that color. Better sit for a moment, to get my head together.

As she sat on her bed, a quiet knock came at her bedroom door. "Sue, dear," her mother's head poked in. "We need to have a little talk." Her mother stepped in, wearing a June Cleaver floral shirtwaist dress and pearls.

Sue was still in her royal purple bathrobe, having had the stomach flu for several days. She was feeling better, but started to run through every possible terrible thing her mother might have to talk about and pulled her robe tightly around her waist. Her mother did not have "little talks" over nothing. "Yes, Mom?"

Her mother joined her on the bed. "When was the last time it was your," her mother paused and looked her daughter squarely in the eye. "Your 'time of the month'?"

"Uh." Sue fidgeted. That question alone was more than she'd ever heard her mother say about the topic. "I don't know. I mean, it has been a while. I know I've been under stress because I have the SAT exams coming up, homecoming, and all that. Other girls at school have missed before too."

Her mother pursed her lips before saying, "I think we need to visit Dr. Haubbeager."

"Oh, no. I don't think that's necessary, Mom," she said in confusion.

"I'm afraid it might be," her mother replied with a hint of disappointment and inner struggle. "He will need to do an exam, but it isn't the type you are used to." She handed Sue a booklet, similar to the one discussing periods, but different. This one covered what to expect with your first female exam.

"What's this? Oh, gross!" Sue was shocked by the pictures she saw. She turned page after disgusting page.

"You and Dan seem very close," her mother said with great and obvious discomfort as Sue skimmed through the booklet. "I am afraid that I didn't tell you what might happen if you were too close."

Sue almost couldn't breathe as she realized what her mother was saying. "You...do you think I'm...that I'm..."

"Have you and Dan become that close?" Her mother looked both dazed and horrified at her own question.

Sue hung her head, the guilt rushing back over her as she sat on there. "I'm so sorry, Mom. I didn't mean for this to happen."

"So, I'm right," her mother let out a long breath. "You *are* expecting." Her mother, so usually unruffled, was clearly upset.

"I think so. Maybe. No. I don't know," she said in confusion. Sue had been concerned that might be the case, but she couldn't be sure and had reasoned it had been stress like her other friends. "Mom, I-" her voice cracked. "I am so sorry." She dissolved into tears. She fell into her mother's arms.

"This is going to be very hard, Susan," her mother said with tears in her voice as she hugged Sue. "Most parents send their daughters away with some kind of an excuse like kidney problems or attending a finishing school, so they can have the baby in peace. Often the child is put up for adoption, but their lives are changed forever."

Sue began to sob harder. "Mom, please forgive me. Please. I-I didn't know this would happen, I wasn't thinking." She broke down and her mother moved in even closer to her, holding her near. They both cried, clinging to one another.

Moments, or was it hours, later, her mother said, "Oh darling." Her mother kissed her head. "Please know, no matter what happens, I will always love you. First things first, sweetheart," her mother moved her hands to Sue's face and held it as she looked at Sue. "We visit Dr. Haubbeager to make sure that it isn't something else and then we'll make plans to see what can be done."

"Mom, could we go to someone I don't know? I don't think I could face him." Sue had known Dr. Haubbeager since she was a little girl and couldn't bear to see the look of disappointment on his face. She couldn't stand the thought of running into their neighbors and having to explain why she was at the doctor's office when it wasn't time for her yearly physical and when she clearly wasn't sick.

"All right," her mother nodded and pushed Sue's hair behind her ear. "I'll make an appointment with Aunt Jean's doctor and we will see about things." Her mother hugged her again. Her mother hesitated. "I need to tell your father." She left the room, calling to her husband as she walked down the hallway.

Sue sat in silence on her bed and stared at the floor, wishing she could burn a hole into the rug and fall into it. She heard her parents walk into their bedroom and close the door. Her throat closed up with tears and her eyes burned as she felt herself breaking at the thought of her father now knowing that she might be carrying a baby. She heard her father's deep rumbly voice exclaim, "What??"

but the conversation became hushed as her mother shared what the two of them had discussed.

Sue wished she could be there to see his reaction, yet was relieved to be alone in her room. Her parents always dealt with issues in this manner, in quiet conversation in their bedroom, the door shut against interruption or eavesdropping, emerging with their decisions made. She heard their footsteps exit from their room and thought her mother was coming down the hall. Through the door came her father and, in one stride came to her bed, pulling her into his strong arms. Sue let out a little sob against his chest and he held her there until she stopped shaking. He let go after several moments, kissed her forehead, and departed without saying a word.

Her mother returned to Sue's bedroom and looked in at her. She said, "Aunt Jean's doctor it is," and closed the door. Sue sat in her room, devastated but thankful for her parents' love and support. How could this have happened to her? She had let them down. She had let everyone down. It was all her fault. She had failed.

Chapter 4

An hour's drive north of Baltimore to where Aunt Jean lived was the price for privacy, and one both Sue and her parents were willing to pay. There was no chance of running into someone they knew. That would only serve to kick start the wildfire of gossip. It was difficult enough that she was expecting a child, not even seventeen years old, but the shame of gabbing mouths was an unneeded added grief.

The appointment was made for one week later, with a test confirming their suspicions. The rabbit died, giving its life to verify her pregnancy. Her mother spoke quietly in the doctor's office as she arranged for her daughter's prenatal care. Sue waited in the lobby twisting her promise ring, as anxiety built in the pit of her stomach. In that moment, as she considered the weight of responsibility that would isolate her from her carefree classmates, she resolved to hurt as few people as possible. In her mind, the choice became clear: She could not tell Dan. But how could she keep it from him?

That evening, Sue and her parents sat around the kitchen table and discussed the steps forward. They decided several things.

Her mother said, "Dear, I know you care for Dan but you need to break up with him as soon as possible."

"Yes, her father said, "this is nonnegotiable, Sue, honey. We can't take the chance that Dan might figure out that you're . . . pregnant."

Her heart was shattered. "Break up? Why? I love him."

Her mother said, "If folks see your expanding tummy, they'll figure out it Dan's baby. If you break up with him now and don't date anyone else, they might not realize you're pregnant. "

Dad said, "We don't want anyone thinking you are a loose girl."

That comment stung to her very core. She *was* a loose girl. She had had a physical relationship outside of marriage. Sue hung her head, than glanced up. "But I don't understand."

Her mother said, "People will think you're just getting fat. You won't be dating anyone and Dan will be history."

Her father added, "Yes. No one will guess that you're … expecting… because by the time you begin to…show…it will have been months since you had a date." He was obviously uncomfortable discussing this delicate issue. It simply wasn't done in that day and age.

Her mother said, "This way, both of you will be protected."

Sue had to protect Dan. If this was the cost, so be it. "Yes. You're right. I'll…do it."

Sue acquiesced to their requests and worries, agreeing with the decisions being made and appearing calm and collected. But below the table, in her lap she held the promise ring that, for the first time, had left her finger since prom and would never return.

She looked at her parents. "I'll tell him I'm focusing on my studies in preparation for getting into a good college," she said. He wouldn't believe it; she knew he would fight it. "That's what nice girls do. I can blend in." She bowed her head and her heart sank. It was clear. She was not what she pretended to be: good.

Though Dan might think the breakup strange, he would figure that her parents had found out about their relationship and made her stop seeing him to protect her reputation. After all, that was the day's culture. The following day, she mailed his promise ring back to him in a manila envelope, along with a short note: "Things have become complicated and I can't see you anymore. Sue."

As she walked away from the mailbox, her eyes brimmed over with tears and her throat tightened with a heartbroken sob. It was all over. As soon as he received the ring, he would know there was no hope for them. She had already stopped taking his phone calls. A few days later back at school, a mutual friend passed her a note from Dan which read, "Please talk to me." Without a sound, she slipped it into a book and walked to her next class.

Two days later, she was getting books out of her locker on her way out of school for the day. She heard some of the other students giggling and talking behind their hands. She knew from the high school grapevine that they had all heard about the breakup, but no one had come right out and said anything about it to her face. She offered no explanation. She was angry at their chatter and slammed her locker shut. Dan. He was standing on the other side, a look of pain in his eyes.

"Sue, please talk to me." His eyes were tinged with the red of tears shed.

"No. I can't. Go away, Dan." Her lips trembled. She tried to move past him but he just moved in closer.

He whispered, looking around at the students nearby, then back at her. "Why'd you do this? What happened? What's wrong?" She moved to leave. He blocked her way.

"Dan, don't make a scene. Just...go away." The other students were moving closer, not wanting to miss a word of the discussion. She sidestepped him. He matched her step and still blocked her passage.

"No. You have to talk to me. Please. Let's... go have a soda. Talk things through." He grabbed her arm, to prevent her escape. She shook it off.

"I...can't, Dan. I just can't." She tried to leave once more but he stepped into her path again. Would he never give up?

"You owe me that much, Sue." He looked down at her, dipping his line of sight below her lowered chin and lifting it with his hand. Their eyes met. "Please."

She couldn't bear the thought of his making a fool of himself, so she quietly agreed to go with him, though only for a few minutes and not long enough for a soda. They walked out of the building together and headed for the parking lot and his car. He tried to take her hand. She refused, grasped her books more tightly across her chest, and walked on next to him but somehow removed. There was a wall between them, a wall of her own making. It felt like a bad dream and she already knew how it would end.

When they got to his car, he invited her inside. No. she wasn't getting into the place where they had shared so much of their love. She couldn't bear it. "I prefer to stay outside, thanks." They put their books on the hood and faced one another.

He talked. She listened to the sound of her own heart, and his, breaking all over again. He had questions. She had flimsy answers about why they could no longer be together. She saw through her responses. Couldn't he? He took her in his arms. He kissed her forehead and hair like he always did. She relaxed into his embrace and returned it, briefly. Oh! That almost did her in. She loved being with him, to be held by the man she desired above all others. But, no. She and her parents had made a wise decision. This could not be. It would not be. She would not ruin his life. Please...

She shook off his embrace and stood back. She couldn't look him in the eyes, not again anyway, focusing instead on his forehead. "Dan, I never want to see you again. I'm leaving. Don't follow me. Don't call me... Goodbye." She grabbed her books, turned, and walked away. Her heart felt like a dagger had struck

50

her very being. He did not follow. How she managed to walk away, she would never know. Tears streamed down her face in silent anguish as she left his side.

Later that month, she heard that his father had been transferred at the last minute and that his family had moved, once more, out of state. Dan did not say "goodbye." In that moment, a sword pierced her heart and she knew that, never again, would she ever love someone as much as she loved Dan.

"It's not just Dan you need to steer clear of," her father said with quiet firmness at their next family meeting. "If Principal Williams sees your...condition, he'll be required to report you." If she was reported, she would be kicked out of high school without a diploma, making life even more complicated. Supporting herself and the child would be impossible without the diploma that would allow her to go to college. School became a fast balance of avoidance and trusting the right people. She hid from Mr. Williams whenever he was due to visit a class or made his routine walks down the hall from his office to the bathrooms and through the hallways.

Her hiding out was enabled by certain rebellious teachers who were known to have compassion on girls like her. There was an unspoken acknowledgement on their part towards the girls that, despite the misfortune of the circumstances, a home for unwed mothers was worse than the alternatives. They excused morning sickness as "extended food poisoning" or "intestinal bacterium," and missed work was made up without penalty. They were just as determined as the girls were with regards to helping them get their diplomas. In the blink of an eye, the attainment of a diploma became paramount in her eyes. Funny thing, she had never thought much about it before all this.

"Give me your skirts as they don't fit and I'll let them out for you," her mother said. Sue nodded. She was thankful, as she carried the baby through term, that her pregnancy was not as noticeable as it might have been, due to her body type. Winter became a blessing in disguise, allowing her to wear jackets or huge sweaters. She regulated her diet with care so as to minimize added baby weight as much as possible. She ate like a pig at school so that everyone would think her weight gain was caused by overeating, but Sue watched her calories with care at home. Right before the end of spring semester, she would give birth so that, when she graduated, she would have been able to shed the extra weight with no hint of the ordeal she had gone through.

To excuse the baby that was living under their roof, her mother would tell people that they had taken the "child of my dead niece" into their home. Sue wouldn't have been able to bear giving up her baby like most girls did. In this action, her parents demonstrated great compassion for her. They decided to raise the child together, allowing Sue to graduate on time and attend Anne Arundel Community College. The plan was solid and agreed upon by the three of them.

A few weeks after she and her parents finalized their plans, Sue retreated to her room and lay on her bed, desperately hoping and praying that people would accept their fabrication. All she wanted at this moment was to disappear into the woodwork.

The plan worked without any complications. She shunned her friends, staying out of sight and silent as much as possible. She overheard them talking, saying that Sue was more upset at her breakup with Dan than they had originally thought. She didn't return their phone calls and didn't accept any offers to go out with the girls she had always been friendly with. They might have wondered, but they eventually gave up on her. That was fine with her. No one must know, not even her former best friend. She dropped out of every club she was in. She left school as soon as it finished for the day. "Whew," she sighed with relief as another undetected day passed. "I made it."

She trusted no one, except for her parents, as she climbed into a cocoon of her own making. The day finally came when her baby arrived. She gave birth right on schedule, slipping into the hospital near Aunt Jean's doctor and then departing a few days later with baby Joshua in her arms. "Stomach bug. Nasty stuff," she explained to anyone who cared enough these days to ask. "I feel much better now."

She began to breathe easier, as she finished her senior year and took final exams. If anyone suspected anything, nothing was said to her face. She got through graduation, avoiding the parties that were given by other students and, of course, not going anywhere near the prom.

A few years later, she walked across the stage at AACC and received her college diploma with her parents and toddler in the audience, beaming up at her. She launched at once into her job at a pediatric office as a physician's assistant and nurse. Her hectic days were filled with work and providing for her son, while he was cared for by her mother during her work hours. She saw Dan in Joshua's eyes every time she looked at him. He was a constant, calming influence for her heart and mind. He reminded her of the young man she had, and still did, adore. Somehow, it was enough for now.

"Sue, you can't continually work and then go home to be a mom to your cousin's kid without any time for yourself!" complained Mary, one of her friends in the office. "You have to socialize! Come on," she insisted. "Come with me to the Naval Academy dance tonight!"

"I don't know, Mary," she said. Sue wasn't sure she wanted any part of it. "Those guys will be awfully young for me. We used to go when I was still a teenager…"

"Oh, Sue, stop worrying and making up excuses," Mary scoffed. "There are some upperclassmen there to keep an eye on the younger guys." She paused. "There are also some officers there, to keep an eye on the upperclassmen." Mary blocked her path from escaping. "That's who we target- the upperclassmen and the officers. Please come with me!"

After much persuasion, Sue relented on one condition: they would leave late so she could put Joshua to bed as she normally would. Her supposed worry and excuses, as Mary labeled them, were in fact her responsibility as a mother; of that, she was very much aware. She saw her responsibility to Joshua as her primary focus, and he needed her to be there as much as she could. Those evenings before bedtime were sacred.

That late spring night, Sue chose her outfit with care. She wanted to present herself in style without seeming to be either a matron or a teeny bopper. At twenty-two, she was a woman with experience beyond her tender years, at the price of lost youthful involvements. She chose a simple burgundy A-line skirt and a burgundy and white print shirt with overflowing long sleeves. She added some comfortable black heels and kept her silky brown hair down to compliment her appearance. People occasionally told her she looked like a young Jaclyn Smith, a real compliment, in her eyes. Looking in the mirror, Sue was pleased with her reflection. She twisted this way and that, scrutinizing her shape. Her figure had returned, thanks to her newly-begun running routine. She considered her appearance again. Not bad for an old woman of twenty-two, Sue, not bad at all.

"Well don't you just look like your mom!" Mary teased as she stepped into the front hall to pick her up. Mary was wearing a hot pink sheath dress. "Adoptive motherhood definitely tempers a person." Then, "I'm kidding! Don't look at me like that!" Mary objected. "You look very... stylish," she said, trying to be reassuring.

"I would rather have the style of Jaclyn Smith," Sue told her friend with a laugh in her voice. "I'm not much of a Joan Collins or Linda Evans type." She sighed. Okay, let's get a move on. Get this over with.

Despite being older than the rest of the young people at the dance, the young women still had a delightful evening filled with dancing and flirtatious mingling. She'd forgotten how much fun it had been when she was a teen, spending time whirling around the hall in the arms of uniformed Plebes. She reflected later that she hadn't sat out a single dance. It soon became a regular outing for the girls; it served to release the tension of the week and start the relaxing of the days of the weekend.

One particular evening, Sue was standing to the side waiting for another partner to lead her to the floor when she caught the eye of one certain young man a ways down the room from her. She looked away, not wanting to seem bold. She always made sure not to hold anyone's gaze, especially when she found the man very attractive. She kicked herself for diverting her gaze, however. The song was good and she wanted to be dancing. She looked up again and he caught her glance once more. She couldn't help smiling at him and his face lit up in return. Before she could second-guess the exchange, he strode across the floor and extended his hand to her with a devilish grin and a wink. Her heart fluttered and she extended her hand to his. "May I?" She nodded as he led her into the crowd of dancers.

"So, Sue," said Mary later, with a suggestive lilt in her voice that made her blush. "You spent a lot of time with that one fellow tonight. What's his name?"

She laughed, self-conscious at Mary's teasing questions. "He's an upperclassman and his name is Kurt Prescott."

"Oh, an upperclassman! How fancy!" Mary giggled. "How old is he?"

"He's twenty-seven," she said. "He'll be twenty-eight when he graduates."

"Oh, doesn't that make him older than most of the other rising seniors?"

"Well, turns out he served in Viet Nam for three years but now that he's home, he can complete his college education. Apparently, he barely made it under the wire, since the rules say a senior has to graduate from the Naval Academy by the time he's twenty-eight."

"You have yourself a brave, capable, fine-looking man there," Mary said with admiration. "You know he looks kind of like that actor from *Looking for Mr. Goodbar*...Richard Gere."

"You're right," Sue laughed.

"Did you get his number?"

"He got mine," she said, quiet and shy. "But I don't know if he'll call."

"Oh, Sue," Mary sniffed. "With a girl like you, he'd be crazy not to!"

A couple of nights later he called, and they made a dinner date for the Federal House in downtown Annapolis, a restaurant they both loved, that was almost on the Chesapeake Bay. Soon they were seeing each other on a regular basis. They never returned to the Naval Academy dances.

"I don't want the competition," Kurt told her with a wink and a smile.

"When are you going to tell him about Joshua?" her mother asked when Sue returned from another delightful evening on the town.

"I..." she hesitated. "I don't know." Things were so complicated.

"Does he know you have a son?" Her mother looked her straight in the eye, unflinching.

"Yes, of course, it's just...," Sue took a breath to collect her thoughts. "I don't know how to tell him about my...situation. I'm afraid it will drive him away."

As Sue came to care for Kurt, she realized that she needed to see how Kurt and Joshua got along before things got any more serious. She had passed Joshua off as the "son from my first marriage," getting closer to the truth with Kurt than with anyone else. Kurt seemed enthusiastic about meeting Joshua. They made plans to go to McDonald's playground for dinner one evening, so they could meet in a setting that the little blonde-haired, blue-eyed boy would like.

"Hey, buddy," Kurt got down on one knee with a big smile on his face. "I brought you this G.I. Joe."

Joshua peeked around his mother's leg, but the lure of a new toy was apparently too much for him. He stepped forward and took it from this very tall man. "Thank you," he said with his eyes glued on the soldier.

"Do you like to play soldiers, buddy?" Kurt smiled up at Sue, nodding his apparent approval of the little boy. Sue beamed back at him.

"Mister, my name is 'Joshua,' not 'Buddy.'" Sue cringed at Joshua's childlike honesty.

"Of course, Bud...I mean 'Joshua.' Sorry about that, chief."

Joshua showed the new toy to Sue and then scurried to the playground. "Sorry, Kurt," she said self-consciously. "Joshua likes to play with other kids whenever he gets the chance. He spends a lot of time with my folks, when he isn't in kindergarten. I know he appreciates your gift, but he *is* only five."

"Hey," Kurt stood up, looking down at her and holding her gaze. "Don't worry about it. I only want to be his friend," he placed his hands firmly on her shoulders. "We have time to make that happen."

Over the next few months, Kurt and Joshua got to know one another better through planned play dates. They went to the National Zoo, the Aquarium in Baltimore, and to the Eastern Shore. They seemed to get along great, and Kurt became the father that Joshua had never known.

After a long day spent with Kurt, Sue put her exhausted little son to bed. As she laid his head softly on the pillow, he said in his drowsy voice, "Mommy, you should keep Kurt." In that moment, as Joshua was lost to slumber, she knew the love of her son had opened the door for her own love to blossom. Soon, she found herself discussing the future with Kurt, one that they would build together.

Sue was not forthcoming right away about the circumstances that had led to her motherhood but, as she came to love and trust Kurt more, she knew she had to explain the true conditions that had resulted in her parenthood. Her mother had warned her over and over to tell Kurt about Joshua's birth situation, and Sue knew that she would either have to show a divorce decree when they got their marriage license or admit she had never been married. The prospect terrified her, but she rested in Kurt's unconditional kindness toward them both. She felt it beyond measure. He would forgive and accept them even so.

Chapter 5

A couple of weeks later, they planned to go to the Federal House for dinner; Sue intended to tell Kurt the whole truth that very night. At first, she had thought she would tell him over dinner, but when the entrée of Mediterranean Royal Sea Bass had come and gone and somehow she found herself savoring a dessert of Lemon and Strawberry Cream Shortcake, she postponed her confession while she summoned all the courage she could muster. The questions she kept asking herself were "Can I do this? Can I pull the trigger on this wonderful relationship?" Her heart groaned at the thought of losing him. Oh, but I must.

After dinner, they walked along the Naval Academy streets lined with identical, pristine houses. The night lights were twinkling. The fall weather was stunning as she looked at the trees turning golden and preparing to shed their leaves. What a lovely night. She swallowed hard and held his hand. He began swinging their hands gently, sweetly. It was time.

"Kurt?" she said, in almost a whisper.

"Yes, darling?" Kurt replied. He lifted their joined hands to his lips and kissed hers.

"There's something that I want… that I need to tell you," Sue paused to gather her fleeting thoughts. "I should have told you months ago but I wasn't sure how to say it."

Kurt stopped and put his hands on her shoulders like he had done the day he met Joshua for the first time. "You can tell me anything, my love. You know you can." She felt the warmth of his touch, seeming to strengthen her for what lay ahead. He drew her close and kissed her forehead. "What is it?"

She drew back. "I love how you're so good with Josh and so nice to me, but you need to know," she closed her eyes, took a deep breath, and prepared for the plunge. "Joshua's father and I... were never married. I was seventeen years old when I had him and so afraid of what people would say." She blurted the words, rushed them out. Kurt's gaze never wavered and he remained silent. She continued, "His father moved out of state before he even knew I was expecting. Mom and I told everyone Josh was her dead niece's son. When he got older, I told Josh that his father and I were divorced so he wouldn't be ashamed. I told him that I had resumed my maiden name and given it to him. He's never known the truth," she said with great misery. "I'm sorry I lied but I was just protecting Josh." Kurt didn't speak. "Kurt, please say something." She was desperate.

"Susan," he said with tenderness in his voice. "It must have been incredibly difficult for you. You were so brave to go through all that on his behalf." He gathered her into his arms and held her head against his chest. "I understand completely," he whispered into her hair. She let out a little sob in relief. "Hey, these things happen" he said, trying to comfort her, and pulling her away to look at her face. He held her face in his hands. "Please, don't worry your pretty little head over this." He wiped a tear from her face. "I love you so much." He kissed her forehead and embraced her again.

***

Kurt smiled to himself as he held her in his arms. He thought: Gotcha! I knew you were hiding something from me. Why do you think I had you investigated? I've known for weeks. I could've saved myself $300 bucks if I'd just held out a little while longer, but this confession was worth waiting for. Dear old Dad always told me to look out for myself. Take care of Number One. Get an attractive wife to have on your arm and then keep her in her place. Dad said I needed to have something on my wife to hold over her forever and you just gave it to me, my lovely Susan. Now, you know that I know. We'll get married and I'll do whatever I want, whenever I want, or I will ruin your reputation. "God Himself will call it justice," as they say. Not that there's a God to worry about. Kurt couldn't stop smiling. You will never leave me, my sweet. Never. Or I will utterly destroy you.

***

Two nights later, Sue planned an evening in with Kurt, Joshua, and pizza. When Kurt walked in the door, he called them over to inspect the pizzas he was charged with bringing. "I want to make sure they're exactly as you asked," he said with a mischievous grin. Kurt opened the box and there was a pizza bearing a simple message written in easy cheese: "Will you marry me?" He knelt down, looked at Joshua, and asked, "Can I marry your mom?" The little boy jumped into his arms, nodding with delight. Joshua looked over at her and yelled, "Mommy, Mommy, say 'yes!' Say 'yes!'"

Sue laughed at the quirkiness of Kurt's proposal and Joshua's enthusiastic reaction. She set the box on the counter so as to wrap her arms around Kurt's neck and kiss his check before saying with joy, "Yes, Kurt, oh, most certainly, yes!"

After eight months of planning the wedding, Kurt graduated one afternoon, and Joshua came down the aisle bearing the rings for his mother and his soon-to-be father, the next. In the Naval Academy Chapel on a beautiful spring day, a little family was formed under the banner of "Ensign and Mrs. Kurt Prescott."

Sue was warned by certain married friends that, as soon as he carried her over the threshold, she would wake up to a brand new man. There was laughter over the assertion, but all agreed that a marriage certificate seemed to be the moment you signed away your best face.

"All those months or years of courtship and engagement are part of a game, you see," one pal said. "Lure the girl in and then, aha! Now we don't have to open doors and kiss hands and flirt with every little comment!"

"Just you wait and see, Sue," said another. "Now that you're married, you'll become intimate with all sorts of attitudes you may not have ever known about!"

"No, you're both wrong. Kurt is exactly the man he seems to be: charming, kind, thoughtful. You're too cynical. Kurt is the best. You'll be the ones to wait and see, not me." She countered their attacks with boldness. She knew her precious hubby much better than they ever would. She shrugged them off with the confidence of knowing she was right. Old fuddy-duddies.

As much as she insisted that their comments would not be the case, it seemed that their pessimistic predications were an all-to realistic fulfillment. His sweet, always-forgiving demeanor was replaced with passive aggression and mild suspicion that came in tiny comments which worked like sand on rock, slowly but surely eroding the surface.

"You meet one man at the end of the aisle, but you walk back down with a different guy altogether" rang in her mind with every caustic remark he made.

One evening a few months later, she sat at her dressing table putting on the finishing touches to her hair and makeup for the military event she and Kurt were attending. He was wearing his formal dress uniform that evening, so she decided to dress herself in a black velvet gown with a gold necklace and earrings. She smiled at her reflection in the mirror as she put in the earrings before turning on her seat and calling, "Kurt, dear?"

"Yes, darling?" he came out of the bathroom in full dress, fiddling with his cuff links.

"Would you be a dear and put my necklace on for me?"

He smiled and said, "Of course!"

He strode across the room and took the necklace in his hands, clasping it behind her neck. His hand remained on the back of her neck as he bent down to look at her in the mirror. "Well, now, isn't she lovely?" he asked with a tease in his voice. He nuzzled her ears and began working his way down her shoulders.

"Oh, Kurt, you silly!" She reached up and caressed his face. She pulled him towards her for a kiss. He started towards her, then stopped abruptly.

"Where did you get those earrings?" he cut in with annoyance.

Sue faltered for a moment. "They were my mother's. Why do you ask?"

"Well, it's just that I've bought you a lot of pretty earrings that would go perfectly with this necklace," he replied. "But if you prefer your mother's plain hand-me-downs, I can stop wasting my money on jewelry for you." He snorted at her.

"Kurt!" she stopped him. "It's not a slight against you...my goodness!" What brought that on? He was acting so strange, different somehow. She was shocked. What's going on here?

"It sure feels like one," he hunkered down next to her and softened his tone. "I know you mean well, but you're mine. I want the whole world to know that and that no one else can touch you." He smiled and kissed her hand.

Sue searched his gaze in confusion. "Well, if it means that much to you," she reached up to remove the earrings.

"It does." He stood and kissed her forehead. "It does." He walked downstairs to wait for her.

She opened the drawer and put the earrings in their place, discouraged by their conversation. She wouldn't look at those earrings the same way, ever again. They were the earrings that made him mad. She didn't have the heart to try with another pair, lest she incur the wrath that seemed somehow bottled up inside him. Forget it. No earrings tonight at all. She slipped on her evening heels and joined him downstairs, where he treated her as if nothing had transpired between them. The entire evening, she noticed he kept careful watch on her, never allowing her out of his sight. He paraded her to all of his friends, joking that she was his latest conquest. Polite to a fault, she laughed along as a supportive wife but, inside, feeling self-conscious about his possessive behavior. Why would he say such things? She wasn't a possession.

"Darling, it's nothing!" he laughed when she mentioned her unhappiness with his earlier actions on their way home. "It's all in fun, I promise."

"But, Kurt, I don't want to be some kind of a possession. I want to be your wife," she said with tenderness.

After a moment of thoughtful silence on his part, he replied, "The war made me afraid of losing that which I value most. I don't want to lose you to a better man."

"Kurt," she whispered, "that will never happen."

Nine months later, she brought a gorgeous baby girl they named Brooke into the world. Kurt was enamored. His entire world seemed to revolve around his daughter. The transformation brought about in his becoming a father to a child of his own was astonishing to her. As life adjusted to the newborn, she relaxed about her worries over her husband. Perhaps new purpose was brought into his life now that he had helped create such a beautiful child. Kurt doted on Brooke and enrolled Joshua in sailing lessons at the Annapolis

Yacht Club. Soon enough, their family grew by one more: a baby boy named Christopher.

Christopher was the only one who didn't remember their old house back in Maryland as he grew up, due to Kurt's transfer to New London, Connecticut, shortly after his birth. It was there that Sue learned Kurt could legally adopt Joshua, since his birth father had shown no interest in the young boy and had not contributed to his support. Dan, of course, had no clue that he had a son, but that was a complication more easily avoided if she simply told the half-truth to the judge. Dan indeed had done neither of those things that would demonstrate his interest in Joshua and had moved away. At Kurt's insistence, they decided to keep things as simple as possible with the adoption and tell the partial truth about Dan's lack of attentiveness to Joshua. She told the judge that she had no idea where the birth father was, which was true, and that the man had not shown any desire to be part of Joshua's life, which was not the case. That was, therefore, why he hadn't signed the adoption papers. The judge bought it.

*** *** ***

Kurt smiled as he heard Sue technically perjure herself when she testified to the judge that Dan wasn't interested in Joshua. He doesn't even know the kid exists! Now I have something else on you, dear Sue! I can get you locked up for some time, should I choose to do so. All I have to do is let the court know that you lied about Josh's father. You are so naïve and such a doormat that I can order you to do anything I want. That's exactly how I like it. The partial truth is a lie, Sue, whether you know it or not. But if you'll lie in court, will you lie to me? I better keep an eye on you, darling wife. And I will. Believe me, I will.

***

As the children grew older, Sue noticed that Kurt seemed to become more irritable. He would return home from work frustrated and on edge. It became clear that he didn't care for Connecticut and so she reasoned that his agitation was due to their location. After all, his unhappiness with everything else in their life was unreasonable. Oftentimes, he would walk into the kitchen when she was preparing dinner and ask with tired agitation, "Why isn't dinner ready? Why are all those toys scattered about in the living room?"

"Well, Kurt, I was making dinner and really needed to not have the kids underfoot, so I sent them to play."

Kurt waved his hand and furrowed his brow as he made his way to the stairs. "Yes, yes, just ...hurry up and get dinner on the table soon, please?"

Sue felt deflated. "Of course." She was so isolated there in Connecticut. Her mother was hundreds of miles away and Sue's support system of both her parents was gone. Kurt didn't approve of long phone calls to her mother, due to the cost, so their conversations were brief and infrequent. The few friends she had previously were at work; those relationships had ended when she left nursing to raise her children. Since he was in the Navy, transfers were common and meant that friendships of any lasting value were unlikely. She had no real friends at all, come to think of it. She was lonely and alone, in the midst of her noisy family.

After dinner, she stood at the sink washing dishes when she felt his arms slide around her waist and his head rest on her shoulder. "I'm sorry for being unpleasant earlier. I was tired, today was so long; I don't know why it got to me."

"It's all right. My day was busy, too."

"Oh, yeah?"

"Yes, I had a meeting with the Ladies' Auxiliary."

"Darling," he yawned, "I'm sure your day was packed but I need to hit the rack. Thanks for understanding." He left her alone to finish her chores.

Some help would have been nice, but she had known for years that there was a fine line between "men's work" and "women's work." Kurt was loath to cross the line. She wished, just once, that he would take an interest in her day, to lend a hand with the chores he deemed suitable only for a woman. It would have been fun to do the dishes with him. She'd heard about her friends whose hubbies offered to dry while they washed the dinner plates. They'd used the time to catch up and talk without the children. Not in their house. She scrubbed the lasagna pan with greater fervor. Why couldn't he at least stay and chat with her?

Okay, Sue, give the man a break. It's been a long day for both of you. He's tired. You're tired. He has to go to work in the morning while you get to stay at home. Calm down. So he's not Mr. Comfy Cozy anymore. He provides for you and the kids, doesn't he? Back off. . . But. . .

She found herself questioning more and more of Kurt's behavior as time went on, yet he seemed to always find a way around the biting remarks, saying that they came from his days in Viet Nam. She swallowed her concern for the welfare of her family. She cared more for her husband being a father to their children than anything else. His sarcasm and unkind behavior was only towards her.

As the years rolled on, Joshua and Christopher became even more connected to their father, while Brooke chose to hang back with her mother. In hindsight, it became clear to her that Brooke had seen more than she was given credit for. Brooke expressed a certain type of protectiveness for her mother when she saw the invisible hurt that was caused by Kurt's behavior. The boys, on the other hand, chose not to see the tension. They desired peace and a good time. Getting in the way of their father seemed counter to those goals, so they ignored his treatment of Sue.

After he retired from the Navy, they chose to return to the Annapolis area. That meant they would be leaving Connecticut, which pleased Kurt to no end. It was one afternoon as Sue was preparing for the movers to arrive that she went into the master bedroom closet and picked up some boxes containing Kurt's shoes. She thought she would dust the closet behind the piles of boxes, so that the movers wouldn't think less of her housekeeping. She accidentally picked up more shoeboxes than she could handle, with several of them careening off her careful stack and crashing to the floor.

"Oh, no! I've gotta get things back the way they were before Kurt comes home and sees the mess...He's become so fussy about things. Say, what's this?" She'd found an old manila envelope had been tucked into one of the boxes. The fall from the shelf made it fly out of the box and onto their bedroom floor. She picked it up, curious.

"The Annapolis Private Investigation Agency? Who are they?" She wasn't given to spying on Kurt, or anyone else, but this was an envelope with a return address she didn't know. She turned it over several times, studying it, and trying to remember if she had ever seen it, but, no, she was unfamiliar with it and with its contents. The whole thing was so curious, she had to look inside. She carefully removed the envelope's contents, after observing that the envelope was not sealed. She found a stack of papers, the first of which was a letter to Kurt. It was dated October 13, 1983. It read:

Dear Mr. Prescott:

68

Per your request, I have been investigating the background of one Ms. Susan Margaret Thomas. As you can see by the enclosed birth certificate, she was born in 1960 to Mr. Steven Thomas and Mrs. Shirley Thomas in Annapolis, Maryland. She is an only child, from what the records show on Mr. And Mrs. Thomas's residency as seen in the United States Census surveys taken from the time of their marriage in 1957 through this year. No other children were born to, adopted by, or fostered by the Thomas family, again using the Census information from that time. I stopped checking for children born to Mr. and Mrs. Thomas after she reached 50 due to Mrs. Thomas's age, which had placed her beyond the childbearing years. However, I did find a Joshua Adam Thomas, born in April 1977. He was reported as a member of the household in the 1980 Census, a copy of which I have enclosed.

On April 26, 1977, Joshua Adam Thomas was born in Mercy Medical Center, just north of Baltimore. I have enclosed a copy of his birth certificate, which lists Susan Margaret Thomas as his mother. She was 17 years old. His father is listed as Alan Jay Merrill. I can find no evidence of this man's existence; however, I do note that these are the first names of three of the Osmond brothers. Perhaps Ms. Thomas was a fan.

I have enclosed a copy of Ms. Thomas's high school and college diplomas. I have examined numerous copies of her high school yearbook. She was quite active in various clubs (Drama, Pep, Spanish clubs; the Student Government Association; and Beta Club) until her senior year, when she stopped participating in all extracurricular activities. She continued to live with her parents after childbirth and graduation; she currently resides with them. She graduated with high honors from Anne Arundel Community College in 1980, getting a degree in nursing.

I believe our next step would be for me to interview some of her neighbors or classmates, though this may be counter-productive to your desire that she not know about the investigation. Please let me know via mail if you wish me to continue my work. I have received your check in the amount of $300.00, which covers my expenses to date. I will need a further retainer of $300.00, if you wish me to conduct interviews with her acquaintances. I do warn you that she may become aware of your interest in her background, since these people would not be under oath or have any obligation to keep our discussions private. I await further instructions from you before proceeding further.

Yours truly,
James Snyder, PI

There was a carbon copy of a letter from Kurt, dated one week later. It read:

Dear Mr. Snyder:

Thank you for your prompt attention to this matter and for your thorough investigation. I am satisfied with the current results and do not require any additional investigation of Ms. Susan Margaret Thomas. I will contact you in the future, should the need arise to investigate her activities further.

Sincerely,
Kurt Prescott

Sue saw the carbon copy of Kurt's signature. It matched all the things she had seen him sign since their marriage license, so she knew it was not some strange mistake. She sank to her knees, and then began looking through the evidence. Yes, it really was copies of all the documents since her birth and Joshua's coming into the world. There were pictures of newspaper clippings of her first dance recital at Miss Millie's Studio when she was four years old and her performances in recitals every year after that. Here was the time she played a turtle in the spring recital; there she was, pictured as a whole note in her fourth grade Christmas pageant. There was a photo of her confirmation in the church at twelve. Every newspaper photo that had ever been taken of her was copied and in her hands.

Was nothing sacred? How could that investigator have gotten ahold of all these documents? Her life was laid out in front of her, found out by Kurt's PI. Before he had even proposed, he had known all about her. She realized that she really knew very little about him.

The Census information...it was all there, in black and white. She felt weak, exhausted. She sat back on her haunches. He had known everything. That thought just kept running through her mind. No wonder he had seemed so calm and collected that night at the Naval Academy! She was telling him what he had already known. The only surprise was the one she felt right now.

What could she do now? She was far away from her family. She had no close friends, none that Kurt had not already pre-approved. They didn't go to church, so she had no pastor to confide in. She could not or would not burden her children with any negative news about their father. They were much too young, anyway. She had no one.

A few minutes later, or was it an hour, she slipped the photocopies and letters back as she had found them. She closed the envelope that bore her story, and placed it back in the shoebox where it had resided for years. She re-stacked the shoe boxes with care, to make certain that Kurt would not suspect she had found his secret stash of her life. She had no desire to dust the closet; she cared not what the movers thought of her housekeeping. She felt totally numb inside. Dead. She turned and walked out of the bedroom, down the stairs, and outside for fresh air.

After several miles of walking, she returned to her home to prepare for the homecoming of her children and spouse. She picked the children up at school, for once not caring about their day. She felt like she was in a tunnel, staring at her chatty children as if they belonged to someone else. Christopher even irritated Brooke by kicking the back of her seat but Sue didn't call him down for it. Brooke looked at her, hurt, but Sue just looked out the window of their car, preparing to leave the school parking lot. What did it matter?

Sue folded laundry by rote, prepared dinner without concentrating, and sleep walked through the rest of her day. Who am I married to? What kind of man is he really? She debated about confronting him but, no. You don't ask questions that you don't want to know the answer to. She would say nothing. Not now. Maybe never. She rallied against her own lack of backbone. I deserve this, if I'm not going to stand up to him. Time went by. The pain subsided but was always present now. I don't know this man. He didn't trust me.

They moved to Maryland. It was uneventful, as the movers came in and moved them; they bought a new home near Annapolis. They all settled into new routines. The kids were enrolled in new schools; life went on. Kurt took a job teaching flying at a former

Naval Academy buddy's flight school in an attempt to regain some of the excitement from his youth. This, however, proved futile after only one year.

"Sue, I'm bored to tears! Don't you understand?" he said in exasperation one evening after dinner. They were sitting in the family room, waiting for the kids to join them for movie night.

"But I thought you would find this exciting and challenging, Kurt!" she handed him the bowl of popcorn, hoping to assuage his anger.

He sneered at her, saying, "the fact that you don't understand tells me I can't tell you anything." He grabbed the bowl and stuck a wad of popcorn in his mouth.

Did he really need to take such large bites? He was libel to choke. "But, dear, don't you think your friend John appreciates your help?" Sue was at a loss over what to say.

"He's done fine without me all these years. The job is tedious and the students are pathetic. I need something that actually stretches my gifts, not a toilet to flush them all down!" He threw the bowl back at her. "There's not enough salt on this. Can't you even make popcorn right? Sheesh!"

"But, Kurt, dear..." She took a bite of the popcorn. It tasted perfect to her, just the way he liked it. She set the bowl on the coffee table. Once rejected, the popcorn would have to be re-made. It was unacceptable. It quickly became irrelevant as she saw his face.

"Susan, you have never really lived a stimulating life, so what would you know about my need for excitement?" He was red in the face now. She had never seen him in such a rage.

She stood. "What do you know about my life, Kurt? You never ask me about it, so how could you know?"

He rose, furious. "Oh, Sue, I know a lot more about you than you think."

The time had finally come. He had brought it up and, for once in her life, she was not going to back off, come what may. Blast it all, she had to finally know. "Is that because you had me investigated before we were engaged?"

"What? What makes you think that?" The veins in his neck looked ready to burst. His face was inches from hers. He looked like he hated her at that moment. "Have you been snooping on me?"

She backed up, frightened. "No, not really."

He closed the distance between them. "What makes you think I investigated you? Huh, what do you think you know?"

She dropped her eyes, frightened. The confession she had hoped for would now come from her lips, not his. "Kurt, when we were getting ready to leave Connecticut, I was cleaning our closet in the master bedroom. I dropped some show boxes and I found... a report that you had apparently paid $300.00 to get. It talked about my life...and Joshua's birth... It also told me that you didn't trust me. You never trusted me." She slouched in her place, shoulders hunched in total angst. Why did I tell him? Am I insane?

"That was absolutely none of your business. A man has a right to know what he's getting himself into. How DARE you look at my things?" He moved closer, if that was even possible. She felt his breath upon her head. What was he going to do to her? Would he strike her?

She lifted her head briefly, then, "Because they were my things, Kurt. I wasn't snooping. I found them by accident." Tears were coursing down her face. Strangely, they seemed to calm him a bit. Oh, yes, submission was Kurt's favorite emotion to draw out of her. That's right.

"Yes, and I found out that the woman I was about to marry was not the person she pretended to be. I had a right to know." Kurt shook off her concern with a shrug.

"I told you before you proposed. I admit it. I should have told you sooner. My mother told me to, but I was afraid of losing you." She was almost begging him to forgive her. She was mad at herself for feeling the need to be forgiven, but that had been her fallback position for years and old habits were hard to break.

It seemed that her admission that she was afraid to lose him was all he needed to know. He seemed comforted somehow by her insecurity and asked in a quiet voice, "So you were afraid of losing me?" The veins in his neck returned to normal; his face lost its redness. He was visibly more relaxed. He sat on the couch and picked up the popcorn. He took a bite.

"Yes, you were so wonderful to Joshua and to me. I knew we had found my husband and his father, all wrapped up into one incredible man." She tried to smile...

"I still *am* that wonderful guy. Come here, woman." Kurt put down the bowl and grabbed her. He wrapped her in a huge embrace.

Her confession of insecurity was enough to calm him down and restore some semblance of peace. It was then decided that he would apply at American Airlines. The company hired him at once. The excitement and joy he had when he burst in the door with the news was almost comparable to the birth of their children. Sue felt satisfied that this might be the thing that gave him the peace he needed. With his military retirement pay and the nice employment package at American, their finances were set. However, since the children were growing older and the demands at home were no longer so great, Kurt suggested she get a job somewhere to occupy her time.

"After all, you don't want to find yourself becoming lazy now, would you?" he joked.

With his advice, she returned to nursing and began work at Anne Arundel Medical Center part time. The income was very minimal, though it paid for the kids to take sailing lessons, but not much else. The job seemed to be merely a way to get her out of the house into an environment that Kurt understood. She soon realized it also guaranteed that Kurt always knew where she was.

Kurt continued to fight his Viet Nam demons, even after he started flying for American. The night sweats, the nightmares, all served to disturb their sleep. Many mornings after Kurt had had a difficult night filled with nightmares, she had to change their sweat-soaked sheets. Every morning, no matter what his dreams had been the night before, their covers were torn asunder from the bed. She tried desperately to get him to open up, but Kurt refused to talk to her about his Nam experiences. He was adamant that he would not see someone for professional help.

She feared that he would harm her with his wild gestures of anguish in his dreams. Oftentimes, she slipped out of bed and finished the night on the floor, rather than have to explain the occasional black eye. Once was enough for that. Now she just moved out of harm's way before he could nail her with a wide swing. She shivered on the floor, and eventually bought a spare blanket to keep under the bed for just such a night. She never told him it was there. He never noticed its presence.

Why didn't he get help? But, no, that would never happen. He would never permit anyone, not even her, to learn what had happened to him during those years of service. There was a wall between them, growing higher and thicker every year. There was nothing she could do to stop it. She was trapped by the isolation in their marriage. She felt powerless to do anything about it. So life went on.

The peace she continued to hope for seemed almost within reach but always disappeared at the last second. His work at American served only to provide an avenue to quench his thirst for adventure but was never enough to satisfy him. He would return home from a trip, greet his children with joy, and then snarl at her. Insidious comments crept into more of their exchanges until it seemed he had become a veritable Dr. Jekyll and Mr. Hyde. She came to dread the sound of his key in the door.

"He's so angry," she thought in despair, "There's nothing I can do to comfort him."

By pure coincidence, she stumbled upon a momentary release for his internal pressure cooker. She didn't know if it was the reassuring sense of order that prevailed in the place, the sight of officers and undergraduates, or his love of country, but he was happier for much longer periods of time after an evening visit to the Naval Academy and downtown Annapolis. Whenever she could feel him moving into an agitated state, she would suggest that they go down to the water and he always agreed. She made a point of suggesting that they go there on a regular basis. It bought her a few days of peace. Annapolis became their haven. For that, she had been grateful. Until that night, many years later, when he told her about Kelsey. Kelsey, the key to the destruction of their marriage. Or was it really this unknown woman's fault?

Chapter 6

Sue wondered how she had made it through the next day, now that she knew about Kelsey. She thought that life would never be the same, from this point forward. Life would now be divided into pre-Kelsey and post-Kelsey days. What hints had she seen that she had somehow missed? She thought briefly, then shook her head at the memories of her years with Kurt. They weren't all bad, she supposed, but they certainly were challenging. Spending most of her adult life walking on egg shells had made her skittish. She didn't even know who she was anymore. Was she even a worthwhile person? She had been such a doormat for so long, it was hard to tell.

Sue glanced at the clock on the far wall of the breakfast room and realized it was almost 11:30 at night. She had lost track of time as she walked down Memory Lane, thinking about the way things had been. She found herself still awake, long past her bedtime. She stood and pulled the sleeves of her hunter green pullover sweater down to her hands. The mid-January day had been chilly, leading her to dress in her favorite jeans, long sleeve burgundy T-shirt, and sweater, for good measure. Now all she could think about was changing into pajamas and falling into bed. Forget the shower.

Early that morning, after going on her run and showering, she had helped Kurt pack for another trip. Her habit was to press his shirts and pants, then give them over to be packed the morning of his departure. This particular morning, a heavy silence hung over their bedroom due to the events that had transpired in downtown Annapolis the night before. Sue felt as though she were walking into a den of fury as she brought his freshly pressed clothes and laid them on the bed. But no, that was not the case. Silence instead, no eye contact, then...

"Is this all of my clothes for four days?" he asked in a low mutter.

Sue nodded, almost unable to speak. She exhaled slowly. "Yes."

He quickly began picking up the shirts and examining them before packing them in his carry-on bag. No matter how well she cared for his things, Kurt had always felt the need to double-check her work. He made it through the pile of clothes with satisfaction, until he came to the final pair of pants.

"You forgot to fix the hem in these," he said without emotion or inflection. He handed them back to her, shoving them in her direction before going into the closet for another pair of pants.

She took them in her hands, astonished by the quiet way he returned the trousers. Most of the time, such neglect on her part would make him blow up, but on this morning, he was flat and uninterested, as if his mind were elsewhere. Perhaps he was thinking of the woman he had confessed or how he had failed to end Sue's life.

Sue left the bedroom before he could remember to be ticked off at her. She retreated to the breakfast room where she laid the slacks on the table and sank into a low armchair. She was certain he wouldn't look for her there and knew that effort would be needed to peek around the corner to find her. Kurt wouldn't bother, she bet. Knowing Kurt, he would leave the house without saying goodbye. Sure enough, he left without another word. She sat there for some time, eyes fixed on the trousers without really seeing them, before she heard the door to the garage door close and the lock click into place. He jiggled the handle three times. Secure.

Kurt always claimed he had to try the lock three times to be sure everything was as it should be. She knew better. His mind was not what it used to be, and he was afraid of forgetting something, though he would never admit it. To counter the feeling he was losing his mental abilities, he installed some checks and balances into his habits. Sue shook her head at the memory of that morning.

But now it was late evening. What had she accomplished today? Who knows? The day was a blur. She had sleepwalked through the hours, thinking and rethinking the night before.

Even at that late hour, she found herself just as apathetic as she had felt all day. She had hoped her daily routine would help her focus on what lay ahead. No such luck. At one point, she sat on their bed staring out the window, watching the cold sky and trees swaying in the wind. A snow storm coming down from the northeast had threatened Annapolis, but it chose to bypass them. She felt mild regret at that, hoping to be snowed in and stopping the world for even a short time.

"A fire would have been nice this evening," she mused as she leaned against the counter in the glow of a kitchen nightlight. She put her empty tea mug in the sink. Though she would have normally washed it and put it in the dishwasher, no one would know if she was a slob this once. The mug could wait until tomorrow. She moved into the living room, to put things in order, though why that was important tonight when the washing of the mug wasn't, she couldn't say.

It took twice as long to get the living room straightened due to her finding an old photo album. She couldn't help but flip through it, remembering happier times. She sank into the couch. She turned her mind outward, focusing on the lives of her children and grandchildren. Turning quickly through photos of their early years with the children in Connecticut and then back in Maryland, she found pictures of Joshua's surprise fortieth birthday party. They had hung a banner over the kitchen table with the words "Happy 40th Birthday" in an arch over the top, and below, "*Dr.*

Joshua Adam Prescott." Ever since he had earned his M.D. and begun his practice as an infectious disease specialist at Anne Arundel Medical Center, he insisted people refer to him as "Dr. Prescott." The bantering over his taking himself so seriously was unstoppable after that.

"I can't call you Doctor!" Brooke had teased.

"She's right," Kurt had added. "If all you're going to do is practice, the best we can call you is 'Coach!'"

The laughter was uproarious, the party delightful. She smiled to herself, looking at a picture of Josh with his arm over his dad's shoulders, both grinning with immense pride for different reasons. Hanging on Joshua's back was his youngest son, with Joshua's oldest daughter peeking at the camera, in the background.

"Four kids," Sue shook her head over the thought of the wonderful grandchildren Joshua and his wife Amanda had given her. She put the album back in its rightful place.

She walked back into the breakfast room, to make sure everything was tidy. As of late, she found herself more distracted than ever and leaving things strewn about in an uncharacteristic fashion. Maybe I should do three walk-throughs of the rooms, just like Kurt jiggles the locks three times, she joked to herself without any joy. She put the mug in the dishwasher, as she should have done earlier. She paused again, her mind wandering into the past again. Joshua was always closer to Kurt, once he came on the scene. Josh was a little boy, in such desperate need of a father. I wonder how our lives would have been different, if Josh and I had been closer. If I hadn't married Kurt. Now there's a thought.

Sue always reasoned that the years without a dedicated father had left Joshua thirsting for a fatherly figure more invested in him than his maternal grandfather was, great though her father had been with the boy. But when she looked at her Christopher,

her youngest, she knew there must be more than just her own submission to Kurt's all-consuming authority in the house, when Kurt took over as a parent.

She picked up the mail from the side-table near her chair and threw away a couple magazines, leaving her with two letters addressed to "Christopher Marcus Prescott." She made a mental note to let him know they had been sent to the house instead of to his current residence. Like father like son, Christopher applied to and was accepted into the Naval Academy where he majored in Oceanography and was now, at the age of thirty-two, in his final year of the Ph.D. program at the Naval Postgraduate School in Monterey, California. Because of his graduate work, his time in the service was extended, though he had no plans to remain in the Navy until retirement. The goal Christopher worked for was a job at NASA. She missed him so much, since he had been out of state for the past six years and came home only once or twice a year. It was weird that mail still came to him at the house.

Part of her questioned why there was so much distance between Christopher and her, given that he lacked for nothing. Perhaps it had been the combination of two things: Kurt's intense desire to raise a strong son and Brooke's natural proclivity to be closer to her mother than her father. Like any set of siblings, there was always a worry that favoritism existed among parents. Brooke told her that she felt it from her father toward her brothers. Maybe Christopher felt it from his mother toward Brooke. Regardless, there was a divide that Sue found difficult to cross without usurping her husband's role. In the end, Christopher seemed to be drawn more by the authority of his father than the affection of his mother. She sighed and shook her head. Perhaps if I'd been stronger. Suddenly, she said in anger, "No. Everything is not always and forever my fault! I refuse to accept the blame." She threw the mail down in anger. Stop being such a blasted wimp.

She took the pants in need of repair upstairs to their bedroom and laid them over the back of a chair near the window. The job would be done tomorrow and she wouldn't worry about it until then. On the desk was a photo of her only daughter, Brooke Eliza Prescott. Sue picked it up. It was one of her favorites, taken when Brooke was frosting a cake. Her brothers had been teasing Brooke, Sue remembered, with Brooke swatting at them with the frosting knife as they attempted to distract her from the task at hand. The cake, though delicious, had turned out to be a visual disaster, due in part to the boys' antics. The bright purple frosting it boasted showed evidence of too much food coloring.

"Don't worry, as long as it tastes good, no one cares about aesthetics," the boys badgered her. True enough, they scarfed it down in less than five minutes flat.

At thirty-four years old, Brooke was a headstrong, confident woman who prided herself on being an observer of life and of people. Her natural perception and inclination for looking out for the underdog were the traits that made her stand out as an exceptional paralegal. Her job allowed her to be close to the law but not have the worries of being an attorney. That was very logical of Brooke, and so much like her.

How fast Brooke had become a woman.

Never in her whole life would Sue have thought her daughter would grow up to be her best friend, but it was amazing how life surprised you. She found a treasure in her daughter, a kindred spirit to whom she felt immeasurably close. They were more equals than mother and daughter. Despite (or maybe because of) her success professionally, Brooke was still single. Though Sue wished for her daughter to get married to a man who adored her,

Sue also knew her daughter was focused on her career for now. Brooke had plenty of time before her biological clock ran out. In the meantime, Sue would continue enjoying hours spent with her.

When Brooke left for college, she had taken the opportunity to move out altogether. Post- college, Brooke moved back to the area and lived nearby, but now with a series of well-deserved raises, was looking for a bigger place to purchase. In the next couple of weeks, the two of them would go shopping for houses or condos, a hunt that they found exciting. The quest would have to wait, however, due to Brooke being on a business cruise to the Bahamas. Brooke's plan was to be back by the end of the week, so the two of them would get lunch and catch up, and then hit the real estate market. Sue was looking forward to their time together.

Sue changed her clothes and crawled into bed. She hoped to fall asleep soon, but her mind was still whirling with the events at the Federal House. The rest of the world thought they were a perfect family with a handsome father, beautiful mother, and three accomplished, grown children. What they didn't know was Kurt avoided her most of the time now that they were at home alone; though this did bring about a homeland ceasefire, the peace was a troubled one. It almost seemed that, like her, the empty house breathed a sigh of relief as soon as he locked the door and flew away on another trip.

She tossed and turned, but found that nothing she could do would make her drowsy and fall asleep. She sat up in exasperation and looked around her room for something she could do that would be productive, while allowing her to sort her thoughts. She spotted the pants draped over the chair and sighed.

"Might as well," she murmured, without any desire to fix the hem for Kurt.

She walked over to the chair and turned the pants over to look at what needed to be done when something fell out of the pocket. Spotting a piece of paper, she bent down to pick it up. Kurt never left anything in his pockets, not even change, let alone trash. He would often comment, being very judgmental, about how some men kept spare change in their pockets. He considered it uncouth, and something he would never do. Trash was the worst offense, especially. Not even receipts were worth keeping. Yet here she found a receipt crumpled up and buried in his pocket. She turned on the desk lamp for a better look. Why he wouldn't have thrown it out? Oh, it was for a fine jewelry store purchase. A $500 necklace. She stared at it in disbelief.

At once, pieces began coming together in her mind. What? Another receipt? How many does that make now? Flowers last month, earrings the month before, but she never got the presents. Shoot, she had totally forgotten about them. She had asked Kurt about the charges once and he had just ordered her to pay them, saying they were going away gifts for some of the flight attendants. He had been given the job of buying them. She had thought it was so strange for him to volunteer to do such a thing, but the receipts' true reason for existence never seemed to make it through to her subconscious mind into reality. Until now. Her heart pounded. How could I have been so blind for so long? Of course. The receipts were for gifts for *her*. What's-her-name? Kelsey.

There had been random moments when she would find dirty clothes in the laundry basket that she never saw him wear at home during a lull in his travel or the detergent lid tightened beyond her strength, even though she was the only one who did the washing. Except that maybe he was sneaking laundry while she was with the grandkids, to keep her from seeing it. It all started to make sense. He would do laundry for clothes he couldn't explain away, since she knew exactly the number of clothes he used at home or on every trip. Usually. She would not question his wearing clothes that she hadn't see him wear, if he washed them. All this time, he had been wearing the extra clothes to look nice for.....her. The other woman.

A voice spoke, startling her. "Hi Mom. It's Brooke. I know it's late, so don't worry about missing the phone. I just wanted to leave a message to say-"

Sue launched herself over to the landline, Kurt's pants falling to the floor, and picked up the handset from its cradle. "Brooke! Brooke!" she cut off her daughter's message. "Hi, honey! I didn't hear the phone ring, sorry."

"Mom!" Brooke said, sounding shocked. "What are you doing up this late? It's almost...1:30 in the morning there!"

She glanced at the digital clock on the dresser and nodded, "Yes, it is. I definitely didn't realize it was quite that late." She paused. She put the receipt on the bedside table.

"Mom?" Brooke broke in. "You still there?"

"Yeah sweetie!" she said, trying not to sound as absentminded as she felt. Good grief. I forgot I was on the phone. "Speaking of late, you don't usually call at this time. What's going on? Are you okay?"

"Oh, yeah, I'm fine. More concerned about you, at this point. Are you sure you're okay?" Brooke said with worry in her voice.

Sue sat staring at the receipt. "Yes, dear. Today's been long and strange, but it's nothing. I sent your father off on another business trip, so perhaps I just," she paused, searching for words. "Wasn't... ready for it to be this quiet, I guess." She lapsed into silence again with her gaze filled only with the crumpled proof of Kurt's purchase. She started trying to swing back into the conversation before Brooke could become even more worried. "I was just about to fix your father's pants since I can't sleep."

"Well, I'll be home soon," Brooke said trying to sound comforting. "And I'll happily break the silence for you."

"Of course, sweetie," she smiled. "So what is it you were calling about?"

"Oh," Brooke sounded as if she had just remembered there was a purpose for her call. "I actually wasn't planning on talking to you tonight; I just wanted to leave a message for you. I guess your landline in your room picks up voicemails. I should've thought about whether that would wake you..." she trailed off.

Sue let the silence sink in for a moment before saying, "Well, lucky for you I was already awake, so there was no interruption. Do you want to talk about it now?"

"No, no, that's fine. I'll arrive in the Bahamas in a few hours and just forgot to let you know that we got off from Florida safely. Are you sure you're okay, Mom? You sound kinda weird and you're up way past your bedtime."

Sue laughed, "I'm fine, just fine. You have a great time, my dear."

"Well, okay, if you say so."

Sue looked at the empty bed beside her. "Maybe we can chat when you get home."

"Sure." Brooke asked, startled. "Anything specific?"

"Let's just say I may have been ignoring some things for a little too long," She continued to stare at the receipt. "But we'll talk when you get back. It's late where you are, and you need to sleep before the ship docks."

Brooke sighed. "Okay. Don't stay up for too much longer, promise?"

Sue ran her finger over the receipt. "Promise," she murmured.

Sue laid the handset into its cradle, and remained sitting in the glow of the single lamp. Kurt's unrepaired pants were still on the floor where they had fallen. I should probably pick them up. No,

87

it's time for sleep. They would wait. If only going to sleep could be so simple, but the past days left her feeling disgruntled. There would be no sleep that night. Sue watched in silence a few hours later, as the sun rose outside her bedroom window, unsure of what the day would bring. Afraid of what might happen next.

Chapter 7

Brooke had been looking forward to her paralegal conference that set sail from Port Canaveral, Florida and landed her on the beautiful beaches of Nassau in the Bahamas. You couldn't ask for more. As soon as the ship settled at its destination, she and her coworkers were swift to find out if time would be allowed for enjoying the gorgeous location. Once the schedule was handed out, it was clear that one particular afternoon would be left open by the conference organizers, to allow for participants to venture out into the beach-loving town. It was quite literally paradise.

On that afternoon, Brooke slipped into a pair of white shorts, a collared pastel blouse, and the navy company blazer. To soften the look, she wore a gold heart necklace, matching earrings, and a dainty bracelet. She fluffed at her thick brown hair before deciding she didn't want to deal with it and swept it up and away from her face in a barrette. Coming to the designated meeting place to find her friends, the three women found themselves similarly attired and laughed light-heartedly over their similar tastes. A trio of pastel collared, shorts wearing, company blazer- adorned paralegals left the ship in good spirits, ready to take on the town and leave work behind.

The group took off their sandals and wandered down the beach, their gazes fixed on the beautiful clear blue afternoon sky and gorgeous water. Everywhere they looked, there were colorful umbrellas and bathing suit clad people. There must have been hundreds vacationing at this time of the year. The group chuckled over the snow birds.

"You know what sounds good right now?" asked one of the women, a gal named Allison. "A Coffee Frappuccino. Why don't we find a Starbucks and then go somewhere we can have a good view of the water?"

They pulled out their phones and located the nearest store. With an objective in mind, the trio began navigating the sidewalk-filled crowds easily, until they arrived at the coffee shop. Stepping inside, Grace and Allison apparently found themselves preoccupied by the new mugs that had come out, while Brooke took advantage of the short line and ordered. By the time Brooke rejoined her friends a line had formed, but Brooke was sipping on her drink.

"Ugh, we shouldn't have gotten distracted," moaned Allison. "You'll wait for us?"

Brooke nodded. Augh!! Man, that drink was cold. "Yeah, of course. There's a bench outside, I'm just going to hang out there until you guys are ready."

Grace and Allison joined the line while Brooke went to sit on an empty bench, to watch the crowds walk by and to enjoy the beautiful weather. What a stunning day. Everyone looked so happy in the lovely town. People-watching was one of her favorite past times and today was no exception. She glanced around, looking for a story; everyone had one and Brooke enjoyed finding folks whose life tales she could create, just for fun.

As she visually browsed the restaurants across the street, she saw in one of the windows a man snuggling with a very attractive, young brunette as they enjoyed cocktails. Brooke smiled to herself as she watched the couple, drawing another cold swallow from her drink. What a handsome couple they made. The woman was stunning and the man was clearly older but still quite handsome, from what she could easily see. The couple kissed enthusiastically, he laughed, and he began nuzzling his companion's neck. Brooke laughed out loud as she watched.

Brooke looked around a bit. Oh, here come Allison and Grace with their coffees in hand. Took them long enough! She shivered and put her freezing coffee on the ground. Enough of that. Thanks but no thanks, due to the chill it gave her. Back to the entertainment going on across the way. She leaned forward a bit, as she stared across the street. That dude looks awfully familiar. It struck her quickly when he turned his face towards her. Dad? What in the world? Huh? No, it can't be. Can it? She looked away, not wanting to believe what her eyes told her.

She noticed that Allison and Grace glanced at her, then looked at each other, then across the street, and then back at her before asking, "Hey, you ready to go?"

"I think that's my dad," she responded as she glanced up briefly, and then returned her gaze to the oblivious couple. More kissing ensued.

"Wait, what?" The two gals quickly seated themselves on either side of her. "Come on, Brooke. Really? Where, exactly?"

"Over there, far right table in front of the long window in the bigger restaurant. The brunette and older guy," she said as she nodded that way.

"That could be your dad, he looks old enough, but the woman," Allison squinted. "She's way too young to be your mom. Your folks have been married a long time, right?"

"I didn't say it was *both* my mom and my dad," Brook said with irritation in her voice.

"They do say everybody's got a twin," offered Grace.

"No, I'm almost 100% certain that's my dad," she said and shook her head. "It makes no sense, though. I talked to my mom last night and he's on a trip."

"A trip here, I guess," Allison took her eyes off the couple and drank some of her Frappuccino. "Is your dad the cheating kind?"

Grace punched her friend, "Allison, that's a horrible thing to say about Brooke's dad."

Brooke stood hastily, "You guys go on without me. I need to check this out." She started walking away.

"Brooke! You forgot your-" Allison yelled...

Brooke heard Allison cry out, but she was on a mission. She walked across the street quickly and pushed her sunglasses onto her head. Her heart was racing and her thoughts scattered as she felt her temper rising. As she drew closer, she saw the man run his fingers through his hair in a similar way that her father often did. Just to be sure, she pulled out her phone and started snapping pictures. Gotta be sure.

Brooke lowered her phone just as the couple was getting ready to leave. The brunette left before the gentleman, likely to visit the bathroom, leaving him the opportunity to lean over and take the last swallow of her unfinished cocktail. As he set the drink on the table, he glanced out the window and caught Brooke's stare. Her brow was furrowed and her eyes ablaze and her face began to steadily grow red as she stared down her father through the restaurant window.

Brooke glared at him for several seconds more. Kurt froze for a moment before leaving the table. He got up, throwing money on the table. Brooke turned and hurried down the street, losing herself in the crowd. She took long, deep breaths as she walked, so as not to lose control. She was crushed and livid. It felt as if all the air in the world had been sucked into that restaurant, leaving her nothing to breathe. She looked around. He didn't seem to be following.

A short time later, she walked into one of her meetings very flustered yet outwardly composed. Her friends tried to get her attention to get some kind of confirmation that she was okay, but she refused to give them any indication of how she felt. She pushed her thoughts down so she could focus on the workshops and not dedicate any more thought than necessary to that man she called "Dad." Brooke closed her eyes, trying to remove the memory of her father and his companion. She breathed deeply and focused. The company was paying a lot of money for her to be here and she had to learn everything about, what? Tort? Real estate law? Who knows? Concentrate, Brooke.

After the meetings were finished for the day, plans were made to have dinner at the Lukka Kairi Restaurant and Bar that evening. The restaurant was known as being one of the most popular eating places with the locals, so one of her colleagues suggested it as a private place where they could get away from the tourist crowds. Agreeing to go, she returned to her cabin to change. She forced away the disturbing images, knowing that if she entertained them, she would be unable to eat and inevitably escalate into a rage. She dressed in a simple black dress, her favorite two-inch heels, and gold jewelry. She brought a soft shrug to fend off the night air, in case anyone wanted to take a stroll after they ate.

After the short walk from the ship, her small group entered the restaurant, where they were seated without delay. Brooke looked around the room, subconsciously looking for her father, when she caught sight of him once again, snuggling the woman. Really, Dad? She was startled yet again by finding him out and about with this woman. What a weird coincidence. You'd think he would be more circumspect, knowing that she was on the island and all. He probably thought there was no way he would see her again. The island's not that big, Dad.

Lifting her phone to take pictures, she worked once more to steady her breath. She knew that confronting him wouldn't be easy. She felt that the photos would stand as even better testimony to the truth of what she was witnessing than her mere, well-chosen, angry words. I guess Dad and his woman friend wanted a place to get away from the throngs of people and have some privacy and a quiet night out. Oh, joy.

Her appetite was nonexistent, even with the tempting entrees the establishment offered. She had been looking forward to trying the restaurant's authentic Caribbean food in the form of cracked conch sliders and tropical curry chicken, having thought about them on the voyage over to the island. She ordered them to be polite, but picked at her food while the affectionate couple continued their display across the way. Absolutely no shame, she thought with disgust. Not even the slightest thought that maybe someone might be watching.

As the couple departed, Brooke lifted her dessert menu to cover her face. She knew she needed to talk to her mom as soon as she returned home, but wanted to give herself plenty of time to prepare for the conversation. Her conference still had two days to go, but she would return home immediately when it was done.

A night owl by nature, she took a red-eye flight and returned to her parents' house exceedingly late at the end of the week, only to find her father reading something on his tablet in his beige recliner. Ever since moving back in with her parents while living in limbo between homes due to her first condo selling faster than anticipated, she had been grateful for the time to reconnect with the both of them. At this moment, however, connecting with her father was the one thing she couldn't bear the thought of doing. Not now. Seeing her father sitting there, smiling as if nothing was wrong as she entered the living room with bags from the same destination he had snuck off to like a snake, made her blood boil. To say she was unimpressed was a gross understatement. She was livid.

"Hi Brooke. Want help with those?" he asked. He started to get up.

"Not particularly, no," she replied with an icy tone. It was enough to reseat him.

"I can explain-" He threw his hands in the air.

"No," she stopped his feeble explanation. "No, you cannot. I saw you. I was there. I was in Nassau for a conference, and you were there with another woman!"

"Brooke, honey, please," he tried to stop her.

"No, Dad," she said. She drew a long breath and quieted herself for the sake of not waking her mother who, more than likely, was asleep upstairs. "I don't want to hear it. I have spent the last two days and an entire flight agonizing over how to talk to you, let alone even look at you. How do you tell someone what you had seen them doing, something that wasn't acceptable for a married man, much less for your own father?" she asked, her voice cracking on the verge of breaking down. "What could you possibly have to say for yourself?" Tears slipped down her face.

His face was drawn and his eyes glued to the floor. "Forgive me."

"Never," she whispered.

She took her bags upstairs to the guest room and crawled into bed without changing, holding her pillow against her chest as tears fled down her cheeks uncontrollably. Nothing her father could do would repair the damage he had just done. In a split second, a wall had been built between them. Shut down. Shut out. She knew that her relationship with her father had changed forever.

Chapter 8

Sue stood at the stove slowly stirring a second batch of scrambled eggs while waiting for a kettle of hot water to come to a boil. When she woke up, she'd found her daughter's car sitting out front and decided to make breakfast for her when Brooke was up for the day. Sue hadn't heard her entrance the night prior, so she could only assume that it was an incredibly late arrival. After making Kurt's breakfast and sending him on his trip, she set about preparing breakfast for Brooke.

"Good morning," Brooke came yawning down the stairs and entered the kitchen, her hair sticking out at right angles.

"Brooke!" Sue exclaimed in delight just as the tea pot began to whistle. "You're just in time. The water is boiled and the eggs are almost done. Go ahead and make the toast."

Brooke came around the counter, giving her mother a big hug from behind and a kiss on the cheek before putting bread into the toaster and pouring herself a hot mug of tea. "You're the best, Mom. Thank you, thank you, thank you."

Sue chuckled. "I'm always happy to serve you whenever I can. And I have to say," she scooped eggs onto a plate and set them before Brooke. "I quite like having you around again, even if it is only for a little while."

"Me too, Mom," Brooke took a bite of her eggs. "It feels like before I left for college. I miss waking up and finding breakfast made for me." She winked at her mother in jest.

"You silly goose," Sue chuckled.

"Only here to bother you," Brooke said and grinned. "You ready to go house hunting today?"

"Always." For some reason or another, Sue took great pleasure in searching for real estate, comparing prices, and taking tours. She poured herself a mug of tea for herself before asking, "How many properties do you want to see today?"

"Only two," Brooke stood and pulled out the orange juice. "I don't need to see any others. I already know they're not worth the time to look at it. And honestly I'm pretty sure I'll go with one that I'm most interested in, but I figured I'd give them both a fighting chance."

"So, what's your plan?" Sue asked.

"I have the agent scheduled to meet us at the first condo by 10:30, then go to the second by 11:45, giving us a buffer so we can talk through the details on the way, maybe grab coffee before getting there. Then we'll get lunch, discuss the options, and afterwards I'll make a decision and move forward from there!" Brooke grinned at her mother.

"Well, you sure have it all figured out!" She laughed, taking her daughter's empty dishes and beginning to clean up.

"I've been waiting a while to finally buy a bigger place. You bet I've got it figured out," Brooke chuckled. "Let me go shower and get myself together and we can leave in...let's say 30?"

"I'll be in the breakfast room," she said.

Brooke stepped over to her and planted a kiss on her cheek. "You're wonderful."

When they headed out, Sue noticed with surprise that, not only was the door to the garage unlocked, but the garage door had been left open. Since she hadn't been outside after Kurt left for his trip, she could only imagine that he had left it open. Now, why in the world would he do that? Just to make sure that the house was secure before she and Brooke left for the day, Susan walked around the house and noticed that every door in the house was unlocked. Now that is really strange. Susan locked everything up tight and left with Brooke.

As Brooke anticipated, the walk through of the condos went by very fast. The first was Brooke's initial choice, based upon her online research. The location was ideal for her commute to work and, from what Brooke could tell by the pictures, the space was just big enough for the furniture she already had. After walking through it, however, it became clear that not only would there not be enough room for her things, but the bathrooms were much smaller than she wanted.

"Does it really matter if they're that small, though?" Sue asked, unsure if that was a concern.

"It's not a deal breaker, but if the second condo has bigger bathrooms and I don't have to get rid of furniture to fit in it, then I think that's the winner," Brooke replied. "It's amazing how different things look in person."

They stopped to get coffee on the way, as planned, then proceeded to the second property. Sue could tell her daughter was thrilled with the space as soon as she and Brooke walked in. At the first property, Brooke had been asking questions about every tiny detail like the paralegal she was. Here, however, her imagination seemed to have run away with her, and Brooke couldn't help but suggest where all of her things would go with excitement in her voice, as she disappeared into the next room.

"I think we have a decision?" the real estate agent asked Sue, with laughter in her voice.

Sue smiled back and said, "We'll get back to you after we've had some time to discuss it. But, yes, it looks that way."

"I'm surprised," Brooke said, shaking her head as they sat at their Panera Bread's local restaurant, with cream of chicken and wild rice soup and tuna sandwiches. "I honestly thought I wouldn't need to see the second unit, but it is, by far, better than the first."

Sue nodded. "I have to agree with you. The space seems to fit your lifestyle and you really felt like it was home, didn't you?"

"Oh, yes," Brooke said with great enthusiasm. "I could just see my things in the second condo. I can't wait to move in and start decorating."

"Are you sure the longer commute isn't a problem, though?" she asked.

"No," Brooke took a spoonful of her soup. "It's only a ten- or fifteen- minute difference and that's nothing in the grand scheme of things. I'd rather keep my couch and take a longer drive to get back to sitting on it," Brooke laughed.

Sue chuckled. "Fair enough."

A moment of silence passed between them. Sue knew the conversation Brooke had hinted at the other night was about to happen, but she didn't want to initiate the subject. Sue took a bite of her sandwich and watched the traffic through the window.

"So," Brooke said, girding herself. "You know how I have been in the Bahamas this last week."

Sue nodded. "Yes, that's what you had said before you left. I still can't get over your business trip being at the beach. The line between work and play seems incredibly blurred. Did you get a chance to enjoy the beaches?"

"Yes, two of my colleagues and I went out and enjoyed what the town had to offer. Although, it seems I'm not the only one who has a hard time finding the line between work and play," Brooke paused, clearly gathering her thoughts. "I saw Dad with a strange woman in a restaurant while I was there."

Sue's heart dropped and her stomach tightened. "I see."

"I wasn't sure if it was him at first," Brooke's voice was quiet and she struggled to make eye contact with her mother. "But I saw him twice, I know he saw me the first time, and I spoke with him last night."

Sue folded her hands and rested her lips against her fingers before responding, "So he knows you saw him with the girl."

Brooke nodded, apparently unsure of what her mother would do. "You ...know about her?" she finally asked.

"Your father admitted his affair to me last week." Sue toyed with her soup stirring it without excitement, not really hungry anymore, now that the thing had been spoken. She put her spoon beside the still-full bowl.

Brooke stared at her. "He...he did?"

Sue nodded. Silence fell over their table as each processed the information shared between them. She'd accepted the facts of her husband's admission, but hadn't dreamed one of her children would happen upon him in full embrace with this mystery woman. It was obvious his longer trips weren't always for work as she'd been led to believe. The information struck her like a lightning bolt and left her wondering how many other blind spots she had.

"Mom?" Brooke asked with worry in her voice.

"I'm okay," she reassured. "I just didn't realize how much I've chosen to ignore."

Brooke's brow furrowed and she asked, "What do you mean?"

Sue took a breath before answering. "Well," she began. "There have been a lot of...indicators. Kurt started becoming excessively flirty with younger women whenever we would encounter them, sometimes even saying to me, 'I've still got it.' Of course, I ignored it simply because he needs reassurance that he's attractive and I suppose he doesn't exactly get it from me."

"Mom," Brooke protested.

Sue held up her hand to stop her. "Then it was him getting upset over my spending as if I was frivolous. But one day I started finding receipts for flowers, clothes, and jewelry that I never received. Again, I assumed that he simply forgot to give them to me. Eventually, I asked if maybe someone might have stolen our charge cards, but he just waved it off and told me to pay the bills. He claimed the money was spent on going-away presents for employees leaving the company. Like he would be the willing shopper. You know how your dad hates going to the mall, much less going out of his way to buy presents for people from work."

"Yeah, right. But, Mom, you should've told me," Brooke shook her head.

"I had no evidence that there was anything wrong," Sue insisted.

"That's not true, there was plenty-"

"Well, what's done is done," Sue interjected. "And it got worse. There were flyers for cruises we never went on, requests for him to take surveys for the cruises he apparently did take. Travel guides were sent to the house. He had no explanation and would blow up at me when I asked about it. He refused to tell me what was going on, until recently. I was entirely at a loss." She shook her head. "What a fool I've been. All in the name of keeping the peace." Tears found their way down her cheeks. She glanced around, concerned that other people in the restaurant would notice. No, apparently no one did.

Brooke took her mother's hand in hers. "We'll figure it out. Okay?"

Sue nodded. She knew she couldn't tell Brooke about the events that had transpired in Annapolis several nights ago. Her concerns were all based on discomfort and unsureness. Mere feelings of tension and angst were not enough to bring worry on her daughter. Nope, she would keep that incident to herself.

The distressing conversation was put on hold over the next few weeks, in lieu of purchasing the condo. They began the process of moving Brooke's things in, a project for which Sue was very grateful. The ample distraction from Kurt's lascivious activity was just what she needed to allow for Brooke's moving. Brooke was establishing her brand-new home and Sue didn't want the deterioration of her own household to affect such excitement. One evening after a hard day of work getting Brooke completely settled in, Sue returned to the breakfast room wondering how to proceed with Kurt in light of his ongoing adulterous activity. She wished so much to save him, to save them. But any chance of such a thing happening was more than she felt capable of. Only time would tell.

Chapter 9

Winter turned to spring as Sue and Kurt continued to negotiate their space with one another. He did not return to the topic of her death; he seemed anxious to be nowhere near her. He moved his things out of their bedroom, preferring to sleep in the guest bedroom. His clothes, down to the last item of clothing, were put away in the guest room dresser. His clothes hung pristinely in the guest room closet. He refused to let her wash his clothes and their days of packing his travel bags together were gone. When not at home, he kept the guest room door locked, preventing her from even changing his sheets. He started doing his own laundry. While it saved her a lot of time, it seemed a very strange, uncomfortable way to live.

Sue noticed that he had refused to eat her meals more than once, loudly banging pots and pans well after she had put away yet another meal he rejected. He began cooking what few meals he ate at home, taking them into his study and eating with the door shut. The only remnants of his meals were a stray piece of silverware he sometimes neglected to wash when doing his own dishes. He would silently leave a check at her place at the table twice a month, to pay for any incidentals she might need. He took over all the bill paying. She no longer had any control over their joint bank accounts.

Sue noticed that, like his first post-Kelsey trip, he left the doors to their house unlocked whenever he went anywhere. With the crime rate in their area going up, Sue was surprised by his forgetfulness. Or was he just hoping for someone to come in and accomplish what he had not? If a robber broke in and killed her, it would save him the trouble, she supposed. Sue got into the habit of checking all of the doors and windows when Kurt left the house, no matter the time of day or night. She needed to. Time moved on and summer came upon them. She felt more alone, isolated, and insecure than at any other time in their marriage.

The sky was a soft purple gray as Sue set out on her run that early summer morning. The rain the previous night left a damp, fresh smell in the air that refreshed her mind and filled her lungs. As she made her way down the road, she returned to a recent discussion she had with Joshua and his wife Amanda. They were getting ready to send their fourth child off to kindergarten that fall, leaving Amanda free to return to work full time. She would be helping out with the running of Joshua's medical practice in the Lesly and Pat Sajak Pavilion at the Anne Arundel Medical Center. Due to transitioning back to part time work while the kids were still young and dependent, Joshua and Amanda had previously asked to her to help out by driving the girls to their high school and middle school activities while their parents worked.

"You're already babysitting the boys in the afternoon, so we don't want to add too much more to your responsibilities," they added, apparently trying to be considerate.

"It's no problem." Sue shook her head and smiled. "I'm happy to help."

This did add to the amount of running around she needed to do. Sue had gotten back into the nursing profession after Christopher headed off to school full time, so she understood the complicated juggle that might take place with shuffling people to their respective destinations. She hoped that her daughter-in-law would enjoy going back to work as much as she had. Alas, Kurt insisted she retire a few years back. She had loved getting back into the nursing profession, realizing how much she had missed using her skills. But being at home for Kurt seemed to be the better option, it was certainly what he wanted at the time, and she complied without complaint.

Joshua and Amanda were very grateful for her stepping in, and she was happy to help out as she could. Sue closed the door, leaning against the door jam, and watched them drive away from their chat that afternoon. She was somewhat dismayed that they didn't offer to help pay for her gas. She couldn't help but feel taken advantage of, but couldn't muster the guts to suggest their chipping in every once in a while. It would have been nice for them to at least offer, but she guessed they thought she always had plenty of money. Wrong. Kurt has money. I have whatever he gives me, which lately hasn't been much. She sighed and walked into the kitchen.

What should she do? She couldn't co-exist with Kurt like this, if it could even be considered a co-existence. They were like two individuals on separate paths. Those ways might even be parallel but she really couldn't tell because they rarely saw each other anymore. I'm so very alone; I don't want to burden Brooke with this pain. She thought often about where she would go, what she would do. There didn't seem to be an answer. No real friends. No paying job. Out of date skills. A husband who didn't want her. A husband who did want someone else. No money. Perhaps it would be best if I.....but, no. Then Kurt would win. That wasn't the way to handle this. Maybe if I took a step back into being the old Sue, he would see what he's missing. Yes, it was worth a try. She couldn't continue doing nothing.

That evening, she decided to surprise her husband and make his favorite meal. Maybe he would actually eat it, spend some time with her. She spent several hours preparing the food so that, when he came in through the door, he would be met with the wonderful smell of homemade lasagna kept warm in the oven, the sight of a colorful fresh salad, and Italian bread sliced and ready for the oil and spices she had prepared. As a surprise after the meal, she would go to the refrigerator and pull out what her friends called her "famous cheesecake." The finishing touch would be to set the table with their fine china and her mother's lace tablecloth. As soon as all the food was prepared and there was only twenty minutes left before Kurt's arrival, she went upstairs to finish doing her hair and makeup and put on a pretty dress and the pearls he had given her for their anniversary some years before. If he dumped her, it wouldn't be because she didn't go down fighting.

"Hello, dear," she greeted him as he stepped through the door. She went to take his flight bag and jacket and allow him to take in the sights and smells of the kitchen.

"Did you forget to tell me about a dinner party?" he asked in confusion. He scowled.

"Oh no!" she replied after hanging the jacket and putting aside his things. "I thought we might have an evening together, just the two of us."

Kurt walked past her and took a slice of bread, swiped it across the dish of oil and spices and took a bite. Silence. Sue felt deflated that his first inclination was to inspect the food and not to notice how she dressed for him. The evening would likely turn out to be a failure just like any other. She braced herself for the worst. Outwardly, she smiled. "It's nice to have you home. I hope your trip was a good one." Seriously, Susan Margaret? A boldfaced lie, if you ever spoke one.

"You finally have a free evening," he remarked, taking another bite of bread. "That doesn't happen very often. Must have had to shoehorn this into your schedule, I guess?"

The remark stung. What in the world was he talking about? He hadn't given her the time of day in months. No, Sue, play nicely. Ignore the insinuation and just answer the question. He is calling this your fault, so just go with the flow. "Well, Joshua and Amanda are so busy with their jobs. They need me to get the girls to rehearsal for the play at the Bowie Playhouse and the boys need to be watched, since they're still in elementary school." She sighed at his ignorance of her responsibilities. "We don't want the kids to be in daycare, now, do we?" she asked with a wifely tone in her voice. She gestured towards the table. He complied with her unspoken request and sat at his place. Stiffly.

"No, but you don't have time to do things with me if you're so busy with them," he snarled as she sliced and served the lasagna for him. "It would be nice if you could carve out some time for me. You're always so busy with other things and other people. How long is this going to keep up?"

Carve out time for you??? You haven't wanted to be in my presence in months. Why so concerned about my schedule now? Brother, what about me? No, she wasn't going to think that way. Play nice, Sue. Stay calm and act like you hadn't noticed he's moved out of your life. You can do this, girlfriend. Breathe.

"I don't know," Sue replied, seating herself next to him with her own plate. "Maybe after the girls' play closes they can watch their brothers after school. But I really don't mind helping," she tried to reassure him. He looked at her with what seemed to be suspicion. She sighed and began picking at her lasagna. Her goal was to keep Joshua and Amanda happy, spend time with the grandkids, and try to make Kurt happy as best as she could. She was often reminded of the plate spinner on Ed Sullivan's show so many years ago. One plate was finally spinning and suddenly another was thrown at her, while the others seemed destined to crash at her feet. Would the insanity never end? Good news, he seemed to like the lasagna. He was certainly scarfing it down.

"What're they doing now?" he asked, while serving himself another plate.

"*Fiddler on the Roof* at the Bowie Playhouse," she replied; she swallowed her first bite. Why did she always feel like she was on the defensive?

"That's a *reasonably* good play. I suppose we can go." He took a long gulp of his sparkling cider, which appeared to relax him.

Good. At least I have a commitment from him for the next month or so. We must keep up appearances, at least as far as the boys and grands are concerned. Neither of them knew about the sleeping arrangements or new, separate lifestyles of their parents. Sue hadn't told them and Kurt, being Kurt wouldn't have risked telling the boys about Kelsey. Brooke, of course, already knew, but had held her tongue. Appearances, to Kurt, were everything. So be it. Sue smiled sweetly at her husband, all the while being a bit more aggressive in her tone. "I wouldn't miss it for the world."

Kurt looked at her for a moment with mild confusion before shrugging in reply, "How much is this going to cost me?"

"I'll check into it and let you know. Not much, I suppose."

The following weekend, they were in charge of the grandchildren while Joshua and Amanda were away for an infectious disease conference. Kurt had slipped out of their master bedroom Friday night, after making sure that the grands were asleep, and then got up for a morning run before they stirred. None of them suspected a thing, from what Sue could tell.

Since the meetings that Joshua and Amanda were attending were held over a weekend, Sue was making a special breakfast for everyone that Saturday while Kurt got ready for his day. The girls were helping mix blueberry pancake batter, stir scrambled eggs, and turn bacon while the boys were upstairs watching their grandfather shave with his electric razor. Fresh-squeezed orange juice waited in the refrigerator as large plates were carefully piled high with pancakes and bacon.

As Sue worked on her own preparations, she could hear the racket in the bathroom. If the boys were reacting as usual, they were climbing about on the master bathroom counter as they watched Kurt use his electric razor on his face and neck. They were yelling with delight as they saw this event occur before their eyes. She grinned at the thought that they never seemed to tire of watching Grandpa Kurt shave, no matter how many times they had seen it. Kurt loved to be the center of their attention, so she was sure he was eating it up.

She and the girls could hear them all the way downstairs in the kitchen. Her granddaughters were not impressed by the unnecessary noise, and could not understand what the boys saw in watching someone shave.

Madison said, "It's disgusting, Grandma."

Abigail added, "Yuck, that's gross."

"They want to be men one day, just like your dad and grandfather. Grandpa's doing something out of the ordinary for them, since your dad uses a disposable razor. It's unique and intriguing for them. I think it sounds like buzzing bees, don't you?" Sue smiled as she poured the last of the pancake batter into a pan.

The girls only scrunched up their faces and shook their heads. Madison told her, "They make too much noise!"

As she flipped pancakes, Sue thought about her hubby upstairs. Kurt was still very handsome and, when he was relaxed, she couldn't help but find herself just as attracted to him as she had been when they first met. There had been one particular evening about ten years ago that she often looked back on to remind herself that, somewhere in the callous nature of her husband, was the Kurt she loved and adored. They had been getting ready for a formal evening out; she couldn't help but comment that he looked like Richard Gere. His eyes had softened, and he approached her from behind, put his hands on her arms, kissed her head, and remarked that she herself looked like Jaclyn Smith, albeit later in life. Little moments like those, though few and far between, reminded her to try giving him more grace, knowing something was wrong in his mind that she could never fix.

"Sue," Kurt said later that month, coming into the breakfast room. "I think we should go on a trip for our anniversary."

Sue looked up at him from her book, so shocked that she almost fell off her chair. To cover her confusion and buy some time, she took her reading glasses off before responding. "What?" Her brow was furrowed in confusion. He can't stand to be with me. What gives with this? We haven't talked since....when? The weekend that the grands were with us? Yep, that was the last time they had exchanged any words at all. Now he wants to go on a trip with me?

"We have the extra money and I think it'd be nice for us to get away and go somewhere. Together." He looked at her with determination in his eyes.

She didn't know what to say, confused as to why he would want to devote any time to her and spend the extra money. Her mind raced as he proceeded to explain how he had set everything up, and that they would be leaving later that month. She was at a complete loss to understand why they were going on the trip. What? He hasn't wanted to spend time with me all year. Why would he do this? This makes no sense whatsoever.

Sue fought the idea, preferring to stay home and be with the rest of the family. What gives? But he had everything planned with no input from her, only to say before retreating to his downstairs

110

office that they would be leaving right after the girls' play on Saturday afternoon and returning on Wednesday.

After a moment spent gathering her wits, she made her way to the office to confront him about the matter. As she entered, she glanced around the room, proud of the way she had decorated it in true "man cave" fashion, with dark bookshelves, hunter green wallpaper, and pictures of the planes he had flown. He loved it, or at least, that's what he told her when the job was completed a few years back. She found herself disappointed that he never noticed the office anymore, let alone pay any attention to her. Perhaps the room was as dated as she was.

Kurt was working at his computer, per his tendency, and clicked out of a window as she entered the room. He sat back and folded his arms. She stood at the corner of his desk, afraid to sit in one of the chairs and presume she belonged in the room. He looked at her and appeared to be waiting for her to say whatever it was that happened to be on her mind.

"Kurt, why must we go out of town?" she asked. "It's just that this is such a busy time and Josh and Amanda need my help." She felt like she was groveling, but she didn't want to go on the trip and this seemed to be the only way to put the brakes on it. How could she bear a long trip with him? The thought of spending extended time with her angry and unkind husband was overwhelming. She tried not to shudder visibly.

He removed his reading glasses to scowl. "They can do without you for a few days," he grumbled. "If something happened to you, they'd have to adjust their precious schedules. A mere five-day vacation should be a lot less trouble. I've made all these plans and I can't cancel anything without losing thousands of dollars. Like it or not, we're going."

"Can I at least see the reservations for where we're going, so I know what to pack?" she asked desperately.

"We are going out west. Pack accordingly. I'll give you the travel documents before we leave," he said as the final word. "Other than that, there's nothing else to tell you. You like surprises, and I'm giving you a surprise. Shut the door on your way out of the room." He put his reading glasses back on and turned back to his computer screen. He commanded, without looking at her, "Now."

She left the room, carefully closing the door behind her. The clatter of the keyboard resumed at once. She knew he would remain there until sometime in the middle of the night, stealing into the guest bedroom, once he was certain she was asleep. She heard his laughter as she went into the kitchen for some tea. I wonder what's so funny.

Sue seated herself at the kitchen table, thinking about the strangeness of this trip. He used to give me all of his travel plans a week ahead of time. Then she remembered the one time she suggested meeting him in Dallas for Valentine's Day a few years ago, and he got so upset. The trip came up at the last moment, he told her, although she found herself not believing the story. He would leave the day before Valentine's Day and return the day after. Once his flight landed in Texas, she decided to call him.

"Kurt, I can meet you in Dallas, so that we can still have our Valentine's Day together."

"What?" He paused. "Are you planning on staying overnight?"

"Yes, dear. Of course. I thought we could have a nice dinner and then go back to the Crown Plaza, where you already have a room."

"Well, I'll have to change hotels, then," he said, quite angry at her idea.

"Why? We can stay there."

"No, Sue," he said. "We can't."

"Why not?" she asked again. "You always stay there when you're in Dallas. I'm sure it's a lovely hotel, if that's where you go so frequently."

"No, absolutely not," he said. She remembered thinking that it was confusing whether he was saying "no" to her coming or "no" to the hotel being nice. "If you're coming, I will simply have to move. What time does your flight arrive?" He was obviously upset at her news.

She sighed. "Never mind, Kurt. I really can't afford the cost to come. I'll just stay home this time." As a pilot, he could have gotten her a free trip. But, no, he never offered.

A long pause fell over the phone. "Fine then," he said and hung up. He never stayed in the Crown Plaza again.

She ruminated over the rest of her tea. Ever since then, he gives me his flight schedule at the last possible moment. I guess he doesn't want unexpected company. She took a drink of her tea. But why would he withhold this information from me when I'm going with him? That makes no sense at all. She finished her hot drink and headed up to the bedroom, walking without sound, past the room where Kurt would be holed up for the rest of the evening.

A couple of days later, he was watching the evening news in the family room. She waited for the commercial break and then asked how the travel plans were coming along. She wanted to alert Joshua and Amanda to the trip so they could make alternative plans for childcare.

"I already told them, and I already told you when we were going to be out of town," he said, obviously trying to control his tone. He got this "look" when he was trying not to get angry. She knew it well, after thirty-five years of marriage. He would take a deep breath, glare at her like she was an imbecile, and speak slowly and carefully as if explaining something to a small and not very bright child. She hated that look. He would gaze at her, attempting to appear loving. Not now. "Don't worry your pretty little head about it." He sneered.

"Kurt." She didn't appreciate how condescending he sounded. "I'd really like to know more details, so that I can look forward to the trip. You know how much fun anticipation is."

"You are going to be surprised, like it or not," he threw his hands into the air in exasperation. "Don't try to control our trip Sue. Your thoughts about the itinerary aren't important because it's all been decided. I'll say it again: we will be gone next week. We leave right after the girls' play on Saturday afternoon. We will return on Wednesday. That's all you need to know, so just...leave me alone." He turned back to the anchormen, sank deeper into his chair, and shut down any hope of further conversation. She left him to his news.

She went outside for a walk to steady her nerves, confused by his snide comments and unsure as to how she should handle this. It was just as much her trip as it was his, why all the fuss over nothing? Why did she feel so badly about leaving with him? Why the feeling of unspoken dread? It was as if, she couldn't pin it down, some secret horror awaited. Maybe it was like waiting for the other shoe to drop. He didn't want her. Why would he spend the money on a trip for her, unless... What was that he had said? "I'd rather you just died." As she walked down the street watching the streetlights come on, she could not have guessed that it would be the last time she ever walked on that street as a home owner.

Chapter 10

The girls' matinee performance of *Fiddler on the Roof* at the Bowie Playhouse came to an end, leaving just enough time for Kurt and Sue to quickly congratulate them on their performance before heading out on their vacation. Kurt grabbed Sue's arm and hustled her outside to their car. "That's enough of that." He dropped her arm as soon as possible and got into his side of the car. Kurt slammed the car into gear; he murmured under his breath, "Hurry up, you old cow. Let's get this show on the road." As Sue buckled herself into the vehicle and they pulled out of their parking spot, Kurt heard her sigh, he guessed at their having to leave. This irked him. Sue had been incessantly complaining about the trip and making up excuses for why this was a bad idea. She even had the gall to remark that normally she would reward the girls for the show by going home to make cookies, but that he had made that impossible. Ungrateful battle-axe that she was.

She'll regret those comments, Kurt thought to himself. She thinks she's such a hero for being submissive. What a doormat!

After hearing on WTOP that traffic was backed up on Route 3 North, he made a quick decision to take Route 450 to Annapolis and hop on Route 97 to get a straight shot at the airport. He was a stickler for keeping to schedules and the time spent sitting in traffic was far worse than the extra time spent on a longer route. He could be flexible, within limits. Given Sue's present attitude, the silence of the drive allowed his mind to drift back to the recent vacation he and Kelsey had taken to Hawaii, where they were "married."

Kurt recalled the day he set off for the airport, where he would meet Kelsey. It was stressful due to the weight of its secrecy. He told Sue it was an unscheduled job and that he would be back in a few days, but in reality, he took time off to make the trip feasible.

"I won't be calling you while I am gone," he informed her. "My cellphone service will be sporadic so it would be a waste of time to even try to reach you."

This was a tactic of his over the years, so Sue would not be at all surprised. Even so, he knew that this time it was a lie covering a bigger fib, which made the telling seem more precarious. She believed him without any trouble, no back talk. That's all that really mattered.

Sue misses a lot, he often thought. She assumes even more to make up for what she misses. It truly baffled him that she hadn't seen through everything yet. He couldn't help but shake his head. It was so obvious; she was thick as a plank and blind as a bat. Granted, this definitely had its advantages, especially once Kelsey arrived on the scene. Their little girl Cassie had been a bit of a surprise, but he doted on the love child he and Kelsey had created, believing that the perfect woman had created a perfect daughter. Kelsey had arranged for the toddler to be taken care of by her nanny during their get-away. Again, quite the cost but Sue was none the wiser. Admittedly, mistresses could be pretty costly, but was well worth it, with Kelsey.

The few days he and Kelsey had in Hawaii were beautiful. They checked into the honeymoon suite of their Oahu beachfront hotel. She was stunning, as always. Her beautiful long brown hair was gently blown by the breezes. Her complexion was smooth and graced by a slight tan. Her perfect figure was encased in top-of-the line clothing that showed her curves to their best advantage. Her only downfall that he could see was her love of huge purses.

Hey, they coordinated with her outfits. So what if she spent a lot of time transferring her "absolute necessities" from one bag to another? That could be easily forgiven. Her low-cut shirts that left little to the imagination, short shorts, and high heels always sent his heart racing and put his libido into high gear. Kelsey knew how to dress, that's for sure.

Kurt spent a lot of money on the trip, but excused the spending due to the special nature of weddings. You only get "married" to someone once.

They ate dinner at Michel's At the Colony Surf before walking out to the beach in their wedding attire and bare feet where his friend showed up to "marry" them. The gorgeous young woman who adored him stood there in a white chiffon wedding gown, draped in flowers, while he wore the traditional Hawaiian thin white shirt and white pants. The sand felt cool between his toes and he heard the pounding surf as they exchanged vows. He slipped a Love Cut diamond wedding band that matched the two-carat pear-shaped engagement ring on her finger. The inscription inside said it all for him: "My one true love, 2013." He might have added, if there had been room, "Kurt and Kelsey forever."

"I, Kurt, take you Kelsey to be my soulmate and my wife. You are the woman of my dreams and my beloved companion. I adore you in all our waking hours and every hour in between. I promise to love, honor, and cherish you all the days of my life."

Kelsey placed a plain silver wedding band on his finger. The matching inscription inside meant everything to her: "My one true love, 2013."

"I, Kelsey, take you Kurt to be my soulmate and husband. I love you more than life itself and am proud to be the mother of your child. I cannot wait to spend the rest of our lives together. I promise to love, honor, and respect you all the days of my life."

"I now pronounce you husband and wife. You may kiss the bride" said the friend-turned-fake-officiant.

Kurt drowned any thoughts about Sue, choosing rather to focus on his love for Kelsey. He found in her everything that he thought he originally had in Sue. Sue was worn and spineless and past her prime, whereas Kelsey still had her best years ahead. He wanted to be there to enjoy them with her.

Spending so much money on Kelsey was no small feat, but he managed it flawlessly, which was further proof of Sue's willful ignorance. Had Sue always been that way? Uncaring and unthoughtful, always concerned about her own affairs, never interested in actually knowing and loving him, yep that was Sue for you. Sue paid some of the bills and had access to their accounts in the past, yet she still never realized that money went missing all the time. These days, he controlled the money entirely on his own, which made it easier to funnel hidden money to his bank. He had always insisted that Sue sign over their joint income tax refunds every year, even though she had worked almost the entire time they were married. Sue never suspected that he stashed the money in his own private account. For times just like this.

To smooth the wrinkled story, he told Sue about various home projects he was going to pay for with the money they got back from the IRS. To get out of the projects, he either had them done on the cheap, or neglected to do them altogether due to his busy schedule. With enough time between stories, Sue always forgot about the money he took. He pocketed the balance and counted himself wise. On the rare occasion that Sue questioned him, he simply responded, "So you don't trust me? After all these years, you still don't trust me?" Immediately, she would become guilty, apologize, and walk away. How did a man like him become shackled to such a pathetic woman? She made him ill.

Cutting costs all over the house, he built a sizable nest egg for his life with Kelsey. One hundred and fifty dollars here, two hundred dollars there, eventually Sue had become accustomed to overlooking the missing funds as if they had never been there in the first place. His plan worked like a champ, though this far from surprised him. It wasn't just his personal brilliance that made it work so well. Sue simply did not think for herself.

Kurt did have to wonder if Kelsey cared that it was a fake ceremony and honeymoon. I mean, Kelsey knew he was still married to Sue. He couldn't have married her for real if he'd wanted to. And he did. It worried him a little that perhaps it wasn't good enough, but they went to one of the top-rated most romantic, expensive restaurants in Oahu and topped off their nights in the bridal suite of an upscale hotel. What did it matter if there was a legal form proving their union or not? In his book, he was married to one woman on a beach in Hawaii, 2013.

Sue won't be around to bother me much longer, if I have anything to say about it, he thought as he navigated the roadway. With his current track record of hiding their joint assets and taking from their financial reserves each month to pay hyper-inflated bills, she wouldn't have the money to hire a lawyer and do anything about it. He tracked her expenses, checking her accounts with care to ensure that she was 100% dependent on him. He made sure everything was in his name or, in the very least, both of their names, such as the house. She couldn't even call her phone her own. And now this trip. Sue wouldn't know what hit her. He was coming home but she...wasn't. He smiled at his genius.

Kurt smirked at just how gullible Sue was. What was she thinking all this time? Was her faith in me really that total? Did the woman even have a brain? She clearly couldn't care less about how much things like electricity, insurance, property taxes, and water cost. Obviously, she was incapable of figuring anything out on her own. Nothing was as expensive as I told her, but it all went right over her head. He sniffed, trying to control a chuckle.

"Kurt, are you all right? Do you need a tissue?" Sue handed over a tissue, which he didn't take. She finally put it back in her purse.

"I'm fine," he responded. "Leave me alone." He got back to his thoughts. The heck with Sue. Focus on Kelsey. Where was I? The wedding, of course.

The professional photographer he hired also cost a bundle, given the massive number of pictures he took. When they received the thumb-drive containing the files, it came to at least a couple hundred photos. There went this year's tax refund, all on one thumb-drive. He was thankful that it didn't go to waste, since Kelsey ended up with some great pictures to display in her condo. They went back to the restaurant for drinks before heading upstairs to an incredible wedding night and luxurious honeymoon.

What a woman! He smiled at the memory.

For the rest of their stay, they took on a nocturnal nature, staying in most of the day with room service and venturing out for moonlit walks followed by romantic dinners for two. Michel's certainly deserved its reputation for luxury wedding packages. The hotel's primary form of communication was through email, ensuring that Sue would never find out about the reservations since she didn't have his password. He was safe, and he knew it.

If only it hadn't ended.

His thoughts drifted as he recalled the news that Kelsey shared on their last night there. "I'm pregnant again, Kurt," she said as she beamed at him. "Cassie is going to be a big sister."

He was quite surprised, but pleased by the news that he and Kelsey had conceived again. They really meant it when they said men were fertile all their days. "Oh, honey, I couldn't be more pleased," he said as he pulled her into his arms. "When are you due?"

"Seven months. Kurt," she said, dropping her eyes. "Are you really happy?"

"Yes, my darling," he lifted her chin to meet her gaze. "I've just married the woman of my dreams and you have given me a wonderful wedding gift." He kissed her sweet mouth.

Kelsey giggled and admitted, "I was a little concerned, since Sue isn't willing to move forward on the divorce yet."

It would seem if you have to lie to one side of a love triangle, you have to lie to the other. To appease Kelsey's worrying mind, he had told her that Sue was unwilling to move forward with the divorce. In reality, he hadn't talked to Sue about a divorce, except to say he didn't want one at all. Nope, that old has-been would be better off if she was simply....dead.

"Don't let that woman take up another thought in your pretty little head, my love," he stroked her cheek. "You know how she can be. She'll come around to our way of thinking, eventually." His kisses seemed to soothe her concern, leading to a late exit from the hotel and almost missing their flight. He smiled at the memory.

"Kurt, watch out!" Sue screamed.

At the sound of Sue's shout, he was startled out of his reverie. They had just rounded the curve a mile east of Rutland Road when Sue cried out. He saw a large white delivery truck careening directly towards them, seemingly out of control. He made a split-second decision and turned the wheel hard, placing Sue's side of the car in the truck's direct path. The truck was unable to swerve. The vehicles collided with a huge crash, leaving their car crumpled beyond recognition. The truck, hanging on the road's barricades, remained on the roadway. It hadn't gone down into the ditch or into the nearby pond. The truck driver pounded on the passenger

121

side door, trying to free himself from his vehicle. The truck didn't release him very quickly.

Kurt treated himself gingerly, as he groaned a bit to get Sue's attention. No response. Kurt looked over at Sue, rolling his head along against his head rest, finding her passed out and bleeding profusely. For a moment, he could have sworn she was dead. He threw his hand over towards her to check for a pulse, hoping she might have expired. No. Not yet. The pulse was weak but still there. Tough luck.

Better make sure I'm okay. Ouch. He touched his midriff. Not feeling too good there, but it didn't seem to be anything serious. His legs were aching, but he ran his hands down them and couldn't find any signs of broken bones. A little blood on his forehead, but head wounds bleed a lot. Okay, I seem to be okay. Not great, but okay. Good enough, or bad enough, that is, for a convincing cover story. He hadn't planned on wrecking the car, but this was better than his original vacation plan. It had certainly been opportune, timely, even. But what about Sue? This would be a great time for her to expire. Very convenient. Better check on her again, to see if I can help her out...of this life.

Kurt picked up a jagged piece of glass from the window and leaned towards her. His plans could fall right into place, right in that very moment. No one would know that the accident had not been Sue's cause of death. If he jabbed the glass into her throat to pierce her jugular vein, she would bleed out in about thirty-five seconds, from what he'd heard. Good. Gotta be careful, so I don't hurt myself. This piece of glass isn't my friend, and it won't be Sue's either, in a minute. He got closer to his wife.

The trucker was finally successful in getting out of his vehicle. "Yes, I'm reporting an accident on Rutland Road," Kurt heard the southern drawl of the trucker say.

"Drat the luck!" Kurt glanced out the cracked windshield only to see the unharmed trucker running towards their vehicle with his cellphone to his ear and a worried look on his face. Serendipity seemed not to be on his side, so Kurt tossed the shard of glass on the floor of the car. Blasted luck. Helpful Herb here is going to make this all for naught. Kurt watched as Sue regained consciousness briefly. Kurt climbed out of the car from his side. Not the easiest trick in the book but I don't want to get stuck inside, if the whole thing blows up. He limped a bit, for effect. Made it. Kurt hobbled around to Sue's side of the car.

The trucker grabbed Sue up in his arms to pull her from the wreck and noticed a bad gash across her neck. Kneeling on the ground, the man tried to staunch the blood flow as they waited for emergency vehicles to arrive. Kurt groaned and fell to the ground, to excuse not helping the trucker with his ministrations. If Sue's bleeding was bad enough, perhaps he might have just gotten lucky after all. Kurt cursed the help under his breath. He crawled closer to her, to see how things were going and to appear to be the concerned husband.

Traffic began to build, its way halted by the tangled wreckage ahead of it. Some individuals tried to help, but most just got in the way. The sound of sirens split the afternoon air, forcing the vehicles to move to the side of the road as best they could. Moments later, the ambulances and firetrucks showed up at the scene, EMTs running to help. Sue's skin was turning blue as she passed out again. Kurt quickly reached out to grab her wrist.

The emergency crew told him, "Don't worry sir. She's still with us."

Kurt nodded, speechless. Did they really interpret his gesture as caring? Good. He pretended to wipe away a tear and sobbed for effect. So much the better. He'd just wanted to check to see if she was still alive or if . . . No such luck, her pulse was still there. Blast it all. He dropped her hand carefully, so as to make appear that he was being gentle. He wiped at his face again, seemingly to remove more tears.

The EMTs loaded her onto a gurney and hooked her up to oxygen and an IV.

"Sir, if you'll just come over here. We need to get you to the hospital for a look-see, yourself." An EMT took his arm and gestured towards a waiting ambulance. As Kurt continued to watch the ambulance, the EMT said, "Please, sir. Not to worry. They're taking good care of her."

Kurt watched as they closed the doors of the ambulance and drove off. He nodded and went with the man, limping and groaning a bit, for sympathy. He could play the distraught husband quite well, if he said so himself. He allowed himself to be lowered onto a gurney. They drove away. While the EMTs were focused on his readings, Kurt spoke to himself.

"Let her die soon and make it permanent," Kurt whispered into the late afternoon air.

Chapter 11

Sue jumped awake with a jolt in the pit of her stomach as if she were falling out of bed. What in the world is going on here? The most recent thing that she could recall was driving through the woods with a man she knew well. Suddenly things went haywire and now she found herself in a very dark, muffled place, waiting. It's so tight in here. Where am I? What's happening to me? Why is the world so dark, black, even?

That was when the weirdness really began. She was squeezed over and over. The black slowly started fading into a dull red until it seemed like light was trying to shine through her eyelids. Her throat felt so funny in those first few seconds until she realized that she was screaming at the top of her lungs while pictures were snapped, and people talked or laughed.

"Well done, sir, Ma'am," a man's voice said.

"Hip, hip, hooray," said a woman who was nearby. Applause broke out in the room.

Sue was completely baffled by it all. What in the world is happening? She felt so cold, suddenly. I'm naked! Oh my goodness gracious! Cover me up, for Pete's sake.

"My love, well done! She's beautiful, just like you!" exclaimed a man. He was quite a handsome fellow and he seemed familiar, somehow. But where did she know him from?

"You don't mind another girl? I thought you might wish for another son." A gorgeous woman looked at her husband tenderly as she held Sue, now wrapped in a blanket, in her arms. Sue knew the woman's voice quite well, having heard it all the time when she was....Sue was what? Or where?

"Nonsense, my sweet wife. I am delighted that our daughter is perfect and you are well. How could a man want more than that?" Sue noticed the man hugging and kissing his wife, right before.... darkness. Sleep, apparently. It had been a long day.

A couple of months passed, or so it seemed from the strange sense of time Sue had. She was lying in her crib one day, when she hit herself in the head with- what was this?- her fist. Where have you been, dear hands? She began sucking on her right hand, with all of her strength and concentration. Wait! Why in the world is this so fascinating? Since when did I start eating my own hand? A short time after that, her feet gave her hours of enjoyment. Seriously? I would love to know what's going on here. I've tried to be patient but my patience has been tried. She was startled by a loud and sharp sound. She let out a wail.

Blasted bagpipes, she thought to herself. "What is the British fascination with them?"

What am I doing here? She tried to remember how she had gotten herself into this situation. Of course, over the course of these last few months, that was all she had been able to do: think. Every time she opened her mouth, the sounds were babbles as if she had experienced a stroke and couldn't communicate the thoughts in her mind with any degree of coherence. It was the equivalent of baby-talk, which made her even more confused. It wasn't just that she couldn't form words, but the gibberish itself didn't even resemble the original words. Pure baby-talk came from her mouth. Get me out of here! Am I going stark raving mad?

"Oh, my, hello, little one!" said a woman leaning over the side of the crib. Sue looked up at the brunette and smiled at this lovely person. "Mummy will be back for you in a little while, all right?"

The woman walked away and at once Sue was filled with any uncontrollable need to sob. Where was Mummy going? Would she be back? Sue refrained, however. That was something she'd been working on for months. For some reason, controlling her emotions was near to impossible. If she was hungry, she cried. If she was thirsty, she cried. If she was missing a certain toy, she cried. If "Mummy" walked away, she cried again. And she cried with gusto when her diaper was dirty.

"A diaper," she moaned to herself, mortified. Has it really come to this?

She'd been wearing a diaper ever since she could remember, and it was one of the worst sensations in the span of her not-so-long memory. It was embarrassing having a complete stranger take it off and clean you up without your permission, especially when you couldn't at least comment about the weather or the local sports team, anything to distract from what was happening. How humiliating. If she hadn't known better, she would be asking everyone when she had been transferred to a nursing home. But then that would require being able to speak and, if not able to speak, at least be able to write a message. Alas, however, that was another of the many things she was no longer able to do. Eye-hand coordination was definitely a no-go and walking had been reduced to pulling herself across the floor in an Army crawl.

What have I become? She looked down at her pudgy little hands and started playing with the lace fringe of her frock. Guess I'm just easily entertained. Pathetic. More months passed.

Two little brunette-haired children came running toward her and peeked over the top of Sue's crib. She stood, to greet them. The boy was named George and his sister was Charlotte. That much she had gathered. What confused her most was the insistence that she was called Victoria Susan Anne. This, of course, was untrue, but there was no way of telling them they were so mistaken. My name is Sue.

The children ran away, and she watched them disappear down the corridor as she began sucking on the railing of her bed. She hadn't seen much of the building, considering she had this terrible habit of falling asleep all over the place. There wasn't a single place she wouldn't take a serious nap. Mummy's arms, Daddy's chest, on the floor, in a crib, in a pram, in a play pen, you name it, she'd taken a nap there.

"Okay, Sue, focus," she said as she dropped to her bottom. She headed towards the sunlit part of her crib. It was warm on that particular spot and she planted herself right in that area. "What do we remember about life right now? Let's start with the most recent stuff."

She had a new set of parents. Mummy and Daddy loved each other so very much. It was quite a comforting thing to know you were part of such a beautiful relationship. None of these present circumstances made any sense to her, but at least she was warm, dry, loved, and fed. Speaking of fed, she suddenly felt her stomach growl. Her brow furrowed as she stood once more, with the help of the wooden slats and looked over to find Mummy. Right on cue, Mummy entered the room with a bottle in hand. Lunch. Outstanding. Sue began a little jig. Well, it could hardly be called a dance. Bending her knees and popping upright was more like it.

"Hello, my darling. Were you waiting for me?" Mommy bent down and lifted Sue out of the crib.

They went to a big comfortable chair and Sue took the bottle in her hands, eager to do something, anything on her own. In through the other doorway came the two brunette children from earlier. They seemed to take special delight and interest in her when she happened to be eating. Sue paused in her eating to give them a quick smile. Nice kids.

"George, what do you think of your sister?" asked their mother.

"Is she still too small to play ball? You said she was when you first brought her home, but she's gotten so big now!" George replied, with hope in his voice.

"You can roll the ball to her, but you can't throw and expect her to catch. But she will grow, just like you and Charlotte did."

"Can I give her the bottle, Mummy?" asked Charlotte. She was always so shy.

"I think Victoria is doing fine, little Lottie," Mummy answered with affection.

"Can we take the lift up to the roof and play in the garden?" George cut in.

"Oh yes, Mummy!" exclaimed Charlotte, apparently setting aside her original request. "And can we bring Lupo?"

"Of course, dears, run along," their mother smiled. After Victoria finished her bottle, she began to squirm in her mother's lap, trying to join her older siblings. She loved Lupo, their adorable cocker spaniel. Mummy told Sue, "No, darling, you need a nap."

"Shall I take her to her crib, Ma'am?" asked the Mary Poppins-like woman known as Nanny Marian who had just entered the room along with Daddy. Nanny curtsied at Mummy.

"Thank you, Nanny, but I think you would best be up with the children in the garden. I don't believe anyone went with them," Mummy replied as she handed Sue over to her father.

"Of course, Ma'am," Nanny Marian replied, offering a brief curtsy and proceeding to disappear out of the room.

"Would you take her to her crib?" Mummy asked Daddy.

"Of course, my love."

As Daddy carried her off, Sue found her eyes becoming difficult to keep open. Placing her heavy head on his shoulder as he walked, she couldn't help drifting off to sleep in the strength of his safe, warm embrace. She couldn't be more content, despite wanting to play with Lupo in lieu of taking a nap.

**

Sue, aka Victoria Susan, measured her pace against her father's as they followed the winding paths through the parks and gardens. She couldn't quite match him step for step, but three strides put her right foot on the ground at the same time as his. At ten years old, she was fast and kept up with her dad on their early morning runs without trouble, even pushing him to go a little bit further. When she first asked if she could go running with him, she overheard her mother suggest "taking it easy with Victoria." Sue was determined to prove she could keep up and succeeded with self-confidence.

The pair went racing down the path in the early morning air. Her ears were filled with the sound of her feet hitting the gravel, when she decided to put in the last spurt of energy she had. She picked up her pace and sped all the way back, coming to a stop and breathing hard as she waited for her father to catch up.

"Quite impressive, Miss," said her tutor, a large man, who was sitting nearby on a bench. Mr. Matthew, as she had always called him, came early in the morning every weekday to work on her studies. Sometimes he would arrive just as she was returning from her run.

"Thank you, Mr. Matthew," she grinned.

"Well done, Darling Daughter," her father said, coming to a stop near her, giving her head a quick kiss. He had given her the nickname when she was very little. She had always been very smart, even smarter than her older siblings. It was her ability to negotiate that had kept her out of the day school that her older siblings attended. She had convinced her parents that, with her brain, she would have a better chance of excelling with a private tutor. Her arguments had been convincing, hence the presence of Mr. Mathew in her life. So, not only was she fast physically but she was sharp mentally, as well. "I was surprised to see you pick up such speed."

"I must always keep you challenged, Daddy Dear!" she said.

"You certainly do that" he said. "Now, don't keep your poor teacher waiting."

"No rush," Mr. Matthew held up his hand. "I was just going to see if I could find a cup of tea with Nanny Marian. Get ready, m'lady, and you will find me in the library as is our habit." He nodded twice, once to each of them. "Sir, Miss." He turned on his heels.

Sue made sure to take as long as possible in cleaning herself up and dressing for the day before grabbing her books and going down to meet him. Her parents had first begun the lessons when she was four years old and by the end of the year she was doing basic mathematics, reading at a second grade level, and studying French. To say the least, she was considered brilliant by everyone. Her proficiency was accidentally discovered by Nanny Marian when Sue was using magnetic letters to form words she shouldn't have known at her age, correctly writing "Mummy" before she'd ever officially learned how to read or write and singing back the rest of tunes Nanny Marian would start to hum. Of course, Nanny Marian was the only one initially aware of the differences between Victoria and other children the older woman had cared for, and Nanny made sure to tell Sue's parents.

"Blasted snitch," Sue grumbled to herself as she pulled on a sweater.

Sue was far from enthusiastic about going downstairs and spending hours on her studies, though she usually adored learning.

It was simply too beautiful a day to be spent cooped up inside. Most ten-year-old children didn't need any of this. Why did she?

"Good morning, Princess," Mr. Matthew greeted her as she entered the library, standing and bowing to her with great solemnity as he laid aside the book he was reading.

"Good morning, Mr. Matthew," she replied with respect.

"You do not seem very chipper this morning," he noted as she set her books on the table.

"True enough, I must confess," she sighed.

"Ah," Mr. Matthew looked at his young pupil in amusement. "What seems to be the content of your confession, Princess Victoria?"

"Several things, not the least of which is that I am far ahead of my peers in study, so why don't I take a break and let the rest of the world catch up," she suggested, with the hope of getting a break. Not forever, heaven forbid, but surely a day or two at the most would do no harm. The day was so gorgeous and she longed to be outside, enjoying it.

"I'm afraid I have very strict instructions from your parents that I teach you everything I possibly can until you go to university," Mr. Matthew replied.

Sue sunk deeper into her chair in a dramatic fashion, even to the point of throwing herself against the seat cushions. Surely Mr. Matthew would realize that she needed a break, wouldn't he? She realized that she was being a Drama Queen, but there was no other choice, if she was to get a reprieve from her studies. "That is a great unkindness and I am gravely wounded," she moaned. Was she going over the top here? Oh, well, carry on. You're committed now. Look pathetic.

"What is your other trouble?"

Sue sat up. Okay, that didn't work, drat the luck. Might as well get on with it. The studies won. Maybe I can at least distract Mr.

Matthew a bit, changing the subject I assume he will raise. "These old ancient fellows you have me studying. Can't we go a little more contemporary than 2500 years ago?"

"Princess," he sighed.

"I realize that they were important to modern literature and public speaking. I have the upmost respect for that but can we please move on? Or, in the very least, Mr. Matthews, can you please answer the questions I have been asking you about remembering what you shouldn't be remembering, situations where you have a certain, I don't know, knowledge, of something. But you couldn't possibly know it, and yet you do? And then there's the idea of reincarnation. I really feel that it is a possibility that we must consider, yet you always dodge my questions," she said.

"If this is a convoluted way of getting out of your studies, Princess Victoria, I'm afraid you will not succeed in changing the topics at hand," he shook his head.

"Do you think reincarnation is a real possibility?" she persisted.

Mr. Matthew took off his glasses and she gulped. When he took his glasses off, she knew she was in for a very serious answer that held the possibility of being long and drawn out. Oh, my stars. Not again. Perhaps he can be brief. Or not.

"I'm not here to teach you religion, Princess Victoria. Just everything else." Mr. Matthew looked firm. Unmovable.

"This isn't religion; it's just a question," she replied.

"Once again, you are trying to distract from my planned lessons for today. We will approach those questions and answers another time," he answered sternly. "Now, we really must focus, Princess Victoria."

"Please call me Sue," she answered.

"I certainly will not, Your Royal Highness," he looked her squarely in the eye. "You were born into a family which holds my highest respect and adoration. You must hold your head high by bearing the honor and dignity that this family is endowed with. I will not stoop so low as to refer to you by a shortened secondary name. You are Princess Victoria Susan Anne, and I will call you such, if that is what it takes to convince you of your incomparable worth as a princess of royal blood and lineage. You are worthy of your full name and an abbreviation, even in one such as 'Victoria,' is not enough to denote all that you are. Now let us turn to your books, Princess Victoria, before the rest of your peers have completely caught up!"

The rest of the tutoring session was overshadowed with the previous tension. Sue had always struggled with the level of respect she received daily. Inside, she felt that it was undeserved. My parents and grandparents are wonderful and Great-Granny is supreme, but what did I do to earn or deserve the bowing and scraping I get? Nothing. Zip. Zilch. Nada. Where did that come from? I know those words but can't remember when I heard them. It's all so strange. Shrugging, she turned back to her books.

Several hours later, Nanny Marian entered the library, curtsying and then saying, "Princess Victoria, Ma'am?"

Sue lifted her head to the woman. "Yes, Nanny?"

"You must leave your studies for the time being and go for your visit," she announced.

"Thank you, Nanny," Sue replied.

Nanny curtsied again and disappeared through the door as Victoria organized her things to be left on the table. "Return soon," Mr. Matthew instructed.

"I cannot control how long we will be gone. I mean, how long I will be gone," she answered, groaning. This royal "we" stuff was catching. Heavens to Betsy. What? Where did I get that expression?

"We have much to finish here, Princess," he looked at her over the top of his glasses.

"Yes, indeed, Mr. Matthew."

She exited the library as fast as possible, knowing that he would pull out one of his weighty tomes to indulge in during her absence. Despite his apparent aversion to her leaving, she knew deep down he was relieved for a few moments of uninterrupted silence. Meanwhile, she made her way to her suite, where she found Nanny Marian alone. Victoria changed into her third outfit of the day. Boy, royals sure blow through a lot of clothes. I wouldn't want to do the laundry for this group.

"Nanny?" Sue asked as the woman brushed her hair.

"Yes, Princess?" she answered.

"What do you think about having memories that aren't really yours?"

"I don't quite follow, Princess," she replied.

Nanny Marian was oftentimes slow on the uptake. She was so consumed by her position that she seemed to almost forget that she was a person. "What I mean is..." Victoria thought for a moment, searching for a simpler explanation. "Do you think you can have memories from a different life?"

"It depends on whether you think you can have a different life," Nanny answered brusquely after tying a ribbon in her hair.

"Like reincarnation?" she asked.

The woman pursed her lips before responding, "Well, it isn't my place to say what is and what's not, but," Nanny took a breath. "I think it's only fair that people have a chance at doing better in life and once doesn't seem to be quite enough. But you can't do better without remembering what you did wrong before." Nanny furrowed her brow before shrugging her shoulders and continuing. "So, I suppose it would only be right that you keep memories."

Victoria thought back to the strange dream-like memory she had of the familiar man in the car and driving along before there was pain. She watched as Nanny Marian hung up the clothes she had just changed out of. She knew she couldn't tell Nanny about the strange memory. One way or another, it would make it back to her parents and they might think she was nuts. Perhaps reincarnation was plausible, but it didn't seem to fit the beliefs her parents had instilled in her. If this life wasn't reincarnation, what in the world was it? A dream?

"Run along, Princess, you have to go!" Nanny Marian urged, looking at her watch. "Mustn't be late."

"Of course not. That would be rude," Sue said as she hurried out the door.

It was a tradition of the family to make regular visits to the less fortunate and offer comfort in their time of need. They had to be careful in their visits, offering love and support while not appearing to pity those less fortunate. Victoria became quite good at this, offering true friendship and kindness. Other royals had not been so sensitive in the past and had appeared to be looking down on those they visited. The press had had a field day with those less sympathetic royals, painting them as opportunistic individuals looking for a photo op rather than being sincerely concerned for others. Victoria truly enjoyed being "with the people" as some of the other royals called it.

The destination today was a wounded veterans' home where servicemen were recovering from traumatic injuries. As they made their way to the location, she couldn't help imagining men lying about with limbs missing, just like in the makeshift hospital tents of World War II movies. Oh, my. When did I watch any World War II movies? There were none in the palace. Of course, the movies she had seen were nothing like the actual building they found themselves walking into. The home was clean and well-lit, with big windows surrounded by gardens and recreational fields. As they walked the halls greeting the service members, she spotted one man in particular who was sitting in a wheel chair. He was a double amputee with two prosthetics resting on the foot pieces. She thought he looked sad.

"Hello, sir," she greeted him with respect, sitting on the settee next to him.

"Good afternoon, Your Royal Highness," he replied in like. "I would stand--"

"No problem" she answered. Studying his face, she asked, "Do you hurt?"

"Phantom pain sometimes," he answered. "Otherwise, it's a long rehabilitative process."

"Phantom pain?"

"It's a pain you feel, but it's not really there," he explained. "My brain believes I haven't lost my limbs and feels the pain they would feel if they were still with me."

"I see you have prosthetics. Are they painful?" she asked.

"Not as much as they used to be. I've had these prosthetics for about eight months. I'm getting better at getting around, but I'm still not very good at using them, though," he sighed in frustration.

Sensing his unhappiness with his current situation, she changed the subject. "Did you like to run before...this happened?"

He laughed, trying to lighten his mood. "You certainly are a curious one, Your Royal Highness. Yes," he smiled in memory. "I did like to run."

"I go running with my daddy regularly in the mornings. He says I'm very fast, but I'm sure you would be even faster than me, if you got your legs to work."

"We'd have to do a test run to see if that's true," he grinned.

"Then it's settled," she replied with determination. "Practice as much as you can and, when you're able to run, let's have a race."

"You're on," the man replied.

Four months later, she returned to the home, ready for a race around the on-campus track. Certain members of the press came to watch the race between the Corporal and the princess. The princess and the military man raced around the track, keeping an equal pace. She ran her hardest alongside the soldier. They rounded the last bend in the track; she put in her classic last spurt of energy, and reached the finish just ahead of the double amputee. He came to a slow gallop before stopping beside her, breathing deeply. They both knew he had let her win, but the truest win was his. Over the course of the past four months, he had worked hard in rehabilitation and come back strong and ready to race.

As a result of the effort she observed in the Corporal, she formed a foundation at the tender age of ten, aimed at helping wounded heroes get back on their feet, literally as well as figuratively. Her parents were very accommodating. The press was remarkable, offering their full support to her efforts. The news coverage they offered was a great boon to the organization.

**

Five years later, Mrs. Patricia Minghella, Victoria's ladies' maid was hanging up the dress Sue had just taken off and she said, "Your work has been quite impressive, ma'am." As Sue had made her way into young womanhood, Nanny Marian and Mr. Matthew moved on to other children who needed their attention and skill. In their place came formal education at university and Mrs. Minghella to wait on Her Royal Highness.

Sue was sitting at her dressing table, deciding which jewelry would be appropriate to wear that evening. "What has been remarkable is the work our heroes have done," Sue said. "It's been a wonderful journey, watching our heroes make their way back to life. I'm glad to be home from university for the weekend so that I can go to the gala celebrating their accomplishments."

"If I may be so bold, it is extraordinary that someone at the age of fifteen is giving speeches and raising money, not to mention being at university" replied Mrs. Minghella.

"Fair enough," she conceded. "Regardless, I should be getting ready for tonight's celebration of the Foundation."

Mrs. Minghella looked at her watch. "Princess, it's going to be a late night. May I suggest a brief nap before we get you dressed? You may be grateful for the rest, once the gala begins."

Victoria agreed. University had been very busy lately, what with her double degree program and preparing to begin her master's degree. "Perhaps 45 minutes would suffice." She pulled on some lounging shorts and a T-shirt and slipped into bed, as Mrs. Minghella closed the blinds.

"Princess, I will return promptly in forty-five minutes. Rest well."

Sue lay between the covers, closing her eyes and focusing on resting. It was not to be. Only a few minutes into her slumber, there came a horrid nightmare. She was in a tiny room, dark and foreboding. She could hear the laughter of someone, a man, standing near her. She was prone on a bed or couch of some sort, as the man whispered in her ear.

"You will not get away this time. I will see you dead." He laughed.

Sue jumped. That voice gave her the creeps. That laughter- she knew it but couldn't place it. It made her sweat, just hearing that terrible, horrible sound.

She heard the shuffle of feet as more people apparently came into the room. They were talking; a woman was pleading with someone, Sue assumed it was a doctor, about not removing, what? A tube of some sort.

Sue grabbed at her throat. What was this? She clawed at her throat, trying to stop what was happening, even though she wasn't sure what was going on. Her hands were pushed away, held down by stronger hands than hers. She smelled familiar cologne, and turned her head away from the memories it invoked. Horrid stuff, that. She thrashed her head about.

The man with the recognizable scent held her head firmly in his strong hands. "Go ahead, doctor. I've got her. She can't move."

Sue strained to get away from that horrid man. If only she could escape. A sweat poured over her body, soaking her clothing.

She tried to speak, but only nothing came out. "Help.....help me, please." Her thoughts were not making a sound. There was no reply, except the laugh again.

She became more aware of her surroundings. The sound. What was that? A swishing noise. She realized that her chest was rising and falling in sync with a machine. Breathing. It's breathing for me, but why? She tried to hold her breath, to no avail. The machine was all in all, forcing air into her lungs and then allowing the air to escape.

"Go ahead, doctor. Do it." The man with the unkind voice sounded more firm, almost angry at the delay. "Now."

Then, it stopped. Silence. The machine had been turned off. The tube was pulled out of her throat. She coughed, choking. She almost vomited. Then, she gasped for air. Breathe, Sue, breathe in. Gotta breathe on my own. Come on. She choked and sputtered for air. She sucked in the air, desperate to get oxygen. Then, she fainted.

Sometime later, it could have been minutes, hours, days, from what she could tell, she awoke in her bed. The sheets, her clothing, were all drenched in sweat. What happened to me? Where am I? Her heart pounded. Her adrenaline was on high alert.

Looking around the room, she started to calm down. I'm home. She deliberately slowed her breathing. She mopped some of the sweat off of her brow, using the edge of her sheet. She reached over to her bedside table and checked the clock. Thirty minutes had passed. It seemed like so much longer, or did it?

Mrs. Minghella would be back in fifteen minutes. She can't see me like this. Sue got up, slowly stretching, and headed for the bathroom. Gotta take a shower. Yes, that's the thing. Shower, wash my hair, unwind a bit.

Once in the bathroom, she turned on the hot water, getting under its spray as soon as it warmed up enough to comfortably do so. Augh, it feels like I haven't showered in months. Feels so good. She washed her hair, letting the crème rinse sit on her locks while she lathered up. She took her time, feeling great relief from the trials of her dream. She grabbed the luxurious bath towel and dried off, hearing Mrs. Minghella come into the bedroom. She heard the woman call housekeeping, asking that Sue's bedclothes be changed, pronto.

A discreet knock came on the door. "Princess, are you all right? Your bed is quite disturbed. I have ordered the linens changed. Are you feeling well?"

'Yes, thank you, Mrs. Minghella. I had a bad dream and am afraid that my sheets bore the brunt of it. I'll be with you momentarily."

Sue walked into the bedroom, dressed in her undies and a thick robe. "So sorry to have worried you, Mrs. Minghella. We will need to dry my hair and redo my makeup. I appreciate your help, even though, quite frankly, I have gotten quite used to doing my own hair and makeup at university." She tried to laugh, but the laugh sounded strange, even to her own ears. Mrs. Minghella seemed not to notice anything but the time.

"Please, Princess, we must work quickly. We are a bit short on time."

"Yes, of course." Sue sat on her dressing room stool, waiting for the hair drying to begin.

Several minutes later, her hair was dry and her makeup was expertly applied. Mrs. Minghella was certainly gifted in that way. Sue stepped into her gown for the evening, a royal purple ball gown that was her all-time favorite. The color might have seemed a bit harsh for anyone who did not have her pure white coloring. The purple displayed beautifully against her dark brown hair. Mrs. Minghella added a small jeweled headband that Her Majesty the Queen had lent Sue for the evening, it having been delivered to her suite while she was showering. Once ready, they headed downstairs to join her parents for the trip to the gala. The limousines dropped the family off at the banquet hall, photographers snapping away as the royal family walked the red carpet and headed inside.

"Congratulations on five excellent years, Princess!" congratulated a gentleman, as he bowed his head to Sue's father, mother, and to her.

"Thank you, I couldn't have done it alone," Sue replied. "Our heroes are the ones to be congratulated."

"We are so grateful to your work, Your Royal Highness," said the wife of an officer, offering a brief curtesy. The woman curtsied even lower to Victoria's mother and father, as was the custom.

"It is my pleasure to have been of some help," Sue remarked with pleasure. As agreed, the family split up, each taking a section of the hall, to meet and greet as many donors as possible.

Sue welcomed more people than she could remember and walked about, seeming to be in a dream. The ladies curtsied while the gentlemen gave her a brief neck bow, as protocol dictated. She received them all, still charmed by this old world tradition. Compliments were given on her beautiful gown, the lovely evening, and the incredible achievements of her work in the community at large. To say the least, she was feeling overwhelmed by their kind attention. Sue loved it but was still getting used to their admiration.

"I'm going to step out into the garden," she said to one of the security men. "I need fresh air."

"Of course, m'lady," replied the gentleman. He bowed.

Sue walked out onto a patio and began making her way down one of the stone stairways, feeling the evening breeze on her face. How refreshing. It was a bit hot in the ballroom. Suddenly, she was exhausted.

"I'm so tired." Sue sank onto a bench near a rose bush.

"Why haven't you died yet?" A man's voice asked her.

She jumped off the bench and looked around, trying to find the speaker? "What? Who? Who's there?"

"You weren't supposed to live. How could *anyone* live through this?"

Her heart almost stopped beating and her skin began to crawl. The male voice sounded familiar but she couldn't place it. "What are you talking about," she whispered. "What have I lived through?"

"You're costing me a fortune. I have a wife, a daughter, and another child on the way."

"That's perfectly fine, go on your way now. Please don't hurt me," her eyes welled up with tears as she frantically looked around the rose bushes for the culprit. Where was the man? Where was her security detail? Oh, why did I leave them behind?

"Just hurry up and die; put an end to this."

"I can't, I can't, I'm so scared," Sue began to sob. She had to get out of here but seemed frozen in her tracks. She couldn't move.

"Withdraw all food. Stop all medications. I *insist* that you listen to me. I am her husband. I have rights."

"What," tears cascaded down her cheeks. "No, stop. I must have food. I'm not on medications. I don't need any money you have. I don't even have a husband!" She finally came to herself, able to move. She ran around the bushes. Who was the man? Where was he hiding? She began screaming. "Where are you?! Where are you?! Leave me alone!" She became hysterical as she tried desperately to find this evil man.

"There will be NO physical therapy from this point onward. I'm not paying another dime!"

"Keep your money; you can keep your money!" Her face reddened. "Go away!"

Sets of footsteps came running towards her. "Princess Victoria!" yelled her bodyguard, followed by three other gentlemen, her parents, and Mrs. Minghella. They ran towards her hidden bench.

"He's going to kill me. I can't let him kill me!" Sue yelled back at them. "Please don't let him kill me!" The three gentlemen fanned out on orders from her bodyguard, searching the garden. Her parents ran towards her.

"Wake up. Please wake up!" another voice, a female said.

"I've been trying, I've been trying," she screamed, her voice cracking in sobs. She fell to the ground and curled up in fetal position. "Go away, please just go away. Leave me alone."

"Victoria!" yelled her father, racing down the stairs, falling to his knees, and grabbing her into his arms.

"I can't wake up! I can't wake up!" Sue tried to wrestle her way out of her father's arms, arms that still felt so far away. "You're not close to me!"

"I'm here, Darling Daughter," he held her tight, his own voice cracking in confused tears. "I'm here, baby girl." He put his arms around her, encircling her with his love.

"You're not! You're not! You're not real," she wailed. She flailed at his chest, to no avail. She collapsed back on the ground in exhaustion, slipping out of her father's arms.

"Mom, please! You have *got* to respond. He wants you dead and the courts can't see that you are still in there. Please!"

Sue jumped, surprised by the female voice that was so familiar. "Please don't kill me!" She buried her face in her father's chest. "Hold me, Daddy."

"I will sweetheart. I will protect you. No one will get you," he said, desperate. He began rubbing her head, stroking her hair. "I'm here for you. Everything will be fine." He rocked her back and forth, kissing her forehead and hugging her close. "I have you, darling one."

"She needs to be taken to a hospital," Sue heard her bodyguard say as he returned from the search. "There's no one in the garden, sir."

"This can't get out to the public," said her mother, rushing to her daughter and husband as they sat on the ground. She joined her husband in encircling Sue.

"I can't be taken to the hospital, no!" Sue yelled, breaking free of her father.

Her mother looked up and spoke to the bodyguard. "Bring medical staff to the palace. She mustn't be seen like this."

Sue jumped to her feet and ran around in circles. Where am I? Where am I? She fell into the yard once more, tearing her dress, only to rise again.

"Please, Mama. Come back to us," said an invisible female voice so close to her heart.

"I'm here, baby," Sue sobbed, stumbling to run further across the lawn.

"Call the doctor; we need to get her sedated," yelled her father, trying to catch up with her.

Sue suddenly heard buzzing around her head. "Bees! Daddy, there are bees!" She began frantically batting the air around her face. "Get them away, get them away!" They were so close to her head, she knew they were real, like the voices.

"Victoria, there are no bees!" Daddy tried to grab her hand. "Please, honey, come to me. Let me help you."

"I don't see what you see. She's not there anymore. Let her go," said another deep voice.

"No, I'm here!" she screamed, unable to see, as swarms of bees flew around her head.

"Mom, please help me help you. Move your arm if you can hear me. Talk to me, anything! Please, Mama!" said the desperate female voice.

"Get out of here," the first male voice, the malevolent one, said. "You have no right to be here now. I command you to leave before I call security."

"Mama, I'll be back soon. Stay with us," the female sounded desperate. Footsteps faded away.

"I'm trying," Sue screamed; her throat was burning as she batted at the bees. She felt as if they were climbing into her head; the sound of their buzzing got closer and louder. Help me! Someone help me!

"No, not again," she murmured, suddenly becoming worn out. "Please, don't let me go...I want to stay..." Sue began to breathe deeply as she became drowsy. "Help me, someone. I want to stay..." She felt her body heavy against a cushioned surface. "Please, don't make me go...I want to stay..." Darkness.

Chapter 12

Darkness. Everything was pitch black. Then Victoria Susan saw a small light. She focused, squinted, and saw a lamp on a bedside table. Its tiny light made everything appear in shadows. Her eyes did not immediately accustom themselves to the dimness, but she realized that the bees had moved away. The buzzing was still there but it was now at a distance.

Laughter. She heard the sound of a man's laugh, a familiar noise but one she did not relish, though she could not say why. She smelled the man's cologne. She sniffed. It was bit too strong for her taste. It was familiar, but not one she remembered with happiness. The buzzing stopped. More laughter followed. She heard him say, "Serves you right." She could not respond. She was still waking up, feeling like she had been asleep for a very long time. Lying on her left side, she stretched with moves that were stiff, slow, and silent. She knew that she didn't want his attention, so her moves had to be slow and deliberate.

The garden was gone. Her family was no longer near her. They had vanished; this she somehow knew. She felt her way, touching her surroundings as if blind. She needed to take stock. She touched her chest. Her beautiful gown had vanished, replaced by a nightgown, one that was flimsy at that. Unfamiliar to her touch. She rolled the fabric of the gown in her fingers. Where did this old thing come from? She never bought anything that felt like this. It was rough, wrinkled, and open at the back. The air conditioning that chilled her back revealed this information. No modesty here, apparently. In self-defense, she flipped quietly onto her back. That's better, temperature-wise. Okay, what else was there to be discovered?

Diaper- oh, no, not again. Bra, no. She rubbed her feet together. Socks, maybe some kind of booties but no shoes. Where am I? What happened? She felt along her side. Her hands stumbled. They fumbled as she groped, but they become her eyes for the time being. Ah, a bed, a metal railing, sheets, two pillows, and a thin blanket. Pathetic.

Her eyes continued to adjust to the lack of light. She became mindful of being in a room, much smaller than the room that she once shared with her Nanny Marian. It was definitely not the one she had as a teen at the palace. This room contained a single bed, a dresser, and a couple of chairs. The lamp was there, of course. She strained to see more. There was a television set, but it was not turned on. There were curtains but they were closed against the daylight that crept around the edges of the drapes. The whole place smelled of antiseptic and urine. The man was still there but his back was to her as he wiped something from his clothing with one hand. He held something boxlike in his other hand. She couldn't tell what it was.

Sue continued to peer around the room for any hint of where she was. There were a few pictures on the walls, though nothing was framed, just snapshot photos of some little girls and boys and a couple of adults, taped into place. Crooked. Stuck on the wall. Not her normal decorating style at all. Pitiful.

An air conditioning unit kicked on again, bringing new air circulating into the room. It moved the curtains just enough to illuminate a small portion of the wall. A bulletin board caught in the light shared the thumb-tacked news: "It is Tuesday. The weather is seventy degrees and sunny. Your charge nurse is Linda S." What charge nurse? Where was she?

Her room was dim and silent but she could hear people moving about beyond her walls. She realized she was on a hospital bed. She looked around, not recognizing anything in this strange room. Her fingers searched as they made their way over her body. What's this? It was a tube going into her stomach, but the end of it revealed that it was not attached to anything. Yuck. She dropped it pretty fast, moving her hands to her sides. She stretched again, being careful not to alert the man standing nearby. She somehow knew he was not her friend. Her limbs were so stiff. Ouch! She straightened her arms and legs, moving slowly. Her arms and legs refused to fully cooperate. She reached up and touched the top of her head. Stumble met her fingers. No hair. What? Where had her hair gone?

"Mummy! Mummy, where are you? Where am I?" she tried to croak out. No sound. With the man there, it was probably just as well. Mummy didn't come, anyway. Neither did her father nor Mrs. Minghella.

Her eyes accustomed themselves some more to the shadowy light. She saw that there was hair all over the bed and floor. She was covered with a thick coat of it. Part white hair, part brown hair. The large man turned back to her and was standing over her, holding an electric razor. It wasn't on but had hair stuck in the blades. Her hair? Perhaps. She felt so strange. She knew she knew him, but how? Somehow, the man looked very familiar. Unkind, almost wicked. No, it was unfair to judge him without speaking to him. Perhaps it was this strange situation she found herself in. Maybe it was just the lighting.

He complained, "I thought you were dead."

Before she could respond, she heard someone say "What's going on here?" The overhead light snapped on, instantly blinding her. Ouch! Her hands flew to her face. She peeked out from behind them as a young African American man rushed into the room, asking, "What have you done, Mr. Prescott?" Prescott? It was Kurt! She peered out between her fingers, to watch Kurt's reaction.

"I've taken care of your problem with her hair, Michael. This will be much easier to manage. Now clean this mess up." Kurt smiled. Sue recognized the sarcastic grin on his face. She shuddered. Now I know where I am- somewhere Kurt is. I'm not in England anymore.

The young man seemed to be in shock at the massive disarray. His head swiveled between the state of the room and the patient lying on the bed, bald.

Sue groaned, hoping to gain the attention of...what's his name? Michael? She coughed, anything to get him to look at her, really look.

Michael turned back to her and their eyes met, "She's awake!"

"No. She's supposed to die!" Kurt was livid. His face turned beet red. "Don't touch her!"

Michael pushed the call button on the bed. "Get me the doctor on call stat and bring me some water. Our sleeping beauty is awake."

Kurt said, "You can't feed her. I have a court order. We'll see about this!" He stomped out of the room, yelling as he went.

This was so confusing. What was going on here? This Michael person wanted her to live but Kurt was adamant that she should..... She remembered what he had said that night at the city dock. "I'd rather you just died."

Michael pulled out his cellphone and punched in a number. "Hello, Miss Prescott. This is Michael Bench, the Nursing Supervisor at Chesapeake Court. You need to get over here right away. Your mother just woke up." Michael listened intently. "Yes, she's awake. She's looking at me, even as we speak." He winked at Sue and waited. "Yes, yes, it's wonderful, blessed news. See you soon." Sue felt a few tears flow down her face. Her Brooke. He had called her Brooke. Sue knew Brooke would be here soon. She would be safe. Relief. She winked back at the young man, Michael, was it?

After changing her bedding, Michael sat her up ever so slightly, using the bed control and pillows. A CNA brought in some water, obviously astonished that Sue looked back at her and nodded. Michael told her, "Now, Mrs. Prescott, I need to do a swallow test before I can give you any food. What I need you to do is to drink this water. Don't rush it now, but do wait until I say "go." Understand?"

"Yes, I understand. Say when." She croaked out the words, her voice rusty from lack of use. Sue lifted the glass to her lips, albeit with a little help from Michael. I'm so weak. That's pretty sad when I can't even lift a glass to my mouth.

Michael looked at his watch. "Okay, go."

Sue was easily able to finish off the glass. Of course, being extremely thirsty did help. She noticed that Michael was still looking at his watch. What was up with that?

After a minute, he looked at her and said, "You didn't cough even once. Well done, Mrs. Prescott. You passed the test with flying colors. Now it's time for some food." He buzzed for the nurse to bring in food. Michael revealed to her that Kurt had been successful when he petitioned the court to have her feedings stopped, so she had been given nothing for several days.

While they were waiting, Brooke came running into the room. "Mom! You're back!" Sue's and Brooke's tears began flowing very freely. "You've been gone so long!" Brooke hugged Sue and didn't let go until a CNA brought in the food Michael had asked for: cream of wheat, applesauce, and scrambled eggs.

Brooke wanted to feed her but Michael explained that, "I need to monitor her eating very closely. You can stay here, obviously, but I need to do this. Why don't you sit down and just enjoy your mother's company while I help her out?"

"Yes, of course. Thank you, Michael." Brooke sat next to Sue's bed and watched the progress. Her tears had stopped but the joy on her face was apparent as she held her mother's hand. "Mom, Joshua is with a patient but will be here very soon. Christopher is in a class but he'll be over once it's done. I know they'll be excited to see you."

Sue nodded. "That's good." She squeezed Brooke's hand and turned her attention to what Michael had for her. Food. I'm hungry.

Michael didn't give her much, just a few teaspoons of each one. A sip of apple juice. Yummy. She had been in a coma, he told her.

The act of eating exhausted her.

"Must sleep." She lay back and closed her eyes.

Sue awakened to the sound of an angry man: Kurt, again. He was standing nearby. She understood from his red face and bulging neck veins that he had been yelling for some time before she woke up. It did him no good to prevent the nurse from feeding her, but he brought in his own outside doctor to see about medicating her, from what she could make out as she moved from slumber to alertness. She stretched, trying to relieve her stiffness. Ouch. Wake up, Susan Margaret. This is important, if you want to live. Focus.

The men were discussing her high blood pressure. She guessed that it might be high due to the stress of Kurt's uncontrollable anger. He was talking about pain medication and how she needed to have it. The man he was speaking with approved giving Sue some morphine, to make her "more comfortable."

Sue shook her head from side to side, wild. "No!" She remembered that she was very sensitive to medication- and she wasn't in any pain, anyway.

Her voice was not yet fully cooperating but she managed to squeak out, "No, no... No morphine... Please." She coughed as she recovered from saying too much too soon. "Nothing ...hurts."

"But Mrs. Prescott, we don't want you to be in any pain whatsoever. Now, we'll just give you a few milligrams to calm your blood pressure. That can sometimes be elevated by discomfort. You're still recovering from your car accident, you know."

"But, Doctor..." She curled up on her side and pulled her arms to her chest to make the medication harder to administer. He wasn't giving it to her if she had anything to say about it. No way! "No."

"Give it to her, doctor. I insist you give her morphine. Now!" Kurt was using his most authoritative tone of voice. She'd heard that tone before, countless times.

"No!" Grabbing the physician's hand, white-knuckled with her effort, she said, "Don't...want... it." Again, the coughing started as she tried to communicate with this unfamiliar doctor. Drat the luck. Voice, cooperate. She pulled back her hand before he could entrap it.

"Well, you do seem to be in full control of yourself, Mrs. Prescott." He turned: "Mr. Prescott, I really don't see any need for morphine. Your wife seems a little weak but otherwise in her right mind. I'm going to refuse your request."

"We'll see about this! I'll find someone else to medicate her, then." Kurt stormed out.

Just as Kurt left, Joshua came running into the room. "Mom! Oh, Mom, you're with us again. It's wonderful to see you!" He hugged her, even as she relaxed into his embrace. There were some tears, much as there had been with Brooke, who was standing at the door. Brooke started crying again, overjoyed with the reunion. A few minutes later, Christopher came in and hugged Sue; he wept a little, as well. "Mom. Welcome back."

Sue laughed, "Group hug."

Michael came in. "Folks, I'm sorry to break up the family reunion, but the nursing home's doctor just arrived and asked to do a complete physical on your mom. Is there any way you can come back in a little while? She'll probably need a nap afterwards, but can we say, come back in two hours?"

They agreed. Joshua said, "Mom, Amanda and the kids will want to see you, so I'll bring them when I come, okay?"

"Sure. Absolutely." Sue smiled weakly at him. More hugs, then the doctor arrived.

"Surprised" was a mild word to describe how he found her. She was awake and responsive. He said that the brain trauma she had experienced in the crash had subsided and his exam found her in "amazingly good shape," from a mental standpoint. Sue tried to be as cooperative as possible but, good night, she was ready for another nap well before he was finished. Blood was drawn; tests were performed. Though her injuries from the accident had been quite severe, they were healed. The doctor left soon afterwards, with the promise to return and check on her the next day.

I'm glad that's over. She slept again.

Later that day, she awakened to some familiar faces. Christopher was at the head of her bed, Brooke was seated by her side, and Joshua stood at the end of the bed. Joshua's wife and children were seated across the room.

Sue said, "It's so... good... to see you all." She smiled, glad that Michael had brushed her teeth at some point in time that afternoon, though she couldn't remember exactly when he had done it. Time to get some information about this whole mess.

Brooke said, "Mom, it's super to see you, too."

Sue reached out and held Brooke's hand. She asked her daughter, "How...long... was.... I...not...here?"

"Just shy of six months, Mom." Brooke pulled up her hand and kissed it.

"Oh, my. . . goodness." How could she have been asleep that long? Then again, was it really that short a time? Her life as Victoria Susan lasted fifteen years, as she recalled. Or was it? She was still muddled, confused by what had just occurred. She shook her head, trying to clear it.

"Yes, we'd just about given up hope." Brooke gave her hand a squeeze.

Christopher stammered, "Mom, I really thought...that the end had come." He reached out to touch her head but withdrew his hand as it met stubble.

Joshua smiled and put her chart back on the end of her bed, then said, "So did I, but, Mom, you remember the kids. Kids, come say hello to Grandma. Amanda?" The grandchildren and Amanda crowded around Sue. Though she recognized them, they had grown so much while she was...away. They were strange with her. Even Amanda looked uncomfortable. Sue tried to put them at ease.

"You've all... gotten... so...big! Missed you... so...much. I look horrid. I must have...run into an electric razor... or something." They all laughed, embarrassed for her. She ran her hand over her head. Ouch.

Sue was humiliated by her appearance, which was reflected in the shock she saw in their faces and had seen reflected in the nurses' glasses. Dreadful clothing, dried out skin, encrusted yellow teeth, bald head, and no makeup. Not her best day, for certain. She read in their faces they didn't expect to find their grandmother looking like this. She was "not up to her usual standards of excellence," as Kurt used to tell her. Blasted Kurt. He would eat this up with a spoon, if he saw her. He was always at his happiest when she was at her worst.

Sue was somewhat aware that Michael had changed her sheets after she came back to reality, though it seemed to have happened as she was taking one of her many naps that day. As she touched her new sheets, she saw some fragments of the hair that were still in bed with her. She picked some up and held them near her eyes to examine them. The remnants of the hair which had been cut off were completely white on one end, while they were brown on the other. The long locks of brown hair that she'd always kept in such pristine condition were gone. She tossed the hairs aside, taking care that they didn't land on anyone. Mustn't make a mess for anyone to clean up, least of all her kids.

Sue shrugged. "Sorry, folks. Guess... I'm just... an old baldy... now." She dropped her hand back on the bed and tried to smile at them. Not good. Her teeth still felt slimy. The family exchanged self-conscious grins. It appeared that no one knew what to say, so they didn't speak. Awkward. Then, "what's new...with... you?"

Brooke talked about her work as a paralegal. Christopher shared how his classes were going at the Naval Academy. Joshua and Amanda told Sue what the kids had been doing, the girls having been in another play and the boys doing sports.

Brooke kissed Sue and gave her a huge hug. Then, to her brothers, "Guys, we'd better head out now. Mom's obviously tired." To Sue, she said, "Mom, I've missed you so much. I'm so grateful you came back to us."

Joshua and Christopher embraced her, murmuring their love. Christopher told her, "Mom, we thought the end had come. It had been so long and you showed no signs of life. I'm sorry we let Dad stop feeding you. I'm glad you aren't....dead."

Sue said, "Me too."

Joshua said, "Mom, people don't usually come back after six months, so I agreed to the decision Dad made about your feeding tube. Please forgive me for not believing you would wake up. It just doesn't happen that often, but I'm really glad it did."

Her daughter-in-law Amanda and the grandkids gave shy hugs to her, this woman they obviously couldn't recognize, as they prepared to leave the tiny room.

With the family now departed, Sue turned her attention to her situation. She felt the top of her head. Michael came back to check on her again.

"Who . . . did this . . . to me, Michael?" She wasn't given to outbursts of temper, but someone had done this to her. She seemed to remember it was Kurt, and she was downright angry about it. Royally ticked off, as they say. I don't want to judge him harshly if it was someone else, since I was just coming back from la-la-land, but if it was him, he would jolly well pay for it, somehow.

"Kurt...Mr. Prescott. You deserve to know the truth. I'm not going to sugar-coat anything with you, Mrs. Prescott." Michael moved to the side of the bed.

"When?" The nerve of that man. What a rotten bum Kurt turned out to be, as if I didn't already know that. Blasted son of a gun. She tossed a piece of hair down the length of the bed, or tried to. The hair didn't cooperate. Figures. She shook it out of her hand, taking several attempts to get the nasty stuff off of her fingers. Disgusting.

"Right before you woke up. I came in and found him standing over you with the electric razor still in his hand." Michael tried to help her with the quest to be rid of the hairs clinging to their prior owner. Then the hairs stuck to him. They both laughed as he faced the same problem she had. He went in to the bathroom and washed his hands. Success! No more hair.

Sue thought. The bees. "Of course. . . I . . . remember now." Kurt's act was ...horrible and there was no reasonable explanation for it. She shook her head in disbelief at the defiling of her body by this man she called her beloved for so many years. How could he do this to her?

Michael hesitated. "Mrs. Prescott, I hope you don't mind but I told your family that your husband did this to you. I thought they should know. I'm the only person who witnessed the razor in his hand. He stuck it in a backpack when other people started coming into your room."

"Thank you, Michael." Her voice seemed stronger now. "It's a long story . . . but the *Readers' Digest* . . . condensed version is that. . . I always thought that his razor. . . sounded like a swarm of bees . . . I was being bothered by . . . a swarm of bees. . . right before I woke up. I guess it was . . . part of a dream. And then I came to. . . and found myself. . . hairless."

Michael said, "That makes sense." He relaxed a bit and smiled. "You know, there've been several studies indicating coma patients have been known to dream while they are...out of contact. I guess you're one of them."

Sue replied, "Well, I'm living proof . . . that they do. What a dream. . . I was having, Incredible! I had a very. . . happy life in... the other place."

"I'd love to hear about it sometime but I don't want to tire you right now. Is there anything I can do for you? Your family will be back in a few hours but if there's anything you need..." He hesitated, then began tucking in the sheet around her.

"Yes, Michael, there is. Please help me take. . . stock of myself. What kind . . . of shape am I in? What road . . . lies ahead?" She wanted no nonsense, just get down to facts. She looked at Michael, kindly but firmly. "Give me the. . . unvarnished truth, please."

He banged his hands lightly on the bed railing before speaking. "Well, Mrs. Prescott, you're going to need physical therapy to regain your core body strength. You've been lying here for almost six months with very little physical therapy because Mr. Prescott refused to let us do much. Brooke did try- I showed her what to do to help you. She was faithful about moving your arms and legs, but it wasn't enough to get you in very good shape. When she came in to visit, which was every single day, she turned you every hour. Our staff did it when Brooke wasn't here, but she was a huge help to us, knowing that Brooke would be able to do it for a few hours a day. That kept you from getting bedsores, which most coma patients have a bad time with. You got off without them because of her diligence."

"Bless her heart." What a wonderful daughter she had.

"Yes, she's been incredible with you, doing everything she could so that, if you did come back, you wouldn't be riddled with infectious sores all over your body."

"My daughter's an . . . amazing woman." She smiled as tears threatened to stream down her face once again. She looked at Michael and winked, in a vain attempt to control her emotions. It was fruitless, so Michael handed her a tissue and waited while she wiped away the tears. She composed herself. What a big baby I am. Get your act together, Sue.

"Yes, she is," Michael said. "Do you remember the accident?"

"Not really. What happened?" She looked for a wastebasket but couldn't find one. Michael realized what she was looking for and offered a nearby trashcan for her used tissue. He returned it to the floor. "Thank you. Please, take a seat, Michael."

He did as she requested and then told her the basics. "Well, Mrs. Prescott, I'll let your family tell you about it later, but the accident caused extensive internal injuries. Your chart indicates that your internal problems have healed but there might be some residual damage. We'll have to wait and see."

Sue asked, "Will I recover? Get strong again?"

Michael replied, "Yes, ma'am but it's going to take some time for you to regain your strength. We'll start you on a regimen of strength-building exercises. They won't be very comfortable but they'll get you back on your feet. It'll take you some time to be able to walk again, so you'll need to be patient with yourself."

"I was a runner. . . Will I be able . . . to do that again?" She flexed her legs. Ouch!

"I don't see any indication on your chart of why you couldn't do that, Mrs. Prescott, but you probably need to ask your doctor. You appear to have been pretty healthy, looking at the comments Brooke made when you were admitted. Understand that I'm not your doctor but I've seen a lot of patients come through here in worse shape than you and they regained the use of their bodies."

"That's good news then." She was weary at such a long conversation. She sank back on the pillow, worn out.

Michael arose. "Mrs. Prescott, you've made a lot of progress today, but I see you're tiring. Before I leave you to rest, is there anything you need?"

"Water?"

"Sure thing, Mrs. Prescott." He gave her a cup, holding it as she gulped it. "Mrs. Prescott, you need to take small sips. Nothing too fast. Not too much now. You can have as much as you like, just not all at once."

She drank her fill, then, "Just rest now."

"I'll come back later and check on you."

"Thank you, Michael." She lay back again on her pillows as the handsome young man left her side.

After her nap, the curtains in her room were opened and she saw outside. Her eyesight was blurry at first, and she found the light dazzling. She peeked into the newfound brightness. There were bushes and trees that she was able to see from her bed. She didn't

160

have any idea where she was, but Michael had stopped by again, briefly, and told her that she was in a nursing home in Annapolis, the Chesapeake Center. The name didn't sound the least bit familiar. Her room was decorated in beige nursing home colors. Beige wallpaper layered on beige paint on beige baseboards. Was everything in this place beige? Bland, compared to what she was used to. Boring. The decorator in her was appalled at what passed for decorating in this place. Banal.

Brooke entered her room a couple of hours later and brought her up to date. "Mom, after the accident, you were in the hospital for a couple of weeks. Dad was treated and released the next morning. The hospital did all they could for you, but you were in the coma and didn't show any signs that you'd wake up. They asked us to move you into this nursing home/rehab center because your needs were ongoing, and they didn't want to deal with them."

Sue, feeling more clear-headed after her nap, asked, "What happened then?" So far, things sounded pretty reasonable. *Give Kurt the benefit of the doubt. She wasn't expected to wake up, so he did what needed to be done, I guess. Okay. Not so bad. But the razor and taking away her nutrition. That didn't sound very nice. Maybe I've been giving him the benefit of the doubt for too long.*

Brooke replied, "I tried to get you into physical therapy but the therapists couldn't do much with you because you were unconscious. They did do some exercises to prevent you from getting too stiff, but then Dad put a stop to it and tried to get you off the ventilator. The judge agreed..."

"They removed it. Yes, I felt that. I thought it was an asthma attack...even though I never had asthma in my life. It felt like someone was . . . yanking on my throat." She grabbed her throat, bunching up her nightgown, in explanation. "It was horribly uncomfortable." *That wasn't very nice of him. Why would he take*

161

away my oxygen? Because he's a nasty creep who obviously wants me dead. Wake up, Susan. Put your big girl pants on and face life. She looked at Brooke. "Go on, honey."

"Yes, well, I was here when they removed it. I begged them not to but Dad insisted. He thought you would stop breathing but, after a few moments, you started breathing on your own. We were so surprised." Brooke wrung her hands.

"I imagine *he* was surprised. Shocked. Disappointed. Mad." She was really starting to get to know who her husband was, for the first time. What she learned didn't please her. How could she have been married to someone for thirty-five years and have no clue as to who she was dealing with? Was she that ignorant or just plain blind?

"Yes...I kept doing the exercises with you when Dad wasn't here and no one was watching. Michael helped me." Whispering: "I think Dad has someone keeping an eye on you and reporting to him, but I can't figure out who it is."

"Sounds like him." Sue shifted in her bed, trying to sit up a bit. Brooke helped her adjust to a sitting position, shoring her up with extra pillows. It made her a little dizzy but it had to be done if she was going to regain her strength. And she was, if she had anything to say about it.

"So, then, he went before the court and asked that you not be fed. You were on a feeding tube from the time you were hospitalized because you couldn't eat. I begged the judge to not consider his request...we went back and forth a few times...it took several months of wrangling... Then, last week, the judge decided that you weren't going to wake up, and he stopped your feeding as of two days ago."

Sue said, "I imagine that... pleased your father."

"Yes, Mom, he was so happy. I tried to give you ice chips but the judge threatened to put me in jail, so I couldn't do that. At least Dad let me visit you. I was taking a little break to go home and shower when you woke up. I'm so sorry about your hair...it was pretty and white at your roots, but dark on the ends...not like you're used to, but nice. Michael told me that Dad came in with his electric razor while I was gone. You were dying, so I don't know what the big deal was."

Sue shook her head, "One more humiliation." Kurt is completely pathetic.

"Yeah, I guess so. Anyway, Michael called me when you woke up. I came right over. I've been here every day."

"Brooke, you are my heart. Thank you so much." She and Brooke embraced, thankful that they were able to do so. Brooke left soon after, telling her to rest.

Lying there in bed, Sue spent some time in self-reflection that evening as she sorted through her life. She had been such a doormat for all those years. When she was Victoria Susan, she was like a whole new person. I liked being her. She was gutsy, ambitious, unafraid. Sure, it was partially because everybody saw her as a princess – I mean, she did have gallons of perks, like great clothes and boatloads of money and the respect of everybody and....and... and.., but it was fun being her. Just plain fun. The girl had guts.

Sue pulled the covers up to her chin, shifting her weight in the bed. Victoria Susan helped others all the time, not just because she could, but because she genuinely wanted to. I want to be more like her, like that kid who had her whole life ahead of her. Sue turned over, ready for sleep but more unwavering than before. Who knew what was ahead for her? She didn't know for sure, but she was determined to embrace it. No one would walk all over her with her permission anymore. Nope, never again. That time in her life was finished, kaput. She might be weak now, but it wouldn't last forever, if she had any say in the matter. Tomorrow would be a new day, a day of adjustment and learning to cope with the new normal in her life. She couldn't wait to see what lay ahead.

Chapter 13

The next day, right after breakfast, Sue was sitting up in bed, barely, when a couple of muscular men came into her room, accompanied by Michael. She glanced at them, then back at Michael. Who were these people? Bouncers in a nightclub? From the size of them, she wouldn't want to anger either one of them. Each of the men was wearing a black back brace on top of his scrubs. "Hello, gentlemen. What's up, Michael?"

Michael said, "Mrs. Prescott, let's get going. We are here to get you 'up and moving.' Doctor's orders."

Relief. They weren't here to throw her out. A female physical therapist walked in, a Ms. Tapscott. They began with simple leg stretches and movements. Ow! Man that hurt. It brought tears to her eyes. Sue panted a bit, then said, "Ms. Tapscott, we need to do that again."

The attractive brunette told her, "Yes, Mrs. Prescott. We will do it many times."

Michael spoke up, "Ladies, I will leave you to your work. Mrs. Prescott, I'll be back to check on you later. You're in good hands with Ms. Tapscott and her two helpers. Enjoy." He walked out.

She wasn't strong enough to stand on her own, but the two men working with Ms. Tapscott picked her up into a standing position. She almost passed out. The men grabbed her, standing her up again for a few seconds and then gently putting her back on the bed in a sitting position.

The physical therapist explained, "Mrs. Prescott, it will take some time before you can stand on your own, but my associates here will come in several times a day to stand you up. They will do all the hard lifting until you're able to put some weight on your legs on your own. Basically, we're patterning your body to remember what it used to do. Don't get mad at yourself for not being able to stand up and walk today or tomorrow, but do work with us as much as possible."

"How long will this take?" Sue was getting impatient already, mostly with herself. Her body wasn't working like it used to. Rats. What in the world ailed her legs? Why couldn't she just stand up and walk around like she always did? What a bother.

"It could take as much as a few months. It's hard to say, really, but we're here for you. Trust us and we won't steer you wrong."

Sue looked at the therapist and said, "Okay, Ms. Tapscott. Whatever you say."

The men got Sue up once again. She tried to stay upright, but the difficulty was too great. The men laid her gently in the bed. Ms. Tapscott nodded at the men and they departed.

Sue and her PT gal worked that day until Sue thought her muscles would simply refuse to move. The two men returned, as promised, several times each day. Sue struggled to support herself, sweating ferociously but determined to stand alone.

Each day got a little better, but there were some days when she almost gave up. No! She would fight this thing with every ounce of strength she had. Kurt automatically won if she quit. That wasn't going to happen while she had breath in her. Nope, he had won often and for long enough. There's a new girl in town and it's me, Buddy Boy.

Finally, she was able to stand alone and was permitted to wear her own clothing once more. She was very happy to trade the unattractive hospital gown for her own things. She learned that Brooke had brought some of her clothing from home the day after the accident. Nothing fancy, just some nightgowns, dark pants, and collared shirts, but they made her feel like a new woman. Her own panties would replace the diaper as soon as she could throw herself onto the potty chair next to her bed without knocking it over.

The days passed as she learned to walk again. Patience, Susan Margaret. You didn't learn how to do this overnight the first time, or the second time for that matter, and you won't do it right away this time. Ugh, this whole thing is the pits. Imagine yourself launching towards Kurt. If you can walk, you can go slug him. Yeah, that's the ticket. Go slug the ornery son-of-a-gun. She launched herself in the direction of the portable potty, successfully this time. Made it! Way to go, literally! She laughed, an unfamiliar sound. I need to laugh more; make a note of that, Susan Margaret.

Brooke, Josh, and Christopher stopped by as often as possible and they worked with her, to re-pattern her body movements, even though the professional physical therapy sessions had already been done for the day. Everyone was so helpful, but she became impatient with her own body. She began working out as if she were an athlete.

She re-trained her mind by reading everything in sight. Brooke brought in old magazines that her friends and co-workers were finished with, just so she could rejoin the world sooner rather than later.

Sue was sitting in an armchair one afternoon as Brooke came into her room.

"Ugh, Brooke, honey?" Sue dropped the magazine in her lap.

"Yes. Mom?"

"Sweetie, this National Geographic is from forty years ago. Doesn't your legal group change magazines more often than that?"

Brooke squinted at the date. "Oh, my gosh, Mom. I didn't realize...One of the partners is into old magazines. I guess he thought you might be too."

"Brooke, look here. They have a picture of the space capsules and astronauts from the 1960s and 70s. Alan Shephard, John Young, Gus Grissom. Look how young they all are. Short, too. You know, honey, the original astronauts had to be short because the capsules were only as big as the front seat of a Volkswagen bug." She looked through the journal in her hands. "I'll keep them after all. There's a lot of history here. I'll really enjoy looking at these magazines. They'll be a trip into the past. Thank your boss for me." She pulled another magazine from the pile on the bedside table as Brooke kissed her and left for the day.

Crossword puzzles became her obsession as she tried to expand her vocabulary. Hey, she wouldn't be doing anything but lying around anyway, so why not learn something new? Brooke played endless games of Scrabble with her.

The day finally came when Michael teased her with the idea of a shower. "Mrs. Prescott, are you tired of sponge baths?"

"Oh, my, don't you know it, Michael."

"Well, you know there's a shower in your room but we have a bigger one down the hall. When you can make it down the hall, we will have a CNA give you a hand with your first shower in a long time. What do you think?"

She looked at him, with the joy of a potential shower in her eyes. "That sounds wonderful. Okay, let's give this a try." She wanted that shower! Let's get moving, Sue.

"Upsey daisy." Michael helped her to her feet.

She worked very hard to walk again, though her initial solo effort took her only across the room. The next day, she made it down the hall a bit. She took a break on a nearby bench before rising to her feet again. Michael stopped by to check her progress. "A shower...how long has it been since I stepped into a shower? Seven, eight months? Longer? Michael, point me in the right direction. I'm going!"

He laughed. Michael said, "Mrs. Prescott, hold on a minute. I'll go get a female CNA to give you a hand. Be right back."

A few minutes later, Sue scooted down the hallway with the CNA at her side, picking up speed as she got closer to the shower. Her effort paid off. A few moments later, she was under the flowing water.

"Oh, my, the shower feels so wonderful! This is absolutely magnificent!" She let the warm water run over her body, just enjoying the feeling of clean. What little was left of her hair was given a good scrub. "Delightful! Thank you so much!" The CNA smiled and helped her back to her room. Sue needed a nap, having exhausted every ounce of energy on that glorious, wonderful shower. It was worth it.

Best of all, her shower removed the vestiges of nursing-home urine/feces smell from her skin. She was able to use her normal soap, thanks to Brooke's ongoing thoughtfulness in bringing her the preferred bar, so she smelled like herself again. She noticed yesterday that Brooke had left a bottle of her beloved Charlie Red on the dresser. A few squirts of her favorite cologne added to her sense of Sue-ness. Heaven on earth! Or perhaps she was just easily entertained.

She'd lost a lot of weight over the months as her muscles atrophied no thanks in part to Kurt's court order to stop her feeding. Her clothing hung on her, but she knew she'd regain her muscle tone as her rehabilitation continued. She moved from her bed to a chair numerous times a day and tried to spend hours sitting up, flexing her feet to increase her range of motion. The endless supply of books and jigsaw puzzles helped keep her interested in remaining upright as much as possible. Daytime television was the pits. How could people watch that stuff? Seriously.

Her rehab continued in earnest. It would take some time to restore her former strength and physical fitness. She sometimes became confused by the instructions her physical therapists gave her. They told her that it was understandable that she was befuddled, given the time she had been in a coma. She began wearing makeup and street clothing every day, so she looked relatively normal, albeit, hairless.

Her family came to see her every chance they got. They were so excited for her regaining function and her normal appearance, yet she felt that there was an undercurrent. They were not telling her something, but she didn't know what. After a week or so of hedging, curiosity got the better of her, and Sue insisted that Brooke tell her what was wrong.

Sue was sitting on a comfy chair in her room when her daughter came by to say hello. "Brooke, what's going on? Your face tells me there's very bad news. What's happening?"

Brooke plopped on the bed, nearby. "Mom, I don't know how to tell you this, but Dad is divorcing you."

"What? He's doing what?" She shouldn't be surprised, she supposed, but it was still hard to hear. He hadn't visited her since the day she woke up, and he had not been even remotely happy that she was conscious again. Why in the world would he divorce her? There was something that she was still missing. What was it? A...girl? Yes, she remembered something about that, but she couldn't quite connect the dots here.

"Mom, I know you wouldn't want me to sugar coat things, so here it is: I just found out that he transferred all of the money out of your joint accounts into his own account as soon as he could after the accident. He also got ahold of your personal savings account, telling the bank that he needed the money to take care of you. I knew he sold your house after you went ...to sleep... He said it was to pay for the nursing home. Mom, you're penniless."

"How could I be broke? I've never been broke in my whole life. But the money from our house- where's that gone? The house was worth a lot of money and the property was in both of our names. He can't have taken *all* the profits. There must be *some* left." Sue was stunned. How could he have done this to her? No, it can't be true! Tears formed in her eyes and her nose began to run. She grabbed a tissue. No! This can't have happened. It took a few minutes to control her feelings. Brooke waited. Sue knew there was more. She looked at Brooke.

"Mom, I hate to dump this in your lap all at once, but I remember how you always were with pulling off Band-Aids. You always said to 'do it fast and get it over with.'"

"Yes, that *does* sound like me!" She took a deep breath. Get your emotions under control, Susan Margaret. The worst is yet to come, I imagine. "Okay, out with it Brooke, What else do you have to tell me?"

"I had Dad investigated. You may not remember this because of the accident, but he has a mistress named Kelsey. They live in a house they bought a few months ago. They used the money from the sale of your house to pay for the new one. They already have one daughter, and Kelsey's heavily pregnant with a second child."

"I *knew* he was cheating on me. I had suspected, but he was so slick. I couldn't prove anything for the longest time. I just knew it. And then, of course, he told me when we went out to dinner right before...I can't remember when, but he did tell me...it was winter... we were near the docks in Annapolis....he told me about this woman...oh, I seem to have forgotten the details but I know that

I knew about this...when was that? I should remember something so important. What's wrong with my mind?" Blast it all.

Brooke said, "The doctors said it would take some time to get your memory restored. Your brain had a huge shock when you had the accident."

"But I should be able to remember when my husband told me about his mistress, don't you think? What's wrong with me? How frustrating!" Sue felt so hopeless yet, at the same time, angry at her inability to remember when it was She and Kurt had talked about his new love.

"Mom, you might also have PTSD- kinda like the service people get when they come home from the battlefield. You had such a shock when you found out about Kelsey from Dad that your mind couldn't accept what your ears heard, so your mind shut down. I heard it's pretty common with this kind of thing."

"But I just lost a whole evening of my life, Brooke." What am I thinking? Then Sue said, "Well, I guess I've lost six months, too, so maybe one night shouldn't be such a surprise." She shook her head, not believing what she had heard but realizing that it was all true. Unbelievable.

"Mom, are you gonna be okay?" Brooke moved from the bed, to kneel near Sue's chair. Brooke reached out and took her hand.

"Yes, but right now, I'm just ticked off. Brooke...give ...me... some...time to...sort through this, will you?" She leaned over and gave her daughter a hug. What a creep Kurt turned out to be! Good night, that makes me mad. Where can I go from here? Justifiable homicide? Calm down, Susan Margaret. Breathe. Smile at Brooke. Oops, that seemed more like a grimace.

"Sure Mom. Look, we'll get this squared away, I promise... When you're ready to read it, here's a copy of the report I got from the forensic investigator." Brooke pulled a thick packet of information out of her purse and handed it to her mother. "I'll give you some time to process this. Be back later today." Brooke kissed her cheek, and then left.

Sue hesitated and thought – How could the man she loved do this to her? Come on, Sue, pull yourself together. Did you really still love him or did you stay with him out of fear of the unknown? She sighed, and then opened the bulging envelope and began to read.

The document told her that Kurt had transferred all of their money out of their joint bank accounts as soon as he was treated and released from the hospital following the accident. The very day of his release, as a matter of fact. Their total cash assets had been in the hundreds of thousands of dollars, since she'd been very careful with their savings. Her personal savings account was also empty, the funds removed by Kurt, who had convinced the bank that the funds were being used to care for Sue. It was all gone, transferred into an account in Kurt's name alone.

He was, the investigator stated, still maintaining her health insurance; as Kurt's wife, her bills would have fallen to him for payment, had he not kept the policy. Kurt's life insurance policy's beneficiary had been changed to one Kelsey De Luca. Of course, that was the name he'd told her about that night in Annapolis. Kelsey, the young one. Her replacement. Sue turned the page, slapping the papers on her table after she read each page. The nerve!

The report continued. He'd been living in their marital home during her coma, bringing Kelsey and their daughter to stay with him. According to an interview with Brooke, the investigator learned that he had managed to keep his children and grandchildren away, telling them that the property was "not up to standards" and he didn't want them to see the house. "Your time is better spent with your mother than in the house. I can take care of things for now," was his excuse. This was a successful explanation. None of the siblings recounted having gone to the house for months. Only Brooke reported having gone there, once, to get clothing and toiletries for her mother, the day after the accident. Additional visits had been discouraged by Kurt.

Interviews with the neighbors were also carried out. They commented that Kurt and Kelsey had conducted several yard sales, getting rid of all the possessions that the couple apparently didn't want. They mentioned that Kelsey's attitude had been one of being happy to be rid of the items up for sale. The neighbors reported that the siblings weren't at any of the yard sales, leading the investigator to conclude that the siblings were unaware of them. Interviews with the siblings later confirmed this.

The investigator stated that her jewelry, including her engagement and wedding rings, had been sold to secondhand jewelry stores. Kurt had taken her family heirlooms and consigned them at antique shops in the area. The items had all sold, increasing Kurt's bank account by thousands of dollars. Her shoes and clothing had been given to local charities. Kurt had declared the donations on his and Sue's joint income tax return. Bank records showed that he had placed the tax refund in a small joint account and then withdrawn the money as soon as the check cleared.

The report further stated that, as soon as the house was sold, Kurt had moved all of the profits into their joint account and then, a few days later, into to his personal bank account. He purchased a house he now co-owned with his fiancée. He had already engaged a divorce attorney. The report included a side remark stating that "since Mr. and Mrs. Prescott have not been living together for six months during her coma or since her awakening, he was free to file for divorce in the state of Maryland in six months, with or without Mrs. Prescott's consent." The report ended.

"Everything is gone." Sue threw the final page of the report on the chairside table where the other pages had landed as she read them. She couldn't believe it, but the facts could not be denied. She'd been in denial so long during the marriage, pretending that things were not as they seemed. Perhaps her ignoring the situation had led to this report. Penniless or worse. This nursing home wasn't cheap. What was up with that?

Kurt had taken the whole kit and caboodle, leaving her with medical bills and no money. At least he had maintained her health insurance for the time being, but the costs over and above those payments would bankrupt her. She had no possessions, except for a few items of clothing that Brooke had brought to the hospital that first day. Sue felt paralyzed, unable to breathe.

All those years with that mean, adulterous man have led to my having absolutely nothing. My worst fears have happened. What in the world will I do now? She climbed into bed, shattered, and sank back on the pillows. She pulled her legs up to her chest, as if becoming smaller would somehow make this all go away. Broken. Wasted. Exhausted, she picked at her clothing and the sheets. Was this all she had now? A few items of used clothing, a couple of old nightgowns, and hospital-quality sheets that don't even belong to me? Was this really *it*?

Brooke, Joshua, and Christopher came into the room a short time later. Based on the sheepish looks the men were wearing, Brooke had probably warned them that their mom knew the truth about her situation. Sue closed her eyes, still astounded at the news she had received. She rocked back and forth, trying to calm her emotions. Breathe, Susan Margaret, breathe.

"Mom?" Brooke asked. "Are you okay?"

"Brooke...I don't know what to say...I'm speechless...Can he really get away with this?" Her head dropped into her hands. Brooke hurried to her side and embraced her.

"Oh, my dear, sweet mother. There, there." Brooke held Sue in her arms. Brooke touched her mother's short, white hair to comfort Sue, kissing Sue's head as she rocked her mother.

Joshua said, "Mom, there's got to be an explanation for Dad's actions." He started towards them from his place at the foot of the bed, then stopped when he saw Brooke's face.

Brooke said, "Joshua, you have got to face up to the fact that Dad isn't who we think he is."

"Brooke, you're always cutting down Dad. I'm sure that he..." Joshua stopped talking.

Christopher, standing in the doorway, spoke up, "Yeah, Brooke. What have you got against Dad?"

Brooke turned towards them. "Seriously? Are you guys in La-La Land? Wake up, dudes!"

Sue, straightening, said, "Oh, kids, don't argue. That won't help things a bit. Brooke, is there anything we can do?" She looked up at Brooke, pleading for some good news. Anything.

"Mom, I hired an attorney, someone my boss says is tops in the business, weeks ago. Dad covered his tracks so well... and the judge who let him have the house is retired now. The attorney said there's nothing we can do. We can't take Kelsey's house away from her. We might try to sue them but that'll cost money, and we need to spend our cash on your rehab right now. The good news is that the lawyer didn't charge us for the hours of work he put into this. I think he felt sorry for us."

A courier entered the room. "Mrs. Sue Prescott?"

"Yes?"

"This is for you." He handed Sue an envelope, which she opened quickly. It contained a letter from the nursing home. Kurt had cancelled her insurance effective this coming Friday and she had the choice of either paying for her room, board, and rehab herself or she must vacate the nursing home by the end of the week. She handed the papers over to Brooke, who read them and passed them along to her brothers. Tears streamed down her face. Brooke, Joshua, and Christopher sat in stunned silence.

She looked at the courier as she held the documents. "Young man?"

"Yes, Ma'am?"

"I prefer to be called *Susan.*

Chapter 14

Susan's rehab continued as Brooke had scrapped together the money to pay the insurance premium on the policy that Kurt cancelled. It was a temporary fix, but it was enough for now. Susan was moved out of the nursing home and into an adjoining rehab center in another part of the complex. Having been through her experiences as Victoria Susan, she had become stronger mentally, in spite of her current physical weakness. Even now, she was leaning against the doorjamb of her room, talking with Michael about life in general and her life, specifically.

Michael was made the Nursing Supervisor at the rehab center, having transferred there to "keep his eye on his favorite patient." In reality, he probably wanted to keep his eye on Brooke. Brooke was so focused on her mother's recovery and her father's treachery, Susan noted, that Brooke was oblivious to how Michael felt. Susan had seen the glances the fine-looking young man made as Brooke came into her room later that day. It wasn't the first time Michael had timed the end of his visits to coincide with Brooke's arrivals. He smiled as he left the room.

"How are you feeling today, Mom?" Brooke came in, nodding at Michael as he left, and gave Susan a big hug. It was much easier for them both to embrace one another, now that she spent so much time standing and walking around. Hugging Brooke, she suddenly felt defeated.

"I'm doing okay, given the circumstances." Susan tried to smile at Brooke, but life was difficult and there was nothing to be done.

Brooke smiled, "I'll take care of you, Mom."

"Brooke, dearest, I've been thinking about my financial situation. How will I manage? I took care of you kids all those years, only working part time as a nurse. The accident has left my brain a little skittled, so I don't know if I'll ever be able to get back into nursing. Not full time work, anyway. My skills are good but my education needs serious updating. I retired from my job years ago because Kurt demanded it and, at my age, job offers aren't exactly going to be pouring in."

"Mom, try not to worry about that right now, okay? Just focus on getting stronger. You can come live with me when you get out of here." Brooke dropped the most recent old magazines from her boss on Susan's dresser. Susan waved Brooke into a nearby chair and perched on the side of her bed.

"Oh, no. I'm not burdening you with my life, Brooke."

"But, Mom...." Brooke sat a bit straighter, in her "I'm in charge" mode.

"No. Not under any circumstances. Subject closed." Susan got up and paced a bit, though her steps were restricted by the tiny room. She fiddled with the magazines Brooke had delivered, and then returned to sit on her bed.

"Well, Mom, the good news is that you seem very composed about this whole thing. You don't even seem too upset, now that you've gotten used to the idea that Dad stole everything from you. If it was me, I'd be fuming over Dad's actions."

"Yes, I've been through the fire, but Michael's been talking to me a lot lately. He's a man of faith, you know." Susan contemplated things, suddenly feeling much calmer. "Our family was always so busy with life that we didn't pay much attention to spiritual things. There's a peace about Michael. I don't know, but what he talks about makes a lot of sense."

"What kind of things, Mom?"

"I guess you'd call it 'Jesus talk,' for lack of a better description. We just started doing a Bible study together when he gets off work." Susan hesitated. "You could come, if you want."

"I don't know, Mom...maybe I'll join you, if I'm here when he comes."

"Honey, thanks to what Michael's told me, I'm at peace. He calls it 'peace in the midst of a storm.' I know what he means even though I don't understand everything he talks about."

Right on cue, Michael walked back into her room. "Hello, ladies! I wanted to let you know, Mrs. Prescott that, seeing as you have returned to normal, mentally speaking, I'll be turning the care of your case over to your own charge nurse. I happened to be here when you woke up, so that's why I've stayed so nearby. Now that you're getting your sea legs back again, I want to introduce you to someone who will be working very closely with you." Michael pushed a phone number on his cellphone. When his call was answered, he said, "Nurse Ferguson, would you please come into Mrs. Prescott's room?"

A few moments later, a tiny, 50ish Hispanic woman wearing purple scrubs entered. Her shiny black hair was pulled back in a ponytail that hung halfway down her back. "Hello, Mrs. Prescott. I'm Nancy Ferguson. I'll be taking care of you on a daily basis, though I'm sure we'll be seeing quite a bit of Mr. Bench, given the details of your...situation."

"It's nice to meet you, Nurse Ferguson." Susan stuck out her hand automatically, and then pulled it back, seeing the nurse's blue plastic gloves. I keep forgetting that those gloves would have to be thrown away if I shake hands with these folks. Waste not, want not. She waved, instead. They laughed. "This is my daughter, Brooke."

"And you, as well, Mrs. Prescott. Nice to meet you, Miss Prescott." The diminutive gal nodded in their direction.

Susan smiled at the very pleasant-looking woman in front of her.

"I'll be coming in to check on you a few times a day and, if there's anything you need, you just push the call button, and I will get here ASAP. And by "anything," I mean that if you want a snack, I'll bring you one. If you want to take a little walk, I'll go with you if I can, or I'll get a CNA to take you."

"That sounds lovely. Thank you so much." Susan smiled once more at the tiny woman.

Michael told the nurse: "Mrs. Prescott has had a bit of a rough journey recently. She may need to just chat, Nurse Ferguson. We're trying to bring her up to date on the six months of her coma, so you have my permission to visit with her as you see fit or as she desires."

"Certainly, Mr. Bench. I would be happy to do that." Nurse Ferguson and Michael headed for the door so Susan and Brooke could continue their visit.

***

As Susan continued her rehab, she had to figure out what was real and what was not. Her life as Victoria Susan seemed so true, but now she knew it was all a dream. Pity, she thought, that was a really nice life, except for the 'going nuts' part. She was grateful that Brooke had found her some stylish clothes at the mall, instead of those clothes Brooke had grabbed without thinking when Susan first had her accident. Of course, Kurt had gotten rid of all her things while she was in a coma, so these clothes were new but, thanks to Brooke, the items were like her usual style. She was glad to have her regular attire updated: black slacks, a printed collared shirt, and casual shoes. It made her feel more human, instead of having to spend her days in clothes that were grabbed on the spur of the moment. Brooke was so generous to buy them for her, though she knew that her sons helped a bit as well.

Susan shared a bit of her story with Nurse Nancy Ferguson, especially about her time as a princess, one day as they were sitting at a table in the dining room having a cup of hot tea and some of the nurse's homemade oatmeal cookies. The nurse had finished her work for the day, though she was still in her scrubs. They both enjoyed chatting in the large, sunny room that was a part of the Chesapeake Center. Big picture windows framed by blue and white curtains hung along two sides of the room. Trees and a wooded area flourished outside, with frequent visits from squirrels, birds, and other wildlife seen through the glass. Pictures with floral themes decorated the other two walls. The pale blue walls with white trim and the mahogany hunt boards with coordinating tables adorned with cheerful floral centerpieces made the room seem fresh and almost homey. It was a beautiful contrast to the room she was in when she woke up, which was a nightmare in beige. Not Susan's favorite color, by any means. Even her present room was a bit boring, with everything painted off white.

"Mrs. Prescott, that princess story sounds like a dream I wouldn't mind being a part of. All those fancy clothes, big houses, and all those kinds of things." Nurse Ferguson nibbled a cookie.

"Yes, it was lovely. It felt like I was accomplishing great things, for once in my life. I had a major charity I was running at only ten years old, and I was at a university at the age of fifteen. Not bad for a kid, do you think? … Actually, if I told my sons about it, they'd probably think I was crazy."

"Hey, if you are going to be rich and young and beautiful and a princess, you might as well be brilliant!" Both of them got quite a chuckle out of the thought.

"Nurse Ferguson, that's the only way to go!"

"I'm with you on that!" Nancy smiled at her.

Their shared joy was cleansing. Susan felt so relaxed with her friend. It was great to have such a kindred spirit in her life. She wanted to know this pleasant woman better. Susan knew she made great cookies. "Nurse Ferguson, are you married?"

"Oh, yes, I got married some time back. Almost 35 years now. My hubby's name is Patrick. Patrick Davin Ferguson." The look on Nurse Ferguson's face told the story: the marriage was a very happy one.

"Wow, that's certainly an Irish name, if I ever heard one. I was curious why my Hispanic nurse had an Irish surname." They laughed together. "I see you're all dressed up in your Irish green scrubs today."

"Oh, my, yes. My husband has the look of the Irish as well- red hair and freckles. He's a proud man, my Patrick." Nurse Ferguson leaned across the table. "Just between the two of us, he has an absolutely horrible fake Irish accent." More laughter ensued.

"How did you meet?" Susan sipped her tea and then dug into another cookie, hoping for a good story. She was not disappointed.

"We met in high school. High school sweethearts. He was this huge lump of a man at 6'4", Patrick Ferguson, strong and self-confident. I was a tiny Hispanic gal at 4'11", Nancy Manuel, afraid of my own shadow. I was a new immigrant. I barely spoke to anyone even though my English was quite good. My parents had wanted to become Americans since they were small children. They'd been preparing us for the move to the United States from Mexico for five years, while we waited for all of our paperwork to be completed. That's why they gave me an American name when I was born, Nancy Beth. My three brothers also got American names: Thomas, Richard, and Harold. Do you get it? My brothers were named Tom,

Dick, and Harry- how can you get more American than that?" They tittered. "We went to a church where an American missionary worked. She taught us proper English, which my parents insisted we use in our home instead of our native Spanish. Don't get me wrong- we were proud to be Mexican, but my parents felt we had to fit into our new chosen homeland."

"You speak English with a mid-western accent, which fascinates me. I assume the missionary was from the Midwest?" Susan was fascinated by this story, so different from her own life. She felt a bit envious of Nancy's relationship with the missionary. She'd never known any.

"Yes. She was from Ohio." Nancy's smile told Susan that the missionary was special to Nancy's family. "I've met other immigrants with regional accents based on where in America they learned English. Can you imagine me sounding like I'm from Tennessee? I know an Asian gal who was a Vietnamese boat person. She came to America as a small child and was tutored by a native-born Tennessean. She has the most interesting accent, honey child!" More laughter.

"So, I must ask. How did you meet your wonderful Mr. Right?" Susan's curiosity was piqued.

"This is too funny. We were in twelfth grade English class together, and Patrick asked me to help him with his homework. English, of all things. Can you imagine? A Mexican transplant tutoring a native-born American in English!" The memory was precious to her new friend. "It was love at first sight. I worked with him all year. We realized that we were meant to be together forever by the time we graduated from high school. Patrick went on to the police academy and I went to nursing school. We got married right after our graduations."

Susan reminisced about her own high school sweetheart. "If only my own high school romance had worked out...If it had, I wouldn't be sitting here with you right now." She hadn't thought about Joshua's father in years. Or had it really only been days? She shrugged. He had been so handsome, with his beautiful dark brown hair and shining blue eyes. I wonder how the years have treated him, if he ever found true love. I hope so.

As the days passed, Susan came to love her charge nurse. She sensed it was mutual as Nancy checked on her frequently during the day and visited after work on a regular basis. Her Patrick was a policeman, so he worked shift work on a rotating basis. "I have no one to go home to, so I thought it'd be nice to pay you a visit."

"I'm so glad you did. Since you get off work at three, my rehab is finished by then. Brooke doesn't get here till after five, so that gives us a good chance to chat." As much as she loved to see Brooke, Susan was worried that her daughter was giving up too much of her own life to care for her mother. Perhaps if she became closer friends with Nancy, she could give Brooke a little break. She would love to get to know Nancy better. She was like the sister she'd never had. They went for a stroll around the rehab center, enjoying the pictures and talking about life in general.

It was several weeks into their friendship before Nancy confessed to Susan that she was infertile. "Of course," the sweet-faced nurse told her, "it's not as if I could still have children now anyway, at my age."

"I have children. You have hair." Susan's hair was growing as time passed, but it was only two inches long. Susan could comb it, but getting it styled was still many months away.

"Well, now that's a trade-off, isn't it, Mrs. Prescott?" The two women laughed at how their lives had played out.

"You may adopt my dear Brooke, if you like, Nancy. I am willing to share with you, my friend." Her eyes welled up, as did Nancy's. A barrier had been removed, a wall torn down. The offered gift made them sisters.

"Thank you, Susan. Brooke is a gem, is she not?"

"Yes, Nancy, she is." Then, "I would also offer you my sons to share, but they can be a bit...troublesome."

"I noticed. If you don't mind, I'll just stick with Brooke for the time being." Laughter.

"How about my husband Kurt, Nancy?" Susan leaned in for her new friend's answer, expecting hilarity to ensue. She was not disappointed as Nancy grimaced before she answered.

"Oh, my goodness, Susan. That is most definitely a 'thanks but no thanks' moment."

"A wise decision, my friend." Susan smiled, knowing that Kurt would not be a good replacement for Patrick. "Hopefully, my sons will one day see things as they are, not as they have been told."

"We can hope and pray, Susan. We hope and pray." They hugged as Nancy left for home. "See you tomorrow, my friend. Love you."

"Love you back."

Chapter 15

After her new friend was gone, Susan realized that Nancy was the very first adult friend she had ever had. She'd given birth to Joshua in secret, avoiding all of her high school friends lest they guess her story. She had completed nursing school in the social isolation of being a full time student and young mother, and then gotten involved with Kurt on her third visit to the Naval Academy dances. The female friend she had gone to the dances with was not up to Kurt's exacting standards, so she had disengaged immediately from that budding relationship. It hadn't bothered her a bit. Having seen the slinky, provocative dresses her co-worker had worn that first night and those two nights following, Susan realized the woman wasn't who Susan thought she was. Or, maybe, she was exactly who Susan thought. Therein lay the problem.

It suddenly struck home: all of her friends were Kurt's friends. To be fair, her lack of friends wasn't just her husband's fault. The forced isolation of her teen years and the nursing school regimen had lent itself well to her natural shyness. She'd been forced to be private to protect Joshua, which fit in with her quiet personality. Aloneness had become a deep-seated habit, a comfy bedroom slipper she had no desire to discard.

Once Susan had married, she still refrained from developing more than shallow relationships due to the transitory nature of the Navy. It seemed every time she started to get close to someone, either her husband or the other gal's hubby was transferred, and they lost touch. In those days, the internet wasn't there to help them keep track of one another, so leaving and being left meant the same thing: loneliness. Kurt had tried to interest her in getting to know other officers' wives. It had worked until she understood that Kurt's total interest in her social life was geared to the promotion of his career. She wasn't interested in using friendships, or other people, for Kurt to climb the career ladder. Susan retreated into her home life, pulling her relationships with her family around her like a blanket in wintertime. Cozy, snug, comfortable.

Come to think of it, she had not had a single friend of her own since their marriage that hadn't been vetted by Kurt. If he didn't like someone, she ended the friendship. It was a shock when she realized how that had isolated her, making her more dependent on him for companionship. It had also made her more vulnerable. Frequent moves, no contact with anyone, other than what he had permitted. Yes, that all served his purposes. Was she as boring as he said? Perhaps. But maybe that had been because he had controlled her life without respite. She scoffed a bit. When you run another person's life, you shouldn't complain if they aren't the person you want in the end. A lesson for both of us, Kurt.

Susan had Joshua; she had Brooke and Christopher. By staying in superficial relationships with her acquaintances, she had been able to build a wall of protection for her feelings. She was nice to everyone but very circumspect. She enclosed herself in the security of her family. She had been an only child. As her relatives had died off through the years, the size of her world had been diminished. Her parents, aunts, and uncles had passed on one by one until her only friends left were her husband, her children, and her grandchildren.

Kurt never told her about his family, his childhood. He said his family was all dead. End of discussion. So, there were three adult people in her life, four if you counted Kurt- she supposed she couldn't count him anymore-, and four grandchildren. And no one else. Her isolation was so like Kurt. Isolate, control, manipulate. His name suited him: curt. And to think, she hadn't made the connection until this very minute. She chuckled. Wake up, girlfriend. Wake up and smell the coffee.

Until now, her circle of true friendship was limited to Brooke, which she recognized placed burdens on the young woman. As she acknowledged this, she regretted her emotional dependence on Brooke. That had all changed, now that she had Nancy in her life. Nancy's companionship opened a whole new world to her, for which she was very grateful. Nancy was refreshing and fun. Hum... Maybe now Brooke could move on with her own life. Get a boyfriend (she had one in mind!) and get married (and give her more grandchildren to love!). Yes, that would suit Susan's fancy to a T.

The women spent more and more time together, enjoying a cup of tea and cookies in the sunny activity room after Nancy finished her workday. Nancy shared her stories of life in Mexico, and her sadness over being unable to have children. "The day we found out that our home would not be shared with children was the unhappiest day of my life. My Patrick, he has always been so strong for me, but that day I saw how much it would have meant to him."

"Nancy, did you consider adoption?" Poor Nancy. She would have made such a wonderful mother.

"Yes, but it was not to be. Financially, we didn't have the money until we were older, and then we didn't have the youth." Nancy set her teacup down on the table and took a cookie.

"What about foster care?" Susan took a sip of her herbal tea.

Nancy hesitated. "Susan, we did think about it, but Patrick's rotating shift would've made it difficult, and I was afraid I'm too short to care for older children who might've been difficult to handle. We have come to terms with our lack of children. We are at peace."

Susan revealed some of her own sad story about being the unwanted wife of an adulterous man. "I found out two years ago that my husband wanted me dead. He tried two different times before I got here, but he didn't succeed, though he almost did this last time."

"What did he do? I've seen your chart, obviously, but some details were lacking."

"The first time, he tried to push me off the city dock in Annapolis in the middle of winter. This time, it was the car accident that brought me here." She shook her head. What a disgusting human being Kurt turned out to be. She would be livid if he wasn't such a pathetic person. No, she was incensed in spite of Kurt's being so wretched, truth be told.

"Why aren't the police on his trail?" Nancy looked mad. "How can he get away with it?"

"Because I can't prove a thing. You can't arrest someone for *wanting* to push you off a dock and the accident *looked* like an accident. You can't be arrested for that. I can't show he wanted to do me in. It's 'he said, she said,' so there you have it." Susan slammed her teacup down on the saucer more forcefully than she'd planned. Rats! She looked sheepishly at her new friend. "Sorry."

Nancy nodded. "No problem. I understand, but Susan, how do you live like that? Knowing that every day your husband might succeed?"

"One day at a time. Of course, since I've been in Chesapeake Center, he almost succeeded in having me killed by someone else. First, the ventilator was removed..."

"But you lived and began breathing on your own."

"Yes, and then he had my feeding stopped..."

"But you woke up," Nancy said.

"Then he tried to get me overdosed on morphine," Susan told her.

190

"But the doctor refused to give you something you obviously didn't want," Nancy replied. "And he cut off your hair. Don't forget that, though obviously it wouldn't kill you. But, why would he do that?"

"To humiliate me one more time." Susan scowled at the thought. Creep.

"But you survived all those things, and here you are," Nancy smiled.

"Yes, Nancy, but it would have been nicer if I'd awakened *before* he shaved my head!"

"Susan, I definitely agree." They chuckled, enjoying the moment.

"My head gets pretty cold sometimes! I don't know how bald men do it." Susan lifted her

hands and gave her short, white hair a rub.

"They wear hats... I'll bring you a knit hat tomorrow." Nancy looked at her watch.

Susan thanked Nancy. "You're the best, my friend."

"Oops, look at the time! I better get you back to your room before Brooke gets here."

"Yes, and then you'd better head home to your hubby, Nancy! Tell Patrick I said hello."

Nancy walked her the short distance back to her room. They hugged and bid one another a good evening. This wasn't the life that Susan had planned, but she was settling into it while waiting for the next phase. In some ways, she was more content than she had been in a long time. Of course, it was probably due more to Kurt's absence than her presence in the nursing home. Somehow, he always kept things stirred up, keeping her on edge constantly. He was like a teaspoon in a cup of tea. The tea could be very soothing but the spoon was always banging against the cup, making noise and upsetting the smooth water inside. Yep, he was a stirrer-upper, if ever she saw one.

A team of physical therapists still came to see her several times a day. They knew that she needed a great deal of help because the only movement exercises she had gotten for those six lost months were from her visiting daughter. Susan overheard the staff talking. They had heard through the grapevine about her financial situation. She was only covered by medical coverage as long as Brooke could make the insurance payments. She might be on her way out of the home soon.

The staff willingly donated their personal time to help her regain her strength quickly. This was a new role for her- that of being served. Susan had spent her entire adult life serving others and it was difficult to give up that control. It made her feel vulnerable. She valued how the staff cared for her needs, helping her get stronger, better. She was humbled by their attention and very appreciative of it.

Susan improved a great deal over the next few weeks, though she was sometimes frustrated at her inability to do as much physically as she had BA (before the accident). Feeling up to par mentally, she put her full effort into regaining her physical capabilities. If her physical therapists asked her to walk two miles, she tried to go four. If they asked her to do ten curls, she aimed for doing twenty. She realized that she would go crazy if she stopped to think about her financial situation; focusing on how her husband behaved would only cause her to get an ulcer.

Thanks to her talks with Michael, her anger subsided. The peaceful nursing supervisor stopped by every day when he got off work. He entered her room and plopped onto a nearby chair.

"Mrs. Prescott, the very worst thing has happened to you, but God is in control of all things and He won't let you down if you depend on Him." Michael took a sip of the coffee he brought in to their chat.

"Michael, how do I handle all the anger that I feel towards Kurt and Kelsey? They were horrid. He lied and cheated on me for years. She had to have known what he was doing when he wiped out our bank accounts. If I know him, and I do, he probably laughed his way through his...shenanigans." Her face reddened at the thought of all his misdeeds. She was so mad she felt ready to spit. Only Michael's presence restrained that. "I gave Kurt the best years of my life and this was the thanks I got." Piece of work, that dude.

Michael looked at his patient and then glanced at the ceiling. He nodded his head, as if agreeing with something or Someone. Susan was uncertain.

"Mrs. Prescott, God knows everything Kurt and Kelsey did. He knows what you've been through. God loves you and sent His Son Jesus to die for you. Remember, when Jesus walked on the earth, folks weren't very nice to Him. They beat Him, cursed Him, and crucified Him. He didn't deserve it, but that's what He got." He paused to let that information sink in. "There's a reason why you had to experience this. Why you had to go through these humiliating and humbling things. If I were to guess, it would be because God wants you to be His, and this is the only way He could get your attention." Michael smiled at her. "It *is* the only way we could have met. I mean, you wouldn't have stopped by here otherwise, right?" Michael took another sip of his coffee.

Susan listened to every word from Michael. She didn't speak at first. Her mouth gaped at his comments. What insight this young man has, what wisdom.

"You're right Michael. I'd never heard of this place. And I wouldn't have come here without a very good reason. I don't know anyone who would have been staying here... I sure wouldn't have come here of my own free will. What you are saying... it makes perfect sense. I wouldn't have chosen this life, this situation, but God seems to have selected it for me...so, what do I do now?"

"Well, ma'am, I think it's time for us to have a little talk with God. What do you think of that?" He put down his coffee cup and leaned towards her.

"Yes, I've ignored Him long enough. Will He forgive me for overlooking Him?" Typical of her behavior, she began to fret that God would be forever angry with her.

Michael took one of her hands in his. "Oh, yes, Mrs. Prescott, He certainly will. Let's pray."

One evening a few nights later, Joshua and Christopher stopped by with news: Kelsey had just delivered her second daughter with Kurt. They named her Christine. The men waited for her reaction.

"Oh, another girl? Your girls were born first, weren't they Joshua? I guess the apple doesn't fall far from the tree." Susan tried to smile, but the news hurt. Tears formed in her eyes but she suppressed them, blinking them away.

Joshua squirmed a bit. He seemed to realize that she knew he hadn't been on her side of things for years. "Oh... right Mom." He tried to change the subject. He began talking about his family and how the kids were doing. Sensing his discomfort, Susan started asking about his work, his life in general. She then turned to Christopher and inquired about the Naval Academy activities he was involved in. Christopher answered in short sentences, obviously uncomfortable. The men left a short time later.

Two more weeks passed. Susan's strength was increasing. She was steady on her feet now, and was able to walk without tiring, without a walker, for sixty minutes. Her muscle strength was improving, though she still took naps after her PT. Her mental status was back to normal, and she was feeling better than she had in months. She wondered when she would be released. She didn't have to speculate very long. Some officials from the rehab center came to see her. Her medical insurance premium had gone up so high that Brooke couldn't pay it anymore. They were no longer getting paid, so they wanted her to leave. In fact, they insisted on it. "By the end of the week, if you don't mind. We'll let your daughter know."

Chapter 16

Susan was in her room doing a crossword puzzle when Brooke came in later that day after work. She knew Brooke had gotten a call from the rehab center's financial office. The next month's bill had not gotten paid. She knew that Brooke had no recourse. Susan set the puzzle aside and sighed. "Hello, dear."

Brooke plopped down on the bed. "Mom," Brooke jumped right into the conversation, "I know you haven't been in favor of this, but it makes the most sense to have you move into my house. Joshua and Christopher will help us with the expenses."

She'd been wondering how long it would take Brooke to bring up the topic of her moving in. Not long, apparently. Without hesitation, Susan said, "No. We've talked about this before and I am not going to be a burden on you." She reached out and patted Brooke's hand before withdrawing it and putting her hand in her own lap.

"Mom, you have no money to go anywhere else and the rehab center is only giving us till Friday to move you. There is no other option. You have no choice." Brooke reached towards her, to return the pat, as if their touching would make a difference in Susan's decision.

Susan touched the puzzle book briefly, to straighten it on the table while she gathered her thoughts. She looked Brooke in the eyes. "Let me think about it some more."

"There is no 'think about it,' Mom. You have no other alternatives. This is what's going to happen: You're moving in with me." Brooke could be just as stubborn as Susan could be, it seemed.

"You always were a strong-willed child, Brooke!" Susan smiled, hoping to deflect the decision. It didn't work.

"Yes, Mom. Look whose daughter I am. No arguments now. Get some rest. We'll begin making arrangements in the morning. Pleasant dreams." Brooke kissed her and left.

Susan knew Nancy was on a vacation in the Poconos with her hubby Patrick. She would have loved to have had the chance to discuss the decision of whether to move into Brooke's condo with her friend. Nancy and Patrick had left the day before, and they couldn't be reached this week. They were having time as a couple. She knew they both needed to have this special trip together, so she didn't call her. Because of this absence, Nancy wasn't there to keep an eye on things which, Susan realized days later, gave Kurt the opportunity to do what he had planned.

**

Kurt had to move fast. He realized the need for swiftness as he drove home from work that afternoon. Everything had to be sped up, but he felt ready to move ahead with the plan. The divorce from Sue was taking much too long and he didn't want her to have a dime of the money he had earned. Blasted parasite that Sue had always been. Thankfully, he had an inside spy, a CNA named Jada, who was keeping track of what was going on with his it-can't-happen-too-soon-to-be-ex-wife.

Christopher had been feeding his father information on Susan's progress and the general scuttlebutt going on about her in the rehab center. Kurt knew he had trained his youngest son well, trashing everything Sue said, while still managing to see his father through untarnished eyes. Christopher had let Kurt know about the rehab center's desire to get Sue...or should he say 'Susan,' out of the home in just a few days. Nah, "Sue" it had always been with him and" Sue" it was. Kurt also knew that Nancy was nowhere to be seen, though he wasn't sure where exactly she was. Christopher didn't have that information. Kurt had been afraid to be too nosey. Christopher didn't know what his father had up his sleeve, anyway. Kurt didn't dare raise any suspicion because there was no way that Christopher would buy into what he was about to do.

He and Kelsey had been scheming for some time. How was he to knock off his wife without anyone suspecting him? He realized it'd become a bit of an obsession to him. He shrugged. Whatever. She'd escaped from him before. She wouldn't be so lucky, this time.

Kurt went through all the plans in his mind on the drive from BWI to Annapolis. It was all set up. He had arranged for airline tickets to Vancouver, British Columbia for the three of them, Kurt, Kelsey, and Sue, and the two daughters he and Kelsey had. He would tell everyone Sue was his sister, who was just recovering from cancer, hence the lack of hair, general lethargy, and wheelchair. Yes, he had plans for the height of the mountains in Vancouver. They would make a very convenient drop off point for an unwanted wife. To avoid suspicion, he had purchased return tickets for all of them, though Sue wouldn't need hers. He could get a refund.

He'd been flirting with a CNA at the nursing home for some time. Jada, a twenty-something with long purple hair and multiple piercings, seemed to think that he found her plump body desirable. She'd bent over in front of him a lot, inviting him to view her substantial backside on several occasions. He'd done nothing to dissuade her from that opinion, since he never knew if he would need her help one day. It had paid off in spades. He needed her help to kidnap Sue, drugging her enough to make the snatch possible. Jada had played right into his hands! What a stupid young thing she was! He snorted.

Jada had been reporting to him daily on Sue's progress at the home. The cash he was giving her made a nice supplement to her scanty income. He wanted drugs to use on Sue. Jada provided them, telling him that "the old man in 221B doesn't need them as much as he thinks." Jada arranged to let him in a side door after the visiting hours were over that evening. She told her co-workers she was going out for a smoke, per his instructions, but he and Kelsey came inside and headed for Sue's room. Jada promised to drug Sue's evening milk, to make sure she couldn't fight back or call out. Kurt told Jada to make sure Sue drank it before putting on her night clothes. That way, they wouldn't be bothered by having to change the clothing of an unconscious woman. Yep, this would work. He had it all figured out.

Kurt smiled to himself. I've kept Jada on the string long enough to make sure she still thinks there is hope for us.....what a fool she is. I have Kelsey. Why would I want Jada?

Things went according to plan that evening. He and Kelsey, dressed completely in black, were let in by Jada who informed the couple that Sue was sleeping, after having finished the milk Jada delivered to her earlier. Jada accompanied them to Sue's room, where she had stowed an extra wheelchair.

"Kurt, Sue's sacked out on her bed. I made sure she didn't change her clothes, just like you said," Jada told Kurt. Jade smiled her most charming smile.

Kurt returned it, just as he spotted Kelsey's bag. Good night! He noticed the luggage Kelsey had with her. Why in the world did Kelsey have to bring along that monstrosity of a handbag with her now? She dragged that purse, or one just like it in a different color, with her everywhere, but you would think she could have kept in the car this once. I guess not. Women! He shrugged. But, back to the business at hand, Kelsey's purse with them or not.

Kurt pushed on Sue's arm. No response. Sure enough, Sue was out of it, having a small head for medication, especially the strong stuff Jada doped her with. Kurt laughed at Sue's inability to do anything but sleep. Such a bother! It wouldn't be long before this pain in his neck would be history. The threesome lifted Sue out of her bed. Whispering lest they be caught, he ordered the two women to "be careful, don't drop her. Steady now." Her deadweight was more of a problem than he anticipated. Was the old woman gaining weight? Kelsey dropped her share of Sue several times.

Kelsey's purse spilled open and the contents were scattered on the bed and floor. "Big Yikes," Kelsey said, as she smiled halfheartedly at Kurt. "Sorry, baby."

"Pick that stuff up," Kurt muttered sharply to his beloved. Kelsey tried to keep one hand on Sue and the other on her belongings, but the room became a mess pretty quickly. Kelsey grabbed her own purse, he noticed, and then picked up Sue's as well. "What the heck do you need that for?"

"Kurt, honey, you never know when something in Sue's purse might come in handy" Kelsey dimpled at him.

"I suppose so- just keep it out of my way. Let's get going."

After several minutes of struggling, they loaded Sue onto the wheelchair and scurried out of the room. This took longer than he thought it would, and they would have to hurry to make it to the airport on time. They rushed out the door as best they could, and loaded Sue into a handicapped van that Kurt had rented for the occasion. He handed the CNA an envelope containing several thousand dollars in cash. "A little extra something for your trouble. Now get lost before the cops find you."

"Sure thing, Kurt." Jada waved them off as they drove away.

***

Brooke entered the rehab center's business office the next morning, planning to make arrangements with the staff to move her mother over to her condo, when Michael came running in, frantic.

"Brooke, do you know where your mother is?"

"In her room, I assume, why?" She was unsure why he looked so desperate.

"I just went by to say 'hello' and she's gone."

"What?" Her heart was in her throat. What happened to Mom?

"The room's a mess and she's nowhere in sight."

"Oh, no!" She ran off towards her mother's room, with Michael coming along.

They raced to the room; Michael dialed security on his cellphone. They searched as fast as they could for some clue of what had happened. Bedclothes and belongings were soon flying through the air as they made a wild examination of the room. Brooke found Kelsey's boarding pass among the bed linens.

"Vancouver? Why would Kelsey be going there?" She was in tears. Michael looked very concerned, as well.

The security detail entered. Michael told them, "Go over last night's tape and see if you can figure out where she went. Notify the police stat. She's missing, and we need to figure out where she went." The men nodded and hurried out.

***

Kurt turned to Kelsey as they drove down the road and away from the rehab center, after they topped their black shirts with colorful white, green, and blue Vancouver Canucks jerseys. He didn't want them to look suspicious at the airport, so he'd insisted that they show team spirit for a sport they never watched. "Okay. Things are back on track now, after bothering with this ton of bricks in the back of the van. I swear she's gained a lot of weight.

201

We just need to pick up the girls from your folks, get to the airport, go through security, and onto the plane. Since Sue can't say much, this should work according to plan."

"Kurt, honey?" She was rifling through her purse, which always annoyed him.

"What?" He was driving the van with little caution. They needed to get going, now.

"Have you seen my boarding pass? I thought it was in my purse, but it's not here."

"Look around some more." Why couldn't she keep better track of her things? "When did you see it last?"

"Right before we left home." Kelsey smiled at him, but the smile did not reach her eyes. She looked worried.

"Go through it again. Maybe you dropped it at home. You **were** in a bit of a rush after you left the girls at your mom's house. Here we are- go in and get the kids. I'll wait here with Sue. DO NOT bring your folks out here to the van."

"Yes, my darling." Kelsey ran into the house.

He waited, tapping his foot so hard his toes started to hurt. He was sure, absolutely certain, that she did not drop the boarding pass at the rehab center. That would be too inconvenient. Nope, everything was fine. I'll just print out another pass at the airport. She's gorgeous but sometimes not too bright. It's not her brains I'm after, anyway. He laughed.

Kelsey came out with their daughters. She strapped the kids in their car seats and they headed towards BWI. They only had about an hour and a half before the last flight left for Vancouver. He'd gotten the last possible flight on purpose, figuring that they could all get some sleep on the plane.

He re-printed Kelsey's pass, checked their luggage, and headed for the TSA folks. Going through security would've been a problem for someone else, but the guards recognized him as a pilot and let him through with his "sleeping sister who has been ill with cancer and is on her last legs but wants this one final trip" without too much hassle. Kelsey had actually been right to insist on bringing Sue's purse. He needed her ID to get through TSA. What was I thinking? Guess I slipped up on that. Okay, Kelsey, score one for you. My missing something so important doesn't happen often. We'll use fake passports to get into Canada, but these TSA folks know me by my rightful name. Can't pull the wool over their eyes. It would not be good to have them wondering.

Fortunately for him, he had automatically renewed Sue's driver's license, even as he got rid of all her other possessions. Good insight, Kurt! His "sister" got through the checkpoint without any problem. Meanwhile, Kelsey smiled her way through security, babes in arms. They hurried for the gate. Safe so far. He smiled at his own genius.

A short time later, they buckled themselves in for the overnight flight. He cautioned the flight attendants not to disturb his "sister," since she needed her rest. Of course, he slipped an absorbent drug under her tongue to keep Sue knocked out for the flight. Those drugs Jada gave me have done the trick. "Home free now," he mused to Kelsey as the plane taxied and took off.

***

Brooke got on her phone to the airlines, looking for the next flight to Vancouver.

She was told "Miss, there's nothing available for this morning. The Vancouver Canucks National Hockey League championship series is on because they won their final games and are in the playoffs. The first flight I can get you on is late this evening. Will that be sufficient?"

"No, I have to get there NOW." Brooke drummed her fingers on the counter at the nurses' station. Michael stood by her shoulder without speaking.

"I'm sorry, miss. The best I can do for you is this evening, late."

Michael told Brooke, "I'm going with you. Get reservations for two."

Trying to talk with two people at once, she informed the reservationist that she would take the flight, while turning Michael down.

"I can handle this on my own. You don't have to trouble yourself."

"No, you need me to go with you, Brooke. I can handle your father while you get your mother out of there. I'm not allowing you to change my mind."

She gave in and turned back to the phone, "I want the next-available flight for two." To Michael: "We can't get a flight until late tonight."

"Okay. That will get us in in the early hours of tomorrow morning. That's not ideal but we need to find out where in Vancouver they went. It's a big place." Michael picked up his cellphone and made arrangements for some time off while Brooke continued to deal with the airline people.

She told the reservation clerk, "We'll take two tickets." After arranging for payment, she hung up and looked at Michael. "Thank you for being my friend."

He started to answer her when the security detail came back.

"We found something interesting on the security tape, Mr. Bench."

They all rushed to the security department, where they watched as Jada, Kurt, and Kelsey pushed the sleeping Susan down the hall. The external camera picked up the trio and showed as they loaded Susan into the van.

The police were called. Jada's apartment was searched. Jada was long gone. Likewise, the house where Kurt and Kelsey lived with the girls was investigated. Nothing. They tried to contact the Vancouver Police Department, but their Internet service and phones were down. Something about excessive traffic on the system.

**

Kurt and crew arrived at the airport in Vancouver. He passed a fake passport to Kelsey, whispering to her he would explain later. "Just use it and don't ask questions." He gripped his own fake passport, handing it over to the customs agent when asked. He also gave the agent Sue's equally-fake passport. He turned over the fake tickets they hadn't used but that he had prepared, so they would enter the country with the police unable to identify them correctly.

They passed through customs pretty easily, considering the fact that he had an unconscious woman with him. Perhaps it was the gorgeous Kelsey and the precious two little girls that were with him. Who in the world would take a stunning woman and two little kids with them if they were committing a crime? He smiled. The kiddies were the perfect cover.

They got to the car rental area and loaded themselves into the van he rented.

As he prepared to drive off, Kurt said to Kelsey, "Wheelchair, unconscious soon-to-be-ex-wife, true wife, luggage, double stroller, and two little ones. This is no way to kill your wife, unless, of course, you don't want any suspicions cast your way! I've really outdone myself, if I must say!" He kissed her hand and laughed. He had done well.

He stopped at the Greyhound bus station near the airport. He'd rented a locker the last time he was in town, filling it with things he would need as soon as he arrived. He pulled out a nondescript black bag and headed back to the van.

Once inside, he got duct tape, black hair dye to cover his white hair, a red wig for Kelsey, and a brunette wig for Susan.

"Put this wig on Sue, Kelsey. We can't have anyone recognizing her, just in case someone's looking for her. I'll grab some food for us at that McDonalds over there. I'll run into the bathroom and comb this dye through my hair quickly, first. It should dry by the time we get to the hotel."

"Sure, sweetie." Kelsey smiled at him.

Kurt hung the moon, in her eyes. He saw it every time he looked at Kelsey. He was a genius and a lucky man, to boot. Maybe there would be time to.....no, not now. Focus, man. Save the love for later.

"Okay, from here on out, you are Mrs. Kelsey Preston, I am Mr. Kurt Preston, and Sue is my sister, Ms. Sue Preston. The kids still have their same names, just in case Cassie slips up."

"But Kurt, why are we using those names?"

"Because of the monograms inside my shirtsleeves. We can't have anyone wonder, just in case they see my clothing. We also need our same first names, in case Cassie questions it. It really makes it easier for **us**, in case we slip up." He really meant "you." He didn't slip up, ever.

A short time later, they reached their hotel, where Kurt had arranged for an early check-in due to "the kids needing their rest." It cost a little extra, but it was worth the expense, so he could have some time to relax before kicking off his plan. They had adjoining rooms so he could keep a close eye on Susan. The thirty-minute ride after their two stops had been uneventful, though getting everyone settled into their rooms was a bit of a handful. Susan's dead weight continued to be a problem.

"Aren't we gonna put her in pajamas, Kurt?" Kelsey asked.

Kurt groaned. "It amazes me how you are always so concerned about fashion, Kelsey. No. Let's stick her in bed and be done with it. Who cares what she's wearing? She's unconscious and I couldn't care less." He pulled her out of the wheelchair and pushed her onto the bed. He wasn't standing on ceremony for that woman. He almost dropped her. Oops. Gotta be more careful or someone might hear her falling body and call security.

Susan was starting to come around. Kurt decided to let her regain consciousness, since she didn't know where she was, and he had removed all references to their location from the room when they checked in. He also unplugged and removed the phone. She was in no shape to fight him. He kept the "do not disturb" signs on both their rooms, and locked her inside her room, duct taping her doorjamb shut from the inside. If she attempted to open the door, the sound of ripping tape would alert him, even though he was in the next room. He threatened her with more drugs if she didn't "keep her big mouth shut." He smiled at his own intellect. The threat worked, as Sue cowered in front of him, like usual. Doormat!

They were all getting a bit hungry, so he called room service. "This is sure different from the last time we ate room service food," he told Kelsey. He took some food to Susan, who ate it, telling him that she hoped it didn't contain more drugs. It didn't. Not yet, anyway. Kurt gave her only a spoon to eat with, so that she couldn't use the silverware as a weapon.

Early that afternoon, he and Kelsey decided to take Cassie to the pool, since it was an unseasonably warm day. The little girl had been cooped up long enough and was getting very antsy. He warned Sue not to try anything. She was still very weak, he noticed, so she agreed to "be good." Kelsey planned on breastfeeding Christina while they were poolside. He pushed Sue in her wheelchair, stationing her in the shade with instructions to "keep your stupid mouth shut. I will be watching."

***

Susan had known that she had needed to eat something, so she had forced herself to eat the food Kurt had brought her. It would give her strength and hopefully get some of the drugs out of her system. Why had he given her this kindness? It must be because it was vital to getting her drugged again, though not now, for some strange reason. Kurt played at life as if it was a huge game of chess. I wish I knew the next move. She ate, though it almost choked her.

She felt her strength returning, even as they had gone to the pool. Her wheelchair was positioned so that Kurt could easily see her. She played woozier than she actually felt, nervous that he would succeed in his plans. She looked frantically around, searching for some hint of where they were. She prayed without ceasing, not knowing what lay ahead.

Chapter 17

As Susan sat there in her crumpled clothing, watching the activity in the crowded pool and trying to figure out where in the world Kurt and Kelsey had taken her, she saw that a children's sports team had just arrived poolside. It was a good thing that the heated pool was Olympic-sized. It was getting very crowded in there. In spite of herself, she loved the feel of the warm sun on her face. It must be close to 75 degrees today. That's so weird for mid-February. Must be a record.

She glanced around at the people frolicking in the water. Cassie was wearing her hot pink bathing suit as she played around with a couple of boats in the shallow end. Kurt was by her side but then she noticed he had spotted a water volleyball game going on in the middle of the pool. Competition!

Susan couldn't hear what he said, but guessed that he told Cassie to stay there while he went to join in the fun. He always had a cutthroat nature, but he was getting a bit long in the tooth for those athletes. Those guys must be half his age. What was he thinking? She observed Kurt was holding in his stomach as he walked through the water in his black Speedo and bright red Washington Capitals T-shirt. 'Paunchy Pilot' in the flesh, as she called Kurt and his friends.

Susan saw that Cassie was playing very close to the deeper water. She glanced over at Kurt, who was totally ignoring the child, having joined in the water sport as a "shirt" versus the "skins." Yeah, Kurt, keep your shirt on! Nobody wants to see your middle-aged body! The "shirts" had their backs to the shallow end. That was a dumb move. You were supposed to be watching Cassie, you fool. Susan's head drooped slightly as she swung it around to look at Cassie again. Blasted drugs. She was having trouble keeping her eyes focused, but somebody had to watch the little girl.

She looked over at Kelsey, who was garbed in a deep purple bikini with a white overdress. The woman had a pastel breastfeeding blanket and a massive color-coordinated purse. Susan saw that the young mother was busy feeding and cooing with Christine. Kelsey was assuming that Kurt was with their little girl. Kurt had never been very interested in babysitting, even when their kids were young.

"That's women's work," he always told her, "so get to work!"

How have I put up with him all these years? It would serve him right if something happened to his daughter. When she looked back to Cassie, Susan didn't see her. She called out to Kurt, but he ignored her cry. "Kurt?" Her voice sounded like it was in the bottom of a well.

It was then that Susan saw the little child was in water over her head and was being trampled. The sports team had rushed into the water moments ago and no one apparently saw Cassie sink. The life guard was distracted by a couple of bikini-clad girls.

What should I do? This isn't my problem. It 'serves you right,' as he always told me whenever anything went wrong for me.

Her mother's heart got the better of her as she saw Cassie's bright pink bathing suit at the bottom. The boats Cassie had been playing with were floating away, abandoned. "Cassie!!!" Susan threw herself out of the wheelchair and stumbled to the pool. She almost tripped over her own feet, before jumping in fully dressed. Her clothes became saturated, which made it harder to push her way through the swimmers. She fell into the water several times before reaching Cassie and plucking her from probable death. It was then that Kelsey at last noticed what happened to her daughter. Kelsey screamed. Kurt turned around after a victory celebration over the point he scored and comprehended that something bad just occurred.

Despite being a little groggy from the drugs she had been given, Susan made her way to the edge of the pool. She lifted Cassie out of the pool, and began mouth-to-mouth resuscitation. Cassie coughed a few times and started crying. By this time, the life guard made his way to her side, calling for help on his radio.

Susan might have expected thanks, but Kurt shoved her aside as he took Cassie, pushing Susan back into the pool.

"Get out of my way, woman," Kurt screamed.

Kurt grabbed his daughter, taking Cassie into his arms as Kelsey stood by, helpless, holding Christine.

Susan sputtered and coughed as she stood, not expecting that he would be so unkind to someone who had saved his daughter's life.

Kurt refused to take Cassie to the hospital when the paramedics arrived, but Susan begged him to let them transport the child.

"Absolutely not." He was adamant.

"But, Kurt, if she has any water in her lungs, she'll drown when you put her to bed tonight. You have to let the hospital take a look at her. Please." Susan was used to begging him for things, but did she need to do this to save his own child? Yes, she guessed so. So be it, pitiful though it was. It wasn't Cassie's fault.

He finally relented after the emergency crew left, having tired of their nagging when Kelsey joined Susan in her plea. The couple changed their clothes quickly, putting on dry things before preparing to head to the emergency room. Kurt threw Susan some of the clothing that he brought along. Susan realized she couldn't be seen wearing the same outfit every day, since the Westin Bayshore was a very nice hotel. One pair of dark pants, one long-sleeved pink collared shirt, appropriate foundation garments, socks, and tennis shoes. Boring, predictable, but at least it wasn't sopping wet. Or wrinkled.

Susan came into the adjoining room where the family was. Kurt, Kelsey, and the girls had much nicer things on than her outfit, but then, she surmised, they could afford it. Lord and Taylor for the little girls? Must be nice. I never had such nice things for Brooke. Kelsey's outfit was also a Lord and Taylor creation, Susan was willing to bet. Lovely. Color-coordinated purple velvet running suit with matching tennis shoes. Gold jewelry...I wonder if the $500 watch he bought her with our money is among her travel jewels. Kurt's clothing had certainly taken a huge leap forward- I bet that's a Nordstrom outfit she has him in. Oxford blue monogrammed long-sleeved shirt, gold cufflinks, Nordstrom label dark pants, and shoes. Yeah, Kurt, fiddle with your sleeves... you look like Prince Charles when you do that. She looked at her own humble wardrobe. Well, an unwanted wife was not going to be dressed as nicely as the mistress of the hour.

Kurt threw a running suit at her. "For tomorrow," he told her. "Go put it on your bed so I don't have to bother with it later." They left for the nearest hospital, getting directions from the front desk.

While she was at the hospital, Susan looked around a bit and discovered that they were in Vancouver. The number of Vancouver T-shirts and the talk of the other patients was the dead giveaway. The playoffs were the main topic of conversation. Why would Kurt take me here? And with Kelsey and the girls, of all things. She had no phone and no money, so she couldn't call Brooke. In spite of Cassie's problems, Susan noticed that Kurt kept a very close eye on her, so Susan had no opportunity to escape. He had frightened her too much for her to say a word. Gotta figure out what he's planning before I make my getaway.

She sat with Kurt and Christine in the emergency room waiting area. She saw a nearby woman was knitting, but observed that the woman left her things behind while she went to the ladies' room. She noticed that Kurt was temporarily distracted by Christine's fussing, so she slipped the woman's knitting into her own large handbag as Kelsey returned with Cassie.

Cassie had indeed gotten water in her lungs; it was successfully removed, saving her life a second time. They headed back to the hotel, but first they made one stop at a local grocery for Kurt to get some toiletries. Sample sizes.

He told her, "Take a shower and use these. The hotel didn't give us any sample deodorant products for you and you're not worth the fancy shampoo and soap they give out. We get them. You get these cheap store brands. I hope they work because you stink." He shoved them at her.

Susan gratefully accepted them and showered at once upon their return to their rooms, putting on the T-shirt and running suit he had given her earlier in the day. Relief!

Why did I steal those knitting things back at the hospital? I'm not a thief. She was surprised at her actions, but remembered how much she used to enjoy watching MacGyver on television.

Maybe I can use these things later to get out of here. Where is MacGyver now that I need him? Cancelled, that's where.

That night, as she lay on her bed, she heard voices coming from Kurt and Kelsey's hotel room next door. It wasn't like when she was Victoria Susan, no. The hotel had no air conditioning and the sliding glass doors leading on to the balcony were open to bring in a breeze. Their voices traveled into her room. She stepped outside to hear more clearly.

"So we have had a little setback here but I think we can move ahead with our plans for tomorrow. Jada sold me enough drugs to send Sue to La-La-Land again. In the morning, you'll give Sue her orange juice. It'll have a small amount of drugs, just enough to keep her quiet. Make sure she drinks all of it. We'll head out to sightsee and we'll slip more drugs into Sue's water bottle. It'll be easier to get her out of the hotel if she's mostly conscious, but we'll drug her more as soon as possible." Kurt laughed.

Kelsey seemed to hesitate. "What then, Kurt?"

"We'll take her to Vancouver Lookout and push her off. The locals and all of the tourists will be at the championship pre-game activities. No one'll be around the Lookout. No one knows she's here and no one'll miss her, least of all me. Her body will be eaten by wild animals before she's ever found. We'll take the next flight out in the morning with our fake passports and no one will ever know we were here. We dump the fake passports as soon as we no longer need them. No one will be the wiser." He laughed again, as usual.

"But Kurt, honey, she saved our baby's life today. Twice. How can you keep talking about killing her?"

"How can you not? She stands in the way of our every happiness. She's a burden, washed up, a total waste of space. She's kept us apart for years and might actually get some of our money if she

214

lives. One sympathetic judge is all it will take. We've worked so hard to get where we are. No. We move on with our plan. She's history."

Tears rolled down Susan's cheeks as she heard Kurt's distain for her. How could she have been so blind for so many years? How could she have not seen how he really felt? She slumped against the door frame, almost afraid to breathe lest they hear her. The conversation continued.

"Kurt, Cassie is alive right now because of Susan. I won't hurt her."

"Don't be such a fool. Of course, you'll help me. You and I have come too far to stop now. Drugging her. Kidnapping her. Taking her out of the country. Using false names. Do you have any idea how much time we'll serve unless we keep going? She must be silenced, and we will do it."

"I can't do it," Kelsey sobbed.

"You can and you will."

Kurt made lovey-dovey sounds. Kelsey accepted his attention.

Susan stood there in stunned silence. A short while later, she went back inside her room, and pulled the sliding door closed. She had no desire to overhear the actions of her husband and his lover.

Susan didn't sleep. She couldn't believe that Kurt would really kill her, but what she heard made it obvious that he would. The old Sue would have fumed through the rest of the hours till dawn, becoming more and more angry but not sure if all of her anger was towards Kurt and Kelsey or if she was angry at herself for being so gullible. She would have been passive in the long run, even if it meant her own death.

Not any more, my friend. The new Susan reacted differently. She had to think up her own plan, and she did, thanks to MacGyver. First, she noticed that Kurt had left all of the room service plates from the last four meals in her room. The leftover food began to smell and he didn't want it in his room, so he dumped everything in hers. He left the plates, spoons, and lids with her, keeping the knives and forks in his room. Lids...metal lids... Hum... what can I do with these? Think MacGyver here. Plates...spoons... what else do I have with me?

She had the yarn and knitting needles from her hospital theft and, by threading yarn through the room service plate covers and placing the metal spoons inside the lids, she created something that would be very noisy out on the balcony. If I could stack them on top of a pillowcase on the little table outside and rip it off at exactly the right time, it would be a distraction when Kelsey came in with the tainted juice.

Susan opened the sliding door quietly, and snuck out onto her balcony while Kurt and Kelsey were sleeping. She was able to set things up so that pulling the end of the yarn would release the covers. She wrapped several strands of yarn together, making a tight cord that would be strong enough to pull the covers off of the table. Kurt and Kelsey had brought her purse on the trip, and she always kept a pair of fingernail clippers inside. They were strong enough to cut the yarn but only if she put the yarn between her teeth, twisted the yarn around her toes, and pulled on it to stretch it thin. Yep, that worked like a champ. What now? Hum....

What else do I have in my bag? She dumped it out on her bed. She pulled out the normal contents of a purse: tissues -nope, they won't help-, some loose change -hey, I might be able to do something with this-, and a baggie of Advil and Tums -nope, this wouldn't help unless Kurt got a headache or a tummy twinge. Why would I care about the condition of his stomach? Nope, no more, Buddy boy.

Wait a minute. Why do I have a couple of bags of marbles? Oh, yeah, I asked Brooke to get me some gifts for Joshua's boys for when they come to visit me at the rehab center. I totally forgot they were in the bottom of my pocketbook. They would come in handy for something! She laid them aside until she could figure out what to do with them.

She put the stacked lids and spoons on top of the balcony table, moving the chairs away from their normal location. She laid the yarn on the floor, bringing it inside the sliding glass doors and next to her bedside table. She would eat her breakfast there-yes that should work.

She took some of the smelly food from their plates and placed it on the balcony's floor, so that Kelsey would step in it and be distracted for a longer time. She knew the woman well enough to realize that Kelsey would take time to wipe off her feet before coming back inside. That might be just enough time for her to do something to slow down Kurt.

Well, that would take care of Kelsey, but what about Kurt? She went to work on making a trip wire for the doors that adjoined their rooms. It had to be flat when Kelsey came through but she had to be able to pull the yarn and raise it as Kurt rushed in to see what was wrong.

She spent an hour on the project, but it didn't seem to go very well as she tried first one thing and then another. Nope, that wouldn't work. Neither would that. She looked carefully at the yarn in her hands. She was happy that it was the same color as the carpet because that made it easier to hide – but what were they thinking? The horrid green color reminded her of the avocado green of the 60s. The hotel must have been decorated by someone stuck in the past. But why would that woman from the ER knit something in such a ghastly color? She felt sorry for whoever was going to get this scarf. She worked for a little while longer before abandoning the idea. She dropped the whole mess on the floor in frustration, slumping. Nope, this wasn't going to work. Drat the luck!

She straightened. Wait a minute! Could she rig the scarf so that it fell down, rather than trying to get something to come up? It could hit Kurt in the face, just enough to distract him, and then she could throw the knitting needles, her coins, and the loose marbles on the floor to trip him. If she tossed some of the yucky plates in his face, maybe that would be enough for her to get by him and run out of his room. Her door was duct taped closed, so that probably wasn't the way to head. Humm...She might be stretching it to think she had enough time to throw plates in his face, so maybe she just needed to keep it simple. She would keep the plates on hand, just in case she did have time, but she wouldn't plan on it. Yeah, that might just do the trick.

She rolled the scarf up and placed it on top of the door that adjoined their rooms, having wound several strands of yarn around it. The scarf would fall when she pulled on the yarn tied to the lamp that was on the dresser against the wall. She moved so as to not disturb the sleepers in the next room. It was a good thing the dresser was so big and so close to the adjoining doorway. She could reach the doorway and set things up with just a little st-re-tch-ing.

The sounds of Kurt's snoring filled the room, so she knew he didn't hear her. She wondered if Kelsey wore earplugs like she had needed to. Kelsey would still be able to hear the girls but not Kurt. Susan was so thankful she didn't have to put up with that cacophony anymore. She smiled at having found something good out of such a horrid situation. But the plan... she must stay focused...

Maybe she should hit him on the head with the lamp while he was laying low. It would be a close call but it was a good thing that she kept working out at night at the rehab center when they thought she was going right to sleep. She'd been doing her PT faithfully, too. She'd pretended to be weak and drowsy around Kurt since he snatched her, but she was probably stronger than she had been before the accident. He wouldn't expect it, so the element of surprise would be to her advantage.

Okay, it was time review what needed to happen in order. Kelsey would come in with her breakfast. Susan would pretend to eat some of the eggs, but would lean over as if in pain. That would give her the chance to pull the yarn that was attached to the service lids and spoons. Kelsey would be startled by the racket. Kelsey would run out to the balcony which had slimy leftovers on it, while Kurt would come in the door that was between our rooms. Susan would leap up, throw over her table, which should block Kelsey from coming back in very fast, and grab the lamp off the dresser, which would make the scarf fall down.

The knitting needles, change, and marbles...hummmm...where can I keep them? Oh, behind the lamp. Kelsey wouldn't notice them. She would talk to Kelsey to keep her looking at her instead of the dresser. She would pick up the lamp that triggered the scarf and then pick up and throw down the needles and other stuff. Let's give this a try. Oh, oh. Wait a minute. She was about one hand short here. She would have to either lay down the lamp to pick up the other stuff or throw the lamp right away. Okay, minor change.... throw the lamp at his head and toss the loose stuff at his feet. She practiced, without letting go. Yeah, that should work out okay.

If I need to, I could hit Kurt with the dishes I have piled up on the dresser as I go around him and run out his door. Good thing she liked to play Frisbee as a child. A little wrist action would go a long way. Those dirty dishes were an option, but she couldn't depend on having the opportunity to throw them at him.

What can I do about my lack of time? This action has to happen very quickly. I'd like to shut Kelsey on the balcony but I don't have time to close and lock the door. The decaying food on the ground should be a help, though, in keeping her outside. There were several unknowns here but she had realized in the last day that Kelsey was a fashionista who would be horrified by having food on her feet. Kelsey would have to wipe it off.

Susan would have to take the element of surprise into consideration. Adrenaline would also be a factor. I'll be fighting for my life and they won't. 'Trust in the Lord with all your heart,' like Michael always said. She needed to pray this all worked, or she would be dead... Of course, that was Kurt's end game anyway, so there was nothing to lose here. It was a lose-lose proposition. Or it could be a win-lose, depending on if everything worked out. Please, Lord.

Yes, the plan was a fairly good one. Now she needed to get a little shut-eye before this plan kicked off. "Lord Jesus, please deliver me from this evil man and keep me safe. In Jesus' name. Amen." Michael always told her that prayers didn't have to be long to be effective. She sure hoped he was right.

Chapter 18

Brooke needed to figure out where the fugitives were in Vancouver, or if the runaways had just flown in there and then headed somewhere else. Michael suggested calling hotels to "extend their stay" as "Mr. Kurt and Mrs. Kelsey Prescott." They got to work, each taking a group of hotels to phone, not having much luck until the telephone operator at one hotel was not very fluent in English and misunderstood what Brooke had said.

The woman repeated, "Mr. Kurt and Mrs. Kelsey Preston. Yes, it would be our pleasure to extend your stay. The hockey playoffs are just starting but we have enough room to let your residency in the two double-doubles continue. When do you plan on departing? Wednesday? Yes, that would be fine. Would you like me to send you a confirmation email?"

"No. That won't be necessary. Thank you for your time."

"You are welcome, Mrs. Preston. Enjoy your continued stay."

To Michael: "Got them. They are at the Westin Bayshore under the name 'Preston.' It's a good thing that woman doesn't speak good English." What a relief! Brooke could feel her adrenalin pounding in her chest. I couldn't live through this every day, that's for sure.

Michael dropped her off to pack a few things for herself and Susan. He told Brooke to "get packed and try to get some rest. I'll pick you up in a couple of hours."

Brooke spent most of the afternoon pacing throughout her condo, trying to convince the police that Susan needed help, and praying that they would be in time to save her mother. The local police said they would write a report but that there wasn't much they could do for someone out of the country. They would be in touch. Frustrating!

True to his word, Michael pulled up in front of her home later that afternoon; Brooke met him at the curb with her carryon bag and jumped into the car. "Let's go!"

"Right on, Brooke. Our flight leaves in three hours." He tried to smile as they pulled away from the curb. "Any luck with the police?"

Brooke told him, "No. It's out of their jurisdiction, or so they say. Mom's kidnapping is not their problem, though they did say they would write it up. Like that would do some good."

Michael told her, "Brooke, I'm so sorry. But if the cops won't get involved, then rest assured we will take care of things ourselves."

"Michael, thank you so much for everything." She hadn't noticed before what a good friend he was. He was the best. She was glad he was with her, relieved that he was on her side.

"I'm glad I can be here for you and your mom, Brooke. Now let's go get Mama!"

Michael sped into the airport's hourly parking lot. They grabbed their carryon bags and got through TSA in record time, heading for their gate.

Once on board, they had a pretty sleepless flight due to the adrenalin rush they were both experiencing. Brooke kept asking herself, and Michael, "What'll happen if we're too late?" He just shook his head.

"Worry about nothing, pray about everything, as the Good Book says," he told her. He squeezed her hand.

They hailed a cab and headed for the hotel.

"Michael, how will we figure out what room my mom is in?" Brooke whispered to him, afraid that the cab driver would overhear.

He spoke low and quietly. "I think that partial honesty is best. We'll talk about the serious illness of your mom- her coma- but we may have to stretch the truth if we're given a hard time. I hate to do it, but her life's definitely at stake, so we don't have much of a choice. May God be with us." He tossed some cash at the taxi driver, and led the way as they ran into the hotel. They approached the front desk, winded.

"Welcome to the Westin Bayshore, Sir, Ma'am." The reception desk gal was wearing the requisite navy blue blazer, gray skirt, and white blouse that marked the attire of most front desk clerks. She smiled the charming smile that demonstrated her hotel-mandated pleasantries were in place.

Brooke said, quite harried: "Excuse me, but you have some people staying here, the Prestons." She could barely make the words come out of her mouth. Mom, hang in there!

"Yes, miss?" Again, the smile.

"My mother has serious health problems and I need to see her as soon as possible." Brooke was already sweating, but now she began to tremble. What if they were too late? No, I must focus on the positive. We will make it in time.

"I'm sorry, Miss, but I cannot give out guests' room numbers." A stern look, but not an unfriendly one.

Michael said, "Young woman, I am Mrs. Preston's personal nurse. I have medication that she needs immediately." He pulled out his rehab center ID and a prescription bottle and waved them in front of the front desk clerk. "She is recovering from a coma and may slip back into a persistive vegetative state without it. Please give us a hand here."

Somewhat frazzled at this news, the front desk woman looked through her records and replied, "The Prestons are in rooms 830 and 832." The gal looked at her computer screen. "I believe the lady in question is in 830 because there are baby cots in the other room. Let me phone her room and see...." The woman allowed the phone to ring several times before saying, "The phone rings a bit oddly. Almost like it's off the hook or unplugged. How odd."

Brooke almost shouted, "Oh no, poor Mom."

Michael held out his hand, stern but forceful. "I'll need her key, in case she has already lapsed into a coma. I'll need to give her the medication, even if she is unconscious."

"Sir, I just don't know…." The clerk was apparently considering the repercussions she would endure if she complied with his request. "I'll phone security to help you. They should be able to meet you here in a few minutes."

"This is critically important, Miss. My patient might not have a few minutes. We have to get to her now." Michael's face revealed his inner turmoil.

"Please, my mother's life is at stake." Brooke was about to jump over the counter and grab the keys herself. This gal better make a decision soon or she would make it for her.

"Well, just don't tell anyone. I could lose my job." The woman still seemed to hesitate, not immediately handing over the key she'd just made. She started to pass it over to Michael and then pulled it back. "You must assure me you won't tell anyone." Her emphasis on the word "anyone" was clear.

"Absolutely not. My patient's life is hanging in the balance. You are saving her from certain death. Did you say 830?"

"Yes, sir, here's the key." The gal finally placed the key on the registration desk.

"Thank you so much. You've saved her life." Michael grabbed it before she could change her mind.

"Yes, thank you!" Brooke smiled her most radiant and genuine smile, relieved that the gal gave the key to them but praying that they were in time to save her mother.

"Oh, you're welcome, Sir, Ma'am. Enjoy your visit at the Westin Bayshore and do come again." The last sentence was said to their backs.

They rushed for the elevator, pushing the 8th floor button. They raced down the hallway to the room, praying that Susan was still there and alive.

***

Susan was already dressed in the blue track suit, white T-shirt, and tennis shoes that Kurt had given her yesterday, when Kelsey entered her room the next morning. Susan was still angry but played up to Kelsey, to distract her from the stacks of stuff on the dresser. It worked. So far, so good. Susan greeted Kelsey pleasantly, hoping that the young woman would change her mind about joining in with Kurt's plan.

"Good morning, Kelsey. What a lovely jogging outfit you're wearing. I love that shade of teal. It looks so nice on you." She hated gushing, but it must be done. I'm glad Kelsey's feet are still bare.

Kelsey focused her attention on the floor. Guilt made the younger woman unable to meet her gaze, Susan supposed.

"How is Cassie feeling today? Did she sleep well?" Susan Margaret, you are about to make me throw up; you are really laying the sweetness and concern on with a trowel. Oh, well, Kelsey didn't appear to be the sharpest knife in the drawer. Maybe she wouldn't notice the baloney that was being dished out.

"Fine. Hehehe. Thanks for asking. We're all going sightseeing today, so here's your breakfast. It's a long time till lunch; eat everything up. Here's your orange juice."

Susan began eating her eggs and bacon, avoiding the orange juice she knew was tainted.

"This is a pretty busy hotel, don't you think?" Susan said. "I noticed that the hockey fans are all over the place." Keep Kelsey talking. Buy some time. "My, these eggs are yummy."

"Yes, uh... Susan, thanks for what you did yesterday. You saved Cassie's life twice in one day. I'll never be able to thank you enough."

Well, not killing me today would be a massive step in the right direction. "You're welcome, Kelsey. I'm sure that......"

"Susan, you'd better eat fast. Kurt doesn't like to be kept waiting." Kelsey seemed nervous, distracted. "Uh....Drink your orange juice. You don't want to . . . uh . . . get dehydrated."

"Oh." Susan bent over, as if in pain. At that moment, she pulled on the yarn that removed the pillow case from the balcony table and sent the room service lids and spoons crashing to the ground. A cacophony ensued. Kelsey bolted from the room and headed to the balcony, to see if someone was there. Kelsey's yelp told Susan that she had stepped into the decaying food with her bare feet.

"Oh, no! What's this? Augh! Big yikes!" Kelsey was adding to the racket on the balcony with her whining.

Susan smiled and yelled, unable to restrain herself, "Yes!" then, "Lord, be gracious unto me... And help me."

Susan jumped from her seat at the breakfast table. She pushed the table over in front of the sliding glass door, threw her food tray on the floor, moved the large dresser lamp, and triggered the falling scarf she had strung between the connecting door to Kurt and Kelsey's room. She threw the paraphernalia she had gathered in front of the door. She didn't have to wait long for Kurt to show up.

Kurt stormed into the room, dazed by the scarf in his face. He was in his stocking feet and stepped on the knitting needles, coins, and marbles. He began to fall, unable to catch his balance. "What the...?"

Susan laughed at his predicament, "Yes!" Nervous tension was built up so much, she moved quickly into stage two. She began pelting him with the room service dishes, plates, cups, glasses... she was on a roll and enjoying herself, in spite of the situation. She threw everything she could get her hands on at Kurt, releasing years of pent up frustration and anger.

"You lousy slime ball. What do you think you were doing to me? Huh? Take that and that! I would hate you, but you aren't worth it." She was yelling at the man. She picked up the lamp but just before hitting him with it, she realized that her goal was to get out of there, not beat him up with anything handy. She also had no desire to commit a felony. Murder would certainly qualify, even though it would be justifiable homicide.

"What the heck?" Kurt was sprawled on the floor with decaying food in his hair.

"Nice look, Kurt. You ought to wear old food more often."

He saw Susan with a lamp in her hands and flinched. She glared at him with a look in her eyes she knew he'd never seen before. The doormat is gone, Kurt Prescott. Forever. Don't mess with me or you **will** regret it.

"Kelsey, where are you babe?" He didn't try to get up. He kept looking at Susan, unable to comprehend what was happening.

Susan still had the lamp ready for action, though she hesitated using it on him. Her goal was to leave, not murder him, no matter how tempting that option was. Tempting, it certainly was.

A bang came on Susan's door and she heard the sound of the door handle being jiggled. Brooke yelled, "Mom. Are you okay?" Relief flooded her. Brooke was here!

"Brooke!" She couldn't believe that Brooke actually found her! "Help me, please!" She lowered the lamp.

"**No**, you are not slipping out of my hands this time!" Kurt crawled closer to Susan, leaping towards her feet. Susan backed up and ran into Kelsey who had re-entered from the balcony. Kelsey grabbed Susan and threw her on the bed.

Kurt shouted, "Get her, honey! Hold on to her." He jumped up, apparently planning to harm Susan.

"Brooke, hurry!" Susan fought off Kelsey, who wrapped her in a bear hug from behind. She elbowed Kelsey in the ribcage and grabbed Kelsey's hair. Her grasp only seized a handful of wig. Oh, that stupid wig! The next clutch hit pay dirt: Kelsey's real hair. She jerked on the hair. Kelsey screamed and immediately turned her loose. Kelsey tumbled onto the floor next to the bed, crying about her painful head. Susan jumped up from the bed, avoiding Kurt's snatching hands as she ran towards the door.

Michael pushed the door in, having hit it squarely with his shoulder. The duct tape was ripped from its place. Brooke rushed to her mother, crying as she went. Brooke grabbed her, hugging her tightly in her arms. Michael took a hold of Kurt, who had risen to his feet, placing the older man in a strangle hold.

"Thank God, you made it here in time. Oh, Lord Jesus, thank you." Susan could say nothing else, so relieved was she that her prayers had been answered. "Thank you, Lord." Tears flowed down her face. "Thank you, Jesus."

"Mom, I thought you were dead." Brooke was sobbing and hugging at the same time, as she kissed her mother repeatedly.

Susan finally spoke. "No dear, I'm fine. A little tired, truth be known." She collapsed against Brooke, exhausted and out of adrenalin. "It's been quite a morning. And a horrid day yesterday." She slumped to the floor. "I'm so glad you came."

Michael said, "I'm calling the police." He jerked back on Kurt's head. "You're going to jail, buddy."

From her place on the floor, Susan said, "No, Michael. There are two little girls in the next room who need their parents. Both of them. Let's just go home." She wanted Kurt back in the States, to face the court system there. She was not a legal eagle but it just made sense to let him re-cross the border, thinking she was such a doormat that she wouldn't press charges. Now who is the stupid one, Kurt? I'm **so** done with you. As for Kelsey, she's a blind fool, just like I was. Okay, well, not exactly like I was, but pretty stupid, all in all. She stared at the two of them, feeling both pity and anger.

Brooke said, "But, Mom, Dad tried to kill you. Kelsey was his accomplice."

Michael said, "I think letting this son-of-a-gun go is a mistake, Mrs. Prescott." He jerked up on Kurt's body, causing the older man to grunt in discomfort. "The police station is where he belongs, followed by a nice stay in prison."

"No, Michael. Let him go. He's my husband and the father of my children. As for Kelsey, I think she was just as blind as I was, once. She can leave, as well. Don't harm them." Susan rose slowly to her feet and smiled at her friend. "Michael, can you fix the door?"

"Yes. It's just a little duct tape. The door was already unlocked with our key." Michael didn't loosen his hold on Kurt. Michael's face showed the disbelief he was obviously feeling.

"Then please do it, and let's get out of here before security shows up. The playoffs are still going on, so we should be able to get a flight. I understand Kurt, Kelsey, and the girls have a flight arranged for later today. They didn't plan for me to accompany them. . ." Susan was a bit out of breath.

"Mom, are you sure?" Brooke was still holding on to her mother, just as Michael was still holding her father in a death grip.

"Yes, dear. I am absolutely certain." She turned to her daughter's helper. "Michael?"

"Yes, Ma'am?"

"Please fix the door while we get ready." She and Brooke headed to the bathroom, to try and fix her bedraggled appearance. Fighting one's hubby was hard work.

"Will do." Michael relaxed his grip on Kurt, who lurched out of his arms.

***

Kurt swaggered a bit as he left the room, adjusting his shirt as he went. I defeated her, again. I have all her money, all her property. She has nothing. She's letting me go! She can't stand up to me, even though I tried to kill her yet again. What a fool. I will succeed the next time and what a victory that will be. He went into the room he shared with Kelsey. Ha!

***

Susan came back into the room and looked at her husband's mistress who was still on the floor where she'd fallen after their tussle. The girl looked worse than Susan had before Brooke's ministrations. Kelsey's wig was lying on the floor and her natural hair looked like it had been combed with an electric mixer. Her lipstick was all over her face. Her mascara was running in rivers down her cheeks. Her feet and legs were covered in rotting food. Kelsey had been cowering in the background once Brooke and Michael broke in. Kelsey left the room to tend to the girls, who were both crying, and to pack. Kelsey was bawling; she didn't look at the others as she left Susan's room.

"Michael?" Susan felt renewed, revitalized.

"Yes, Mrs. Prescott?" Michael was straightening his clothing, its having gotten pulled askew by Kurt's wrestling.

230

"I need to stop by Vancouver General Hospital."

Brooke asked, "Mom, are you okay? What's wrong? Are you hurt?"

"I'm fine, dear. I just need to return something I took. They should have a "lost and found" – I'll leave it there, with a quick note of apology for my theft of some knitting." She began to gather the knitting needles, yarn, and a definitely-worse-for-wear scarf. "I hope the lady can fix this. I'm afraid it is a mess."

"What in the world, Mrs. P.?"

"I borrowed some lady's knitting when we took Cassie to the ER yesterday. I want to give it back...with twenty dollars, if you don't mind loaning me some cash, Brooke."

"Sure thing, Mom." Brooke shook her head with a laugh. "Anything you say."

The motley crew took their leave of the hotel, with Kurt in a sullen mood, Kelsey humbled and bowed with care, Cassie squealing as little girls do on their way to an adventure, and Christina sleeping, for once. Susan, Brooke, and Michael were overjoyed to be together again, though she knew she looked as exhausted as she felt. It had been a very long couple of days.

The hospital drop off was made as Brooke ran in to return the stolen items. After a short trip to the airport, they got on an earlier flight for BWI than Kurt had originally planned for, post-murder. Because of the playoffs, there was only one flight out of Vancouver that morning, but it was readily available. Susan, Brooke, and Michael tried to catch up on lost sleep. Kurt and Kelsey had their hands full in the back of the plane with two little ones who were very determined to **not** sleep.

Susan looked out the plane's window and offered her thanks again, for the Lord's watched care. Where would I be without you, Lord? In the bottom of a ravine, most likely, and on my way to eternal separation from You. What should I do about Kurt? In her heart, she felt the Lord tell her to trust in Him to redeem the day. Susan slept.

Chapter 19

The flight landed at BWI. Susan, Brooke, and Michael headed to Joshua's home. Christopher had finished his Ph.D. in California and was staying at Joshua's while waiting to close on his new home near the Naval Academy, where he would be teaching Oceanography. Michael and Brooke had taken Michael's car to the airport and had parked it in the hourly parking garage because it was closer to the terminal than the daily garage. Kurt had arranged for a rental minivan to take his family home, so they had to get to the rental car facility. Kurt had to get their luggage, two car seats, and the children loaded up.

The only thing that Susan could figure out later was that Kurt was afraid she would arrive at Joshua's first. Since Brooke had texted Joshua and Christopher telling them a little about the recent events, Kurt was probably determined to get his side of the story told in person first, knowing that the boys always supported him against their mother. Pitiful.

**

Kurt had to beat Susan to Joshua's house. He **had** to get his side of the story told before Susan and her pathetic companions had the chance to foul his reputation. He must get there first, knowing he could manipulate the boys enough to believe his story, no matter the appearance of his own bad behavior. To do that, Kurt would have to make very good time. The flight had been a full eight hours, and eight hours with two whinny kids and a load of unrealized dreams had made him very antsy. Kelsey was periodically sobbing, probably feeling guilty about her part in the activities of the past few days, or so he guessed. That irritated him even more. He snapped at Kelsey for the smallest thing as they drove away from the airport towards Route 97.

"Woman, you are really starting to bug me. Give Cassie a juice cup, feed Christine, and give me some peace and quiet." Kelsey stopped whining at once when she saw him scowl at her. "We have to beat Sue to Joshua's and I can't listen to your mindless chatter and weeping for another minute." He was driving 70 in a 50 mile per hour zone but it couldn't be helped. They had to catch up. He floored it, swerving around cars unfortunate enough to be in his way.

Kelsey had unbuckled her seatbelt and had lifted Christine out of her car seat so she could feed her and was ready to re-buckle her seatbelt when she spotted Sue in Michael's car. Kelsey moved Christine slightly in her arms and excitedly pointed. "Kurt, baby, there they are. I see Sue in the backseat. Do you see her, honey? We're almost up to them."

"Hold on. If we just run this light......"

Their white minivan went through the very red light. Kurt had been so busy plotting how he would beat Sue to Joshua's house and deciding what he would say to the boys that he failed to notice the eighteen-wheeler coming through the intersection until it was too late. "No! Hold on!" He stood on the brakes and tried to swerve, to no avail. Kelsey screamed.

The van was struck on his side, towards the back. The vehicle spun around a few times and flipped, sliding down the road. Kelsey was thrown wildly around the vehicle, as the air bags deployed. The unrestrained infant flew through the window. Cassie was sitting behind him when the truck hit their side of the van.

**

Susan, Brooke, and Michael heard the crash. They pulled a U-Turn and returned to the site as quickly as possible, thinking that Michael might be of some immediate help. The devastation was incredible. There were van parts and shards of glass everywhere. Susan was horrified as she realized that Kurt was in the van, spotting his white hair through the window. Michael and Brooke got out of the car and ran to the crumpled van, but Susan just sat there. Should I try to help? Why would I help my adulterous husband and his mistress? They tried to kill me, for Pete's sake. She was shaking all over, unable to move.

It was then that she saw the small, crumpled body lying on the side of the road. What if that was one of my children? She unbuckled her seat belt and stumbled towards the infant. Her own sobs caught in her throat. "Dear God in heaven, help me know what to do!" Christine was still breathing, just barely. Susan picked the infant up, unsure if that was the medically correct thing to do or not. In the world of motherhood, it was exactly right. The little lungs were trying hard to pump air into Christine's body, but to no benefit. Susan felt so helpless. She screamed towards the sky. "What can I do for her? Dear God, please help me!" Tears ran in rivers down her cheeks.

The baby was only semi-conscious. Thank God. Susan calmed down a bit. I'm glad she isn't aware of what's happening. The little hands grasped her finger...then...relaxed. Christine's head pitched to one side. Gone. Susan hugged the child close, and then realized that Cassie was screaming from inside the mangled van. Susan laid the infant down on the grass and ran to the little girl.

As Susan lurched toward the scrunched van, she noticed that Michael was trying to help Kurt. Brooke and the truck driver were working on Kelsey. None of them appeared to be having much success. Kurt was trapped. Michael was apparently trying to reinflate Kurt's collapsed lung from a very awkward stance, from what she could see. Michael was hanging upside down through the window of the van. Kelsey was lying on the side of the road with Brooke and the truck driver walking around the injured woman, apparently uncertain how to help her. Brooke told her later that they were afraid to move her for fear of making her worse but they were concerned she might bleed out somewhere if they did nothing.

Both of the adults were unconscious, bruised, and bleeding. Traffic was beginning to back up as vehicles were unable to get by the contorted mess. Susan moved on, her Jello legs almost failing her. A small voice called out from the back of the van.

"Mommy! Mommy, where are you? Help me!"

"Cassie, sweetie, it's me, your...uh... Aunt Susan." Well, that's kinda true.

Susan looked in where the window once was, seeing that Cassie was covered in her own blood and broken glass. Oh, no. She's in trouble. Big trouble.

"Mommmmmmmy......"

With each breath, Susan saw blood spirting out of Cassie's neck.

"Hold still, honey. I need to hold your neck." She reached towards the child but couldn't get a good grip on the squirming child. If only Cassie would stop wriggling so much! How can I get ahold of her with her moving around? Gotta stop the blood.

"I want my Mommy!" Cassie was flailing around but unable to go anywhere because of her car seat.

"She'll be here in a minute." She looked over where Kelsey was. The woman was in very bad shape; her leg protruded at a weird angle. Kelsey regained consciousness briefly and started thrashing about. Susan looked in Kelsey's eyes but, from what Susan could see at this distance, they were glazed, unaware. Kelsey was out again. Kelsey wasn't going anywhere anytime soon.

Suddenly, Cassie began coughing, gagging...blood was everywhere.

"Hold on sweetie." No, she's gotta stay conscious! Think, Susan, what do I do now? I haven't been a nurse for so long. How can I help her?

Her nursing skills stepped in but the situation was hopeless. She saw that Cassie was beginning to turn blue...the child stopped screaming. Her eyes rolled back in her head...her throat made a gurgling sound. Susan gently slapped the child on the cheeks, hoping to stimulate her. Susan was finally able to pull her out of the car seat. Susan cradled the child in her arms.

"Honey, stay with me. Please, Cassie!" The child went limp. She held her tightly and did not let go. "Cassie! Dear Cassie! Not you, too! No!"

Susan burst into tears; she kissed the child's head. Cassie's curls were a mess of blood and debris from the crash. Not both of these precious babies. Please, Lord. Not these babies.

The paramedics arrived. Susan pointed to Christine. Part of the emergency team went to check on Christine, but just shook their heads. Susan continued to hold Cassie's lifeless body until the nearest paramedic removed the child from her arms. She sobbed as the emergency workers took the children away, laying them on the ground, and covering them with blankets. Susan rose and walked towards Cassie and Christine, not wanting to let them lay there unattended. "Dear Lord, not my will but yours. Receive these two little ones. Heal their bodies and help them live with you forever. Amen."

An EMT approached her, "Ma'am, can I have a look at you. Where do you hurt?"

"Huh? Oh." Susan was enveloped in the girls' blood but she assured the man that she had been a bystander, a belated witness to the tragedy. "I'm fine. I wasn't in the accident. Help their parents, please." The EMT handed her a towel, to wipe off some of the blood. "Thank you."

"Please stay here, ma'am. You were a witness and the police will need a statement from you."

"Yes, of course." Susan stayed near Cassie and Christine, though the children's need of her was gone.

Michael and Brooke came to her. Michael offered Susan a report on the situation.

"Both Kurt and Kelsey are seriously injured. Kurt's body was crushed by the impact and one lung collapsed, and…" He hesitated, knowing that Susan as still Kurt's legal wife.

"And, Michael?" Susan had to ask. "What then?"

"I knew what to do and I restored Kurt's breathing by the time the paramedics arrived. There was so much blood everywhere that I was uncertain where to start, at first. I stabilized Kurt as best I could and then asked Brooke to watch her father while I worked on Kelsey."

Brooke spoke, shaking over the tragedy. "Mom, I held Dad's hand but didn't speak. Mom, there was nothing I could say to him. I felt so lost and alone. I'm sorry, but I couldn't talk to him at all. There was nothing I could tell him, nothing I wanted to tell him that would have helped." Brooke sobbed. Susan held her tightly.

"It's okay, my baby. It's okay." Susan rocked her back and forth, just like when Brooke was a little girl.

The situation looked glum. Two officers approached the trio, to get their take on the matter. Apparently, Kelsey had been thrown out of the vehicle because she had removed her seat belt to tend to Christine, from what the police could guess. Her left leg was broken, possibly shattered.

Michael gave them his own assessment on the family. "I feel certain that Kelsey has a concussion and internal bleeding, though it wasn't absolutely obvious from the short assessment I did. Kelsey was tossed, I'm guessing, at least twenty feet, so I know that things could be very bad for her. The good news is that she didn't seem to have become paralyzed because I tested her reflexes and they were working fine."

The men thanked him and moved back to the injured couple.

Brooke asked Michael, "What happens now?"

"The paramedics will arrange for them to be airlifted to Shock Trauma in the University of Maryland Medical Center." He hesitated. "Brooke, I don't know if they will survive." He reached over and hugged her. "I'm so sorry."

They overheard the trucker tell a police officer that he had seen his light turn green from fifty yards back and had not slowed down as he approached the intersection. "I'm so sorry officer. I didn't see the van until it was too late to stop. My light was green. I swear, it was green."

"Yes, sir. Thank you for your statement." The policeman conferred with his colleagues.

Susan and her companions stayed with the children's bodies while the police pieced together what had happened. Sometime later, the trio was free to go. They left the scene in stunned silence. Their conversation about the accident and injuries was very stilted as they made the ride home. What had happened was incomprehensible.

Michael helped the two women into Brooke's condo. Shock had set in and they weren't thinking straight. Susan felt very fuzzy and she noticed Brooke was dazed.

Michael said, "Let's all grab some showers, and then I'll pick you up and we'll go to Joshua's house. Be back in thirty minutes." He started to walk out.

Susan grabbed his arm and said, "No, we need to go there right now. I don't know why you brought us here. What was I thinking? We should have gone straight to Joshua's."

Michael replied, "No, Susan, we're covered in blood. We'll scare Joshua's kids, and everyone else. I'll be back soon. Go get showers, both of you."

Brooke told him, "Michael we need to get to the hospital or call Joshua or something. I don't know."

Michael comforted Brooke, saying, "Kurt and Kelsey will be in triage, so we can't get in to see them right away. It could be hours. We'll head to Joshua's after we all shower. I'll call Joshua on my way home and give him the *Reader's Digest* condensed version, like your mom always says. I promise, I'll be back soon and take you wherever you want to go. Deal?"

Susan and Brooke nodded. He hugged the women and left.

"Momma?" Brooke seemed to have become a child again.

"Yes, dear?" She looked at her blood-stained daughter.

"Are they gonna...die?" Brooke began to cry again.

"Oh, honey, I don't know. It doesn't look good...maybe." She hugged her beloved daughter tightly. They were both crying again.

Brooke began to sob even harder at the thought of losing her father, despite the kind of man he had turned out to be. Brooke stumbled into the kitchen for a glass of water.

"I just always thought Dad would be there..."

"Honey, you really haven't faced death, except for when your grandparents died...but that was such a long time ago. You haven't seen anything like this before." Susan brushed Brooke's soggy hair out of her face. "Let's get some showers and then go see Joshua and Christopher. We really need to tell them what happened."

"Michael said he would be back in thirty minutes. He'll drive us over."

"Good. I'm not sure either one of us could make the trip without him."

"He's a good man, Mama."

"Yes, he is, Brooke." Susan hugged her daughter again for a few moments and thanked God for the young woman, and for Michael.

By the time Michael returned, they were almost ready to leave. Michael had called Joshua, as he had promised, to let them know about the accident. They agreed to meet up at Joshua's house and then have a caravan to Shock Trauma, where Kurt and Kelsey had been taken. While time was of the essence, they knew that the couple would have to be triaged before the family could visit, so it was not vital that they rush.

Once the trio arrived at Joshua's, Susan gave them a shortened version of the events of the previous days. She also told them about the horrific accident that had taken the girls' lives and that now threatened their father's and Kelsey's lives.

Joshua and Christopher seemed skeptical about what had happened, but they were eager to see their father, so they hurried Susan through the tale. Joshua did seem to be softening towards her given Brooke's and Michael's testimony, Susan felt, but Christopher remained adamant that his father was merely misunderstood. *I'm glad Joshua finally understands, at least a little, but what about Christopher? What can he possibly be thinking in the face of this evidence? I just don't know my own son.*

The family and Michael caravanned to Shock Trauma in the University of Maryland Medical Center, with Joshua and Christopher riding together and Susan, Brooke, and Michael

241

following behind. Amanda thought it best to remain home with the kids, planning on telephoned updates from Joshua. Brooke and her brothers went in to see their dad, but the men asked Susan to remain in the waiting room with Michael. She noticed Brooke's apologetic glance back at her, but Susan stayed behind without a word. Now was not the time to assert her independence. Michael brought her a cup of tea and took up residence in a nearby chair. He reached over and took her free hand. "Mrs. Prescott, things will work out. Have faith."

"I know, Michael. Thanks so much for being here with me." She asked Michael, who was a gentle man to pray with her.

"Sure thing. God in heaven, we come before you now, humbled by what we have witnessed this afternoon. Thank you, Lord, for protecting Mrs. Prescott from those who would do evil to her. Thank you for upholding her in Your righteous right hand. Father, we pray for those precious babies that went to be with You this afternoon. Thank you that they are whole and saved and in Your presence right now. Thank you, Father, for that. Oh, Lord God, we lift up Kurt and Kelsey to you right now. Lord, these two people have lost their way. They have gone astray and have not known You. Oh Lord God, it breaks our hearts to know that, if they were to pass on right now, they would not spend eternity with you. Lord, no matter what they have done, we lift them up before You right this moment. We pray for healing, if it is part of Your almighty plan. We pray for their salvation. We pray for them to feel Your presence in their lives. We know, Lord God, that it is not Your will that anyone should perish. We pray that You will help us to be good witnesses for You. We thank you and we praise you. In Jesus' name. Amen."

"Amen." Susan looked up. "Thank you, Michael."

Just then, Brooke and her brothers came back into the waiting room. Susan rushed to her side. Michael also came nearby.

Brooke said, "Mom, we could only see Dad for a few minutes. They're taking Dad to ICU. Kelsey is doing okay, all things considered, so they're putting her in a step-down room. They told us to go home. They'll call me if we need to make a trip back. It's getting late. Let's go home."

Neither brother spoke. Joshua gave Susan a quick but affectionate hug. Christopher's A-frame embrace was considerably shorter. They mumbled their goodbyes and headed out. Susan left with Brooke and Michael very soon thereafter. What could be said? Nothing, I suppose. She determined that she would return the next morning. Alone. Freed from the restraints of Kurt's overbearing personality. For now, a bed at Brooke's condo would be a welcome respite from the drama of the past few days.

Chapter 20

Susan read the full emailed police report the next day as she sat eating breakfast in Brooke's kitchen. Susan read the police report. Kurt had tried to swerve to avoid a head-on collision with the eighteen-wheeler, once he had seen it, but had been unsuccessful and got T-boned instead. The huge truck crossed through the intersection and demolished their van. From what the doctors at the hospital told her when she called them first thing that morning, he was not expected to survive his injuries. He was lying in intensive care with so many physical problems that they hardly knew where to begin to put him back together. She got up to wash her dishes.

Susan suddenly sagged onto the countertop at the thought of him dying. What did she feel? It was hard to tell, since he'd been so mean to her for so long. She tried to sort things out in her mind but felt like she was hitting a stone wall. Was she sorry for him? Certainly. Did she pity him? Yes. But would she be sad if he did die and was no longer around? To be perfectly honest, she wouldn't mourn him at all. At least, she didn't think she would. Well, maybe a little. What about his mistress? Kelsey was expected to survive because her injuries were deemed serious but non-life threatening. It suddenly struck her that she needed to visit the couple. Where did that come from? It must be a God thing because she certainly couldn't have dreamed it up on her own. Okay, Lord, if that's what you want.

Susan decided to go see Kelsey first at Shock Trauma, taking a cab because she no longer had a car. Kurt had demolished her vehicle in the accident many months before and hadn't replaced it. In light of what had happened, she thought it best to wear a simple black sheath dress, to play down how she actually looked better than Kelsey did, for once in her life. And, of course, because of the girls. Susan sobbed over the little girls' lost lives. Very sad.

Susan called Nancy while she got ready to leave Brooke's condo. Nancy was back from her vacation with Patrick but had not yet returned to work. Nancy had been surprised- make that flabbergasted- to learn that Susan was no longer at the Chesapeake Center. The news of what had transpired while she was out of town made her absolutely insist that Susan meet her for lunch. Their phone chat was relatively brief, for them. Susan put her dear friend on speakerphone.

"Susan, you have to tell me everything, from the start." Nancy's voice was insistent, to say the least.

"Well, I don't remember a lot of the earlier stuff because I was drugged." Susan sat on the edge of her bed and slipped into her shoes. She walked across the room, to get some jewelry.

"Who did it to you?" The sound of a dishwasher slamming shut came through the phone.

"Rumor has it, and according to the video recordings that Brooke and Michael saw, that it was a CNA named Jada. Do you know her?" Susan put in her earrings- her mother's set that Kurt had refused to let her wear so many years before. She had given the earrings to Brooke several years before, so they had escaped the fate of her other jewelry. Brooke gave them back, recently. Things are changing, Kurt. You'd better hang onto your hat. Susan didn't care if he liked her earrings or not. A little defiance was a good thing, even if he was too injured to notice her earlobes. *She* knew the earrings were there, and that was what was important. Put that in your pipe and smoke it, Kurt Prescott.

245

"Don't I ever. It's a good thing I wasn't around when she did it or I would have punched her lights out. Where is she now? Do you know?" More rummaging around was going on at Nancy's, and she wasn't being very quiet about it.

"No, but, Nancy, I don't have time to go through the whole story on the phone. How about if we have lunch at the hospital? I can be there in about forty minutes. Shall we say, the cafeteria at 11:30?"

"Well, for starters, the University of Maryland Medical Center's cafeteria is not known for its delicious cuisine... But why are you going to the hospital, Susan? Are you okay?" Nancy's voice was full of concern and the background noise suddenly ceased. "Susan?"

"Yes, dearest Nancy, I am fine, more or less. A tad tired, but none the worse for wear... I'm going to see Kelsey and Kurt. They're both in bad shape."

"You're going to do what? Are you nuts, Susan? You're going to see the man who tried to kill you at least three times that we know of and his mistress? Why in the world would you do that?" Nancy appeared to be ready to jump through the phone, judging by the sound of her voice.

"Because they need me to." Susan sat back down on the bed. Perhaps she was more tired than she thought. She shook her head. No, I'm going, and that's all there is to it.

"Susan, are you out of your mind? I totally disagree." Nancy's dishwasher got one more slam and started up.

"Nope, I'm not crazy, Nancy. I held their daughters in my arms as they died. I need to see them both. I owe it to them, and I will do it." She stood, determined.

"Let me at least come with you. We can go right after lunch."

"Okay, Nancy, you can stand in the hallway while I go into their rooms... I would actually appreciate your being there. I'm not sure what to say to either one of them, but I feel that I must go."

246

"Yes, I don't want you to go alone. Does Brooke know about this?"

Susan could tell that Nancy was very worried about her. "No. Brooke is at work- she's got an important case and couldn't take any more time off. I didn't tell anyone I was going. Please don't call her. I promise I'll tell her later." She strode out of the room and headed downstairs. She was going to see this through.

"How will you get to Shock Trauma?"

"Taxi. The car will be here in a few minutes. I shouldn't be driving yet, and I know it. Besides, I don't have a car anymore, thanks to the accident that Kurt and I had. The accident that was no accident, as it turned out." Susan applied her lipstick and made sure there were tissues in her purse. She was going to need them. No doubt about that. She clicked the purse shut.

"Okay, well, I'll meet you at Shock Trauma, and I'll drive you home afterwards, okay?"

"Yes, I'd appreciate that. This whole thing is emotionally draining, and I'll probably need your strength just to get back home."

"Uh, Susan, you are aware that I am 4'11" and ninety-eight pounds, right?"

"Oh, yes, I had noticed that, Nancy. I meant your emotional strength!" She found Nancy's comment so silly that she had to laugh. It was catching. A glance out the front window showed the taxi had arrived. "Gotta run, Nancy Beth. My taxi's here. Love you." Out the door she went.

They met in the medical center's lobby a short while later. Susan felt pretty anxious about what she was going to do, even questioning if she had the strength to do it.

"Nancy, could we maybe just have a cup of tea, and then have lunch after I see them? I don't really have much of an appetite right now."

"Sure thing. I don't understand why you're doing this, anyway."

Susan filled Nancy in on what had happened as they drank their tea in a quiet corner of the cafeteria- the drugging, kidnapping, and hotel stay. She shared how Brooke and Michael had tracked her down and rescued her from certain death at the eleventh hour.

"I didn't have anything really planned after getting out of that hotel room. I don't know...I guess I would have run down the stairs to the lobby, hoping that Kurt and Kelsey wouldn't have chased after me. I couldn't have waited for an elevator to show up, so the stairs would have been my only option. I did have my tennis shoes on, so I might have made pretty good time. But still, I shudder to think what might have been if Brooke and Michael hadn't been standing on the other side of the door right when they were."

"Susan, that is so scary... I doubt you would have had a second chance to escape."

"No, they would have kept a very close eye on me until they killed me, I imagine. This was a one-shot deal."

"Interesting choice of words, my friend."

Susan smiled, "If I'd made it out of the rooms, I would have been trying to get down seven flights of stairs faster than they could have. Of course, Kelsey would have probably stayed behind with the girls, but Kurt was furious, so who knows how fast he would have moved."

"Well, you would have had adrenaline on your side." Nancy was doing her usual job of comforting her.

"Oh, yes, running for my life *might* have made the difference in how fast I moved." They both laughed, then sobered up at the thought of her not making it. She thanked God for His watchful care, yet again, over her life. Tea over, they headed upstairs to Kelsey's room. They embraced. As agreed, Nancy stood outside in the hallway while she went in.

Susan slipped into Kelsey's hospital room. Susan was shocked by the young woman's appearance. In spite of a nurse's clean up job, Kelsey's face was blood red and swollen to the point where one eye was closed. Her hair had been partially shaved off, to accommodate the multiple stitches that marched across the top of her forehead. Her arms were bruised and her legs were wrapped in thick bandages, which were showing signs of seeping blood and pus. Susan was thankful it was a private room so that they could talk undisturbed, and so that another patient would not see how horrid Kelsey looked. Kelsey groaned, and turned towards her visitor. Recognizing Susan, she asked, "What in the world are you here for? To gloat?"

Susan walked towards Kelsey's bed and said, "No, I'm here to help. I know that you've lost two of the dearest people in the world to you, and I'd like to help you through your time of grief. I know what it is to lose someone you care about."

"What do you mean? Who have I lost? No one'll let me see the girls, but they're just in the children's ward." Kelsey's eyes were wild with fear. She began thrashing about in bed.

"Kelsey, didn't anyone..."

Two nurses entered as Susan spoke.

Kelsey yelled at them, "Get this mad woman outta here. She says my babies are dead. She's deranged."

The nurses silently shook their heads, then nodded at Susan. Susan realized that no one had had the courage to break the news to Kelsey about her daughters. Kelsey hadn't known that they were dead until that moment. Susan gulped, not wanting to break the news but knowing that she had gone too far to back out of the conversation. The nurses left the room.

"Kelsey, the girls didn't make it." Tears began filling her eyes. How horrid this must be for Kelsey, learning from the lips of her lover's wife that her babies had been killed.

"No, you're lying." Kelsey screamed from her bed. "When Kurt comes here, you'll see. He won't let you get away with this."

"Kelsey, I know this is hard to hear, but has anyone, anyone at all, told you that they are alive?" Tears began coursing down her cheeks. Her compassionate heart went out to the young mother, regardless of who had fathered the girls.

Kelsey seemed unable to speak. Then, in a small voice, "no." Her eyes were glassy, blinded by the tears in her eyes, flowing down her cheeks like the banks of an over-filled river. "NO!!! My babies!!!!! It can't be true. It can't. Liar!" Kelsey cried, wailed, and beat the bed where she lay. Kelsey bawled, crying out that Susan was wrong.

Susan waited, knowing that the news was devastating. Time went on, though she would later be unable to remember if it was thirty minutes or an hour that had passed since she had given Kelsey the news. Still, Susan waited, praying for the mother.

Finally exhausted, Kelsey's howling changed to silent sobs. Then, almost an eternity later, she choked out, "What . . . happened?"

"They were horribly injured, Kelsey. Christine was thrown from the car. I found her in the grass. She could hardly breathe when I got to her. I picked her up...she died a few minutes later. I heard Cassie screaming in the van. I went to her...she was bleeding from her neck. I heard this morning from the doctors that her internal injuries made survival... impossible."

"This can't be." Kelsey was stunned into silence, sobbing once more. She stared out into space. "No, I don't believe it."

Susan moved closer to the bedside. "Kelsey, I was with the girls when they...went away. They were both so hurt. I held them in my arms because you couldn't be there." She touched Kelsey's arm and sobbed...then, "I am so sorry." Susan wept.

Kelsey could not bear the news alone. She reached out to Susan, who went still closer to her and held the young mother in her arms as Kelsey wept uncontrollably. Moments...hours, perhaps, later, Kelsey got some measure of control back.

"Tell me...I have to know ... more."

With tears rolling down her face, Susan sat in the chair next to Kelsey's bed, and told the young mother about Christine's loss of consciousness. She shared the deaths, how Cassie had been yelling for her mother, and how Susan had gone to be with her in Kelsey's place.

"She wasn't alone, Kelsey. I was there, holding her as she...left us."

"No, no, tell me somehow that my girls live."

"They do live, Kelsey, but not on this earth."

Kelsey was quiet. Susan shared how she knew where the girls were. How Kelsey could one day be with her girls again. This was all information that Michael had told her as she recovered from her own injuries and coma. All the while, she knew she was the unloved wife of a husband who felt he no longer wanted to be with her. She also had the knowledge that her financial resources had been completely decimated by the man she had trusted. But her new faith had become her richest treasure. It had given her peace, she told Kelsey, and it passed all understanding. Kelsey could have it, as well.

Kelsey stammered a bit, sobbed occasionally, but mostly listened in stunned silence. Kelsey seemed amazed that Susan would take the time to come see her, especially with the huge role she had played in Susan's pain. Kelsey fiddled with her sheets and blanket. Susan waited.

"Why're you trying to help me? There's no reason why you should be here. No reason at all." Kelsey tried to shake her head, but was overcome by pain.

"Kelsey, I needed to come because I was with the girls when they died. I needed to share with you how I didn't have any strength to get through the things that happened to me, until I met Michael, and he told me about God and Jesus Christ. I suffered greatly at Kurt's hands...and at yours. But I found out that God loves me and that Jesus died for me. I could understand that. I knew that, no matter what Kurt or you or anybody else did to me, I had Jesus to depend on. That was the only thing that kept me sane."

"Why did your God let such bad things happen to you?" Kelsey sniffled. "Doesn't seem very nice to me. Why would God do that to you? To me?"

"Kelsey, I don't know why He allowed it, but I do know that I would never have met Him if He hadn't." Susan felt her face begin to glow at her discussion about the One who had never let her down. It was He who had held her hand silently in the midst of many years of a trying marriage, the horrible accident, the painful rehab, and the difficult rebuilding of her life. He had never left her or forsaken her, even when she hadn't known Him, hadn't known He was there.

It seemed that Kelsey could not look away from her. Susan knew she was a woman who had every right to hate Kelsey, but she somehow loved the young woman. How can I love Kelsey? This must be what Michael was saying about God's love. Even while we were sinners and the enemies of God, He loved us. Kelsey's shame was met by Susan's love. Incredible.

The injured woman began to wonder aloud what Kurt had ever seen in her, since he had had such an extraordinary woman as his wife. Susan shrugged her off, trying to keep the focus on Christ.

"It's not my doing. It's God's. Kelsey, do you want that kind of peace in your life?"

"Yes." Kelsey looked at Susan. "Yes, I do. I want what you have. Peace."

Susan stood and took Kelsey's hand in hers. "Let me tell you about God and His Son, Jesus Christ." Susan shared what Michael had told her when she was unsaved. She told Kelsey about God's great love and the sacrifice that Jesus had made to save people from their sins.

"I'm not sure I understand everything you're talking about, Susan." Kelsey moved uncomfortably in her bed.

"You don't need to know or understand it all, Kelsey. Here's what's important: Jesus is the Son of God. God sent Jesus to die for our sins. If we confess to Him that we are sinners in need of salvation . . ."

Kelsey squirmed, "No doubt about that, for sure."

"And if we ask Jesus to come into our hearts and lives and take control, He will save us. Does that make sense?"

"Yes."

"He will give you the peace that I was talking about that I have. I'm not the one who's incredible, Kelsey. God and Jesus Christ are."

"I want that."

"Then let me lead you in a prayer," Susan told her.

They prayed together. She understood that Kelsey would tire easily, so she hugged the bedridden woman and left a few minutes later.

"I'll come see you again, Kelsey." Susan smiled at her new sister. "Take care."

"Thank you, Susan." Kelsey settled back in her bed, still crying but appearing more hopeful.

Nancy hugged her as Susan exited. They talked as they walked down the hallway.

"So, from what I could hear, things were a bit antsy, there for a while. The nurses were concerned, but I waved them off. Then things calmed down a bit and seemed to go pretty well, all things considered." Nancy gave her arm a squeeze. "I really admire your willingness to go see her, Susan."

Susan told her, "I'm glad I went. I can't imagine losing my only children. She lost them both in a matter of minutes. I was the only one with her children when it happened, so I had to share their passing with her."

"So, what's next?" Nancy asked.

They had stopped briefly at the elevator. They were on the fifth floor and had to go to the third to see Kurt in ICU. Susan hesitated then spoke softly.

"Kurt."

"Susan, are you really going to go see the man who wanted you dead?"

"Yes, Nancy, I am. He's gravely injured. He might not survive. I don't imagine that his death will bother me, after all I've been through with him, but he was my husband for thirty-five years, and I need to say 'goodbye' if nothing else."

"You're a better woman than I am, Susan Prescott." They got on the elevator and pushed the third floor button.

"No, I don't think I am. I've been pretty angry at him. You didn't see me at the hotel in Vancouver. I was throwing everything at him that wasn't nailed down: dishes full of rotten food, marbles, knitting needles, glasses, cups, anything. I almost hit him over the head with a lamp. That might have killed him. I was swinging really hard until I came to my senses."

"You go, girl! Get the creep!" Nancy smiled at her.

"Yes, well, Nancy, I almost did!"

Their laughter was a release for her from the sorrow with Kelsey, and the tension of going to see Kurt. Susan relaxed a bit.

Nancy said, "I hadn't heard that part of the story from Michael."

Susan laughed. She said, "No? Well, it happened right before Brooke and Michael came in, but they could see the mess I made. We straightened things up as best we could before we left the hotel, but then I realized that the bill was on Kurt's credit card and said the 'heck with it. Let him pay for the cleanup.' For once, I wasn't going to straighten his mess. The creep wanted me dead. I wasn't going to save him a few dollars on his hotel bill."

"You have more gumption than I thought, Susan." Nancy hugged her.

They got off the elevator, turned left, then walked without speaking towards the receptionist stationed outside the ICU. The closed doors leading into the ICU were right ahead of them.

Susan took a big breath. Steady as she goes, Susan Margaret. She told the receptionist, "I...we are here for bed thirty-two."

"Name?" The woman waited, to check her list of patients.

"Mrs. Susan Prescott and Mrs. Nancy Ferguson for Kurt Prescott."

"You may enter but please talk with the charge nurse right in front of the room before entering the patient's room." They were buzzed in.

"Yes, of course." Susan nodded.

Susan and Nancy walked into the ICU, which was set up so that two rooms had one charge nurse whose desk was in front of the double sliding glass doors for each patient's cubicle. Each room had green striped curtains available for privacy. They noticed the curtains were a putrid shade of green, which matched the smell of blood, urine, and defecation that, mixed with the smell of cleaning fluid, permeated the area. Their nurses' sense of smell was on high alert the moment they stepped into the ICU. They made slight faces at one another. Someone who had been very, very sick had most likely passed that morning. Staff was still scurrying about, trying to rid the smell of death from the unit. Thus far, they had been unsuccessful.

There was a brief formality of proving who they were and being given details about visiting an intubated patient. Don't try to get him to talk, don't expect much out of the patient, don't stay too long, don't sit on the bed, and don't overtire the patient. In case of a crisis, they would have to leave pronto. They nodded their understanding. Another deep breath to calm her rattled nerves, then it was time to see her husband. Lord, give me courage.

Chapter 21

They looked into Kurt's room. Susan paused outside the room for several minutes. This was going to be harder than she thought. Much harder than seeing Kelsey, who she had expected would not want to see her, but to whom she had not pledged her life. She had made a vow to Kurt. He had chosen to break it. He did not love her. He had made obvious his utter distain for her. He wanted her to die so that he could be with Kelsey. These thoughts troubled her.

At the same time, part of her still wanted to be married to him. He couldn't just throw away thirty-five years of shared history, could he? Would she somehow be able to convince him that she was, even now, the woman for him? Maybe she could win him back. Maybe her sons were not so far gone that their relationships could be restored. Wait a minute! Was she insane? Why would she want to continue their relationship, especially given their latest history?

Yet, the same things that had drawn her to him so many years ago remained in her heart- he was her Kurt, after all. NO! No, he was not hers and hadn't been for years. There was no use pretending that somehow, some way, everything was going to be fine and dandy. He wasn't fine and there was no fantasizing that he would return, somewhat broken but understanding that they were meant to be together. He was not ever coming back to her. Realize that and accept it, Susan Margaret Thomas Prescott. Grow up, right now. No more la, la land.

Susan's heartbeat increased as she internalized her conflict. She felt her blood pressure rise. She broke out into a cold sweat. She wavered between going in the room and walking away forever.

Should she or shouldn't she? No one in the family would ever know if she chose to leave without visiting. They didn't know she was here and would never know unless she told them. She could change her mind, get a ride home from Nancy, and no one would ever be the wiser. She glanced at her friend.

Nancy waited with her. She squeezed Susan's shoulder, silent, head bowed and apparently praying. Nancy's left hand rested on her shoulders, and her right hand touched the crook of her arm. Nancy's half hug neither forced her to go in nor hindered her forward movement. It was simply there, waiting.

Susan squared her shoulders. She took a big breath; she released it. She willed her heart to stop racing. She shut her eyes and prayed for strength to get through the situation. "Lord, please help me." She calmed down, peace flowed around her. Yes, this was the right thing to do. She resolved to see the man she had loved for so many years. She opened her eyes. He was still there. It wasn't a dream.

At first, the ICU nurses hadn't wanted her to visit him. She would not have normally been allowed to see him, since she was his estranged wife. The expressions of the nearby nurses when she walked into ICU revealed that they knew her story through the medical grapevine. At least, they knew *part* of her story, the part that Brooke had shared with Kurt's doctors. Brooke told her what she had told them the night before. He had spitefully used and willfully abused her, so they probably couldn't understand why she was even there.

 Susan stood in the doorway of his glass-enclosed room. There were tubes everywhere and he was in and out of consciousness. His body was bloated and bloodied. His face was swollen almost beyond the point of recognition. His eyelids were black and blue. His matted hair was partially shaved off; an angry scar covered the left hand side of his head. She came a few steps into the cubicle and halted there, staring across the small room at this totally helpless man who had brought so much pain into her life.

The room seemed to collapse into a tunnel as she stared, with the end of the tunnel being her husband lying on the bed. The rest of the room was blurry, perhaps because of her tears. In the beginning, she was unable to talk. Her voice caught in her throat, almost seeming to strangle her. She gagged briefly at the sight of his bruised and bloated body. His eyes fluttered open and met hers. He tried to glare at her, but was too weak and injured. He could not speak for the intubation tube. She stood there, without speaking, for several minutes. Or it could have been several hours. Time moved away from her. Thoughts of the past thirty-five years filled her mind in sequence. She could not stop them; she did not stop them. She walked closer to Kurt's bed, touched his hand, and simply said, "I forgive you."

She gazed at him one last time, knowing she would never return to his side, that she would never see him again. She patted, then squeezed his hand. Tears flowed down her face as she turned and walked out the door. Immediately, Nancy met her outside the room and hugged her as the astonished nurses looked on. The two visitors left the ICU and headed for the elevator.

Nancy took Susan's arm and led her to the medical center's cafeteria, where they bought a couple of salads and some sweet iced tea. Nancy had insisted that Susan must eat something.

"You probably haven't eaten all day, and it's way past lunchtime. I don't want you fainting on my watch. Sit and eat," Nancy told her.

They took seats at a table in the corner, hoping for some privacy. Since it was no longer the lunchtime rush, the remote table offered them a retreat. Susan's bottled up anxiety spilled forth like a torrent. She told Nancy everything she could remember about Kurt's condition, and how he looked, in spite of the fact that Nancy had been able to see into the glass-enclosed room that housed Kurt. Nancy let her talk.

"Nancy, when I saw him lying there with all those tubes and looking so bruised and bloodied, something in me broke. My heart went out to him. I don't know what I had planned on saying-whatever it was, I forgot everything but the need to forgive him. Why do you suppose that was?"

"Susan, you are still what we call a 'baby Christian,' but I believe that God wanted you to forgive Kurt so that you could move on and grow. You were never a really bad person, but you were a sinner, and God forgave you. You needed to forgive Kurt. And you did." Nancy reached for her hand and squeezed it. "I am so proud of you. You have done what I couldn't."

"Nancy, my life with Kurt wasn't all bad. Why, I remember when we lived in Connecticut. We were pretty active in the kids' schools. Kurt used to get all dressed up in his Service Dress Blues and take Brooke to "Tea with Daddy and Me" parties at school. He would look so dreamy and she would wear the fanciest frilly dress she owned. I would comb her hair and put in pretty bows, put on her necklace and bracelets and newest white socks and her patent leather shoes. You should have seen the two of them heading out the door!"

"One time after we moved back to Annapolis, Christopher got a classroom assignment with something called 'Flat Stanley.' The idea was that the children were to send this brown construction paper gingerbread man to friends and family who were supposed to photograph Flat Stanley in various locations. We all really got into the project, even though it was very time-consuming. We got into the car and drove that little gingerbread boy all around Annapolis, laughing and taking pictures of Flat Stanley everywhere we could think to put him. It was Kurt's idea to take him to the Eastern

Shore and to Washington, DC. It took us a full weekend to get all the shots we wanted to get. We all had the best time, laughing, and driving all over the place. We sent Flat Stanley to all of our relatives, who took turns photographing him in different states before sending him back to us. We had a whole album of pictures for Christopher to turn in. It was so much fun!" She beamed as she told Nancy about it.

Susan continued: "When the boys got involved with sailing, and started to race their sailboats in the Annapolis Yacht Club regattas, we would both be there, cheering them on. We would spend the whole day watching them sail and then we'd take them home for showers and a game night. The kids would be in their jammies, and I would make a huge bowl of popcorn that kept us company as we played Monopoly. Those were the days!"

Her thoughts turned to the children as teens. "Kurt was a good father and husband, usually. Yes, he had his Viet Nam demons... they gave him nightmares and the occasional short temper...well, a short temper a lot, but our lives weren't all bad. We watched the children grow. The first time Joshua drove, Kurt was right beside him, looking so proud. He was there to comfort Joshua when he and Brooke were involved in an accident. Brooke was so upset- screaming, really loud, actually- but Kurt went to get the kids. Joshua told me later how nice Kurt had been about his banging up Kurt's car. Kurt hadn't given him a bad time, just hugged on them both when he realized they were both okay. I had stayed home with Christopher, who was just a little fellow, so that he wouldn't see the kids, if they were hurt."

"Kurt has always been a good provider. I've never wanted for anything. We never starved, and he never went out and gambled or drank our income away or anything. I know women who have done a lot worse." Susan hesitated. "Has our life been perfect? No.

Has he always been a good husband? No. But I really did love him, and I think he, in his own way, loved me."

Nancy hadn't spoken the whole time she was talking, she just listened. Susan really appreciated that ability of Nancy- to just listen and not judge.

"So, Susan, what do you want to do from here?" Now that the torrent of words was over, Nancy asked and then took a sip of her tea. So did Susan.

"I didn't plan on ever seeing him again, once I left his room today. But I want to minister to him, if he'll let me. I know that he'll probably leave me for Kelsey once they get out of the hospital, but he is still my husband...does that sound insane? I know it must." She put down her cup and shook her head. Had she really said that? She wanted to minister to Kurt?

"Susan, I think you need to face the fact that he might not be coming home, wherever he chooses that to be." Nancy reached over and squeezed her hand.

"Does he seem that bad off to you, Nancy? I mean, I've been a nurse, so I've seen some things but I was a nurse in a doctor's office attached to the Anne Arundel Medical Center. We mostly dealt with runny noses and the flu. Don't know if I'm up to it, but I want to try."

Nancy said, "I think it's a real possibility that he's going to die. You need to face that fact. You also need to face the reality that he might not decide in your favor, if he does make it out of here."

Chapter 22

After his bothersome wife left her message, Kurt slipped into sleep, having a very strange dream. A very tall, brown-haired man dressed in radiant white entered his room. That was weird! The man seemed to come in through the wall. Kurt didn't recognize him, though the man greeted him by name.

"Hello, Kurt." The man walked further into the room but still remained near the door.

"Who are you...wait a minute, I can't talk. I'm on a ventilator." He twisted and turned in the bed, suddenly able to move. "What the...?"

"That's one advantage of dreams, Kurt. You can talk right now, though you can't get out of bed."

"Well, if I can talk to you, I can jolly well get out of bed. Just watch me." He tried to rise but found himself bedbound. Seriously? Get me out of here.

"No, Kurt, you can't get up because I don't want you to." The man stepped closer to him but was still several feet away.

"Well, we'll see about that...hey, what's wrong with my legs? They aren't working!" Kurt began flailing around in the bed, only able to move the top part of his body. Am I paralyzed? No, I can feel my feet. I just can't move them.

"Like I said, you can't get out of bed right now because we need to talk, and I want your full and undivided attention."

"I demand you let me up!" Kurt tried to thrash around in bed again, but nothing would cooperate. His arms and legs wouldn't cooperate. What in the world was going on?

"You aren't in a position to demand anything, Kurt." The man spoke quietly but with authority.

"Who are you?" Kurt was very angry over his loss of control. Why was his body not working right? What right did this guy have to barge into his room uninvited? How dare he?

"My name is Thomas. In case you're wondering, no, you don't know me, but I do know you."

"What do you want? Why are you here? Tell me and then get the heck out of here."

"I was asked to come." Thomas smiled at him and moved closer to him. Now he was standing at the foot of Kurt's bed.

"By who? Who told you to visit me?" His visitor's kind countenance really bugged him!

"Michael and Susan made a special request."

"I might have guessed that annoying black guy from the nursing home and my equally annoying soon-to-be ex-wife had something to do with this." Kurt pulled himself into a curled up snit at the thought of Michael and Susan having anything to do with this man's presence.

"Susan will be a widow before she is ever an ex-wife. That 'annoying black guy' has been praying for your recovery, so don't count him out yet."

"I want nothing to do with either of them, so you might as well leave." Kurt tried to turn his back on Thomas; he was unsuccessful. He still couldn't move. What was it with this sudden paralysis? What gives here?

"That's not your call, Kurt. For once in your life, you have no choice about my being here. Shall we get my visit over with by getting on with it?"

Kurt waved his hand for a reply. Hey, at least my hand works! "So, what do you want?" He couldn't get rid of this fellow fast enough.

"I want to talk with you about some decisions you have made." Thomas was at the side of his bed now, which made Kurt uneasy.

"If you must. Go on, then." Maybe by pretending to go along with Thomas, Kurt could get rid of him sooner. He smirked, certain that the man wouldn't have much to say. He always considered his decisions with care, plotting things out as if life were lived on a chess board. How else had he won the game as he moved and counter-moved against his sniveling wife?

"You mistreated your wife Susan for many years, turning the hearts of her sons against her." Thomas spoke quietly but firmly.

Thomas's comments were not fresh news to him, but he was uncomfortable at the man's insight into his character. He jumped to his own defense. "She wasn't what she pretended to be! Everyone thought she was the perfect wife, but I knew the truth- she had an illegitimate son. She had no right to pretend she had been married."

"Susan was very sorry for a childish mistake she had made. She trusted you to love her."

"She had to pay. I bought damaged goods when I got her for my wife." He shrugged. Susan had gotten what she deserved, nothing more or less.

"Yet you knew ahead of time that she had made a judgement error- you had Susan investigated before you even proposed. It wasn't like you didn't know. She confessed her sin before you got engaged."

"That was simply good management on my part. Know the competition and all that. It gave me a foot up in keeping my wife on the straight and narrow." He felt pride at his brilliance.

"It gave you ammunition to hold over her head."

"That, too. A guy can't be too careful. Gotta keep your wife in line and under your thumb."

"In your heart and under your protection would have been better." Thomas did not smile at the words.

"That's not the way I operate." What was it with this man? How did he know all this stuff? Kurt wanted to get rid of this dude. The sooner, the better.

"Not how you operate? That is certain, Kurt. But let's move on. Through the years, you reminded her of her dependence on you yet, when she aged, you didn't want her."

"She was boring. She was getting saggy. She worked out, but it didn't help much. I was tired of her. There are millions of women more interesting, younger, and prettier than she was."

"You shouldn't have been noticing."

"Hey, a guy has the right to look. If your wife isn't living up to your expectations, you have every right to move on. That's all I did. There's nothing wrong with replacing a wife whose old and worn out." Kurt nodded his agreement with himself.

"But, Kurt, one reason she was so 'worn out' as you say is because you mistreated her."

"Tough stuff. I'm the guy. I do what I like, no matter what Susan thinks." No woman was going to get the better of him. No, sir!

"So you moved on."

"Yes. Have you seen Kelsey? She is one stunning woman! Young, interesting, everything that Susan isn't." He smiled at the memory of his mistress.

"Well, you might be right that she isn't Susan, but that isn't necessarily a good thing."

"When I get out of here, I'm going back to a great life with the woman I love. That woman is NOT Susan Prescott. Not on your life! No thanks, if that's what you're selling."

"I'm not selling anything, Kurt. I'm not a salesman. I do have something you can have for free, if you want it."

"What's that, big man?" He felt on top of things, now. This fellow was not going to out-smart Kurt Prescott!

"New life in Jesus Christ."

"Nope, not for me. I decided years ago that the 'holier than thou' life is not my cup of tea." He threw up his hands to dismiss the whole idea. No way! There's no God and that's the bottom line. These goodie-two-shoes Christians were not for him. Not on your life. He had done quite well for himself, in his book. Who needs God?

"Your choice, Kurt. But I'm not in the tea business, anyway." Thomas smiled.

Kurt thought Thomas seemed rather amused by their interchange. "Look, I like my life. I'm rich, I have a beautiful wife-to-be and two gorgeous little girls. All I need is to get back on my feet and Susan Prescott is history." Yep, definitely on top of the world again. The current circumstances he found himself in were a mere inconvenience. A temporary situation. Nothing to be concerned about, long term.

"You have money that you stole from your wife Susan. You have a woman, who is not your wife, lying injured in a hospital bed on two floors away, and two little girls in heaven."

"What? What do you mean? Cassie and Christine....."

"They didn't make it, Kurt. They died at the scene of the accident."

He was silent for a moment. For once, he didn't know what to say. "Well, Kelsey and I will have more children, then. It's sad but nothing we can't overcome." The whole dead-children-in-heaven idea was already dismissed. He would take care of it. Problem solved.

"Kelsey's injures mean no more pregnancies, Kurt. She is unable to have any more children. She would be unable to carry the pregnancy to term. The two babies she had are all she ever will have."

"Then we'll take up traveling around the world. She'll be sad for a while but I'm all she needs. She's resilient. She's young and can serve me the rest of her life." Okay, this is not ideal. I hope Kelsey won't be a pain in the neck with this grief stuff. If so, she's easily replaced. Plenty of young things will find me attractive. Well, maybe not right now, but later.

"Kurt, you really don't get it, do you?"

"Get what? What are you saying?" Thomas was starting to get on his nerves.

"You have lived your life as a liar and a cheat. The woman you love no longer resembles the woman she was two days ago. On top of that, your children with her are dead. You are in serious condition and might not live. You have twisted the minds of your adult sons..."

"Wait a minute, here. Only one of those boys is my real son. The other one is as fake as his mother." He had already decided that Joshua had been a drain on his energy long enough. He was history, just like his mother. He thought that Joshua was starting to see things from his mom's point of view, at least to some degree. That would never do. Joshua might turn Christopher from him. Maybe it was Joshua's wife Amanda who had started feeding Joshua the idea that Susan might not be as horrid as he had led Joshua to believe. He would watch and wait and dump the stepson he had not fathered when the time came. He only needed Christopher, anyway. And Kelsey, of course.

"Joshua doesn't know that his parents were never married."

"He will, if I have anything to say about it. It's time he knew that I only have one son- Christopher." He had been more than a father; he had been a living ATM. He had kept track of all the money Joshua had cost him through the years. It was time for a little pay-back in his book. Maybe the birth father could be found and hit up for a little cash- to keep feathering the nest he had with Kelsey. It was worth considering, anyway. A little embarrassment for the deadbeat dad...this could get financially rewarding. Kurt smiled at the thought of more cash for a kid he had raised. Yep, this might pay off big time!

"And what about Brooke?"

Kurt snorted. "I haven't had anything to do with her since she saw Kelsey and me in the Bahamas. That's no loss- she's just like her mother." He shrugged off his daughter. Unfortunate, but he could do without her. Christopher was the important offspring, in his mind.

"Kurt, you really **are** fouled up beyond all recognition, aren't you?" Thomas stood beside him, shaking his head.

"I'm not messed up- I see everything very clearly. If anyone's messed up, it's you." What did this man think he was? His conscience or something? Where did Thomas get off, confronting him? The nerve!

Another man, shorter than Thomas and dark-haired, dressed completely in black, entered the room through the wall. "Hello, boys."

Thomas turned to look at the newest entrant into the ICU cubicle. Thomas said, "Hello, Damian."

"Oh, boy, another persuader, I assume?" Kurt was getting very angry. What was it, with these guys coming in through walls? Did they misunderstand the use of doors?

Damian said, "Oh, no, Kurt, my work with you is almost done. I haven't had to persuade you of anything you weren't already totally on board with." To Thomas: "I see you couldn't do anything with him. You should have given up before you even came in the room. Kurt and I have been working together for years. You didn't have a chance." Damian smiled. His teeth were yellow, slimy.

Kurt had never seen such a creepy smile in all his life. Damian approached his bed. He wished the fellow would keep his distance.

Thomas said, "There's always hope."

Damian replied, "Not in this case. He's too much 'in' to ever listen to you and your pathetic offerings." The man laughed.

Okay, now that's a strange laugh. It reminds me of the weird laughs in those old horror films. Better pay attention. Who knows what this guy is up to? What about the smell? The room had taken on the scent of burning....what was that? Flesh? Gross! At the same time, Kurt was almost livid. "Hey, guys, I **am** here, you know. What are you talking about? Who are you Damian? What's this 'in' business, Damian... if that's really your name."

Damian said, "Oh, yes, Kurt, that's really my name. You and I have had many conversations, though you weren't aware of it. It was my idea to have Susan investigated so many years ago. I have guided your mistreatment of her for all of your marriage. You listened to me completely and bought into everything I said." Damian stretched as if to relive himself of a burden. "Oh, it has been so sweet to watch you work, Kurt. You're good."

"What? I don't know what you are talking about. I never laid eyes on you before."

"You didn't have to see me; you just had to listen, Kurt. And listen you did. Every mean and hateful comment that you spoke to her. Every time you locked yourself away in your study to ignore her for the evening, I was right there with you. As you spent your evenings on Skype with Kelsey, I encouraged you and you always listened." Damian laughed again, and drew closer.

"No, I wanted to talk to Kelsey." This guy needs to back off a bit. Go away, buddy! He was repulsed by him. At least Thomas smelled nice.

"Yes, you certainly did. I helped you figure out how to cheat your comatose wife out of house and home and you bought into

270

it fully. And all those murder attempts? My ideas completely." Damian laughed.

Thomas said, "I think he's had enough, Damian." To Kurt: "So, Kurt, what will it be? New life with Christ or the future with Damian and his buddies?" Thomas waited.

"I don't know. I need to think about this." Anything to get both of these weirdos out of his room! Buy some time, yes, that's the thing to do.

Damian said, "Sure thing, Kurt. Take all the time you need." He smiled. Yellow teeth protruded from his mouth. Disgusting.

This guy was giving him the heebie-jeebies. Go away, both of you. "Yes, time would be nice. I'll get back to you." Kurt tried to smile but it didn't work. He was actually a bit scared, the truth be known.

"Damian, I said that was enough. The man didn't even know you existed a few minutes ago and here you are dumping his whole life in his lap." Thomas moved closer to him. Kurt was glad the man was there.

"Kurt, I'll be around, buddy." Damian treated him to one more smile then turned away.

"I'm no buddy of yours!" He said it to Damian's back. Suddenly, the man was gone, vanished. Totally weird. Good riddance!

"Sorry about that, Kurt. Damian has a tendency to show up at the most inopportune moments."

"Yeah, you can say that again." Kurt wiggled, trying to remove the feel of Damian from the room. It didn't help much. The stench lingered.

Thomas seemed to relax a bit. Thomas sat down on the bed, but Kurt felt no pressure from the man's weight on the bed. This is so peculiar!

Thomas continued, "Okay, Kurt, so you need to decide what you want for the rest of your life. Do you want to ask forgiveness from God, from Susan and your family and be reunited or do you want to keep going your own way? There are only two choices here."

"I, uh...I don't know. Like I said, I need to think about it." Time for Thomas to move on. Let him go bother some other poor schmuck!

"You're running out of time to think, Kurt. You're in what humans call the 'put up or shut up" time of life."

"No, I have to think about this. I don't want to make a hasty decision. I need to think about my options." Anything to get Thomas out of here!

"You only have two options, Kurt. And you really do need to decide." Thomas's smile seemed somewhat sad to him.

Too bad, buddy, you don't get a recruit today! "I'll think about it and get back to you...How's tomorrow sound?" Kurt gave the man one of his condescending smiles. Charm always worked before; that might be the way to go here.

"I think it sounds like a horrible idea." Thomas looked distressed at his decision to not decide anything; the visitor rose to his feet. Good, he's almost out of here. Keep going, Thomas! Shoo.

"Well, like it or not, that's what you've got. That's my option for **you**, Thomas." Kurt smirked at Thomas's discomfort.

"As you wish, Kurt. I tried." The large man started to turn away when Kurt stopped him.

"Hey, how about showing me your wings? I'm guessing that you are an angel or something. How about a little wingspan viewing? I am a pilot, after all." Kurt was very amused at his own sense of humor. This was starting to be fun, but the man needed to hit the road.

Thomas looked around and then shook his head. "Kurt, this tiny cubicle could not hold my wingspan. Goodbye. I don't know if we will ever meet again." Thomas turned and headed for the wall. He vanished.

"Goodbye." And good riddance. He awoke, eagerly awaiting his next pain medication. Whew, I'm so glad that was just a dream! That was eerie. I'm glad none of it was real. I have plenty of time. This is just a temporary condition; these tubes and pain and hospital stay will be over soon. Kelsey and I can get back to our lives. That will be sweet! He was ready for this all to be over. It would be shortly, he felt certain. Hold on Honey, I'm coming home!

Kurt was right about one thing: It was over shortly.

Chapter 23

Two mornings later, Kelsey lay in her bed, drifting in and out of consciousness. She felt so blue. Her kids and lover were all dead-the nurses had come in to her room and told her that Kurt had died during emergency surgery. Funny thing, she wasn't as upset at his passing as she thought she *should* have been. Or maybe, as upset as she thought she *would* have been. Why don't I care? That seems so strange. I would have done anything for him, but now I just feel...empty. Numb.

Her life didn't seem worthwhile. Kelsey didn't know where to turn, who to talk to. She threw herself about on the bed, then regretted any fast movements. "Oww....blast it all." At the same time, she was unable to get comfortable with these new thoughts that were flying through her brain. She was uncomfortable in both mind and body. Her injures made it hard to move, and the medication she was on wore off before the next dose. The bed was so...hospital-like, the pillow was not like the one she had at home, her pathetic hospital-issued blue/gray nightgown was bunching up in all the wrong places, and she wanted a shower more than anything. Mid-day television was horrid. How did people watch that stuff, really? Most of all, right now, she hated her life.

It was fine to pray with Susan. Kelsey had been glad for the comfort that brought, but she had no idea where to go from here. She had no friends, no family that wanted anything to do with her. She hadn't worked in years, though she did have plenty of money- she and Kurt had planned well in that respect. But it was no comfort to her now. She sobbed intermittently throughout the never-ending hours. Pain and misery were her life now. She felt soul-sapping sadness over the deaths of her children, a deep longing to have a happy future, and complete regret over the actions she had taken. What was she to do?

As she was coasting off to sleep yet again, she became aware of someone's presence in the corner of her room. A very tall blonde man, dressed in a radiant white shirt and pants was standing there, looking at her with love. What compassionate eyes! She didn't recognize him. Had they met? Maybe in a bar or at one of her many boyfriends' numerous parties? No, she didn't think so. He didn't look like the bar type.

"Who are you? What do you want?" Kelsey mumbled towards him, in the midst of her deep depression and sadness. He didn't look like a creep, but you never know. Just looking towards him made her neck hurt.

"Hello, Kelsey. My name is Andrew." The man looked at her with great compassion, but not pity. No man had ever looked at her like that before. He wasn't hitting on her, she felt certain.

"Do I know you?" Who was he? One of the bartenders at that restaurant she and Kurt had visited on one of their trips? Likely not. Again, not the type.

"No, we've never met, but I know you." Andrew came out of the corner, and walked towards her bed. He stopped a few feet away.

"Get outta here or I'll call the nurse." She was very nervous about the guy. She fumbled in the bedding. Where was that call button? Oh, it's on the bedside table.

"Fear not. Kelsey, it's okay. I'm not here to hurt you. I'm here to help."

She started to reach for the call button, but then decided to humor the man. He wanted to help her? Well, maybe she could use a little assistance here. Okay.

"What'd you want? Andrew, was it?"

275

First, she was scared. Then she felt a little uneasy. This is so strange- what gives with me? Then he began walking towards her again. Okay, scared again. She drew away from him.

"Yes, Kelsey. Andrew. We need to talk. Undisturbed."

She tried to call out but her voice didn't cooperate. A squeak came out, but not loud enough for anyone to hear her. "Help..." No real volume. "Help, nurse..." Nothing that would reach the hallway...what could she do? He was closer still!

"Like I said, my name is Andrew. Mind if I sit down?"

He sat on the edge of her bed but, though she saw him do it, his body did not create any weight on the mattress. There was no indention.

Oh, this was so bizarre! What's going on here? Yet, at the same time, she felt a sense of peace now that he was closer. Humm . . . "What do you want?"

"I've been asked to talk with you, indirectly speaking."

"I have no idea what you're talking about. Who asked you to talk to me? Why?" She was, once again, somewhat unnerved by the man and his closeness. She needed to get rid of him, pronto. Yep, that should be her course of action.

"Susan. She and Michael have been praying for you ever since the accident and my Boss told me to come and visit with you for a while." He was very relaxed, in comparison to her obvious discomfort.

"What? Why?" Keep him talking till someone comes by. Sooner would be better than later. Come on, nurse, where the heck are you?

"Because you need what He has to offer. Susan has already told you about God. I know you prayed to receive Christ. That's wonderful." He smiled.

What a glorious smile. She relaxed a bit. What an incredible smile. But then...

"How do you know about that? Who told you? I thought what Susan and I talked about was between the two of us. Is she a gossip?" What the heck-was this some kind of a weird joke? She wasn't laughing.

"No, no, it's okay, Kelsey. Susan didn't betray your confidence. But we need to chat, you and I, for a little while.' He patted her arm. She felt enveloped, somehow. "I know you're disappointed about some things in your life that haven't always gone so well. I want you to understand- really understand- what you have now that you never had before." He was smiling again.

"I'm not....sure.....what do you mean?" What does he know about me? Has he been following me or something? At the same time, he really seemed nice.

"Kelsey, you've never been one to be introspective, but I know that you have had some difficult things to face about your life in the last couple of days. How about if you tell me about it? Then I have some really good news for you. Let's talk a while, okay?"

"It doesn't seem like I have a choice." She shrunk down in her bedclothes, trying to distance herself from him. It had been hard enough to face her life when she thought about it, much less share it with a total stranger, albeit, a handsome one. You know, he's one nice-looking dude. Well, this might work out. Besides, it wasn't like she was busy doing other things right now, anyway. Except for her babies. Grief and pain welled up. She started to cry again. What was this Andrew dude saying?

"Interesting selection of words, Kelsey, since you have made plenty of choices throughout your life. Some of those choices were good, while others were not. Let's start with college."

"Why in the world . . ." What was this going to accomplish? What's the big deal about her life in college? She didn't make any connection. She shrugged. Ouch! That shoulder...

"Humor me, Kelsey. You did well in the academic world…"

"Yes, I graduated from college, the pride and joy of my parents. I was the first person in my family to even go to college, and there I was, graduating with honors." Well, that wasn't so bad. Okay, I can do this. It's weird but do-able, I suppose. She smiled at the memory. Yes, college was a good time. She sat up in the bed a bit.

"Yes, you did very well. You worked hard and deserved the honors you received. Do you remember what happened next?"

"Sure, I got that wonderful first-job-out-of-college gig with the biggest public relations firm in Baltimore. I was on my way to great things. My parents were so very proud- bragging about me all the time. I was working my way up the corporate ladder so fast. I knew what people wanted and how to give it to them." Her smile became broader. She was happy thinking about everything she was planning to do way back then. Life had been busy but sweet. She sighed.

"Yes, your folks were very pleased with how you turned out. They bragged about you to all of their friends. You were the top new recruit in the company. Everyone was so happy for your success. You were nice to everyone, did a great job, and really deserved the recognition."

"And then I met Tony . . . that older guy really had the hots for me. We met when I was working on a new campaign for his business. He promised me the moon. He was fabulously wealthy and could have almost bought the moon…" she shifted in bed, trying to get more comfortable. It didn't work. "I knew he was married, but I went out with him anyway… He gave me some awesome gifts- like my first huge diamond, the most stunning wardrobe, and a BMW convertible. He made it so I didn't have to work at a nine-to-five job anymore." Her speech slowed as she thought about what had occurred. "Being with him was easier than scrambling all the time to do better than I had before. All I had to do was be available to travel with him and play like I was a dumb brunette. Older guys don't like smart women, you know." She looked over at Andrew. "I guess they're intimidated by brains and are going just for looks. Which I had, by the way." Okay, that wasn't what I planned on saying. She shook her head. What makes me so willing to talk about my own downfall? What makes me so open with this dude? This is definitely not my style. I need to keep my blasted mouth shut.

"Yes. What happened next? It appears like your life took a turn for the worse."

Kelsey shivered in her lightweight hospital gown at the thought of the two years she spent with Tony before he moved on. "He preferred younger twenty-somethings. 'No offense,' he told me after I turned twenty-five. He bought me a condo at the beach in Ocean City, to say goodbye. I guess he felt guilty about taking up my time...no, bag that. He never felt guilty about anything. It was a 'keep your blasted trap shut' gift, I guess. Okay, so I should have expected it. Tony wasn't good at faithfulness. I knew that before we got . . . together, but it seemed like a good way to live the good life without having to work. It was fun...while it lasted, as my Mom used say." She alternated between trying to smile and grimacing. Awkward! It was a toss-up whether she felt worse when she smiled or when she didn't. Her injuries were really bugging her, for sure. She stretched out her arms, trying to unwind the knots that she felt. Oh, that wasn't a good idea. She shifted in the bed again, but that only made her legs feel worse. She groaned.

"How did you feel about it, Kelsey? The life sounds like you might have enjoyed yourself, but did it lead to true happiness?"

"No, I didn't feel very happy when it ended. Tony didn't think he was doing anything wrong. He had no guilt, no shame. Tony considered his wife a free-loader he had supported for years. In reality, she was probably a faithful wife." Kelsey adjusted herself in the bed, painfully. She reached for her water cup. Andrew held the straw to her lips. Refreshing.

"She, you know, raised his children, took care of his home, and loved him. Tony was a total jerk. She knew about me, he said. I hurt her, Andrew." The last few sentences came very stilted as she thought about how she had caused another person's unhappiness. That lady hadn't deserved what she had gotten, any more than Susan had. No way.

"Kelsey, this may be hard to understand, but you are forgiven. When you prayed to receive Christ, He took away this sin. God knows your heart." He paused to look at her. "What else is troubling you?"

She thought about the men she had...been with. What other lives had she screwed up? Tony, Bill- "Wow, Bill. He almost succeeded in stealing everything from his wife while we were together. His wife was such a wimp- he told her to sign papers without reading them. And she did, at least at first. Finally, she realized that he was moving all of their money off-shore and put a stop to it."

"And then?"

"She had him investigated and found out about me. Boy, that was quite a scene! We were at my place, in....bed. She showed up one night, yelling at both of us. What a racket she made. That lady could scream! Her brother got ahold of Bill and wouldn't let him go until Bill agreed to give her all the money that he moved out of the country." She thought for a moment. "Bill did gift me with some land in Williamsburg, Virginia. Another broken relationship, but that's okay. I got a great gift. It turned out to be worth a bundle! Yeah, that land sold for a lot of money a couple of years later. I stuck the half a million dollars I got from it into an annuity that'll take care of me for the rest of my life. No worries, financially speaking." She stopped suddenly. She still wasn't happy after Bill, not really. She was rewarded with a boatload of money, sure enough, but Bill and his wife...

"Kelsey that, too, is forgiven. You sincerely repented two days ago. That sin is forgiven and forgotten."

She needed to tell Andrew more..."Bill...he almost died the night his wife's brother got a hold of him. I found out later that his wife wanted to kill me, too! My lifestyle of.... being with other men . . . almost got me killed." That knowledge had been mind-blowing at the time: someone wanted her dead. Served me right, I suppose. "In my line of work, or lack thereof, I really shouldn't have been so shocked that Bill's wife wanted me 'off-ed.'"

"Yes, that is true enough."

She was deep in thought by now and barely heard Andrew. His comment only registered in the back of her mind.

"Then there was...what was his name? He bought me that HUGE diamond ring, and the jewelers accidentally sent the appraisal to his house. His wife opened the mail and wanted to know where her ring was. He scurried to the jewelers, but they couldn't match it, even though he begged for an identical ring. Mine was one of a kind. He got one that looked kinda like mine, and tried to give that to her, but that lady knew her diamonds! He took my ring back so that he would have one to give her, promising me an even better one. He managed to cough one up, but the whole thing was a real mess." She shook her head in disbelief. What a mess she'd made of things. Screwing up one marriage after the next. Why couldn't I hang out with single guys? 'Cause the married guys who wanted to play around were the ones who had the money. I like money.

Kelsey continued, "He had put a West Palm Beach condo in my name, which was nice of him. I got to keep it, and she never knew about it. They were divorced pretty soon after that, but I lost interest in him when he lost half his money. What was his name?" She pondered for a few minutes but came up dry. I guess he didn't mean as much to me as I thought... "No, I don't remember his name. Sorry." She looked sheepishly at Andrew.

"Kelsey, the man's name was Steven. His wife was Samantha."

"Oh, yeah. Their marriage fell apart shortly afterwards. He lost his job when his wife told his CEO, who happened to be her brother, about our being together. She got a great attorney and took him to the cleaners. He did get a little money with the divorce, but he bet it all on one roll of the dice- what turned out to be a Ponzi scheme. He lost his shirt. He's living in a small town in Florida now." She wept, distraught at the memories. Andrew patted her hand.

Kelsey continued, "He'll have to work for the rest of his life. He barely makes it. His fancy house is gone, sold; he lives in a hovel of a home. His children and grandchildren want nothing to do with him. He called me a few times, wanting to get back together. I think he wanted me to support him. I turned him down cold." She was, all at once, very unhappy at how she had treated him, post-rich. She could have been nicer, given Steven a little of the money she got from the sale of the condo he'd bought her. But, no, she hadn't spared him a dime.

"I know. You weren't very happy to hear from him..."

"No, I wasn't. What did I want with a loser dude? Big Yikes. That would have been a bummer." She hesitated to say more. Then, "What happened to him, do you know? We lost contact a few years ago, after I refused to answer his texts." She found herself curious about the man. What was his name again? Oh, yeah, Steven.

"I think you'll be surprised at what happened next, Kelsey. He was invited to a neighbor's house for dinner. They became good friends, and the neighbor asked him to church. He went. His life has never been the same. Yes, he's living in what you called a "hovel of a home," but he's truly happy. He's been reunited with his children and grandchildren, who have seen an amazing change in him. He's doing fine, Kelsey. You don't have to worry about Steven anymore. He has forgiven you and is at peace. He's happier than he has ever been. Even Samantha no longer thinks of him as an enemy."

"Oh ...I ... didn't know." She was stunned by this news. "So, did they get back together, then?"

"Time will tell. Perhaps they will one day, though not yet. He has prayed that you'll forgive him. He knows what he did was wrong."

"Forgive him? What do you mean? I took his money happily and turned my back on him when he needed me. Why should he forgive me? I should ask the opposite. Can he forgive me?"

"Kelsey, he did it years ago. He bears you no ill will, none at all, for taking his money and running."

"What about Samantha? Has she, you know, forgiven me?"

"She is no longer as angry. She has a ways to go before you will have her total forgiveness, but I would say she's on the right path. Steven is talking to her. She sees such a change in him that it's very likely that she will forgive you, some day. Hopefully, it will be soon. The important thing is that God has forgiven you. Forgive yourself, dear daughter of God."

She lay there in stunned silence. Steven's okay? He's not mad at me? She couldn't understand how that could be. She hadn't been very nice to him at a time when he needed her so much. Tears rolled down her cheeks. "I don't deserve his forgiveness, Andrew."

"True, but you have it. Rejoice!" Andrew's smile seemed to light up the entire room. It was so bright that she almost shielded her eyes, yet she could not bear to look away. It drew her.

"Andrew, what about Tony? Is he okay?" She was suddenly concerned for the man who started it all. Maybe he…he was okay? Any chance of that?

"We all have choices to make, Kelsey. You had no control over his actions. Tony died of an STD a few years ago. He apparently got less selective with the women he dated as time went on. His wife divorced him years before that. It wasn't your fault that he continued down the wrong path. Forgive yourself. You're blaming yourself for his continued adultery, but you had no part in that, Kelsey."

"But . . ." She had thought she was to blame, but Andrew said not. How could this be? She was forgiven? She didn't deserve it, she hadn't earned it, but she was forgiven . . . it was hard to comprehend. More tears.

"He was going the wrong way well before he met you. You're only responsible for what you did with him. You're truly remorseful, Kelsey. That's enough."

"Bill, what about Bill?" Maybe things were better with him.

"He's living in a rehab center, Kelsey. Bill's brother-in-law shot him in the back one night, after finding him with yet another woman. The bullet struck him, hitting him on the C-four vertebrae. Bill is a quadriplegic; his brother-in-law is in jail. It's very sad, but again, not your fault. Humans all have to answer for themselves."

"What will happen to them? Is there any hope?" She felt so bad for Bill-it would probably drive him crazy to have no use of his arms or legs. It would drive her crazy, for sure. It was making her mad right now, what with every movement causing such horrid pain. How would Bill, the active man she knew, feel?

"Kelsey, I appreciate your concern. Bill has … gone through some difficult adjustments, but he met a man named Michael

Bench who told him about the Savior. Bill is more "all right" now than he has been in a very long time."

"Wait, I know that name . . . Michael Bench . . . how do I know him?" She was puzzled. The name was so familiar, but she couldn't place it.

"Michael Bench is the Michael of Michael and Susan who have been praying for you. They asked me to come see you, indirectly, as I have told you."

"I didn't know his last name." *Who is that guy? Boy, he sure gets around.*

"Yes, Kelsey. Michael, as you might imagine, does indeed get around. Bill came to the Chesapeake Center a few years before Susan did. Michael is a faithful witness. He's a good man who has led many people in his care to the Lord."

"And Bill's brother-in-law?"

"The jury is still out on that one. He'll be in prison for many years. He has had a little contact with a prison ministry, but I don't know if he will accept Christ or not. He's a bitter man, who saw the shooting as retribution for his sister's years of unhappiness with Bill. His sister, while we are on the topic, visits him regularly. She's become a devoted Christian since the shooting. She forgives you."

This conversation shocked her. "I'm not sure what happens next. Andrew, where do I go from here?"

"You've already asked Christ to save you, and He did. You asked Him to forgive you. He did. He remembers your sins no more. Now you need to forgive yourself, Kelsey. That's the real road to healing." Andrew looked at her with sympathy. She was obviously still devastated by the events of the past few days.

She wept again, remembering her precious babies. Thinking about the horrible person she had been. Andrew waited, silently, by her side.

Through her tears, Kelsey said, "Andrew, I'm not very proud of what I've done with my life. I wasted it. I let my parents down, destroyed one marriage after the next. And I'm a wreck. I mean, just look at me." She picked at the cheap-looking gown she was wearing. "I've worn such beautiful clothing, such wonderful lingerie, and now I'm reduced to this?" She sniffled and wiped her nose on the sheet. Her pride was gone. "Some pastel unisex hospital gown that's open in the back and makes me chill? This is the pits! My life has been the pits." She tried to cover up with the flimsy white blanket on her bed, but it wasn't enough to warm her up. She shivered. "My babies are dead. I'll never get them back." More tears followed. Andrew waited again.

"Kelsey, I know that things don't seem to be very good right now. Let's move on for a few minutes. What can you tell me about your relationship with your family?"

"My parents rejected me and my life and stopped talking to me years ago. I had fun, in spite of their . . . rejection. I got to travel wherever the wife of my man-of-the-moment didn't want to go. My parents never went anywhere, except to see her mom once a year. Mom was always saying she wanted to travel, but Dad never took her to any fun places. I got to go all over the world, but they didn't want to hear about my trips when I got home. I offered to send them places, after I got financially well off, but they refused to go. They called my income 'sin money' and wanted no part of it- or of me." Back into the doldrums, Kelsey slumped deeper into the bed clothes.

"Why do you think that was?" Andrew looked at her tenderly.

"Because my trips were with married men?" How could I have been so stupid? Payday always comes, and now it had come to her. She was an . . . an . . . she couldn't say it, not even to herself. Then,

"I was an escort to men who were not available." She wept bitterly. "I'm a real mess."

"Your parents didn't approve, did they?"

"No. I was an only child, so they didn't have anyone to fall back on. I was their shining star, the example that was supposed to do them proud. It worked out fine for a while . . ." She slouched deeper in the bed, humbled by the weight of this discussion.

Kindheartedly, "And then, what?"

"They found out what I was up to when an angry wife called them. I was important, Andrew, at least a little. I knew famous people and went to all the best parties." She tried to redeem herself, in spite of her remorse. It wasn't working.

"How impressive was that?" Andrew asked.

"Well, it seemed like a good idea at the time. I also got more expensive gifts as the men I was with moved on to younger women. The presents let me build a nice bank account for myself." She nodded with her own agreement. Yes, as far as money was concerned, she was doing just fine. No hovels for her, thank you very much.

"What have you done with that money, Kelsey?"

"Well, there came the day I knew would come. I knew I was "over the hill" as my parents always say. Men were looking for younger women. I was washed up. Still attractive, mind you, but men want younger and younger women these days, even the really old geezers. My mid-thirties hit me hard, but I had saved a lot of money and could live off of it for the rest of my life." Only in her thirties, and she was already a has-been . . . or maybe a never-was. It was hard to tell which was more accurate.

"What happened next?"

"That's when I met Kurt." She tried to smile but her face felt frozen. Kurt, another married man, another attempt at permanence. Another failure. Another wife's life destroyed, or almost destroyed.

"Tell me about it."

Chapter 24

As she sat at Brooke's kitchen island that morning sipping her cup of tea, Susan reflected on the strange twists and turns of life that had happened over the past two days, ever since she had visited Kelsey and Kurt in the hospital. She remembered how that day had gone. She had gone to see the couple, which was weird in and of itself because who in the world ever goes see her husband and his mistress as they lay in beds of their own making, after they had tried to kill her several times? That was odd enough, yet her day ended in ways she had thought about every once in a while over the past few years, but she never really expected would happen. Susan thought about it now, trying to relive it, to see if she had missed anything.

She and Nancy had gone to Brooke's condo after Susan had visited Kelsey and Kurt, to make dinner. Patrick was working late that night, so Susan had invited her dear friend to stay for the evening. It was just as well. Susan had experienced a very stressful day and was happy for the company. Nancy was good at sensing her discomfort, as always, and Susan was glad for the diversion of the silliness she knew would ensue.

Susan brewed the two of them a cup of tea and then told Nancy, "Don't tell anyone, but let's eat dessert first. I never let the kids eat cookies before dinner, but . . . "

"I'll never tell!" Then Nancy smiled as Susan put them in front of her friend, "Susan, Mickey Mouse chocolate chip cookies? I feel like I'm about ten!"

"Hey, Nancy, I also make some pretty mean Mickey Mouse pancakes. You ought to hang out here on Saturdays!"

"What have I been missing out on?" They laughed, knowing that it wasn't really that funny, but they both needed to "chill" as Joshua's girls loved to say. They chilled. They also ate a *lot* of chocolate chip cookies.

As they finished off their tea, Susan got serious about making dinner. Into the freezer section of the refrigerator she went, at least her hands went, as she sorted through the freezer's offerings. She glanced at her watch. "Let's see. It's three o'clock now. Yep, we have time for a meatloaf, mashed potatoes, and a salad. What kind of veggies do you want, Nancy? Courtesy of Birds Eye, we have a choice of broccoli, sweet corn, or mixed vegetables. What strikes your fancy?"

"Susan, why in the world did they name their company Bird's Eye? That sounds pretty disgusting when you think of it." Nancy spoke from her perch on the stool near Brooke's kitchen island.

Susan turned towards her friend. "I never thought of that before … that's the kind of veggies I always buy, but I never stopped to think about the name. I mean, they could have named it Bird's Feathers, Birds Fly, Birds … what else?"

"Susan Prescott, did you spike our tea?" Nancy looked into her cup, suspicious.

"Uh … nope, Nurse Ferguson. It's not even the time of year for eggnog! But I digress. Just stick with me on the thought process here. For example, did you ever buy any *Sag* Harbor clothes from Kohls or Penneys?" Susan slammed a frozen bag of broccoli on the countertop.

"What in the world is that? The clothes, I mean, not the broccoli." Nancy felt the need to clarify, apparently, what she was referring to.

"Nancy, you never heard of Sag Harbor? It's a clothing line for middle-aged women. Bad middle-aged. Get the idea? Sag?" They laughed like silly school girls as they prepared the meatloaf and peeled some potatoes. The meatloaf went into the oven, while the potatoes simmered on the stove.

"So, what does the stuff look like?"

"Actually, my dear Nancy, it's really quite nice. I understand that they're still in business, but I don't fathom how that name has caught on. Am I the only person who gets it?"

After the meatloaf was snuggly in the oven, they played a long and very spirited game of Mexican Train Dominos. The timer on her watch gave Susan the countdown to meatloaf completion. Fifteen minutes to go. "Okay, Nancy, my dear, we need to get the dinner show on the road. No more time for dominos." They put the game back in the box as Nancy told her, "You always shut things off when I'm winning, Susan!"

"How do you think I keep from being skunked by you, dear Nancy? Strategy is everything. My timing is always impeccable!"

The ladies were laughing when Brooke's land line phone rang. Susan jumped, not expecting any calls. She saw that the caller ID was from Shock Trauma in the University of Maryland Medical Center. "The Medical Center? Oh, my."

Nancy said, "I wonder how things are going."

Susan picked up the phone. "Hello?"

"Mrs. Susan Prescott, please." The woman's voice sounded serious.

Susan replied, "This is she speaking. Who's calling, please?" she shook her head at Nancy. "Not a good sign."

"Mrs. Prescott, this is Nurse Parkinson from Shock Trauma. We tried reaching you through your cellphone about an hour ago, but it went straight to voicemail."

"Oh, I am so sorry. I was visiting my husband this afternoon and didn't want to be disturbed. I forgot to turn it back on." She

291

fumbled with her cellphone, turning it on as she spoke. "I hope you weren't too inconvenienced."

"Mrs. Prescott, your daughter had given us this number as an alternative. Mr. Prescott's doctor needs to speak with you. Please hold for Dr. McNeice."

Susan turned to Nancy, "Kurt's doctor wants to talk to me." Nancy moved closer. "I'll put him on speakerphone."

"Hello, Mrs. Prescott. This is Dr. McNeice."

"Yes, Dr. McNeice. What can I do for you?"

"I'm sorry to inform you that your husband began bleeding out about two hours ago. We hoped to bring you in to see him before we rushed him to surgery, but we couldn't get ahold of you. You and your family will probably want to come to Shock Trauma very soon, so that you can be here when he gets out of the operating room."

"What? What happened?" Her hand flew to her neck. Oh, no. I didn't want him to get worse.

"Well, Mr. Prescott had some bleeding from an uncertain source, so we made the decision to operate. He's undergoing exploratory surgery right now, to determine the cause of the bleeding and fix it, if possible. Again, I must stress the need to have you and the family here, in case decisions need to be made."

"Yes, of course. Thank you, Dr. McNeice."

"Certainly. I hope to see you soon."

Susan hung up, in a tizzy. "We have to go. We have to get there now." She began rushing around, unsure of what needed to be done. Get her purse. No wash her hands first. Where's the dishtowel. Oh, over there.

Nancy came over from the table, which she had been setting for the evening's dinner, and took her friend by the shoulders. "Hold on, Susan. Slow down a minute. Focus. Our dinner is cooking; it will be out soon. I'll get things ready to take to the medical center. We may be there a long time. We don't know how long Kurt will be in surgery, so we might as well have a good dinner with us."

"What? How can you think of food, Nancy? We need to get over there right now!" She was panicking while Nancy seemed so calm.

"No. We have enough time for you to call the kids and get them to come. I'll get the dinner packed up, and we'll take a little picnic with us. We have enough for the whole family to enjoy, so no guilt trips about not feeding them. I'll cook a few extra veggies I found in the freezer and pack some paper goods that we can throw away when we're done."

"But, Nancy . . ."

"No if's, ands, or buts, my dear Susan. It's important to keep your strength up- I saw the pathetic salad you sort of ate for lunch. Then you had that massive amount of cookies a little while ago. They won't keep you going for very long. You aren't going to faint on my shift, dearie." Nancy stopped to let her words sink in. "We may be at the medical center for hours. You make the calls. I'll get the food ready, and then we'll leave. Move it, Susan."

Susan made the calls quickly, explaining to first Brooke, who was at work, that her father had been rushed to the operating room. Brooke would meet them at the ICU. Joshua was called next. He was busy with his office hours in the Lesly and Pat Sajak Pavilion, but would contact Amanda, who was off that day, and pick her up on his way to Shock Trauma. The neighbors had volunteered to watch the kids if need be, when they learned of Kurt's hospitalization. Amanda would take one of the neighbors up on her offer, since they didn't want the children to be exposed to a dying or newly-dead grandfather.

Susan knew Christopher was just finishing up a class at the Naval Academy, but she left an urgent voicemail. Her message was the same with all of her children: Kurt had massive internal bleeding requiring an immediate exploratory operation. They needed to be at the medical center as soon as possible. Nancy would drive her, along with the now-massive dinner the ladies had prepared. The plan was that they would probably be there a long time according to Nancy, whether for good or ill, but at least they would be well-fed.

The family met in the lobby, having arrived within minutes of each other. They headed up to the ICU waiting room. Dr. McNeice met with them, explaining the seriousness of Kurt's condition. He had just gotten an update from the surgical team, who were busy clamping off bleeds, only to be met by another one.

Kurt underwent six hours of surgery that afternoon and evening. He did not survive.

***

Susan didn't know if she would ever eat meatloaf again without thinking about Kurt's hapless end. She felt numbed, shocked by the end that, yes, she had thought about many times during their troubled marriage. Truth be known, she had often wondered what it would be like to be free from him. Now she was.

She felt stunned. She felt relieved. There was emptiness in her heart, a void in her very being. She sobbed at first, but it was more because of the lost potential for their relationship, rather than over his passing. We could have been such a great team, if only things had been different. Why wouldn't he let me into his heart? What had been the stumbling block that created the wall between them? I guess I'll never really know, never fully understand what made him hold me at arm's length all those years. Our marriage died so many years ago. Now it could never be restored.

It seemed that she was on an emotional seesaw as she thought about what had transpired. How am I supposed to react? Should I mourn him? Should I jump for joy? The man is dead who wanted me dead. He tried to kill me and almost succeeded. I tried to help him, against his will, but he died. It's over. I hope he doesn't come back and haunt me. No, that's silly. He's... gone.

Life was so uncertain for her now. She had no means of support, but had responsibilities to perform for her legally-wedded husband. Was he an organ donor? Did he have a will? Who was his attorney? What paperwork did she need to file? What were his desires for his body disposal? Did he want to be buried or cremated? How would she pay for it, since it was her legal responsibility? She did sign consent forms for organ transplantation, allowing the doctors to take whatever they could use to help someone else. She sure hoped that his personality would not be transferred to the recipients! To get things over with as soon as she could, she requested cremation, though she considered donating his body to science so that she wouldn't have any expenses at all. Since he was so battered by the accident and then the exploratory surgery, she wasn't sure that they would take him anyway, so she went with the path of least resistance.

Brooke's boss's law firm did handle family planning issues, so she was able to make an appointment to see them a couple of days later. She was thankful that they gave her a greatly-reduced rate as a professional courtesy to Brooke. That fee was waived by the attorney put on her case as soon as he realized what had happened. He walked her through the minefield of legalities, but Susan was still stunned by the whole predicament. The good news was that she could apply for Kurt's Social Security. The bad news was that it would take some time to kick in. In the meantime, her children stepped forward to pay for their father's cremation. She felt horrid having to call on them yet again, but Kurt really had wiped her out. She hoped she would never have to live through two such terrible days again. It was a relief when they ended.

It occurred to her that maybe Kelsey didn't know about his passing. Susan knew that the young woman didn't have anyone in her life and felt that maybe another visit was called for. She called Nancy to tell her of the plans to go, to see if she could ease Kelsey's burdens a bit. Nancy said she was nuts to go a second time, but Susan felt compelled to go. She would reach out to Kelsey, who she had led to Christ. Susan would go in obedience to God.

Chapter 25

Kelsey told her visitor, Andrew, the story of her relationship with Kurt. "I was a passenger on one of his flights when I spotted him. He was the spitting image of Richard Gere, a real live look-alike. I was immediately attracted to him. He was so charming and obviously thought I was beautiful. We went out to dinner the first time we met. It was the beginning of our long relationship. Kurt was happy to take me into his life. He had been married for some time and was bored with Susan." The memories, given the circumstances now, did not please her.

"Was that boredom enough reason to cheat, do you think?" Andrew leaned towards her a bit. She wasn't afraid anymore, so she didn't cringe at his nearness. Somehow, she felt comforted by his presence.

"Well, he said that he hadn't strayed before, that I was the first. I'm wondering. Did I really, truly know him? He said that Susan was such a horrid woman, but that's not what I've seen. She's kind, tender-hearted, and cares about people. Even me . . ." She just shook her head. Susan had been there for her girls, even though they were the children of her husband and his mistress. How could Kelsey have been so totally blind not to see through Kurt? Not to mention that no one could possibly be as bad as she had been told Susan was? "I'm so sorry for hurting her, Andrew. Do you think she'll ever forgive me?"

"Yes, Kelsey, Susan has forgiven you, and she even cares about you. That's why I was sent to talk to you."

"Like you said, Andrew, I am not used to . . . what did you call it?"

"Introspection. You don't usually stop to think through how your actions have affected others, but I think it's actually working out better than you think today."

Kelsey continued to muse, fiddling with her bedclothes as she did. "I gave birth to Cassie, hoping that she would win Kurt to me and away from Susan forever." She sighed. "I was so tired of ending up alone. My biological clock was ticking, and I wanted to have children before it was too late."

She looked at Andrew. "The other men I had been involved with had warned me that any pregnancy would lead either to abortion or with them walking away, with no financial support for me or the baby. Kurt apparently thought I was "taking care of that" or that I was infertile." She shook her head. Men. And she was the one who was supposed to be dumb.

"What did he say when you told him you were expecting Cassie?" Something about the way he asked made her think that Andrew already knew the answer, but wanted her to think about it.

"He'd been totally surprised when I told him I was pregnant the first time. He immediately began talking about divorcing Susan, but, you know, it never seemed to happen. I mean, I wonder if they ever really discussed it. He said that they had, but who really knows?" It was the first time it occurred to her that Kurt might have lied to her. After all, he lied to Susan all the time. Why wouldn't he lie to her as well? What a thought! It never crossed her mind that he might be a serial liar. But she was Kelsey, after all. All those nice things he had said to her...the future they had planned. Was anything true? Their marriage . . . their fake marriage . . . it was all fictitious. She knew as they stood on the beach that the whole thing was a farce. She had bought into it because she had wanted to. What in the world had she been thinking?

"They talked about many things, Kelsey, mostly his unhappiness with Susan and his desire for change. He mentioned divorce only to say that he didn't want one. He talked about killing her, or somehow causing her death . . . and she knew that he wanted her dead. He also told her about you."

"When? How?" He told Susan he wanted her to die? "How could Susan live with that?"

"Yes. Susan knew. She didn't know what to do about it. She hadn't supported herself in years, and she was no longer a young woman. She had no idea how she would manage as a single woman. Kurt had taken her to their favorite downtown Annapolis restaurant . . ."

"The Federal House?" Kelsey asked.

Andrew told her, "Yes. It was a dark winter night, shortly after Cassie was born. He told Susan about you during dinner. She was devastated, as you might imagine. Shocked. Afterwards, he walked her down to the end of the dock while she was still numbed by the news. All those years of marriage and he wanted to be rid of her. He even mentioned killing her as they walked, thinking she didn't hear him, but she did. He tried to lure her up on the end of the city dock, but she refused to step up on the dock's main platform. That refusal saved her life."

"I didn't know that. He never told me. I don't know what to say . . ." Kelsey stammered.

"You almost killed Susan as well, but you had remorse. I don't think you would really have gone through with it, Kelsey. Not after she saved Cassie."

Kelsey just lay there, hearing Andrew again as if through a tunnel. She was talking more to herself than to him. She shook her head firmly. "He pulled me into it with the Vancouver trip. I don't know how I could have been so blind." Augh, what was I thinking....again? What did I expect? Did I really think we could get away with murder? What a fool I was!

Andrew said, "There is a saying: 'There is none so blind as he – or she- who will not see.' But you see now, Kelsey. Your eyes have been opened, and I sense a real sorrow at your actions. That's tremendous growth. You have to know- God has forgiven you."

"Okay. Good." She had never felt so utterly hopeless in her life. What was going to happen next?

"Kelsey, let's move on. Tell me about other people in your life."

"What other people?" Kelsey had no idea what he meant.

"You know, your friends."

She thought for a moment. "I haven't got any friends. Most of the married women I know are afraid I'll be after their husbands next. The few like-minded women I've known through the years are as shallow as me. We spent more time caring about our appearance, our outfits, and the next party or trip, than any of the popular social causes. We had to keep up appearances, Andrew, or we were history...and we knew it. We had to have shiny hair, thin thighs, a trim backside, and flawless makeup all the time. We had to be the ultimate of womanly perfection."

"That must have been tiring." Andrew smiled.

"It was. Every single day, I had to be ready at a moment's notice. I could never, ever have a bad day, never take a day off. Sometimes I think it might have been easier to work a full-time job than constantly keeping track of my own looks." It was pretty exhausting, always prepping to be looked over like a piece of meat.

"What about men?"

"Most of the men I've been with don't care if I live or die or even know I'm in the hospital. They care so little that the ones that do know- I called a few of them- haven't stopped by to see me. But

300

my parents? They hung up when I tried to call them yesterday. They threw me away years ago." She began to cry.

"Is there truly no one?"

"No one loves me. No one at all." She hesitated to be this honest, this incredibly vulnerable. "It's all my own fault. I made this life for myself. I have no one else to blame." She hung her head in shame. Tears ran unhindered down her face and onto the cheap-looking hospital gown. She didn't lift a finger to brush them away.

"Kelsey, there is Someone. You have already met Him, thanks to Susan, who, by the way, should hate you but doesn't."

She looked up in shock. "What? She doesn't? Susan is an amazing woman."

"Yes, but her being amazing comes from her relationship with Jesus. God is her Rock and Fortress, in spite of what others do to her."

"Andrew, you're here because she asked God to send you to me? Right?"

"Yes, Kelsey, she prayed that God would send you a comforter. I'm here because of her prayers."

"That's incredible. Why would she care about me?" Kelsey was amazed.

"Susan does care, Kelsey. That's the kind of person Susan is: loving, caring, not wanting anyone to have a rough life. That's why I came, Kelsey."

Kelsey thought deeply, perhaps for the first time in her life. Her children, her pride and joy, were gone. Her lover had died two nights before. The nurses had tried to show pity over her mother loss, but their words couldn't reach the bottom of the pit she had dug for herself. She thought back to all the things that had happened since she met Kurt. The secret meetings, the clandestine trips, the gifts of jewelry and clothing that he should have given his wife, the fake marriage, the shared house bought with money that belonged at least half to Susan. Kelsey turned back to her visitor.

"Andrew, you mentioned some good news. I could really use some. What is it?"

"Cassie and Christine are fine."

"What???? Susan lied to me about their deaths? Everyone lied to me???" Kelsey sat bolt upright in the bed. Unbelievable! Her tears dried up on the spot.

"No, no. Calm down, Kelsey. Yes, they died. But they're fine. They're in heaven and are well-cared for. I just wanted you to know that. Because you're a Christian, you will one day be reunited with your girls."

"And Kurt?"

"No, I'm sorry, Kelsey. He kept postponing his decision to follow Christ until it was too late. You'll never see him again. Neither will Cassie or Christine."

"How do you know that?"

"When Susan prayed, she also prayed for someone to come to Kurt, not just you. One of my, uh, colleagues, for lack of a better word, went to Kurt right before his operation. Thomas told me that Kurt died an angry man who refused to make a decision. Alone. Without God."

Kelsey sank back into her bed. Then, "Oh. Where is he?" She had heard where folks went who rejected God when she was a little girl at Vacation Bible School. It didn't sound like fun- she guessed that *not* deciding **was** deciding.

"He is eternally separated from God in a place called Hell."

She was speechless. That was the cost of denying God? The price was way too high. "What now, Andrew? Where do I go from here?"

"Kelsey, I think you're on the right path. You understand what you've done and have truly repented of those sins. You are

302

forgiven. Be encouraged. You've grown greatly today. Some more good news: Susan will be coming to see you tonight. She forgives you and wants to bring you comfort. Listen to her. She's your friend." Slowly: "You will never be totally alone again. Remember that, Kelsey. Remember that you are the child of a King. I must leave now." He got up and smiled down at her. "Goodbye."

"Andrew, do you have to go?" She wanted him to stay, to never leave her.

"Yes, for now. I'll be back sometime in the future, but it isn't for me to say when." He turned and walked slowly towards the wall. Without warning, Andrew was gone.

Kelsey awoke, surprised that only thirty minutes had passed. It'd seemed like so much longer. She thought long and hard about what had transpired. She remembered her relationship with Kurt, which had gotten her into this present mess. She blamed herself for her naiveté in thinking that everything would work out for her own good. Though she felt comforted by Andrew, and truly happy about the forgiveness he said was hers, she still felt angry about her actions.

I knew he was married! Why did I listen to his love talk? Why did I let myself be charmed by him? The girls. The kidnapping, the attempted murder. What will happen to me? Will I lose my life, after losing my lover and our daughters? What judge will ever let me off, knowing the crimes I've committed? No, there's no happy ending to this story, Susan's God or no God. Who *am* I? What led me to this horrid end? She couldn't think of a single best solution.

Kelsey caught a glimpse of herself later that day, reflected in the glasses of one of her nurses. She was revolted by the sight. Well, my days as a glamorous girlfriend are over. Black and blue face, right eye swollen almost shut, puffy lip, broken body, missing teeth, filthy hair partially chopped off when they stitched up my scalp. Who will want me now? I belong in a freak show.

The nurse came into her room, a syringe in hand. It was then that Kelsey noticed the morphine that she was being given. It was the only thing keeping her from excruciating pain. She recalled that the nurses only gave her some of the medication each time, leaving a good portion of the dose in the syringe each time they injected it into her IV. She asked her charge nurse, "Why don't you give me all of it?"

"Oh, Ms. De Luca, we can't do that. It would stop your breathing if we gave you too much. No, the amount we inject is just right for your body weight."

In that moment, she knew what to do. She had gotten saved while praying with Susan, and understood from her conversation with Andrew that she would go to heaven to be with her girls when she died. Since she was in a really bad way and headed for a long prison term, the best solution in her mind was to "off" herself.

But first, she had something she needed to do. She made a phone call, explaining what she wanted done without delay. The man did as she asked and then visited her. He came for a short visit. He questioned her mental stability, but she convinced him that what she wanted was the right thing to do. He concurred. He brought in two witnesses from the nursing staff. Papers were signed. Then he left and she turned her attention to the next step in her plan.

The next round of nurses was on duty. Her nurse entered, as always, placing the syringe with her next dose on the table next to Kelsey. The nurse turned her back and fiddled with the IV bag, preparing to insert the medication. As was the habit of the medication nurse, she pushed the call button, saying that Kelsey needed to use the bathroom before being medicated. Kelsey reached towards the needle.

All I have to do is inject the whole amount into my IV, and then I can be with my girls. All this pain and anguish will be over. If … I...can...just....reach... the... needle. She started sliding off the bed. It was out of her comfortable reach, but maybe...she...could...grab...it. The needle skittered away because she had only managed to touch the side of it...it slid across the table, coming to rest at the opposite end. So close, but so far away, Kelsey thought.

The nurse turned and said, "Ms. De Luca, whatever are you doing?" The nurse helped her back on the bed. To the aide who had just entered, "Help me get Ms. De Luca into the bathroom. She needs to use the toilet before I medicate her for the night."

Kelsey thought for a moment. Okay. That was just a dry run. I'll try again, next dose.

"All right, Ms. De Luca, up you go!" With one nurse on each side, the women stood her up.

***

Susan walked in just as they were preparing to take Kelsey to the bathroom. Susan had wanted to visit with the young woman again, to see how she was doing. Kelsey stood up, then suddenly groaned. Kelsey turned blue and slipped through the nurses' arms, as she hit the floor, unconscious.

The nurse shouted, "Code blue. We have a code blue." The call went out over the intercom.

Susan stood back as the medical team dashed into the room pushing a crash cart. "Pulmonary embolism" the nurse told them, wasting no words. The team worked on Kelsey for an hour, to no avail. Susan was a mouse on the wall, watching from the side as they worked on Kelsey in vain.

Finally, the doctor called "Time of Death, 5:30 pm." It was then that he noticed Susan standing nearby.

The doctor walked over to her and asked, "Are you a family member?"

"No, I'm a friend," Susan answered. "But I have a medical background. What happened?"

The doctor explained, "When we stood her up, a blood clot that had formed because of her injuries and two days in bed traveled to her lungs and stopped her breathing. There was really nothing we could do, but we hate to give up too easily on someone so young. We did everything we could."

"I see. Thank you for trying to save her," Susan said. She stared at Kelsey's lifeless body.

"I'm sorry we were unsuccessful, but your friend is dead." The doctor patted her on the shoulder and left the room.

***

Kelsey had been standing by the back wall of her room during the flurry of activity that had just taken place, watching carefully as her body was poked and prodded. The bed and floor were littered with used syringes, discarded medicine vials, and other crash cart trash. The bed was disheveled, with bedclothes strewn about in total disarray. The bedside table was covered with rejected emergency medical equipment. The room resembled a messy child's bedroom more than a hospital room. Andrew entered and stood next her. Still looking at her own body on the bed, she commented to him.

"So, I'm dead."

"Yes. I knew that it wouldn't be long before I saw you again."

"Andrew, did you know that I would try to kill myself?"

"No, that was not given to me. Only the knowledge that you would be coming with me soon. I was waiting in your room, but you didn't see me after you woke up. That was pretty tricky, grabbing

306

for the needle, Kelsey. I didn't see that coming. I just barely managed to shove it out of the way before you got ahold of it."

"That was your doing? You kept me from grabbing it?" Kelsey looked his way, in shock.

"Yep, in the flesh. Well, not really. That's just an earthly expression. I promised you that you would never been alone again, Kelsey, and I was telling you the truth. I've been here ever since we first met...By the way, nice move this afternoon with your visitor. I'm so very proud of you, Kelsey. You did well. You truly showed the love of Christ." He gave her a quick side hug. She smiled at him.

"It was the least I could do . . ." She noticed that Susan had walked over to her bedside from her former place near the wall. Susan knelt down on the floor with her head on the hospital bed and began to pray. "Why's she doing that, Andrew?"

"Kelsey, Susan is praying for your well-being. She knows that you're going to heaven, but she's just trying to put in a last-minute good word for you, as they say."

Susan got up and pulled up a chair. Tears flowed freely down her cheeks. "Kelsey, I'm here for you." She patted the body on the arm. She took a small Bible out of her purse and began to read, "The Lord is my Shepherd..."

"What's that she's reading, Andrew?" Kelsey turned her head from Susan to look at Andrew, then back at the reading woman. "It sounds vaguely familiar, but I can't place it."

"The Twenty-third Psalm. One of my favorites, especially in situations like this." Andrew continued to look at Susan, while commenting to Kelsey.

Susan had just finished when one of the nurses, the one with glasses that Kelsey had seen her reflection in earlier that afternoon, came in. "I'm sorry, Ma'am, but we need to prepare the body for the morgue. If you don't mind . . ."

Susan looked at the nurse. "Of course, I was just getting ready to leave, if you're sure that someone will be with her."

The woman nodded. "She won't be alone, Ma'am."

"Good. That's good. Thank you so much." Susan got up to leave, kissing her fingers and touching her fingers to the dead woman's swollen blue face. Tears flowed down her cheeks, falling onto the disheveled sheets. "Goodbye, Kelsey. I'm sorry that we met under these circumstances." She turned and walked out.

Kelsey looked at Andrew. "I'm so sorry for the pain I caused her. Will she ever know it?"

"Yes, Kelsey, eventually. One day, you'll tell her yourself."

The bespectacled nurse was working on Kelsey's body when she turned toward the couple standing nearby. Kelsey was shocked by what she saw reflected in the woman's glasses.

"Andrew! Why didn't you tell me? I'm back to normal! I look like my old self again. Hehehe. But, where... did this dress come from?" She hadn't noticed that her blood-stained hospital gown had become a beautiful diaphanous white gown. It shimmered like a piece of translucent fabric, swirling at her feet. Her feet were shod in sparkling white flats. She twirled, laughing. "Oh, my. I feel so young. Is this really death?"

Andrew laughed at her unmistakable joy. "Kelsey, everyone who knows the Lord feels that way when they see themselves after they pass. You were so busy looking back at what you had lost that you didn't see what you had become."

Kelsey twisted and twirled for a few more minutes, simply for the pleasure. She hugged herself and then raised her hands in the air, laughing the whole time. For someone who was dead, she had never felt more alive. Then, with great seriousness, she stopped in her tracks and asked Andrew, "What now?"

"I'm here to escort you to heaven. Jesus is there, waiting for you to come to Him. You also have two little girls waiting to see their Mama again." He put out his arm for her to take. "Shall we go?"

She became more serious and thoughtful. "I'm not worthy, Andrew."

"No one ever is... Come on. Let's go."

Kelsey took his arm, smiling. They turned and walked towards the corner. Gone. Happy. Forever healed. Completely forgiven.

Chapter 26

Susan and Brooke had just gotten her things from the rehab center settled into the spare room in Brooke's condo. She had agreed to stay with Brooke for the foreseeable future because she knew that she was too exhausted to stay on her own, especially given recent circumstances. The rehab center had prepared her belongings for pickup when Susan and Brooke stopped by the day after Kelsey's passing. Susan didn't have any money to go anywhere else, thanks to Kurt. The phone rang as Brooke tidied the new mint green comforter she had bought her mom and arranged the matching decorative pillows on Susan's new bed. Susan was a bit startled by the ring as she rocked in the deep green Amish swivel armchair nearby. Brooke took the call.

"Hello?"

"Good afternoon, ma'am. This is John James. Is this Ms. Brooke Prescott?"

"Yes, it is. Who's calling, please?"

"Ms. Prescott, I am the attorney for Ms. Kelsey De Luca. Are you familiar with that name?"

"Yes, of course. Why are you calling?" Brooke whispered to Susan, "It's Kelsey's attorney. I wonder what he wants."

Susan said, "I can't imagine." *I sure hope her estate isn't suing me for some imagined slight. No, of course not. Don't even think of that.*

"I have a legal matter to discuss with your mother, Mrs. Susan Prescott, but I've been unable to locate her. Do you know where she is staying?"

"Yes, she's currently living with me. How can we help you?"

"Could you possibly bring her into my Annapolis office in the next few days?"

"No, I'm sorry. Mr. James. My mother is in no condition to travel, even across town right now. She has had a very stressful week. However, you could come see her in my home, if you want."

It was arranged that Mr. James would stop by the next afternoon. The two women were curious about the reason for his visit. Not being used to having visits from a member of the legal profession in their home, the ladies decided dark dress pants and pastel collared shirts would be appropriate. They wore matching silver jewelry, agreeing that business semi-casual attire was the order of the day. Brooke was off work for a few days, her big case settled at work, taking the time off to get Susan acclimated to her new home. They were ready a half hour early, wondering what Mr. James could possibly want.

He was there promptly at two pm. Brooke escorted him into the living room, where Susan was sitting on Brooke's couch. As Susan started to rise, he waved her to not get up. Brooke offered him some sweet iced tea, which he happily accepted. After Brooke handed over tea to her mother and Mr. James, she sat down with her own beverage.

The dignified, dark suited gentleman greeted Susan formally, bowing slightly as he spoke. "Good afternoon, Mrs. Prescott. Thank you for seeing me. I am John James. As I mentioned yesterday, I am the attorney for the late Ms. Kelsey De Luca."

Brooke said, "Yes, we know. What does Kelsey have to do with my mother?" Brooke seemed rather abrupt with the attorney.

Susan said, "Brooke, let's hear the man out." She patted Brooke's arm, and then sipped from her glass of sweet tea. "Mr. James, why are you here?"

311

"Ms. Prescott, you showed great compassion and love to Ms. De Luca as she was mourning the death of her …uh…fiancé and their two children, in spite of the fact that you were still married to Ms. De Luca's …uh…fiancé at the time."

Susan said, "I did what I could to help her through a very rough time." Well, this is strange. Kelsey is thanking me from beyond the grave? She looked over at Brooke, who seemed as shocked as she was.

"Yes, well, my client really appreciated that. As you know, Mr. Kurt Prescott had taken all of your assets and combined them with Ms. De Luca's money. He then left a will which designated her as his only beneficiary."

"Yep, that sounds like Dad." Brooke hastened to explain, when the attorney looked surprised. "Not the Dad I knew growing up, but the man he'd become."

Mr. James nodded and then continued. "Ms. De Luca had a will that split her considerable estate between her children and Mr. Prescott."

Susan said, "But they all died before she did." She and Brooke glanced at one another, sensing a trend here.

"Yes, well, Ms. De Luca realized the day you visited her, Mrs. Prescott, she had misunderstood the kind of person you are. She called me and asked me to make some changes in her will. They were quite some changes, indeed. She signed her new will when I brought it to her the day she unexpectedly died. Mrs. Prescott, you have inherited all of Ms. De Luca's estate. She left everything to you."

Susan almost stood up, in surprise. Then she stammered, "What? How can that be?" What in the world? Why wouldn't Kelsey have left the money to someone else? Susan was Kelsey's lover's wife. It made no sense. She shook her head in disbelief. How can this be?

"It's completely true. Ms. De Luca had considerable assets, given her . . . uh . . . previous encounters with wealthy older men . . . and, of course, she also had the money that Mr. Prescott left her. He predeceased her, which left her with his money, and the children were already dead. She only had two other people who might have inherited her assets, her parents, Antonio and Helen De Luca." The lawyer paused as the ladies absorbed the astonishing information.

"Oh, my, I don't know what to say." Susan glanced at Brooke, seeming to question if she had heard the attorney correctly.

"Mom, the years that the locusts have eaten...Michael was telling me about that just the other day." Brooke beamed at the news.

"I just, I mean, it's a bit much to take in right now, Mr. James." Susan slumped back in her seat.

"I understand, Mrs. Prescott, Ms. Prescott. I should warn you- Ms. De Luca's family may make a claim against the will. We need to be prepared for that possibility."

Susan's eyes began to fill with tears. Brooke held her hand, patting it with her other hand. Susan just shook her head. Was God really giving her back what she had lost? Kurt had taken so much from her. It was impossible to believe. She was so shocked she almost couldn't breathe.

"Ladies, I've given you a lot to think about. I've drawn up a spreadsheet with the approximate value of Ms. De Luca's estate. After you have had the chance to look it over, let's get together and go over it in detail. I understand that you will need to bring your own lawyer with you, in fact, I encourage you very strongly to do so. How does that sound?"

Susan said, "Yes, thank you very much Mr. James. I think it would be easiest to just have you represent me, if that's okay. I really don't feel up to going through this entire story with a new lawyer, when you are so familiar with the situation. Does that sound acceptable?"

"Yes, Mrs. Prescott. I believe that can be arranged. I will put myself at your disposal." He bowed.

"Thank you so very much." She nodded.

"I'll say goodbye then. Good afternoon, ladies. I look forward to hearing from you soon." He bowed again. Brooke led him out and returned to her mother.

As she came back into the living room, Brooke remarked, "He likes bowing, I take it." Susan smiled. Then both women got an attack of the giggles. They laughed till the tears flowed.

"Oh, my, doesn't he? I think it's rather quaint...rather charming, to tell the truth."

"Mom, let's cut to the chase. What's the bottom line here?" Brooke plopped down on the couch next to her.

"Let me see here." Susan shuffled the papers. "Oh, Brooke... It looks like Kelsey left me . . . I can't believe it . . . it can't be true . . . She left me property and cash worth . . . five million dollars!"

Chapter 27

Susan and Brooke met again with Mr. James a week later and were handed the keys to Kurt and Kelsey's home. They drove to the downtown Annapolis area, wondering for a short time if they were even in the right place. How could the couple have afforded a place downtown?

"Mom, I guess those gifts from the wealthy boyfriends of Kelsey, combined with all of the things Dad sold that belonged to you, and the sale of your house, made them able to buy one of these downtown mini-mansions."

The white colonial with a green door and matching shutters was gorgeous. The plaque on the front said that the historic house was "The Carriage House to the John Brice III House, erected 1766." It had been newly renovated.

"Prince George Street. I always wanted to live in downtown Annapolis, but your father always said we couldn't afford it. Mr. James's spreadsheet . . ." she shuffled through some papers . . . "valued this house at $1.2 million." She looked in awe at Brooke. "I guess your father and Kelsey were living my dream."

"Mom, are you thinking of living here?" Brooke looked at her, startled at the thought.

"No, no, the house will be sold. I don't need it and couldn't stand to live in it, knowing that they had been here . . . no, I'm not keeping it." Susan couldn't fathom becoming a permanent resident there. "This is a 'den of iniquity,' as we used to say. I won't live where Kurt cheated on me. Not in a million years!"

"Whew! That's good to know . . . Shall we go inside?" Brooke offered her arm, but Susan brushed her off.

"I'm not totally feeble, you know! I am perfectly able to get in there under my own steam, thank you very much!"

Susan walked up the three brick steps to the front door, supported by Brooke's presence, though not her arm. It was difficult to imagine her husband laughing and loving and living with Kelsey here, but she tried to shrug it off. It was made more difficult by what she found there. Everywhere she looked, there were professional pictures of Kurt and Kelsey and the girls.

***

Brooke noticed that one wall of the narrow entrance hallway was filled with wedding photos from Kurt and Kelsey's Hawaiian wedding. Susan almost collapsed when she saw them. Brooke, on the other hand, just got mad. Brooke pulled several of the photos down, slamming them together as she put them in her large purse, and taking photos with her cellphone of the walls filled with other shots of the happy little family. Wait until Joshua and Christopher see these!

In the upstairs master suite, Brooke found Kelsey's huge pear-shaped diamond ring, along with Kurt's wedding band, which they had left behind on their trip to Vancouver in order to avoid calling attention to themselves. Kelsey's ring was definitely noteworthy. A bit gaudy, if you asked her. Brooke pocketed the rings, planning on showing them to her brothers later. After walking through room after room filled with high-end decorations, she had seen enough.

Brooke was totally disgusted by her father's . . . well, she wasn't sure what to call it, but it really ticked her off. All her mother had put up with for all those years, and her father had showered Kelsey with all this...stuff. She told her mother they were leaving. They walked back to the car and drove home in silence, stunned by the gallery of unfaithfulness they had seen adorning the walls.

Brooke got her mom settled in for a nap, but was unable to stop pacing in her kitchen as she contemplated what she'd seen. She muttered to herself. How could Dad do that to Mom? Mom had never owned such nice things, even after all those years of marriage. Why did Kelsey rate? It was horrid. She needed to talk through it with Michael, but knew that he was working a double shift that day. Their conversation, and his soothing demeanor, would have to wait. Knowing Christopher was staying with Joshua while waiting to purchase his new home in Severna Park, she called to ask them to come over soon. During the phone call with Joshua, Susan entered the kitchen, also unable to rest. Susan started pacing the floor, doing laps of the kitchen, like she did when something was bothering her.

Joshua responded to Brooke's call, saying, "Oh, I was about to call you, Brooke. Can you and Mom take care of the boys? We're going to Dad's and Kelsey's memorial service. We don't think that the boys will want to come, and it's really not good for them to be exposed to the idea that Grandpa was living with someone and having babies while he was still married to Grandma. The girls are gonna hang out with some friends. We'll explain it all to them when they get older."

"Oh, when is the service?" Brooke put Joshua on the speakerphone, so that Susan could listen in.

"Tomorrow at one. We can drop the boys off about noon. We didn't tell you and Mom about it because the De Lucas have asked that she not come. I figured you wouldn't want to come either, since you were always siding with Mom and against Dad."

"You're right. I don't want to come. You know, Joshua, Dad wasn't who ..."

317

"Brooke, don't start that again. Mom simply was not supportive enough of Dad. It's her fault he strayed. If she had been more understanding of his needs . . ."

Brooke was almost shouting at him, "Joshua, don't you speak one word against Mom. Yes, we will watch your boys. Yes, you may drop them off at noon. When you get back from the service, please plan on stopping by for a few minutes. I have some things to show you."

"All right, all right. See you at noon. Bye."

Brooke dropped her cellphone onto the kitchen counter with a thud. She shook her head at her brother's thick headedness. Susan finished her lap of the kitchen.

Susan said, "Well, that was a bit noisy. Not that I was able to sleep, anyway. Listen, Brooke, what do you have planned? Don't blacken your father's memory. No matter what he did, it's not good to speak ill of the dead."

"Mom, there are some things that Joshua and Christopher simply have to face up to. I'll be kind, but they need to know that we're their family and we love them. We're not the enemy...we're also not made-to-order babysitters." They spent the rest of the day puttering around the house, trying to forget that Kurt's funeral was the next day and that neither one of them was welcome to attend. Forgetfulness did not come to either of them.

The next day when Joshua dropped off the boys for them to babysit during the funeral, Brooke noticed that the boys were dropped off precisely at noon. Black-suited, Joshua came in briefly, but hurried on his way. A few hours later, he and Christopher returned, refusing to meet her eyes. Susan was in the back room, doing a puzzle with the boys.

Brooke said, "I have something to show you guys. Look here." She handed them a couple of the photos that had previously hung in Kurt and Kelsey's home.

Joshua asked, "What in the world . . . where did you get these?"

Christopher, spoke with defiance, "Yeah, where did you get these made?"

Brooke said, "Wake up, gentlemen. You just attended the funeral of our father, his mistress, and their children. Do you *really* think he was as pure as the driven snow?" She shook her head in amazement at their pig-headedness.

Joshua said, "Well, Mom drove him to it. He never would have even thought of cheating on her if she wasn't so . . . frigid."

Brooke replied, "There are pictures all over their house, pictures of Dad and Kelsey over the years. This has been a long-term affair, not something that just popped up when Mom was in the coma. Wake up and smell the coffee here." She felt about to burst. When would they finally understand what had transpired?

Christopher said, "Yeah, but we overheard Mr. and Mrs. DeLuca talking at the funeral. They said that Dad and Kelsey hadn't gotten involved until Mom was in a coma. They said that he thought she was going to die and was just moving on." He shrugged off her comments.

"How do you explain the fact that Cassie was four? That Christine was born two months after Mom woke up? Mom's coma was only for six months, and it just happened this past year."

Joshua said, "You don't know for sure that Cassie was Dad's child. Maybe Kelsey was involved with someone a couple of years before him."

Brooke held out her cellphone: "Here are some pictures of the other photos in the house. Cassie's birth- Dad is standing right there. Cassie's christening- there he is again. Their wedding and

319

honeymoon in Hawaii. Christine's birth and christening. Oh, wait a sec." she scrolled through some pictures, settling at last on the photos from her paralegal trip. "Here are some shots I took when I was in the Bahamas for my paralegal conference last October. I'd forgotten that I even had them, what with Mom's illness. You can see the date stamp on the photos. They were clearly taken before Mom's coma. Come on, guys! Don't be so blind!" Brooke put her pictures right in front of them. Surely they could see the handwriting on the wall.

Joshua said, "I guess it does look bad, Christopher."

Brooke reached into her purse: "And these rings- read the inscription." More proof that they could not ignore, at least in her mind.

Christopher turned the engagement ring over in his hand. He said, "Oh, man, what a rock! That must have cost $60,000 if it cost a dime." Then, "'My one true love, 2013.'" He dropped the rings back in her hands, unable to meet her eyes.

Brooke said, "Look, I don't want to harm Dad's memory. He was always good to us, but he wasn't who we thought he was. He cheated on Mom. Mom did everything for him, and for us. Her love and trust were thrown back in her face. He mocked her- you know he did. He belittled her at every turn- you've seen it with your own eyes, heard it with your own ears." She dropped her defensive stance and pleaded. "All I am asking is that you be reconciled to Mom and start to see her as I always have. She's a good woman and has always been a good mother. She deserves a lot more than she's gotten."

Joshua and Christopher didn't speak for several minutes. Brooke stared at them, waiting for some kind of confirmation that they had heard her plea. Had they listened at all? Joshua was the first to speak.

Joshua cleared his throat. Then, wavering, said, "She's got to be mad at us. She has every right to be furious with how we treated her." He looked very uncomfortable with himself. "I, uh, guess I was so eager to have a father that I bought into everything Dad told me. Even..." Joshua shifted from one leg to another... "as an adult. That's pretty pathetic, I know, Brooke."

Brooke nodded and turned to Christopher. "Well, Chris? What do you think?"

Christopher hesitated and then said: "Yeah. I didn't, ugh, treat her very well, I guess." He shrugged. "What can I say?"

Brooke said, "Ask her to forgive you. Start afresh. She has always loved you- nothing could change that." She tried to encourage them to talk with Susan.

***

Susan and the boys were playing quietly in the back bedroom. They'd been putting puzzles together, but she sensed the boys were ready for more action. She was just preparing to take them outside when Joshua and Christopher came in. Joshua asked the boys to go visit with Aunt Brooke for a few minutes before they headed home.

Joshua turned to her and said, "Mom, ugh, Brooke showed us the pictures of Dad and Kelsey. And the rings. We . . . we were wrong about Dad."

Christopher told her, "Yeah. All those years, we thought that Dad hung the moon, but I guess he wasn't what he always appeared to us. We were pretty dense."

They both looked very embarrassed. Susan smiled at them. They were her sons, after all.

Susan said, "I couldn't tell you. You wouldn't have believed anything against your father. Besides, people have a tendency to shoot the messenger." She continued, "He wasn't who you thought he was, but neither am I. I've changed since this all happened. I'm stronger. I'm not a doormat and never will be again!" She gained strength from her own admission, feeling justified in her innocence and in Kurt's guilt.

Joshua said, "I don't know why we were so tenacious about the whole thing. We were like a couple of bulldogs holding onto a toy we wanted." He ducked his head in shame. "How could we have been that blind? Mom, can you ever forgive us for the terrible way we treated you all those years?"

Christopher added, "We're sorry for the pain we caused you, Mom. Nobody should have had to go through junk Dad dropped in your lap, what with selling your house and stuff and then leaving you in the lurch financially. And me? I should've been more 'here' when I was here. Maybe I should've just been around more. I didn't realize what was going on. You really got a rotten deal, Mom."

Susan said, "I know, I know. You meant no harm." She hugged them tightly. "Boys? I mean, Josh and Christopher, let's make today a new start. You've just been at your father's funeral, and I know that must be very hard for you both." She hesitated to tell them. "I didn't go because I wasn't invited, even though I am- or was- his wife. Mr. and Mrs. DeLucas told me I wasn't welcome. That must seem so strange, now that you think about it."

Joshua said, "Yeah, now that you mention it, but we were so stupid."

She said, "Let's draw a line in the sand. Today is a new day, a new beginning for us all. Let's move on and create something better than before. What do you say?"

They hugged and headed out to Brooke and the boys. Life was finally getting on the right track, or so she sincerely hoped.

Chapter 28

Just as Susan entered the living room a few minutes later, the phone rang. Susan plopped onto the couch while Brooke answered the call. It had already been a long day, so Susan was happy for a few minutes to relax. Joshua and Christopher sat next to her, planning to only stay a few minutes more.

"Hello? One moment, please." Brooke whispered, "It's Mr. James. He wants to talk to you, Mom." She said into the phone, "Mr. James, I'm going to put you on speakerphone. My brothers and I want to listen in on your chat with Mom." Brooke sat next to her mom and siblings, while Joshua's sons ran back into the back room, to play with the Tonka trucks Brooke had there.

Mr. James said, "Certainly. Mrs. Prescott? I just received a letter from an attorney representing Mr. and Mrs. De Luca. They are contesting Kelsey's will."

Susan sighed. It still wasn't over, I guess. Susan replied, "You mentioned before that they might do that." She shook her head at Brooke and the boys. It was tempting to throw her hands in the air, but that was *so* like Kurt. She restrained herself and scooted further down into the sofa.

Mr. James said, "Yes, I wasn't particularly surprised. Since Kelsey wasn't married to . . . uh, your husband, her parents have something called 'standing' in the state of Maryland. That means that they can inherit her money and possessions if they can prove that Kelsey had undue influence in changing her will."

Susan asked, "What does that mean?" She'd never heard of such a thing. She glanced over at her sons and shrugged. Brooke took her hand and gave it a little squeeze.

Mr. James told them, "Well, if they can prove that you coerced her into leaving her estate to you, the De Lucas might be able to get everything. They might try to prove that Kelsey was mentally impaired. But that wouldn't be successful because I was with her, and she knew exactly what she was doing and why."

Brooke asked, "How do you plan on proving that?"

Mr. James said, "I took a video of her on my phone before, during, and after the signing. There is no question that she was doing what she wanted. I even have her apologizing to your mother, Miss. Prescott. I didn't show it to you before because I thought that this was all too new and fresh for your mother and didn't want to overburden her."

Susan said, "But I didn't even see her for two days. I went to see her right after the accident, and then I didn't go back until two days later, when she stood up and died. We didn't even speak that day, though she saw that I was there. How could I have pressured her to do anything?" This was ridiculous. Okay, chill, Susan. Breathe.

Mr. James said, "You obviously didn't. We can prove that pretty easily, but it is going to take a little time. It will also be a nuisance, but hang in there, and we will get you through it, okay?"

Susan said, "Yes, I guess we have no other choice."

Brooke asked, "Mr. James, is there anything else we need to know?"

Mr. James said, "I'm going to contact the doctors and the nurses at the medical center. If any of them heard her say anything about changing her will, other than our two witnesses to Kelsey's signing the new will, they can testify on our side."

Brooke asked, "Did her parents even visit her in the hospital?" Brooke seemed a bit testy. Susan squeezed Brooke's hand.

Mr. James said, "Not according to the medical center's records. According to what Kelsey told me when I went to see her, they haven't even talked to Kelsey in years because they disapproved of her chosen lifestyle as a companion of well-off, older men."

Joshua asked, "So their acts of grief at the funeral?"

Mr. James said, "Were most likely done to garner sympathy from the judge they hope to get on their side. Political posturing, the way I look at it. The newspapers and television cameras were there, as you know. Very sad story of the death of a beautiful family, and all that... Public outcry over the loss... Incredible public relations coup for the sorrowing parents versus the absentee wife who is trying to steal their daughter's fortune...the disgruntled wife is trying to rob them blind...She didn't even show up for her husband's funeral. They made a statement to that effect after the service was over."

Brooke said, "Mom wasn't trying to steal anything. She didn't even know Kelsey changed her will until days after the deaths. What are they trying to do?"

Mr. James said, "They are simply trying to put your mom in a bad light, to strengthen their argument that they deserve Kelsey's money."

Christopher shook his head and said, "They were crying their eyes out."

Mr. James answered, "A pretense and a front to fool everyone. Kelsey told me when I went to see her that they had been estranged for at least ten years. Giving her a funeral makes their claim to her estate seem more solid, especially since Mrs. Prescott was nowhere in sight for the funeral of her own husband."

Susan said, "But . . . they asked me not to come. Said I wasn't welcome. That's why I didn't go. They wanted to pay for the funeral and I don't have any money, so I gave them permission to have his cremated body. They told me he loved their daughter, not me, so they would take care of 'things.' Dag nab it all, he was my husband, for Pete's sake. This whole thing makes my blood boil! What a bunch of crooks!" Susan shook her head. All the garbage I put up with for all those years and now they're fighting me?

Mr. James said, "That was all a part of their plan, which is now playing out. Makes you look like a bitter woman for not being there. They make you look bad, like a gold-digger after her ex's money, and the public forgets that your hubby was a cheater, and that he had two children outside of wedlock while he was still married to you. This is going to take a little time, but be patient, Mrs. Prescott, I will get you through this. For the record, I believe we can win."

They hung up, after making a date to discuss the case further once Mr. James had more information from the medical staff. Joshua and Christopher got up to leave; Brooke called for the boys, who came running from the back room.

Susan stood and said, "I just can't believe this is happening. When will this ever stop?"

Brooke gave her mom a hug and said, "I'm here for you, Mom."

Joshua walked over and said, "Me, too, Mom. You aren't alone."

Christopher also gave Susan a hug and murmured his support.

When Mr. James contacted Susan again about a week later, things looked pretty good for her. The hospital staff confirmed that the De Lucas had not been in to see either Kurt or Kelsey. Mr. James had the video of his visit to Kelsey and shared it with the family. Nancy came over for moral support as they watched the film. Michael was there to support Brooke. Joshua and Amanda came, having left the children with her mother. Christopher was teaching a night exam-preparation class and was unable to attend the gathering. The group gathered Brooke's living room, waiting for the video to begin.

Mr. James told them, "Now keep in mind that Kelsey was very badly injured. I know that you saw her, Mrs. Prescott, but her appearance might be shocking. Well, not to you, Dr. Prescott. I'm sure you've seen patients worse off than this, but I mean the rest of you. If you need me to stop the tape at any time, just say the word. Also, I'll be happy to replay it for you as many times as you like. I have a complete transcript of our conversation and have made copies for all of you." He passed the copies out, giving each person a copy.

Susan told him, "Thank you, Mr. James. I think maybe we should all just take a listen first, and then look over the transcript your staff has prepared."

"Yes, Mrs. Prescott. I think that is a good course of action. Of course, anyone may ask anything he or she would like, because I am certain there will be questions." He took a deep breath. "Shall we begin?"

Susan said, "Yes, please, Mr. James."

"As you wish, Mrs. Prescott." To everyone: "We were in Kelsey's room, number 507, at Shock Trauma in the University of Maryland Medical Center when this was filmed. It was taped on April 29, 2015, at 10 AM Eastern Time. I kept the recording going during our entire visit."

The video began with Mr. James reiterating the date, time, and location of the taping. He showed the audience two witnesses to the taping: Dr. Joseph Marquez and Nurse Selina Atkins. He asked them if they were there of their own free will, to which they both responded "yes." He asked them if they knew they would be witnessing the signing of a new will. Again, they replied "yes." They gave their home addresses, stated the date and time of the recording, and acknowledged that the witnessing was being recorded with their permission. He asked Kelsey, who was lying in her hospital bed, if she was granting her permission to record the visit; she replied "yes." He asked her for her name and then allowed her to talk.

Kelsey said, with surprising strength in her voice, "My name is Kelsey De Luca. I am giving my attorney, Mr. John James, my permission to record this interview. I am a patient at Shock Trauma in the University of Maryland Medical Center, where I am recovering from injuries I suffered in a traffic accident with my lover, Kurt Prescott. In the van with us at the time were our two daughters, Cassie and Christine." She sobbed at the mention of her daughters. She hesitated. "We were returning from Vancouver, British Columbia, where we took Mrs. Susan Prescott, who we had arranged to have drugged so we could kidnap her and take her out of the country. The purpose of this . . . kidnapping . . . was to . . . kill her." At this point, Kelsey broke down in sobs. Mr. James offered her a drink of water, which she accepted. She took a sip. She composed herself after a few minutes and then continued.

"I was involved with Kurt Prescott for five years or so. During that time, I observed him stealing every joint asset he could from Mrs. Prescott. He placed those monetary gains into a joint bank account he had with me." Kelsey shuddered and rested. She continued, "He admitted to me that he had caused the accident that made Mrs. Prescott go into a coma, making it a lot worse than it might have been by turning the wheel of the car so that the impact would hit where she was sitting. He told me he didn't help her when she was injured and actually tried to hurt her even more, but I don't know exactly what he did. He never told me, but there were occasional side comments that made me believe he had somehow tried to kill her while they were waiting for help. He did tell me that the trip they were going on that day was so he could 'get rid of unwanted baggage.'" Kelsey paused again, appearing to be weakened by her confession. She lay back for a few minutes.

Kelsey took another sip of water and then continued.

"During Mrs. Prescott's six months in a coma, I moved into their house at Kurt's request. I brought my daughter with me. I was pregnant with our second child at the time. Kurt managed to keep his grown children away from the house by giving them excuses and telling them to spend time with their mother, who he was convinced would die soon. He did everything in his power to make that death happen, from getting her taken of off the ventilator to having her feeding discontinued. During her hospitalization, we began selling all of her possessions or giving them away for a tax deduction."

Kelsey turned to Mr. James, "Do you want details here?"

He said, "Yes, I think that would be suitable, Ms. De Luca."

"We sold most of her jewelry to secondhand shops. Some of the rings she had were quite nice, so I had them melted down into new pieces for myself. Her family heirlooms went to antique shops, where they were sold on consignment. Her clothes were given away to charities. Kurt declared them on his income tax return, as I already told you. Their joint bank accounts had been cleaned out by Kurt as soon as he got out of the hospital. His injuries were fairly minor, so he was released in a couple of days. I don't remember exactly how long he was in- I'm sorry." Kelsey took another sip to moisten her throat. She had started coughing a bit. After another break, she gathered her strength and sat straighter in the bed.

She continued. "He went before a judge and claimed he needed to sell their house to pay for Mrs. Prescott's care. He didn't really- he lied to get ahold of the equity they had in the house and so we could buy a nicer home together. The judge bought his story and let the sale go through. We sold my place pretty fast, and added that money to the pot. We stayed in a long term hotel for a couple of months while we went through the buying and renovation process and then moved into our new house in downtown Annapolis." To Mr. James, "The house wasn't new, since it was in historic downtown Annapolis, obviously, but it was new to us."

The attorney said, "Yes, Ms. De Luca. I understand but thank you for clarifying. Please continue."

"Kurt sold most of their furniture. We had a couple of yard sales to get rid of some of their junk. The nice stuff was sold through consignment shops. He said his kids didn't need any of the old stuff- he didn't want to have to look at something Sue- Mrs. Prescott- had 'sat her ugly fat butt on' when he visited the kids. Those were his exact words. He didn't want anything in our new place that reminded him of Mrs. Prescott, so he got rid of everything. He really hated her. I think it was an obsession by that time. I thought it was kinda strange to be so hate-filled, but I was so in love with him. I see now that I had ignored all of his faults." She hung her head for a few moments. She sighed, and gathered her thoughts.

She looked up and continued. "We hadn't even told his children that we were selling the house until it was too late for them to do anything about it. Kurt kept everything secret from them- the court hearings on the house sale, his cleaning out of their joint bank accounts- he told them to focus on their mother, and that he would take care of everything financial. And he did."

Mr. James asked Kelsey, "Didn't they notice that the house was for sale?"

"No. They'd all moved out by then. Joshua was married with kids. Brooke was living in a condo on the other side of Anne Arundel County. Christopher was going to school in Monterey, California. No one had really been around since Brooke came into the house, right after the car accident and took out some of her mom's clothing and toiletries. It was just Kurt, me, and our daughter Cassie. We kept to ourselves and the neighbors really didn't bother us. A few questions...not much else. I had our second child, Christine, about four months before we kidnapped Mrs. Prescott." She sobbed at the thought of her little girl's tragic end. "Four months old. That's such a short life." Her tears flowed freely. "I'm sorry. So very sorry. Please excuse me."

"Ms. De Luca, is there anything else you want to say?"

"Yes. There're several things. Mrs. Prescott, I apologize for my role in hurting you so terribly. I was blinded by my love for your husband. I'm responsible for my actions, and I don't blame Kurt, not entirely. I realized when you came to see me two days ago that you weren't the monster Kurt made you out to be. I had believed his lies. Instead, you were ...you are... a loving person who truly cares about others... And I'm not. I cared only for myself." She wept harder. "I've lived only for myself, until my girls came along. I'd convinced myself that having them would make Kurt leave you. I was wrong. They only made him want to kill you so that he could be with us and have all your joint money." She stopped again. She wiped tears from her cheeks. "Please forgive me. Thank you for your kindness to my . . . little girls . . . when they . . . were leaving us. Thank you for cradling my precious babies as they . . . slipped away." Now the tears really came down. Kelsey sipped more water. A few minutes passed.

"Thank you for your kindness to me, Mrs. Prescott. Thank you for visiting me in the hospital. Thank you for sharing your faith with me. Thank you for . . . praying with me. I'm eternally grateful to you." Kelsey smiled for the first time. "There's something I want to do for you." Deep breath.

331

"Now for the important stuff- the really important stuff. I asked my attorney, Mr. John James, to write a new Last Will and Testament for me. My previous will left everything I own to Kurt and then to my girls. As we all know, my daughters . . . died at the scene of the accident. Kurt died two days ago. The only other beneficiaries I have would be my parents, Antonio and Helen De Luca. I have been estranged from them for more than ten years. I have called them, but they refuse to visit me here in the hospital. They will not even talk to me on the phone, in spite of my injuries." She almost broke down, but then composed herself.

Kelsey spoke with a strong voice. "It is my desire and intention to leave my entire estate to Mrs. Susan Prescott. I do not wish to leave my parents one dime. They have repeatedly rejected me. I understand why they did, but they have refused to be reconciled, in spite of my recent change of heart. I, therefore, being of sound will and mind, wish to leave all of my worldly possessions to Mrs. Susan Prescott, in the hopes that she will find in in her very warm heart to forgive my sins against her. I truly apologize. I set my hand to this Last Will and Testament today, April 29, 2015. Thank you for listening." Kelsey signed her will.

Mr. James took the signed the will, and turned to the doctor and nurse. "I have a few questions for the two of you. Do you see that Ms. De Luca is signing this will on her own volition?"

"Yes, sir," Nurse Atkins told him. She was crying as she spoke. She squeezed a tissue, as she dabbed away the tears.

"Yes, Mr. James," Dr. Marquez seconded the thought. He was teary-eyed. He blew his nose and tried to look authoritative, but it was clear he was touched by Kelsey's comments.

"Have you heard her testimony prior to executing this document? Nurse Atkins? Dr. Marquez?"

"Yes, I have." The nurse's voice was shaky.

332

"Yes, indeed." The doctor was back in control and answered with conviction.

"If you believe Ms. De Luca is in her right mind as she signed this document, according to your own experience in the medical field, and that she has not been compelled in any way but does this freely, please state your willingness to sign as witnesses."

"Yes, I believe she is clearly in control of her faculties," Dr. Marquez stated.

"Yes, I agree that Ms. De Luca understands what she is doing and desires to right some wrongs," Nurse Atkins told the video. She nodded.

Mr. James instructed them, "Then the witnesses will please sign Ms. De Luca's will." The witnesses stepped forward and placed their signatures on the document. Mr. James moved forward and signed as the attorney for Kelsey.

To the doctor and nurse, he said, "Thank you." To Kelsey, he asked, "Ms. De Luca, would you like to say anything else?"

"No, I've said everything I hoped to say. Oh, I pray that the Prescott sons will support their mother. She is a wonderful woman who was wronged by their father and me . . . I think that's all." Kelsey leaned back in her bed, exhausted but smiling.

"Thank you, Ms. De Luca. This is attorney John James, ending the recording of this visit with Ms. Kelsey De Luca in room 507 of Shock Trauma in the University of Maryland Medical Center. The purpose of this recording was to testify to the sound mind of Ms. De Luca at the time of her changing her will. The present time..." he looked at his watch, " is 10:43 am Eastern Time on April 29, 2015."

Mr. James turned off the video. He turned to the family. "Questions? Do you wish to see this again?"

No one spoke for a few moments. A few sobs broke the silence, a few noses were wiped. Some straggled coughs were heard. The living room was hushed as Susan thought about what they had listened to. There was no question in Susan's mind that Kelsey knew what she was doing. What would be said in a court of law? Susan had to ask. "Well, Mr. James. That sounded pretty straightforward to me, but I don't know much about the law. What's your take on the whole thing?"

Mr. James told her, "Mrs. Prescott, there's no real thing as a totally air-tight case, but this is pretty close to one. I believe that we should be successful with our response to the De Luca's case."

Joshua said, "Boy, that whole confession thing was certainly damaging to Dad. Mom, I don't know what to say." He leaned forward on the couch to take her hand. "I seem to be in that position, of not knowing what to say, a lot these days."

Brooke said, "I'm in shock. I knew it was bad but I didn't realize just how unscrupulous they both were. At least she repented at the end. I don't know about Dad. I guess we'll never know what went through his mind when he died."

Michael spoke for the first time, "The end was the important thing. She was truly sorry and asked forgiveness."

The general consensus was that their father and Susan's husband had behaved in a manner that none of them could excuse. They also said that Kelsey, who they had not met in her glory days, looked really, really bad.

Susan told them, "Well, for once in my life, I actually look better than Kelsey did."

They had to laugh, which broke the tension in the room. They listened to the recording another time and looked over the manuscript. They asked Mr. James a few technical questions about the situation. Shortly thereafter, he made his departure, bowing and telling the family he would be in touch. Now all they could do was wait and pray, while Mr. James jumped through various legal hoops.

Chapter 29

A few weeks later, Susan waited on the polished wooden bench in the hallway outside the courtroom at the Anne Arundel County Courthouse. She was thankful Mr. James had been able to get an early court date. No waiting for months, to see if the Sword of Damocles would still be hanging over her head. Her thoughts turned to her future plans. Where would she be financially? Would she be living with Brooke the rest of her life? Would she have to get a fulltime job to make ends meet? How would she pay for this court case if she lost?

On a more positive note, she might be living a life of luxury. What would she do if she won the case, as Mr. James thought she would? Would she travel? Would she buy a gorgeous new house and decorate it to her heart's content, totally in her own taste? Could she give some money to her kids, helping them pay off their mortgages? How about scholarship funds for all the grandkids? Donations to her church? Support missionaries across the world and have money enough to visit them? Wow, the possibilities were endless. Yes, think positively, Susan Margaret. God provides all of our needs. He will take care of me, no matter the outcome.

She shook her head. Life had not turned out to be anything like what she had planned. Deep sigh. Such was life. She squirmed over the hardness of the bench beneath her. Some cushions would be nice, if they were going to keep her waiting so long in this hallway. She looked at her watch. An hour had gone by since she and Nancy had come into the courthouse. I sure hope Nancy gets back with our tea soon. Susan turned back to her thoughts about her predicament.

Joshua's gift of a new car had made it easy for her to get around, but she hated to continue living off the allowance he and Christopher gave her. It wasn't fair for them to have to take away from their own incomes to support her. It wasn't fair for Brooke to sacrifice her independence by having her mother living with her. It simply wasn't fair to any of them. Blast Kurt. Why did he have to misbehave?

Nancy had volunteered to accompany her to court so that Brooke and her brothers wouldn't need to take more time off work. Nancy rejoined Susan now, cups of tea in hand. "Here you go, decaf tea with milk and two sugars. How are you holding up, my friend?"

"Thanks, Nancy." Susan took the cup from her friend. "Whew! I was just playing through various scenarios...what happens if I lose, Nancy Beth? Will I ever be able to live on my own again? How will I manage? On the other hand, what if I am suddenly fabulously wealthy? After attorney's fees, of course."

"You're worrying about so many things, Susan Margaret. You know what they say about crossing a bridge before you get to it." Nancy gave her a side hug.

"Yes, I know. That crossing the bridge thing doesn't do any good. Neither does sawing sawdust. It doesn't work out so well."

"Right on. Talk to me, Susan. What are you thinking?" Nancy kept her arm around Susan.

"If only Kurt and I had . . . But, no, I can't second-guess how life would have played out if my hubby had not cheated on me . . . if the man I had loved had not rejected me, tried to kill me. If only I had been wiser or stronger or been someone different, before the accident."

"Lay down these burdens, Susan." Nancy gave her another squeeze.

"Fretting never did anyone any good. You're right, Nancy. Thank you." Susan hugged her back, taking care not to spill their tea. She began to pray that God's will would be done, whatever that would be. She finally found some peace.

Mr. James was in the courtroom talking with the attorney for the De Lucas and the judge. Susan had made a statement. How much more would she have to go through? She second-guessed herself about the statement, as she sipped her tea. Susan wondered what was happening, when the attorneys finally exited the courtroom. The men parted ways as Mr. James came up to her. The ladies put down their tea and stood to greet him.

Mr. James bowed to the two of them. "Mrs. Prescott? Mrs. Ferguson? Sorry to keep you both waiting, but I think you'll agree that it was worthwhile. I gave Judge Sandra Ellingham the statement you had made, Mrs. Prescott. I also showed Judge Ellingham my video of Kelsey when she signed the new will. I produced affidavits from the staff at the medical center, stating that the De Lucas had not visited her, and that Kelsey had told the staff she was estranged from her parents. The De Luca's lawyer had nothing but hearsay and a will that was about ten years old. Judge Ellingham threw the case out of court, saying that she felt that Kelsey was clearly in full possession of her faculties. She berated the attorney for the DeLucas for wasting the court's time. The De Lucas may decide to appeal after they talk with their attorney, but I doubt it."

Susan asked, "So, what happens now?" She was unfamiliar with courts and wills and the like. Things still seemed a bit uncertain but they sounded like she'd won.

"Mrs. Prescott, you have, without a word on your own behalf, inherited five million dollars, courtesy of your husband and his mistress. While it's not generally the way I would personally choose to become wealthy, it has worked in this situation." He smiled at her. "Since everything has to go through the will, you will get the money in about a year. Sorry for the delay, but that's the way things work."

She and Nancy squealed, then hugged.

Nancy said, "The Lord has returned to you tenfold what Kurt stole."

"So all those years of suffering, all the money he stole from what should have been our joint resources have apparently paid off." Susan was stunned at the turn of events.

"In spades, Mrs. Prescott. You are financially set for the rest of your life. I'll work out the details and be in touch regarding the disbursement of the funds. Congratulations." He bowed. "Ladies, I bid you good day." He bowed another time and walked down the hallway. She and Nancy looked at each other, hugged again, then picked up their tea cups and headed out.

Susan said, "He does so love bowing. It's quite charming, actually." They laughed, relieved beyond measure. God is so good.

Forward to From the valley to the Mountaintop, Book Two in the Prescott Family Chronicles

"My Mommy died two days ago." Kurt Prescott stopped and wiped away a tear as he wrote in the journal his teacher had given him the day before. "Daddy and Mommy had been drinking and were fighting again after dinner. They always fight a lot. Sometimes Daddy hit Mommy. I ran upstairs to my bedroom and jumped into bed. I covered my head with my blankets but I could still hear them. Then the kitchen door opened and slammed shut. I peeked outside, looking through the blinds on my bedroom window. I scrunched down real small so that no one could see me watching. Mommy walked towards the creek. She was drunk and it was dark out-why would she go outside like that?"

"I saw somebody big come up and talk to her. I think it was a man, but I'm not sure. The moon was pretty bright but we don't have any outside lights, so I couldn't see very well. The man grabbed Mommy's arm. They might have been fighting, but I couldn't hear what they were saying. They walked around the bend, so I couldn't see them anymore."

"I got real tired and went to sleep. Daddy pulled me out of bed in the middle of the night and told me to come downstairs with him. Peter and Candy were sitting at the kitchen table, waiting for us. Nobody said anything. My pajama bottoms were wet around the ankles and I didn't know why but I didn't want Peter to tease me, so I didn't tell anyone."

"Daddy said that Mommy was gone. That she had left. We weren't supposed to tell anyone that they had been fighting that night. We weren't supposed to say anything at all except that our parents loved each other and we had all been home watching TV all evening. Daddy said that if we told anyone what had happened, we would be in big trouble and that he would bring out the strap. The big one."

"Peter, Candy, and I told him that we wouldn't say anything he didn't want us to, but he kept us in the kitchen for a really long time. I think it was a couple of hours. I was so tired that I almost fell asleep a couple of times but he yelled at me and woke me up. Finally, he let us go back to bed. I went upstairs and changed my pajama bottoms but my bed was wet where my feet had been, so it was real nasty and hard to get back to sleep."

"The next morning, a couple of policemen rang the doorbell. They said that Mommy's body had been found in the creek. She had hit her head on a rock and fell into the creek and drowned. Daddy acted real surprised. Peter and Candy and I cried and told them what Daddy told us to say. I'm real sad. I'm ten years old and my Mommy is dead. Her funeral is tomorrow. I guess she's never coming back."

www.ingramcontent.com/pod-product-compliance
Lightning Source LLC
Chambersburg PA
CBHW072342020726

47506CB00004B/977